W9-ALM-236

Caterva

Juan Filloy

Caterva

Translated by Brendan Riley

 DALKEY ARCHIVE PRESS

Originally published in Spanish in a private edition by Ferrari, Buenos Aires, 1937

Copyright © 2006 by the Estate of Juan Filloy,
c/o Guillermo Schavelzon & Associates, Agencia Literaria
Translation and introduction copyright © 2015 by Brendan Riley
First edition, 2015
All rights reserved

Library of Congress Cataloging-in-Publication Data
Filloy, Juan.
[Caterva. English]
Caterva / by Juan Filloy ; translated by Brendan Riley. -- First edition.
pages cm
Originally published in Spanish by Impr. Ferrari Hermanos, 1937.
ISBN 978-1-62897-036-4 (pbk.)
I. Riley, Brendan, translator. II. Title.
PQ7797.F535C3813 2015
863ʹ.62--dc23
2014031427

Partially funded by the Illinois Arts Council, a state agency
Work published within the framework of "Programa Sur"
Translation Support Program of the Ministry of Foreign Affairs,
International Trade and Worship of the Argentine Republic

Dalkey Archive Press publications are, in part, made possible through the support of the University of
Houston-Victoria and its program in creative writing, publishing, and translation. www.uhv.edu/asa/

Dalkey Archive Press
Victoria, TX / Dublin / London
www.dalkeyarchive.com

Cover: Typography and layout by Arnold Kotra
Art and Composition by Jeffrey Higgins
Typesetting: Mikhail Iliatov
Printed on permanent/durable acid-free paper

"Whatever happened to Filloy?"

Many readers today who happen onto the work of the Argentine novelist Juan Filloy come to him by way of Julio Cortázar, thanks to an oft-reprinted passage from his celebrated 1963 novel *Hopscotch* (Rayuela). In it, Cortázar offers some high praise for his compatriot through the voice of the novel's main character, Horacio Oliveira, who shares an interest with his girlfriend, La Maga, in the clochards, the street people of Paris:

> "*La cloche, le clochard, la clocharde, clocharder.* There's even a thesis that was presented at the Sorbonne on the subject of the psychology of the clochard."
>
> "Could be," Oliveira said. "But they don't have any Juan Filloy to write *Caterva* for them. What ever happened to Filloy?"
>
> Naturally, La Maga was in no position to know, in the first place because she never knew he had existed. He had to explain to her why Filloy, why *Caterva*. La Maga liked the plot of the book very much, the idea that South American *linyeras* were in a class with clochards. She remained firmly convinced that it was an insult to confuse a *linyera* with a beggar, and her liking for the clocharde of the Pont des Arts had its roots in reasons that now seemed scientific.

Hopscotch helped to make Cortázar one of the most famous names of the Latin American Boom but few readers, in Spanish or any other language, really know this novel *Caterva* or its author, to whom Cortázar paid such a singular compliment. Who was Juan Filloy and what, if anything, happened to him?

In a literary career spanning sixty-seven years, from 1930 to 1997, Filloy published twenty-seven novels, hundreds of poems (Hernán Casciari claims Filloy wrote more sonnets than any poet since Petrarch)[1], and thousands of palindromes, more than 6,000 of them comprising his *Karsino*, a unique "palindrome treatise." Yet, Carlos Fuentes's 2011 study *La gran novela Latinoamericana* (*The Great Latin American Novel*), which surveys dozens of Hispano-American authors makes not a single mention of Filloy. An interesting omission but perhaps not an entirely surprising one. Michel Nieva's review of *Caterva*, "Juan Filloy: El eslabón perdido," calls Filloy the missing link of Argentine letters: "Enthusiastically read, on the one hand, by authors like Reyes, Marechal, or Cortázar, while on the other, partly due to [Filloy's] own decision to stop publishing or to do so in small, private editions, he was, apart from rare book collectors who read his work infrequently and poorly, forgotten by the public and the Academy."[2]

In his essay "Joyce's *Ulysses* in Argentine Literature," author Carlos Gamerro claims that "Ulysses is probably the foreign novel which has had most influence on Argentinean narrative fiction . . ." and mentions the enormous impression it made on Jorge Luis Borges, who dabbled at translating some of the "Penelope" chapter, and whose most famous short stories, such as "The Aleph," seek to invoke Ulysses's epic sweep in miniature.[3] Like Carlos Fuentes, Gamerro makes no mention of Juan Filloy. And yet, Filloy's *Caterva*, published in 1937, only fifteen years after *Ulysses*, when so many writers were touched by Joyce's enormous influence, shows a much more clear and obvious imitation of the bittersweet encyclopedic comedy found in *Ulysses* than anything by Borges. Though *Caterva* was published a decade before the first Spanish language translation of *Ulysses*, by Argentine writer J. Salas Subirat, Filloy, a polymath like Joyce, reportedly spoke seven languages and probably

1 Casciari, Hernán. "Lado B: canciones lentas," *Orsai Blog*, August 25, 2004. http://editorialorsai.com/blog/post/lado_b_canciones_lentas

2 Nieva, Michel. "Juan Filloy: El eslabón perdido," in *Soles Digital*, September 25, 2009; translation mine. http://www.solesdigital.com.ar/libros/juan-filloy.html

3 Gamerro, Carlos. "Joyce's *Ulysses* in Argentine Literature" in *Irish Migration Studies in Latin America* 7:2 (July 2009), 177–184. Translated by David Barnwell. http://www.irlandeses.org/0907gamerro.htm

read *Ulysses* in English. Indeed, Filloy's familiarity with English is conspicuously displayed in *Caterva* when the character Longines deftly summarizes an article from *National Geographic* magazine about Arizona's recently inaugurated Hoover Dam, sixty years before the magazine published any Spanish language edition. And like *Ulysses*, *Caterva* is epic in length, scope, and style, scatological, riotously funny, keenly psychological, and fascinated with the minutiae of everyday life. It displays a vast, eclectic scope of humane interest; a short list of its many topics includes: the Armenian genocide; astronomy; auto clubs and road rage; the Black African carnival; criminology; cryptology; enology; herbalism; lepidoptery; hydroelectric dams; lachrymae therapy; epicureanism; railway politics; metempsychosis; Nazi espionage (*au courant* for a 1937 Latin American novel); sartorial elegance; spiritualism; stage magic; stink beetles; syphilis treatments; the advent of the wristwatch; and, of course, being an Argentine novel, the tango's natural predominance over all other dances. Also similar to *Ulysses*, *Caterva* is freely, confidently multilingual and poly-rhetorical. Along with samplings of French, Italian, German, Lunfardo, Cocoliche, and English, Caterva boasts an impressively varied rhetoric that poses a formidable challenge to any translator: acronyms; newspaper articles and editorials; chiastic syntax; cypher; epic catalogue; entomological monographs; eulogies; gravestone inscriptions; industrial labels; comically illiterate receipts; intimate confessional letters; headlines; parables; parody; pastoral lyricism; paronomasia; portmanteau words; and free-form stream-of-consciousness writing. Along with the epic's requisite trip to the underworld, *Caterva* even includes a memorable wake attended by a cast of drunken doctors, nurses, and interns, reminiscent of Joyce's scene with Stephen Dedalus, Buck Mulligan, and some other medical students drinking freely at the Dublin maternity hospital in *Ulysses*'s "Oxen of the Sun" chapter.

Caterva opens with several *linyeras* huddling under a bridge on the outskirts of Río Cuarto, a small city in Córdoba province on Argentina's humid pampas. La Maga's concern that *linyeras* not be conflated with beggars is shared by Filloy's characters themselves. Claiming to be purposeful vagabonds or professional beggars "on an ideal tour for the sake of others," not simply aimless drifters, these *linyeras* get off to a rough start when a pair of detectives try to arrest them all on suspicion of providing money to striking workers. Cagily eluding the authorities, the *linyeras* begin to travel about Central Argentina with a ferocious aplomb which detached expatriate Horacio Oliveira could only imagine.

They travel under suggestive, assumed names: Aparicio, ("specter"; an embittered veteran of the Uruguayan civil wars), Dijunto ("dead man," a Spanish dirt farmer) Fortunato ("lucky man," a former Prague bank manager); Katanga ("dung beetle," an exile from the Armenian massacres); Longines (a genius cryptographer); Lon Chaney (a Parisian jack-of-all-trades); Viejo Amor ("Old Love," a shameless Italian satyr). In one episode, during a collective, full moon nightmare, they all fuse into a *Homo septuplex*; otherwise they are a fractious fraternity, bound together by their tense, contentious desire to deliver justice to the pampas.

Stoic, solipsistic, satirical, severe, and savagely silly, they collectively try to help or avenge people in need, and punish the unscrupulous, but each *linyera* also plays by his own set of rules. The result is an epic tragicomedy that stares long and hard into the abyss, and then, a la *Ulysses*, says Yes to life.

The *linyeras'* ideal tour takes them to a wide variety of locales both rural and urban — towns, farms, gas stations, boarding houses, brothels, general stores, cemeteries, train stations, dams and lakes — in, around, and between Filloy's native Córdoba, and Río Cuarto, the provincial city in central Argentina where he worked and lived for more than sixty years.

During his years in Río Cuarto, Filloy also wrote a daily column for that city's newspaper *El Pueblo*. No surprise then to see how in *Caterva* he deftly, singlehandedly, both shows off and mocks the inflated journalese of small town reporters and editors.

From 1940 to 1971, bracketing his years presiding as a magistrate in Río Cuarto, Filloy wrote ceaselessly but refrained from publishing novels in order to avoid professional conflicts. Therein lies the answer to Horacio Oliveira's question "What ever happened to Filloy?"

In 1971, Juan Filloy ended his long self-imposed hiatus and published two new novels, *Invictus*, and *Yo, yo, y yo*. In the following years and decades he garnered numerous literary awards in Argentina and abroad (some sources claim this included a Nobel Prize nomination) but advanced age did not spare the distinguished author and poet arrest in 1976, at the age of eighty-two, by Argentina's military junta, which took exception to his novel *Vil y Vil* (1975). In a wonderful, real-life twist, one that readers of *Caterva* can relate to the episode in which wily, silver-tongued Katanga sweet talks his way into the good graces of the local magistrate in Río Cuarto, Filloy was released after several hours of questioning during which he only deigned to answer his interrogators with remarks on literary theory.

But Filloy outlasted Argentina's junta, and between 1977 and 1997 he published fourteen more novels. In 1984 he moved back to his native Córdoba, dying there in the year 2000, only two weeks short of turning 106, and fulfilling his supposed desire to live in three centuries. At his death Juan Filloy left behind an enormous amount of writing. Since then three more novels have been posthumously serialized, while an additional twenty-one novels remain unpublished!

In addition to his prolific literary output, Filloy was also a champion swimmer, a boxing referee, and a general sports enthusiast. In *Caterva*, he seems to makes a subtle nod to this fact when his magnificent seven arrive by train to Córdoba and, rolling through the quarter of San Vicente, they spot the Pucará sports and boxing club: "A cloudy tumble of alleys and barking dogs, the suburban quarter opened out toward the city center. Opposite the Pucará, the bend of the Suquía River shone bright as a scimitar. And amid the joyous ringing of bells they reached the asphalt platforms of the train station, thick with imminent embraces and heavily loaded porters." As of 2014, the club still stands on Calle Agustín Garza, just a short walk from the now-crumbling train station and the river.

One of the most peculiar and oft-recited facts about Filloy's novels is that every one of them, with the necessary exception of *Los Ochoa* (1972), bears a seven-letter title, (*Don Juan*; *Estafen*; *Gentuza*; *La Purga*; *Mujeres*; *Periplo*; *Tal Cual*; etc.). Unique among Cortázar's novels, *Rayuela* also sports a seven-letter title (the name Horacio, too, follows suit), further echo, further homage, perhaps, to *Caterva*, whose own seven letters might well be a nod to the seven of *Ulysses*. With its seven letters and tragicomic *homo septuplex*, *Caterva* might be Filloy's most perfectly septualogical novel.

This edition of *Caterva* represents only the second translation into English of a novel by Juan Filloy, the first being *Op Oloop* (translated by Lisa Dillman and published in 2009). "Caterva" is a Latin word which migrated into Italian, Portuguese, Catalan, and Spanish. It means "crowd," "gang," "mob," "faction," "rabble," "throng," "hoi polloi," "the great unwashed." In various Latin uses, *caterva* signifies a flock of birds, a company of actors, a phalanx of soldiers, a troop of gladiators, a dramatic chorus, a band of barbarians. For a time this translation did bear the working title of "Faction," a very attractive solution to the problem of translating such a slippery word, especially because "faction" also contains Filloy's requisite seven letters. However, the novel as a whole reveals two critical facts that strip away some of the attraction from "faction." First, that Filloy's *linyeras*, while fractious and factional, are both more and less than, but never precisely a political faction per se. Second, that *caterva*, in its fullest, most malign, and truly satirical sense refers not just to the seven "professional" beggars but, effectively, to all the characters in the novel which, from start to finish, mounts a trenchant satire on the whole of Argentine society. As in Shakespeare's comedies, especially the so-called "problem plays," no one in the book comes up smelling like roses. Because no single, seven-letter word in English truly captures the full, sinister verve of "caterva" as employed by Filloy, a non-fractious consensus was reached to maintain the novel's original title. It's an intriguing, enigmatic title for a book that is concerned with multiple identities, solving problems, and breaking codes. Nor is "caterva" very tricky for English language readers to recognize, learn, or say, and the word's distinctive amphibrachic swoop trumps the snub-nosed trochee of "faction." There is also precedence in the fact that the title *Caterva* entered into the awareness of English language readers through Gregory Rabassa's translation of *Rayuela*.

Caterva is a brilliant, intriguing, touching, and irrepressibly funny modernist novel which rewards readers aesthetically, morally, and intellectually. My hope is that this English translation does some justice to Filloy's rich, complex Spanish and furthers the introduction of Juan Filloy to the English-speaking world, where his enormous, uncanny, influential oeuvre remains almost entirely uncharted by translators, readers, critics, and scholars.

Heartfelt thanks are due to those patient friends whose knowledge, insights, and suggestions along the way helped to shape the text of this translation: Susana Fabrés Díaz, Álvaro Enrigue, Jeremy Davies, Frances Riddle, Carmen Grau, Thomas Riley, Donald Riley, Sarah Fleming, Lisa Broderick, Richard Cushman, and Alexandra Shaeffer *¡Mil gracias!*

Brendan Riley
San Diego, California
February 2015

Caterva

ca•ter•va [cah-terr'-vah]

noun

Spanish < Latin < [unknown]: crowd, mob, rabble, throng, swarm, multitude, the vulgar, the hoi polloi, the great unwashed; in Latin used in describing a flock of birds; a troop of soldiers; a company of actors; a horde of barbarians; a dramatic chorus; (also used pejoratively).

NOTICE

SEEK FOR NO AGONAL CHARACTER
AMONG THESE DISASTROUS DRIFTERS,
WHO FORM A SHREWD MILITIA
ON THEIR IDEALISTIC TOUR
FOR THE SAKE OF OTHERS.

ASSIGN TO THEIR ADVENTURE
NO OTHER INTENTION
THAN A HOLY HATRED:
NAMELY, AN INCURABLE LOVE FOR HOPE.

A BAND OF TIRELESS ADVENTURERS,
THEIR HEROISM ON THE MARCH ACHIEVES
NOTHING MORE THAN THE CONQUERING OF DEATH
IN THE NEAR RESIGNATION OF LIFE.

J.F.

ON THE ROAD TO ...

MACKENNA	UCACHA
MOLDES	BENGOLEA
BULNES	OLAETA
SAMPACHO	CHARRAS
JAGUELES	CHUCUL
HOLMBERG	HIGUERAS
RÍO CUARTO:	**RÍO CUARTO:**

They were huddled together under the bridge. Not clustered in a heap like stones and boulders that just come rolling randomly along ... but rather washed there by virtue of a secret current. A spiritual current that propelled them along that riverbed, all tumbling together from different places. Though, yes, to outside eyes, simply stones skidded to a stop, purely by chance.

They were huddled together under the bridge.

Tormented sky. A stubborn, nauseating wind blowing out of the north. In the greasy lethargy of the afternoon, the fetid stench thereabouts quickly filled the air; on clear, crisp days the pollution scudded away towards zones more remote.

Stormy sky. Low clouds, scudding quickly from one side to the other, like housewives caught short by the sudden pangs of childbirth. Low clouds, the smell of sex. On the horizon, lightning flashed and illuminated the inner folds of their skirts.

The sickening wind blew insistently. It swirled around the vagabonds like a swarm of flies brazenly pestering their noses. It blew harder, undulating in gracious curves, curling round the spandrels of the bridge. It floated upon the river, the water reflecting its miasmal tulle. It rose up to the railway tracks, threading through the heavy ties cut from *quebracho* trees. It played around the ironwork railings. And flying, flying—a stubborn swarm of flies—the dogfighting wind again returned to scour the vagabonds' nostrils with its sickening stink. To drink the sweat of their ragged clothes. To lick the scabs on the piss-stained walls.

"What a stink!"

"What kind of a shit heap have we landed in?"

"Patience. Just be a little bit patient. It'll pass soon enough. It's the garbage dump over there. They're just burning some trash, old man . . ."

One of the men snapped his newspaper shut and spat out his words in a rage:

"Always the same. You're so tolerant of everything . . ."

"Well . . . what else can we do? If I could go over and piss on the fire to put it out, I'd go. You just have to put up with it . . . Keep reading. In a little while the rain will put the fire out."

"That's what you think. The fire comes from the water. The water fans the flame."

The others fixed their eyes on him. They stuck out their lips in ironic pouts. Then seeing that he'd unfolded his paper again they perked up their ears:

". . . the new king will be named Edward VIII, Rex, Imperator. As prince, he had the following names: Edward, Albert, Christian, George, Andrew . . ."

"Hogwash!"

". . . Patrick, David; Prince of Wales, Count of Cambridge, Count of Garrick, Count of Chester . . ."

"What a big cheese!"

". . . Duke of Cornwall, Duke of Lancaster, Duke of Rothesay, Duke of Cornouaille . . ."

"What a circus!"

"Baron of Renfrew . . ."

"Baron? *Un varón?* 'A man, a warrior...?' We'll see about that. If he's anything like his big brother . . ."

"High Steward of Windsor, Lord of the British Isles . . ."

"Which cattle ranch was that, *che*?"

". . . Defender of the Anglican faith . . ."

"Outstanding. Defender of the errant faith . . ."

". . . Knight of the Order of the Garter, Knight of the Thistle . . ."

"Some knight: quickly unseated by a blow to his shield . . ."

". . . Grand Master of the Order of Saint Michael, Grand Master of the Order of Saint George, Grand Master of Scotland . . ."

"Hold on: look at the river!"

". . . Knight Grand Commander of the Indian Empire, Knight Grand Commander of the Star of India . . ."

"Commander of the other bunch, too . . ."

". . . High Cross of the Order of Victoria, Grand Master of the British Empire, Keeper of the Imperial Service . . ."

"Of the Imperial 'Service'! More like the Imperial Sluice, the latrine, where they shit out Australians, Hindus, Egyptians, right? What an honor!"

"Keeper of the Military Cross, Member of the Royal Society, *Aide de Camp* . . ."

"Ugh! That's enough! Quit reading!"

"*Aide de camp!* What camp? Where? When? What a sham!"

The reader tossed his paper aside. The loose pages spun away, bouncing and leaping over the puddles like school children in their smocks running off to play hooky.

Rattled by his companions' jibes as well as the choking stench from the garbage dump, he cursed between his teeth and fluttered his hands, as if trying to suddenly clear the air.

Then he clucked his tongue. And growled:

"Majordomo ... *Aide de camp* ... Titles. What do these aristocratic pricks know about *el campo*, about living off the land, about regular people? Only how to oppress them. How to squeeze them. All they've got are names, titles. They don't have to wander around the country hoping for work, their hands ready and willing for hard labor. They don't know about overcrowded bunkhouses or sweating out in the fields in bad weather. They don't know about the callouses on the shearer's hands or what it's like choking to death loading grain onto a wagon. They don't go out to the fields dreaming of being free, in the cold, cutting air of dawn, sharpening their hopes into some kind of ideal. Names and titles, that's all they are. They've never done a goddamned thing in their lives. Nothing worthwhile. Nothing really human. They go out to the countryside just to take a ride, nice and comfortable, everything taken care of, with a whole troop of servants. They go out to show themselves off, to con all the suckers with their fancy clothes adorned with chevrons and their Brandenburg greatcoats. Pretending to be men of the land through the cheap illusion of hunting deer that have already been flushed out for them. Or with the arrogant stupidity of winning polo matches against opponents paid to lose ... *Aide de camp* ... they're hollow men. Titles. Farces. Faced with the settlers' desolate unrest, faced with the laborer's useful sweat, they saddle up just for fun. Neighing and whinnying about how they're all so high and mighty. They blow farts and the cretins applaud them. They're nothing but names and titles!"

"Fine: don't get upset. They're just following the code of honor that's been handed down to them, just another page in the aristocratic 'book of etiquette.'"

"Besides: they're far away . . ."

"It doesn't matter. Little boys whose only merit is that they're their father's sons, grandchildren of drunkards, great-great-grandchildren of degenerates, and they rub it in the world's face with all their cynical privileges and their whole long list of names and titles. I suppose it's all written down in their book of etiquette, but it's a book with many pages missing. Because they inherit their names and titles the same way they inherit syphilis. The sap of their family trees runs thick with spirochetes. Noble family histories are rotten with putrid viruses. Blue blood equals putrid blood, their chests flush with enameled buboes and other chancrous decorations. Every name, every noble title is an open sore festering with ignominy."

He broke off suddenly but left no room for interruption. Immediately he switched to another line of reasoning:

"And to think that we've got no name, no word, no title of our own, because we've forsaken even that. To think that when one of us dies, they just put down a double letter X, just like that: XX, two crooked crosses, fallen on their sides, the double incognito of our identity. To think we're just as insignificant to those politicians, out there stumping on the campaign trail. Ask them to spell our names, and you'll get a similar answer: two capital Ns: *Nomen Nescio,* representing their non-opinion of our non-identity: *Nobody. Nothing* . . . But someday this will change. One day their scorn will come face to face with our vilification. There'll be no barriers, no social exclusion, no special channels, sluices, canals, locks, or dikes . . . And to bring this about, we need to strike against them. We need to boycott kings, princes, dukes, and all other kinds of stooges, letting them choke to death on the public's antipathy and the noxious atmosphere of their own public speeches. We need . . ."

"All right, that's enough *of that,* too."

The wineskins in heaven rumbled and shuddered.

Thick drops came pelting down. The rain was preparing to attack with heavy artillery. Then came its liquid grenades, falling, exploding at regular intervals. Here, there, anywhere. On the edge of the wrought iron railing. On the hulking bridge pilings. On the bald heads of the boulders. On the bald heads of the vagabonds . . .

The raindrops grew smaller in caliber. A tight frightening rattling curtain of water came down evenly across the afternoon. A cloudburst of rifle shots and shrapnel. Between the grainy screen of the air, filtered gasses and shafts of light.

"Sonofabitch, look at that rain!"

"Let's get under the bridge."

"Hurry."

They moved away in a flurry of old clothes and curses.

The storm now past, they returned.

Three bald vagabonds.

One with a rounded half-bald head like Socrates. His muttonchops grew down into a beard of grey curly hair that really belonged on his head.

Another man, the youngest, had a rounded bald patch, as if tonsured: holy ground for diabolical ideas.

The third, the oldest, had a sharply crested cranium descending to a curved nose. His loose skin — red and granular — gave him the look of an eagle, plucked bald.

The afternoon was fresher and colder now. But the sky was still white, blank and contorted, with the eye of the sun gouged out . . . Although the stench from the fires at the dump continued polluting, polluting . . .

Odors of snuffed-out garbage. Odors of meconium. Odors of prostitutes' armpits. Odors of hydrocyanic emanations. Familiar sour, bitter smells floated along now, just above the ground, carried on the vaporous wings of humidity.

"Why don't we gather up the gear and move somewhere else?"

"What for? It'll just be the same, Katanga. Or worse . . . At least right here it's not all filthy with garbage. And there's water here. As soon as the wind shifts . . .

"Oh, of course! The wind will now shift direction for our convenience . . . After all, that downpour we just had was trouble enough . . ."

Their two smiles conquered his derision. They stayed put.

Katanga, the youngest man, seated himself on a rough burl of cement that jutted out from the foot of the bridge. He cupped his face in the hollow of his hands, his arms sticking out across his splayed thighs like two crutches. In this way he sat still, staring for a long while at the flowing river.

The riverbank was slick from the rain. A tuft of rescue grass jutting up through the sand flicked its glaucous smear of stalks back and forth, caressing itself suggestively in the fresh breeze. And Katanga murmured:

"Everything is connection and correspondence. A dewdrop for each pore in the earth. A drop of rain for each stalk of grain. A star for every grain of wheat. Everything is connected. Only man is broken up, unsociable, diverse, different. Only man is disconnected!"

"Were you saying something?" asked Viejo Amor, using his right hand to mop up the sweat pearling on his Socratic head.

"The only one without any connection!" Katanga continued, talking to himself, far removed from the others' incomprehension. Yes, indeed! And how can we have any connection or correspondence with anything when we've got nowhere to live?"

Katanga barely raised his eyes. He smiled, his nose curling down as he continued.

"There ought to be something like a poste restante for the soul! Places where the emotions of mysterious metapsychic correspondents can be rescued from oblivion or silence! There ought to be! . . ."

But it wasn't worth explaining. So he went back to letting his thoughts drift along on the diaphanous current. To enjoy the plants' flirtatious coquetry—a smear of glaucous stems in the sand.

His companions were almost all fellow travelers. More capable than most when it came to facing the vicissitudes of life

on the road. But, nevertheless, most of them went about with
their heads stuck firmly up their asses, their minds always hovering at street level, precisely at the height of grocery store and
delicatessen shop windows. They weren't interested in examining things more deeply, or turning their hungry shop-window
eyes to probe the abundant mysteries of their own existence.
What could such grasping men understand of the subtle, inter-
woven correspondences between living beings and inanimate
objects? How could one imbue them with the secret loves that
reign in the pantheism of the world?

He looked out of the corner of his eye. Longines and Viejo
Amor were hard at work preparing dinner.

Katanga's thin lips curled into a disdainful grimace.

Many times in his days of stubborn wandering he had stumbled over some expected enigma, found himself checked by silent warnings emanating from seeming trivialities. And if he
was wont to discover sublime connections therein—among
the banalities of life which inspire no respect, among the mean-
ingless minutiae which the world scorns and abuses—then
what phantoms, what genies, what pneumas awaited him in
the realms of transcendence? Over time his gaze had sharpened
to penetrate deeper into the sense of everything he saw. His vision did not drop anchor like some ordinary boat bobbing at
its designated dock. No. His gaze penetrated to the essence,
to the most arcane depths, to the subtle homeports of *hierar-
chia*: the divine order of the world. Thus, for him, the universe
was not a mere physical conglomerate of earthly beings and
heavenly bodies. He despised the pretense that anything in this
world might be pondered objectively. He loathed the notion
of things being fixed and concrete: that was what vulgar minds
liked to ponder! For Katanga the universe was the footprint,
the track, the wake, the slipstream ... not the electric spark of
the lightning bolt but rather its zig-zag trajectory. Not the river's water but the memory of it gliding around a willow bough.
Not men, but the seamless swath of their actions. Once, in the
thin strands of a spider's web, he read the allegory of his own

life. He felt hobbled by those tenuous filaments that were his true telluric moorings. He spent long, sleepless nights in meditation. Until Rimbaud gave him the key:

Par délicatesse
J'ai perdu ma vie.

Thus he discovered the dazzling seductive power of symbols.

He inclined his head broodingly:

Destiny boasted of its power by lowering its yoke onto his shoulders, by imposing itself upon him, inflicting defeat upon him, slowing him down, hobbling his every step. His sense of personal progress imploded into fantasy: mere superficial vanity. He was a prisoner of his conscience. And in the pain of knowing himself to be sad, through an excess of intelligence, he found a measure of happiness in his own lack of affection.

"*Che*, come give us a hand."

He'd been kicking around Argentina for years. The nomadic life had toned his flesh: stealing it, withering it, making it thin and flaccid. No longer vain or anxious he only nourished one remaining ideal. To die little by little while living as much as possible. To live deeply by locating the soul amid the chaos and struggle of an eternal agony. Thus, when death finally smothered him, he would obtain what his spirit had never achieved. It was enough to overcome even the smallest doubt. Virility overflows the riverbed of doubt. Upon the riverbed of doubt, death engenders the supreme moments of our lives.

"C'mon, *che*: come help."

He slowly withdrew his face from the hollow of his cupped hands. He freed his thighs from the pressure of his elbows. He made a great show of yawning wide while flexing and stretching his arms. At last, wresting himself from his lethargy and standing up, he opened his eyes and greeted the glassy mirror of a splendid evening.

Nine o'clock at night.

"Let's eat dinner. The meat's ready."

"Let's wait. Fortunato, Lon Chaney, and Dijunto will be here soon."

"They should already be here. That was the plan. You're always the same. Always ready to forgive them . . ."

The Swiss unreeled his harangue, while Katanga considered his man's words: strict; precise; thorough. And while innately good and tolerant in general, the Swiss man was implacable in matters of punctuality. They had nicknamed him "Longines" after the brand of watch.

"Let's make an exception. Just this time. If they don't come in fifteen minutes, we'll eat."

"Well, the salad's already got lemon on it. It's going to wilt."

"Well, it doesn't really matter if we don't eat it . . ."

For Katanga, punctuality was hogwash: a voluntary constriction, kowtowing to social expectations; the punctual man always suffers the anguish of waiting, and lives to complain about it. On the other hand, by not being punctual, by not making his private peace with the petulant whims that hold things back and slow men down, Katanga was able to "sympathize" with latecomers.

Longines rejected his proposal.

Slow, tidy, meticulous, he pulled out his combination penknife-fork-spoon-punch-canopener-corkscrew-awl-screwdriver-glasscutter-scissors; "The Ten Commandments" as he liked to call it. The utensil shone clean and bright.

It was more a fetish than a useful tool. A gift from a German official, who stayed in Freiburg during difficult times, Longines carried it with him everywhere he went, like a scapular. Slow, tidy, meticulous, the Swiss moved up close to the edge of the grill. And he started to eat, steadily, without pause, without haste, chewing so carefully, so quietly, that he seemed to be grinding away at his own cheeks.

Now and then Longines turned his face to observe Katanga and Viejo Amor. One of his eyes was always oozing pus, rendering him practically one-eyed, and so he stared the same way parrots do: sideways. Watching the two of them talking away, unfazed by their companions' laxity, his gorge began to rise. He judged their devotion to the latecomers shocking. Fixing his jaws in a motionless clench he resisted the urge to swallow. But then he changed his mind. Their indifference was simply disrespectful. And he swallowed the blob of chewed food—a very soft smooth paste—with the same unwavering pride with which the antifascists, refusing to be broken by the Blackshirts, swallowed the horrid dose of castor oil forced down their throats . . .

His companions kept chatting:

"Look. What a splendid night. You can still see the sun's glow on the horizon. Gold melted into shadows. Fire filtered through shreds of mist. That cloud! . . . Look, Viejo Amor, that glowing silken strip of cloud. It looks exactly like the thigh of a beautiful girl reclining on a couch . . ."

"Where?"

"There. Above the belfry. Right there where the clouds are all bunched up and wrinkled."

"To the left?"

"No. The ones with a sort of satin silvery lining. Just like a fine old suit. Oh, nature is so amazing! Earlier this afternoon the clouds looked as heavy as burlap sacks. And now they look so wonderfully light and gauzy. The stout matrons of the daytime have become graceful girls. Just for us. Look. Look! Doesn't that one look like a naked girl?"

"Where, where?"

"No, man, no. Look up! In the sky . . . There. Over by the city hall tower. Look really close, quick; because the celestial sculptors shatter their figurines just as soon as you get a good look at them. See? A young girl crouching down at a fountain. Her back is all lit up, from her neck down to her ass, with a coppery reflection."

"Wow . . . nice girl! What I'd give to be a cloud! . . . A male cloud, of course . . ."

Viejo Amor kept staring, lost in his contemplation of the

clean, precise profile. Katanga's voice pulled him out of his ecstasy:

"Come on. Those guys aren't coming. Quit sighing. It's too
late for you to be a cloud now. You can't go backwards. That's
the Karmic law, old man! Your whole life is one big cloud anyway ..."

In reality, Katanga was distracted, even as he was distract-
ing the other man. He was distracted by the profound magic of frivolous things. Katanga knew that, in spite of the primitive roughness of his instincts, Viejo Amor had a soft spot for
even the subtlest touch of beauty. Then again, Katanga was also
well-aware of the man's monstrous mentality, which had led to
two trials for statutory rape, and another one for incest. He'd
heard many tales of his homosexual quirks, and seen proof
aplenty of Viejo Amor's current predilection for sodomy. But
the man didn't frighten him. On the contrary, he liked having Viejo Amor around. For the sake of studying him, and an-
alyzing his enormous lubricity—a kind of mental macroceph-
aly—which made his psyche sway and stagger at every step.
And, moreover, because behind the canvas of his emotional landscape, he'd become rather fond of contemplating Viejo Amor's soul, in its moments of sweet satisfaction, pacified,
licking its lips with ineffable tenderness, as if all his past outbursts and excesses, all his erotic violence were, in a word, no
more than the visible expression of his reproductive instinct.

Love stutters in some but is eloquent in others. It's a gift.
Katanga knew this. Through the long years on the odyssey of
impulses he'd played the voyeur, gazing on as one coarse suitor
after another seduced and plucked the finest flowers ... And,
conversely, he'd watched as some of the wisest minds remained
inert, fraught with desire yet unable to experience the delights
of sexuality. The instinct is the same in all men: an enormous
cistern of desires, trapped in the thicket of the self. But for
some, the channels that are meant to flow out freely through
the lips get choked by a mess of emotions.

Viejo Amor was a born stutterer. And although he lacked

the words to persuade, he had, by contrast, more than enough strength to conquer. His brutality made up for his soul's lack of eloquence. And peremptory, ignoring all pleas or promises, he satisfied his whims wherever he liked. Unfortunately for him, however, morals do exist. And for flouting them with such insouciance, he paid the stiff price in prisons and courtroom hearings. But this essential rebelliousness excited Katanga. He'd never captured such a specimen before. Which was why, dissimulating his superiority like a good Samaritan, he condescended, descending from his intellectual throne, to show Viejo Amor the eloquence of love in the lovely things of nature, using short, choppy, staccato words to match the man's stuttering emotions.

The roasted meat was now all dried out.

The perfumed aroma from the ribs, which half an hour earlier had wafted into their nostrils, making their mouths water in anticipation, was now reduced to a thin wisp of acrid smoke.

They barely ate a mouthful.

The stench of burned meat was enough to make one cringe.

Viejo Amor attacked the bread and cheese. Katanga grabbed the bowl of salad for himself. The watercress was tough: its tiny, crisp leaves and fragile stems soaked in the citric acid. From the corner of his eyes he spied Longines peeling a juicy pear. Slow, tidy, meticulous, he seemed to be extracting a spiral of sarcasm from his mouth while he worked, as fine as the golden spiral he was paring from the fruit. Katanga heard him mutter in bitter mockery:

"It doesn't really matter if we don't eat it."

Katanga bellowed a wordless diatribe. Then, ignoring Longines's insult, briskly choked down the bloody pulp of a tomato.

Longines and Viejo Amor were lying down. Their folding cots squeaked as they turned over, trying to find the best position for falling asleep.

But sleep had not yet come. Because sleep enters through

the ears, conducted by phalanxes of wise and mysterious elves as soon as the eyelids surrender and droop.

Both of them were still talking.

The guardians of sleep encircled their heads, infusing them with the monotonous susurrations that soften and distend the flesh, the fluid currents that flood every channel of the brain and dissolve it to a flat, standing pool.

They muttered their good nights.

And the guardians of sleep slipped inside. They stopped up their ears from within. And in a happy, macabre saraband filled them with the slippery bliss of rapture and nightmare.

Katanga unfolded his cot. He stripped to the waist and did some pushups. Then he stepped away to urinate among the weeds.

A soft night, spread out like smooth silk along the horizon line. The crinkled clouds from the storm had disappeared. An obsidian night, with the deep green resplendence of volcanic glass.

Falling upwards! Yes. There are such paradoxical emotions. Katanga fell upwards, ecstatically, into the great void above. A tranquil ecstasy. Reveling in the light spun from the immaterial. But his flesh, bound to the earth, continued with its routine, unaware of his transport. And while his imagination, magnetically attracted by the stars, passed through the sidereal regions, his hand continued shaking his limp penis, following its accustomed task of squeezing out every last stubborn drop of piss.

It's difficult to measure ecstasy with time. Each second spent fused with the flights of stars and planets contains the eternity of the cosmos. And for the duration of the contemplative effusion one's eyes—two wondrous eggs—incubate within themselves the truth of a new and marvelous cosmogony.

In this vision, Katanga saw his father's face. His severed head was the axis of a bloody constellation. It revolved around him, like endless mountain ranges, a necklace of stars with the sharp scintillations of cutlasses and scimitars. A tragic circle of decapitated heroes! Each star was a symbol in the greater narrative of his sacrifice. They had been men of honor from the inner plains of Armenia. And their silvery flash, which leaped out from the ochre of the wastelands, now radiated in the black deserts of the sky.

Katanga trembled: a forgotten memory blossomed in his mind. Barely making a sound, barely moving his lips, he formed the words:

"Almudafar! Almudafar!"

Yes. It was written. It was he! Almudafar: "the Valiant One."

"Almudafar! Almudafar!"

As a boy, one splendid night like this one, on the path outside his tent, his father had warned him:

"It's good, my son, that you believe in yourself; because sorrow will always shadow your steps. I don't fear death because I love life too much. Selfish men, cowards, those who don't know that love is the closest thing to nothingness . . . the instant that the news of death sheds rainbow light across the surface of their skin, they tremble like water in the pools of Azem. I've brought you on these epic adventures so that you will understand, while you're still young, that there is no other law than suffering. At the same time, I want you to be fully aware that when you rage against ignominy, the pain of suffering is sanctified with your cry or filled with the air of song. While the happy poets of Armenia were composing retractions to their Rubaiyats, my life spoke like a rebec accompanying them. Later came the infamous whirlwind of the Red Sultan. Since then, since Abd-ul-Hamid II unleashed his rage and set his dogs loose on furious campaigns of malice and crime, we have taken up arms against this anathema. They have branded us insurrectionists, bandits . . . Men of unbowed pride who openly face the aggressor and fight for the dignity of the oppressed are always called bandits! It doesn't matter. My only aspiration is to come face to face with Abd-ul-Hamid . . . To send him to hell, his face marked with my sword. This is the only way the Red Sultan will pay for his cruel treatment of my fellow countrymen. Just as he reveres the sword more highly than the Koran, I have set my homeland before

my religion. And I will stamp his flesh with my signet, no matter the cost, even if I must wet its characters with my own blood ... It is well, my son, that you believe in yourself, because sorrow will always shadow your steps. Be like Poliorcetes: defend the fortress of your self with courage and determination. When you are grown, you will learn, perhaps, the things we men must do to fulfill our duty. And such things will come easily to you. Learn to contemplate the firmament. Wherever you wander, wherever you settle, learn to contemplate the firmament. Behind its niello, behind its curving steel vault fretted with gold and precious stones, is written the destiny of men. Kismet! Kismet! The trails of the planets, the trajectories of the clouds, the flights of birds, are divine traceries, mysterious glyphs inscribed in the sky by the hand of Allah. Turn your eyes away from earthly writings and read instead only what is written in the heavens. Learn to contemplate the firmament. When you can decipher the intricate plots, written within the rays of moonlight, the edges of the sun and the lightning flash of the storms, be they sublime, ordinary or offensive, then you'll see that all the wisdom of our ancestors lives on in the permanence of their secret. And in the same way that our ancestors inscribed the vault of heaven with Arabic names: Achernar, Mirafeh, Algeiba, Sirah, Deneb, Mirath, Albireo, Unukalhai, Mirfak, Hamal, Mirzam, Alphart, Sadalmelik, Menkab ... from now on, my son, be persuaded that the constellation of your father, Almudafar, "the Valiant," will sprout in the blue meadows on high. Wherever you wander, wherever you settle, look for me. Your eyes will grow weary from gazing upon the celestial deserts. Wastelands of burned-out stars will limn it, and it will be polluted by dust clouds of nebulae; but do not be intimidated. Wander, investigate. There are stupendous oases of stars. There are caravanserai where the spent and discouraged traveler finds refreshment and comfort proffered him by the most splendid houri. Wander, investigate. If you cannot be an astronomer, be a wanderer among the clouds. You will find me! Scan the length of the celestial equator. I have always chosen the longest, roughest road. Do not lose hope. Learn to contemplate the firmament. And your eyes will come to rest on my tent ... on this

tent . . . in this village of brave men . . . while I . . . your father . . .
outside . . . here . . . with astral eyes . . . I will remain vigilant, spy-
ing on the Red Sultan's caravan . . . along the edge of this waste-
land of stars . . . which is the Milky Way . . . "

Katanga felt every cell in his body vibrate with exhilaration,
so drunk on his filial reverie, so absorbed in its magic, that he
could hardly distinguish dream from reality. He felt like the
round, bald crown of his head had expanded right along with
his thoughts to the point that the whole curving night sky was
now floating inside his cranial dome.

His father's counsel was so vivid that it seemed freshly delivered, and not a distant childhood memory. Deep within the
double concavity of the sky and his mind, Katanga's vision remained fixed:

"Yes. Yes. That's it, there's no doubt, the constellation Almudafar: 'the Valiant One.'"

Moving from Sirius towards Aldebaran, he'd scaled the fantastic steps that demarcate Rigel, Orion, the Three Kings which
form Orion's Belt, and Betelgeuse. And there, in Aldebaran,
a third of the way along the trajectory from Nath to Menka-
linan, approximately fifty degrees in the ascendant, he saw a
bloody light dripping from the severed head of his father, amid
a necklace of stars glittering like polished razor-sharp blades of
cutlasses and scimitars.

If, in such circumstances, his mind had not been flooded
with such a sidereal confluence of longings and memories of
a childhood fraught with horror, adventure, sudden flights,
and harsh punishments, perhaps, as he lowered his gaze — still
absorbed in the night sky — his eyes might have discerned a
group of individuals approaching their camp under the bridge,
finding their way along the swampy riverbed by the glare of
two flashlights.

Fortunato. Lon Chaney. Dijunto.

But they weren't alone. Two detectives, revolvers in hand,
swept bright cones of light back and forth, in wide arcs.

The instant one of the lights discovered Katanga's torso, both beams immediately focused on his face. But rapt as he was in his longing for his ravaged homeland, in summoning the faces of ancestors, and watching the stirring legends of those Islamic lands unfold in their distant time and place, he hardly realized what was happening. It was only when he heard one of the detectives ask:

"Who's that?"

And he heard Dijunto's broken voice, in an agonized inflection, saying: "It's Katanga,"

that he finally came to his senses, instantly, philosophically, adding in agreement:

"Abd-ul-Katan ben Hixem . . . Abd-ul-Katan ben Hixem . . ."

But an imperious voice cut him off:

"Don't be a wiseass! Put your hands up!"

"I'm not being a wiseass. I'm Abd-ul 'Katanga' ben Hixem."

"There are seven cots here. One of them is missing. No doubt about it. None of you matches the description we were given. So let's hear it! Where's the other guy?"

" . . . "

" . . . "

" . . . "

" . . . "

" . . . "

" . . . "

"What the hell are you waiting for? Don't you hear the Chief talking to you? Or do you want us to beat the shit out of you? Where's the other guy?"

Fortunato, rattled, stammered:

"Looks like . . . he's moved on . . ."

A hard, stinging slap across his face sealed his ingenuous answer with a red welt.

This provoked a brief commotion among the vagabonds.

"Hold it! Anyone tries to run, I'll blow his fucking head off."

The flashlight beams darted nervously from one face to the next. Behind the light, clutched tight in their fists, each detective's revolver was pointed dead center at their spotlighted targets.

The six vagabonds stood, intimidated, fuming with opprobrium.

"Are you gonna answer me or what, goddammit? Where's the other guy?

The silence was about to explode. Then Katanga, drawing from his burlesque grab bag a mellifluous voice perfect for just such emergencies, declared:

"Gentlemen, please! Don't get upset. We'll tell you whatever you want. We're honest men. We had no idea that you represented the authority of this most cultivated city. Not having introduced yourselves, we weren't able to discern your intentions."

"What the fuck's wrong with you, wiseass? You think we'd waste our time on a bunch of lousy drifters?"

"Neither drifters, sir, nor lousy."

"Shut your mouth! Don't interrupt me."

"I'm not interrupting, sir. Please proceed."

There was another uncomfortable silence.

In the modulation of that "please proceed," the junior detective perceived a whisper of secret malice that deeply mortified him. He scrutinized the offending man out of the corner of his eye, muttering bitter blasphemies. He studied him insidiously. And turning towards his commanding officer, asked:

"Why don't we drag them all in? It's better that way. Headquarters, we'll get them to sing."

"Yes: that'd be better. All right, all of you: get dressed."

While Longines and Viejo Amor, half asleep, grumbled softly about bothersome police behavior, Katanga began reflexively to don his shirt, jacket, and straw hat. He moved slowly, thus gaining a few extra moments to carefully consider the risks at hand. Unless the detectives were just trying to scare them, the situation was becoming serious. His pockets held several compromising letters from some quasi-legal communist newspapers. Additionally, his bags held various books attesting to his political faith. He couldn't suppress a shiver. Words he'd uttered many times returned to his mind:

The snobs, pitucos, *posh* fils à papa, *they're allowed to read and*

dabble in revolutionary literature. But if the cops find any left-
ist book or magazine on me, I'm done: jail, torture, near starva-
tion, and for a long time, too. Freedom of thought! Freedom to ex-
press ideas! . . .

What occupied his memory next were the agents of the
BECEC. He'd once fallen into their clutches, collared on
trumped up charges: "arms trafficking" and "fomenting rebellion." He couldn't help shivering again. His back was tanned
from countless truncheon blows. His testicles had been twisted like a corkscrew. His belly scarred by the terrible electric discharges of the "shock baton." His throat knew the fiery thirst
of being forced to eat salted herrings and other police *gour-*
mandizes . . .

After furtively observing the Chief Investigator, he began
to brighten up. He had the sudden impression that the Chief
was actually a good man, meaning a poor Chief. Aside from
his requisite share of professional roughhousing—the inevitable slaps, blows, and beatings he'd had to administer over the
course of his career—the man didn't betray an instinct to do
any real harm. His eyes glanced around in a natural, relaxed
manner, and his countenance seemed undistorted by the malign, sarcastic glow of the members of that Okhranka *All' uso*
nostro. He had the look of a family man, and so Katanga didn't
consider him capable of any serious treachery. Feeling sure that
he wasn't dealing with one of the many Torquemadas of the
Holy Inquisition Against Communism, he figured his best op-
tion was to try to win the man's sympathy—although the other detective, the Chief's second-in-command, clearly much
sharper and more than a little bull-headed, might snort with
indignation.

Arranging the kerchief around his neck, he approached the
Chief. He swallowed to loosen up his vocal cords in preparation for unleashing his most fawning falsetto.

Like the cautiously probing antennae of certain insects, he
tried to get a sense for the path ahead. He figured that this
evening's unwelcome surprise had probably arrived courtesy of

some fresh blunder on the part of the ever-troublesome "Aparicio." Still, unsure of the detective's true motive for raiding their
camp, he thought it best to first determine whether or not the
aforementioned arrest warrant was simply a bluff to get them
to cop to Aparicio's whereabouts.

Katanga's mellifluous, emergency voice began again:

"C'mon, Longines, hurry up. Don't let your arthritis slow
you down! There's nothing to be done about it. Authority is
authority. What're you doing, Fortunato? C'mon, fold up the
cots. The same for you, old man. No fair pretending to be
asleep!"

"What! We're being taken in along with these useless idiots?"

"Of course. Nobody stays behind. Right, sir?"

"What a time of night to be going to the clink!"

The Chief Investigator—certain to be fired soon thanks
to the coming change in government—had lost his old zeal.
Pride of place no longer mattered to him at all. And his once-
sparkling lynx-sharp eyes were fogged over with the bitter fear
of his impending unemployment. The brief exchange between
these drifters—embellished with well-timed laments and complaints— seemed to mollify the Chief almost completely. The
vagabonds felt his benevolence like a fresh breeze ... They
could almost hear what the Chief was thinking:

Why, we're abusing our power. These poor drifters!

So they didn't get frisked after all, and their camp wasn't ran-
sacked. The cops made a cursory sweep with their flashlights,
doodling about but not making a careful search. Clearly they
were only interested in arresting Aparicio, whom they accused
of being "the professional agitator who'd delivered ten thousand pesos from the International Red Aid to a local union
strike." The result was that the detectives overlooked the peculiar characteristics of the campsite with its cots and folding
field chairs, baskets packed with ingenious picnic equipment,
a collapsible canvas awning, primus gas, Sterno burners, and a
small radio.

The Chief looked down at his second-in-command.

"What do you say we just cite them, order them to report to the station in the morning?"

"Cite them? No, no! Tomorrow they'll vanish. You know these people . . . Here today . . . gone tomorrow . . ."

The younger detective made a nervous flourish in the air. And finished his sentence:

". . . I still vote for the third degree."

"If you would permit me," intervened Katanga, his voice soft as merengue. "I'm happy to provide you with any details you might require concerning our presence in this most highly cultured city. We are unemployed. We used to be among the inhabitants of the Villa Desocupación camp in Buenos Aires, before the Eucharistic Congress started interfering and making life even more difficult for us . . ."

"Interfering?"

"Yes. The Eucharistic Congress "trampled our nest" as they like to say. Their euphemism for raids and forced evictions. You see, the distinguished ladies of the organizing committee were of the opinion that our Villa might be an affront to the pious eyes of the pilgrims. And so, filled with pity, and under the auspices of an enormous cross made from cement and celotex, the Municipality ran us out of Buenos Aires like some festering mob of plague-ridden peasants. Now we are thousands of farflung crosses — suffering, twisted crosses of flesh, left in the hands of God!"

"Hmmm! You all look too clean to be drifters."

"We're not drifters, we're simply unemployed. We heard that they'd be paving roads around here. We're looking for work."

"Work . . . eh? Hmm, let's see your hands!"

Conscious of the danger their companion had landed himself in, Dijunto and Longines quickly stretched out their hands. They knew that Katanga would play dumb and ignore such a demand: it was an astute, oblique line of attack.

His fire dampened, the young detective insisted: "Let's see yours, too."

But he got nothing. Katanga had continued chatting up the

Chief: this latest demand had further inspired his malicious cunning, and he drew this gullible man deeper into his false confidence:

"No, I assure you, sir. You've been misled. Our only relation to the man you mentioned is that we share our food and camp-site with him. Clearly our situation is rather precarious; we're in desperate need, here. How could we be giving away fantastic sums of money when we're starving to death out here in the cold!"

The Detective saw that their investigation was being derailed by this bum's chatter.

Always the same idiocy, he spluttered. *Instead of investigating, the Chief talks. He extends bridges to the enemy, bridges of words so they can flee with impunity. Cretin!*

His fury increased in the darkness. It all reminded him of the *affaire* at the Bank. His hunch had been correct but the Chief thought otherwise. How could anyone have believed that that young manager in training, so submissive and help-ful, with his peach-colored skin and fishy eyes, was innocent . . . innocent! A magnificent triumph, wasted!

Whether from books, movies, or by intuition—God only knew!— he'd learned to question everything. Always. System-atically. He was a professional skeptic. An explorer of lies. A pi-oneer of the absurd. He trusted in his experience which had taught him that reality always dresses in falsities. The more ma-nure on the plant, the more beautiful the rose. The same is true for actions, they say: the most shining, noble and gener-ous acts are born of rotting garbage heaps. Fallacies! So obvious as to be overlooked. Misers may hide their money in trashcans and earthenware jugs, and even in scummy spittoons—there's no better custodian than dissimulation—and by the same logic, the most normal-seeming, naïve, unlikely human has a heart willing to commit the blackest crime. Knowing this all too well, career criminals, not the clumsy oafs who pervert the craft, clearly understand the disorienting power of good faith, candor, and misfortune. For that reason, and wisely, they dress themselves in the highest virtues or the saddest circumstances, pushing away responsibility, injecting it directly into other people's compassionate natures . . .

The camp's inhabitants shouldered their bundles, ready to go. The signal had passed between them to exaggerate their suffering. Every new effort brought forth some mutter of protest meant to confuse the police. Every step was full of creaking bones and angry gesticulations.

As the pack of men began moving out, the night, which sublimates beautiful things, added sordid accents to their collective misery.

The young detective, wise to the vagabonds' stratagem, couldn't hold back:

Farce! Lie! he hissed to himself, rattling with revulsion. *I'd let you have it right now, if it was up to me—a good beating! What a mockery, to let ourselves be fooled like this!*

And he followed behind, bringing up the rear, firm in his doubts, yielding not an inch, his thoughts loaded with more bullets than his revolver.

Reaching the access embankments, the Chief stopped and dabbed at his shoes. The bodies of the unwashed men emitted a sickly cloying odor that was impossible to ignore, a sour, fermented, pestilent stench that dogged his nose. But now they were all assaulted by the overwhelming stench of the garbage thrown under the bridge by pedestrians. A host of additional noxious smells swam into the mix. Rotten fish. Sweat-rotted clothes. Tar and rusted metal. Dirty crockery. Onions and garlic.

As soon as they came out into an open space, the Chief moved a ways ahead, taking big strides along the path. He panted anxiously. He wiped off his shoes again, this time in a clump of weeds. And observing the grumbling shadowy *caterva* of ragged men straggling behind, he pulled his second-in-command aside:

"Seems to me we're creating a ridiculous hassle for these poor bastards. Don't you feel sorry for them? We've got nothing on them."

"What about that guy's cot?"

"So what, a cot ... Look at them! Just a bunch of poor devils ..."

"Meanwhile they're not saying anything."

"Just look at them ... we're gonna be knee-deep in shit over this. Just as soon as the new government's in. All our screwing around, all our mistakes ..."

"Look, Chief: do what you think is best. But I think we should haul their asses in. And crack their skulls open without a second thought."

"That's ridiculous. Besides: we couldn't actually make any charges stick. We're just following up some rumors ... But, listen, I think we might at least arrest that one ..."

"Katanga?"

"Yes: him, he'll do."

"As you like."

The detective turned his face away, towards the shadows.

The heat of shame flooded through him, suffocating him.

The motto of any serious investigator: *de omnibus dubitandum* lay trampled beneath the blind idiocy of hierarchy, as though squashed by the Chief's stinking shoes.

Happiness is an impossible emotion, it refuses to be pinned down. Each person conceives of it according to their own degree of shrewdness or defines it according to their own aspirations. But no one really gets it right. In spite of possessing a permanent ubiquity, happiness is such a slippery idea that men often stubbornly deny its very presence. They don't realize they've been enjoying its protective blessing until the moment has passed. Then they miss it. And because happiness can't be followed back into the past, they shape it into an ideal for the future ...

Unlike most men, Lon Chaney possessed a true sense of happiness. For the very reason that his life had been beset by extreme misfortune, he made the most of any propitious moment, any kindly breach to be found in the otherwise unbroken wall of penury circumscribing his daily life. And letting its benisons seep into him, he would laugh a laugh like the sunshine filtering through the cracks.

When the detectives disappeared into the night, he turned to his accomplices. The stereotypical expression of the sad comedian he'd kept plastered on his face all the while suddenly relaxed and lightened up. And with the great theatrical instinct that they all knew so well, he whipped off his beret, sweeping back a greying, clownish curl of hair. After which . . .

The anticipation was icy.

"Out with it already," someone said.

But this demand went unheeded. Words would have to wait. From inside the lining of his jacket, Lon Chaney withdrew a sheaf of papers. And carefully evaluating whatever tremendously compromising information they contained, he finally let fly with a crafty cackle:

"That was damn close, but we were lucky. Katanga managed to pass these to me when the detectives were distracted for a minute. They're communist letters and flyers. We've got to burn them. Right now!"

"No, not now," said Longines, and hammered his point with precision: "In good time. They might be watching us. We don't want to attract attention. The greater the danger, the greater the caution."

As soon as he stopped speaking, his jaw and right fist closed tightly. On the tip of his tongue and in the handle of his valise he had two secrets that had to remain concealed until an opportune moment.

No one replied. Katanga's refined brand of cunning had allowed him to rise up to be the group's leader; but Longines still possessed a preeminent authority. This attribute in particular seemed to reside in his plucked eagle's head. Thus, while the group had great faith in Katanga's dialectical resources, they still respected the security implicit in Longines's support of a given plan.

Still, no one spoke, and the forced intimacy of the momentary pause began to weigh upon them.

A few yawns tainted the silence.

Some of the men suggested a short nap to relieve their fatigue.

A fair request, but not convenient.

The evening's events demanded the men take on a more appropriate attitude. There was no sense in remaining inactive when one companion had been arrested and another was being hunted. It's true that they had foreseen every possible contingency, and that neither man had anything to fear, really. But it was still necessary to safeguard the success of their common enterprise by means of a supplementary plan, a diversion of some sort.

Each one of them made himself as comfortable as he could for the wait. They formed a somber conclave, phantom Nyctalopes speaking in low voices ... but Dijunto and Viejo Amor began to nod off the moment they sat down on their upturned baskets. The snores of the former prompted a corrective action. A tugging, soft at first, then violent, brought him back to the conversation.

"No napping yet ..."

"I already did my part ..."

"But you must have some other details to report, something you left out, something you're holding back."

"We've explained everything."

"When I left you with Aparicio, in front of the Post Office, I managed to slip into the workers assembly which was preparing to vote on whether to suspend or to continue the construction workers' strike. I learned a lot about the integrity of the union leaders. Good people, courageous and enthusiastic ..."

"Agreed. But what else ..."

"One by one they were informed of our contribution and the method agreed upon for delivering it. They didn't want to believe that begging might be a skilled occupation like any other, and that we were going to help them. They were very reluctant to accept our solidarity, in fact. As soon as ..."

"Can you just come out and tell us what we're missing? I did exactly what you told me to do."

"Come on, Lon Chaney, we need details . . ."

Longines didn't like all this shilly-shallying. From the crest of his head to the point of his nose, his entire profile crinkled into countless wrinkles.

Annoyed by the delay, he repeated:

"Come on, Lon Chaney, details . . ."

"Well, what I mean is I don't know why the Union Treasurer came running out of the Post Office like he did. I had him pegged as being levelheaded. What a blunder! Talk about cracking under pressure. After all, we know that the members of the Pro-Strike Committee are being very closely watched. That's why we decided to hand over the money in the busiest spot in the city so as not to arouse suspicions. Why such a panic, then? Unless Dijunto lost control of the situation, there was no reason for the man to try to flee the scene like that."

"Not at all. We simply didn't count on the Treasurer's completely losing his cool. When he arrived at the appointed spot, wearing the mourning clothes we knew would identify him as our man, he was already wildly, painfully reluctant and self-conscious. I stuck out my hand as though I was begging for some change. That was the signal. Aparicio played his part just fine; when he and the Treasurer bumped into each other, as planned, our friend handed over the ten thousand pesos. There was nobody else in the hallway. Nobody even noticed a thing, until . . ."

"Yes, but they still detained you. And me, too, for good measure."

"Inquiries . . . routine investigations . . . Nothing more. You'll see."

"Maybe so; but the police still found their way out here. Granted, all they did was confirm the existence of an empty cot. And arrest Katanga."

"I say there's no danger. They won't manage to finger any one of us, individually. By the way, I noticed our prearranged signal on a wagon in front of the crossing."

"Was it a *U* or an *S*?"

"What kind of a question is that? It was a *U, Ubi bene.* It couldn't be otherwise. Aparicio will head out tonight on the 3:20 A.M. freight train. It follows our route."

Longines abruptly interrupted them:

"Enough. That doesn't concern us right now. What matters is that we carry out our orders. You've got to learn to eschew simple plans—simple plans give us away and put us in danger. The more we take care to mechanize and synchronize our actions, the better we'll conceal ourselves behind complexity. We're a clock that's running and will not stop or slow down for anything. We're heroes on the road, and no mere organizational error is going to stand in our way."

The secret conclave was at an end. Some of the comrades stood up and moved about—phantom nyctalopes, etcetera— setting up their cots.

No longer sleepy, Dijunto couldn't contain his resentment:

"So tell me, Longines, is it my fault that the Union Treasurer panicked and ran? Lon Chaney, who pretends to be a psychologist, should see things like that coming. Obviously the poor fool didn't trust us to stick to the plan. Even though he saw our efficiency with his own eyes, even with the money already in his pocket, the lunatic ran like hell out of there. And that's the only reason a seemingly ordinary passerby like Aparicio was spotted when he was about to walk into the corner bar."

"So then . . . Aparicio!"

". . . was seen! Yes. That useless fool of a Treasurer stopped to beg his pardon just like some old acquaintance, and their little encounter was instantly spotted by that young detective who was just here. An amazing coincidence! Afterwards, when the rumor about the International Red Aid Fund was going around, Aparicio's face surfaced in his memory. I suppose that's why they're looking for him. Otherwise, why all the excitement?"

"To hell with excitement! When will man learn self-control, to regulate his impulses, to don a coat of impassivity, to conquer himself? Good thing you didn't explain all this in front of the others. Now beat it. I need a moment alone."

Meanwhile, Fortunato was stacking small piles of coins on the base of the pillar.

Viejo Amor was sleeping like a log. A log snoring itself into sawdust.

Lon Chaney lay down and stretched out his limbs.

Their shadows soon melted into the darkness of night. Their thoughts drifted away into the silence. Their breathing matched the rhythm of the breeze.

Dijunto went back to sit down on his basket.

He was Spanish. His durable Castilian honor, and little more, kept him upright and honest on his long hard road. His dirt-brown skin stretched tight over his starving frame, often the only thing he had to swallow was the sharp sword of his honor. But he'd been born and bred to a meager life! He could suffer all the miserable changes of fortune, anything except doubt. He sat on his basket, staring into the distance, staring but not seeing.

In this way, he didn't notice what Longines did next. He never saw the Swiss man open and close his several valises, avidly searching, checking, studying their contents. He didn't see him creep down to the river's edge where he kindled a small bonfire from letters, flyers, and books, then when it was cool, cautiously scattering the fresh ashes on the surface of the stream. Dijunto saw nothing. Only an image of his own wounded pride caught in the strange maelstrom of his turbulent spirit.

Longines continued working, absorbed with his stealthy, complex preparations. Softly opening secret compartments. Silently uncorking flasks. Smoothly unscrewing double false bottoms. Inscrutable stealth of quiet calculation. Working with consummate skill to concoct his stealthy stratagem of diversion ...

Longines knew that Katanga's freedom depended on their ability to act swiftly and prudently. If the man's unexpected arrest made it necessary for them to flee Río Cuarto, their careful plans would be thwarted, and they'd all be wracked with the guilt of failure. It was necessary to stay put and stick to the plan. But they needed the shelter of an airtight alibi, an excuse so perfect, so plausible that its rolling thunder would make them invulnerable . . .

He suddenly glimpsed a single star, previously unnoticed, reflected in the river's dark, shining current, a slipstream of golden flashes suspended in its wake . . . Its bright light seemed the very emblem of dissimulation, an ironic contrast to his dark designs . . .

Grateful for that favorable augury, Longines began his final preparations, carefully combining the various materials spirited out from the secret folds, pockets, and compartments in his luggage. Working by the sputtering light of a candle stub, his nimble fingers quickly and precisely finished the work. The result? Ever so neat and tidy, four slender cartridges of melinite, each one activated by a spring-loaded detonator and timing mechanism.

With his four bombs ready, the rest would be easy enough. Longines only had to needle Dijunto's wounded sense of honor, prod the man out of his lethargy, convince him to carry out this urgent diversionary tactic. He went over to where Dijunto was sitting, still staring into the night, and began to give his instructions:

"Listen, you need to vindicate your behavior today. Prove yourself, make up for your conduct by passing the test I'm about to give you. I want you to go right now and place, at four construction sites, at each of the four cardinal points of the compass, these four little alarm clocks . . . You'll know just where to put them, because you've surveyed those areas yourself. They're all timed to explode simultaneously, twenty minutes after you get back here. We'll certainly hear them, even this far away, and we'll know if you've done your work right. I'm giving you a total of two hours. Be careful! Look closely at the numbers I've written here in chalk! They must be set exactly according to this order, and no other. No improvising! This way, by the time all hell breaks loose, the freight train carrying Aparicio will have already departed. The police will come straight to the camp here but they'll find us snoring away ... And tomorrow Katanga will be freed, and you'll be back in my good graces."

Now readmitted to his chief's trust, Dijunto accepted the mission. His fatigue dissipated as if by magic. And he took pleasure in the rather sexy sort of risk that his behavior had now conferred on him. It wasn't difficult to hide the alarm clocks in his pockets. He said good night and departed, his thorny figure disappearing among the hawthorns along the riverbank.

Longines's good nature happily accompanied him from afar.

Afterwards, he weighed things for himself:

The purity we sometimes glimpse in even the most abject beings is quite touching. They spend their early years crawling through the slime of misfortune, dishonesty, and crime, which somehow purifies them, at a certain point, age sublimates them, grinds, buffs, and polishes them into clear, moral mirrors, uncontaminated zones of the conscience. It's the very vengeance of time! Of time misspent—and all the inevitable misgiving drives a man to display those clear, noble qualities subdued in the first fervors of youth. Old Chronos likes to spin his threads fine: emotions without knots, thoughts without frayed ends ... In such a way, the bearer of each enfeebled soul arises at last to face the evidence of his authentic virtues. He contemplates himself in them. He yearns to slow life's clock. But no, impossible! The record of their wayward youth is inscribed deeply on their faces—they've been had. Thus does one becomes infantilized, wallowing in lachrymose self-comparisons. And, unable to do anything but forgive himself, the prodigal son faces the final steep slope with a harsh frown, bearing as his only map the pristine candor of infancy.

Slow, prolix, meticulous, Longines set up his cot.

His eyes circled around, scrutinizing the camp. Within this rattling concerto of throaty breathing, wheezing, coughing, and snorting, his fastidious character was a baton pointlessly raised to a slumbering orchestra.

He lay down.

He couldn't fall asleep. Duty, the cross he'd always borne, the unforgiving timekeeper of his existence, ordered him to stay awake until Dijunto returned.

Nevertheless, he closed his eyes. The spectacle that they were offering the world was a stupendous one. He felt how much he really mattered, here, helping to lead their close-knit fraternity on a mission towards the improvement of mankind. And as his chest slowly rose and fell, filled with the evening air, he felt the mantle of the night draping him in the same ancient tenderness with which his mother had once enveloped him. And sleep came upon him.

He remembered, then, a peculiar definition of happiness he'd once encountered in the *Contre Sainte-Beuve*: "Happiness is like being sleepy ..." This had intrigued him profoundly. He'd always thought that happiness resided in being as far outside of oneself as possible, beyond all notions of introversion, oblivious of one's own individuality ... and yet he couldn't understand it. Now, though, he'd hit the nail on the head! Now that his duty demanded he not fall asleep ... now that Dijunto's task was going to be seen, visible for miles across the celestial sphere, the red sky of so many dreams and illusions ... he'd floated away, tracing a parabolic arc, rising from silence to glory. And it all meant very little. He knew now that happiness is never content. That happiness cannot be conquered, but instead conquers, like sleep. Sainte-Beuve ... was ... certainly ... right ... "Ha ... ppi ... nesss ... is ... like ... being ... very ... slee ... eeepy ..."

And he slept.

Three whistles.

A sudden jolt.

The train was pulling out ...

Hidden in a fragrant hollow formed by an enormous stack of cedar logs, Aparicio felt safe at last.

Nothing like movement to neutralize fear. However much terror pursues us, we can always evade it by running away. However much we may be hemmed in by our afflictions, we can still liberate ourselves by slipping away. To be in one's right mind, is to be a prisoner. Slip away! To flee is to cut a path through the thicket of reason, to tunnel through the humus of instinct. Sneak away! No better inspiration for self-preservation than a good healthy injection of fear to speed things up . . . and then you can let the wheels of time roll on.

When the train crossed over the bridge, Aparicio slid to the edge of the wagon to look for the campsite. He couldn't pick it out. The din of the rattling train cars hammering the rail joints and the dizzying sight of the tracks and ties speeding past blurred his vision and threatened to overwhelm his senses. Although skeptical by nature, his deference to command helped him remain calm. Unless something unexpected had happened, they would've already noticed the chalk mark he'd left on the wagon. And his decision to move their itinerary forward should be clear.

He made himself comfortable again, curling up inside his cedar enclosure. The weather was cool. His jacket and cap served as a pillow. He'd cut himself free from all ties.

He kept his eyes open, for a long while. Not that it made any difference—the flickering light through the beams prevented him from seeing more than a few inches beyond his face. So, rather than strain his eyes, he closed them instinctively. And right away, as is only logical, his eyes began to look inward, to scrutinize his inner self.

The sheer idiocy of that afternoon's episode bewildered him. He clucked his tongue in disgust. Much as destiny sometimes saves heroes from rumors of cowardice, it often indulges itself by making a mockery of authentic bravery, toying with it as a cat does a ball of yarn.

Why should he, of all men, get tangled up in the Union Treasurer's skein of stupidity during this strike? Why should he, of all men, who had fought alongside the great Aparicio

Saravia—so great he'd adopted the man's name as his own traveling moniker—in the epic civil wars of Uruguay, surrender to the suspicions of some provincial detective? Why should he, of all men—who had escaped the jaws of Eliseo Lamas to become one of the most celebrated cutthroats among the imprisoned members of the Uruguayan Red Party, *los Colorados!*—recoil before the threats of a few clumsy thugs? Why should he, of all men, who had taken part in the violent skirmishes at Tres Árboles, Hervidero, Arbolito, Masaller, and Tupambay, flee the city at the mere insinuation of a fellow traveler? Had he lost his courage? Was his rebellion now perfunctory, insincere? Was it . . . ?

He asked himself no more questions. He clucked his tongue with greater distaste than ever. And gave thorough consideration to the notion that within the nexus of unknowable forces that make up this world there lies some ironical power whose agenda consists solely of cultivating our most ridiculous attributes in order to act as an essential counterweight to any gross exaltation of human values.

Yes: do good and then hide yourself away . . . Lend your hand to a brother in need and then get out of town . . . But why? Instead of wasting our spirit and energy hurling stones and dashing each other's brains out we might, all of us, use those stones instead to build a better, more noble society, for the benefit of all men. Giving, for the poor man, implies becoming indebted to effort and fatigue. For the rich man, giving implies giving back *the illicit gains he's realized from "legal" speculation with his fortune. But now the time has come for our business magnates to demonstrate—and for the dispossessed to convince themselves—how contemptible a thing money is within the great scheme of humanity's eternal aspiration for happiness. Yes, nowadays, money's sole purpose is to be spent in orgies of altruism. It's only in such glorious expenditures that one can truly experience the voluptuous delight of erasing all the privations of saving and all the penuries of labor! The only satisfaction a fortune can provide resides in letting it flow out from the strongbox of our egoism into the cordial coffers of the community. That char-*

acter in Zola, who in his rich, tortured old age, repeats, "One must give back, one must give back!"—he could perceive what true justice would mean: being united as one with every soul, plagued neither by ignominious hunger nor the ignorance and misery of one's neighbors. It would mean filling your sails with love and joining humanity's crusade to better itself. That's why, poor or rich, we should not speak of throwing bricks at one another but of using them to build ... So why then must our efforts be clouded by such sarcasm at every turn if our money is casually donated to save dozens and dozens of homes from hunger; to save thousands of simple people from physical misery; to save hundreds of men from desperation? Is it a crime to be generous? IS IT A CRIME TO BE GENEROUS?

He had no other response than to cluck his tongue once more.

He returned to his conclusion, and had to concede the point. What were the police if not the embodiment of that sardonic principle of life's contradictions. "Yes, in fact, it's a crime to be generous," they would answer. Set firmly at the right hand of those who enjoy all the advantages and privileges of the world, their ideals as well as their machetes are forever massed against any plebe who dares complain or make a claim. They stifle magnanimity among the lower class, but foster its growth among the upper class; because the goodness of the rich is a *modus operandi*, like so many others, meant to iniquitously perpetuate injustice. In this way, they ensure that the tree of misery grows in eternal helplessness, never knowing relief, aside from an occasional watering by wealth ...

The police's contemptuous behavior made him drunk with rage, made him want to tear out his own pubic hair from the sheer bitterness of considering how a poor man's generosity could be cause for suspicion. Whether or not said generosity might well have been made possible by a crime, it should, by virtue of its keeping close quarters with the pith of pain and suffering, be considered holy, most holy. And choking back his hatred, Aparicio hawked his throat clear of the arrogance of the entire prevailing social regime, which deprives the humble of even the most pitiful scrap of cooperation and solidarity, if it might undermine the bourgeoisie.

The train rolled into a station.

The brakes squealing, the wagons shunting, uncoupled his thoughts.

Occasionally, the signalman's red spotlight shot through the gaps between the stacked beams. Greetings or warnings? For a moment he almost believed that the red light was some mystical encouragement—soothing him like a perfect caress—and then he was flooded with happiness. And he murmured:

"Red Aid . . . Soviet money . . . Oh well, let them think what they like! What's certain is that the strike will triumph. Our contribution staved off the hunger that would have otherwise brought them to their knees. And now, tomorrow, instead of having to return to the building sites, holding out their hands to accept whatever meager wages might be offered, the workers will raise the threat of their clenched fists."

And yet, when the train resumed its movement, Aparicio was no longer happy.

Indeed, he was sighing with intense disappointment.

He tried to shatter his insomnia with several clucks of his tongue.

And his face, suffused with the melancholy of disgrace—wounded and weeping—felt the same sadness that overshadows all redeemers.

"All right. Sit down there. Bear in mind, Detective: this man is being held incommunicado."

"Absolutely, Chief."

More than an hour had passed since they'd placed him under observation. Like a pawn sacrificed in a gambit. Katanga kept his cool, didn't get impatient. Being a chess player, he had measured calm, and so, this new wrinkle in their plans brought with it a certain degree of intrigue. Events do not arise spontaneously, he knew. They are the baffling result of both impulses and reasons, reaching the field of our perception, and assuming some recognizable, definable configuration only after being set in motion from afar, like the wave to the dune, a moving changing complexity of oceanic flux and reflux.

Thus, he waited, calmly, and let the circumstances grow and take shape around him. Life had often made him sit and wait. He understood how a confusing confluence of events can unexpectedly lead to checkmate when one attempts either to harvest circumstances too early or too late, yielding produce that, whether green and inedible or foul and rotten, is useless.

Considering his own situation, he repeated to himself the advice he had so many times dispensed to others:

Be careful of stepping into temptation's snare! Beware the intoxicating allure of masochism, of serving as an example for others! Events come to fruition of their own accord. They advance when we have the patience to stand still. They age and acquire their proper flavors in their own psychological climates, without any regard for the desires of those who might suffer or enjoy them. Events, like fruit, must be harvested when the time is ripe . . .

Fatalism was the big brother to his cool remove. So why struggle, then? One had to be tolerant, to endure. So Katanga tolerated the odor of stale ink in police headquarters, the choking sewer stench of their sodden paper, and their rickety moth-eaten furniture.

While he waited, he glanced indifferently at the police sketches and rogues gallery on the walls. What a wax museum of old fogies and has-beens! The oldest drawings looked like they dated back to the days of Johann Kaspar Lavater's *Physiognomy*. The yellowed, discolored mugshots exhibited a variety of criminals posed in ferocious attitudes, a practice stamped out by the so-called "Positivist School." What useless relics!

Katanga couldn't suppress a smile:

I'm sure that the photographer was one of those old shutterbugs who lugged around a load of gelatinized glass plates . . . What a technological throwback! Putting such grotesquerie on display now that Pierre Abraham has sharpened physiognomic science to an in-

credible degree! What ignominy, clinging to the theory of the uomo criminale, _now that_ le maquillage _can convert demons into angels!_

His thoughts flew like a toboggan down a snowy slope, and he considered the gallant hauteur of gangsters, cutthroats of the side streets and silver screen alike, in Chicago as well as in Buenos Aires. Physical beauty had called off its quarrel with crime, and thugs now swaggered in style. The comforts of silk suits and sleek autos were no longer the exclusive privilege of distinguished business magnates. Cosmetic surgery and elegant casinos were no longer the exclusive domains of Cecilia Sorel or André de Fouquières, just as crime was no longer the product of vile Neanderthals, but rather _la fine fleur_ of the handsome, the dashing, the jocund individuals. Stavisky and Baby Face Dillinger winked back at Katanga from the depths of death. What a kick in the guts for Lombroso's theory of anthropological criminology!

It was a quick trip from there to exploring the moral coefficients of modern banditry.

He remembered that he'd been in New York when the St. Valentine's Day Massacre happened. He was already self-employed then, working as a freelance illusionist, after having been disillusioned by numerous dishonest employers . . .

The poster advertising his now remote triumphs passed through his memory like a Dantesque apparition . . . a connection not unrelated to his stage name: Doctor Inhell! . . . But we digress. The crowd at the café-concert hall at which he performed that night—half speakeasy, half _casa non sancta_—wasn't the least bit interested in his tricks. Furtive comments slipped between them by means of a nervous _whisper demain_. Their collective shock over the Massacre produced the most peculiar remarks, just as he, for his part, produced rabbits, flags, booze, and bras from out of his top hat . . . He, then, became a spectator. And descending from the stage into the room, on the pretext of picking out some lucky member of the audience to assist him, he mingled with the dizzy tide of the audience. Katanga's affection for gangsters dated from that evening. The amazing coup pulled off that day by the Chicago Outfit was a heady episode of bravery and audacity. Trifling petty crimes were nothing more than hiccups in the justice system, or else recidivism on the part of small-time degenerates. Those men in Chicago had made an industry out of vice, graft, kickbacks, and contraband. The crime monopolies were at war. Al Capone's cartel versus . . . Buck Moran's? *(he didn't remember too well)* in the eternal competition for primacy and dominion. Nothing more. A clean fight. A lofty fight, albeit in the gutter. An epic battle. What a difference from the Wall Street scoundrels, who speculate with the hunger, health, and honor — essential, indispensable things!—of the underprivileged half of humanity! Not only do the true gangsters manage to exploit the superfluity of a rich minority, they've dignified the profession of the delinquent. No longer sullying themselves with the task of snatching a passerby's meager purse, the racketeers go after the business squids and bank sharks: those who exist to suck away, rend, grind, and chew up money belonging to the people . . .

The detective sat hunched over his desk. Perhaps reading over his case against just such a purse snatcher . . . Or perhaps the file on some cattle rustler . . . The man's suspicious preoccupation with the smallest details of bad behavior bothered Katanga excessively.

Which only served to further darken his ruminations:

Today's gangsters are the direct heirs of Robin Hood, of Schinderhannes, of Cartouche, of Carmine Donatelli Crocco, il massimo brigante del secolo decimonono, *of Joaquín Murrieta, of Diego Corrientes . . . And of so many others who were tired of waiting for the law to protect them, and so ended up cursing it. Of so many others who wielded the dagger and carbine to impose a more ideal justice: the kind engendered by the pain and sorrow of injustice . . . Gangsters are the heroes of these turbulent times. The twentieth-century cult of heroism requires something more than audacity: the moral scope of a soul well-tempered by life's inequal-*

ities. An indispensable requisite for being a modern hero is to be able to identify, in its purity of sentiment, the lively aspirations of the cries of the popular conscience. Regardless of their individual fate, gangsters are never haunted by ridicule or shame. Even when they fall they garner respect. They elude the ignominies suffered by so many two-bit rogues who have their reputations warped by penny operas and street-corner poets. Fra Diavolo accompanied by Auber's sol-fas, for example; or Juan Moreira beset by scribblings from every last criollo *bard.*

His sarcastic appraisals sweetened his mood and fueled his thoughts:

Besides, mustn't we appreciate the true beauty of the criminal's cold, clinical insolence? Nothing of paradoxes à la maniere de . . . *Nothing truly underhanded and dirty. They prefer actions that are simple, precise, and terrifyingly effective. And to that end they adorn their transgressions with high passions, not base, bloody savagery. Not content to be mere public enemies, they aspire to be worthy adversaries, to be properly hated, to be judged completely, to be killed spectacularly, they signify frankness in resentment, vertigo in the conquest of achievement, clear sacrifice in action.*

Katanga paused in his thoughts, sighed deeply, then flowed on:

During the Depression, the only public acts of generosity seen in the United States were those enacted by gangsters. After the Crash of November 1929, *the philanthropy expected from potentates was suddenly in short supply. Publicly, their so-called conscience restricted the generous open hand to stingy, scheming legerdemain. Lock–outs. Shrinking salaries. Unemployed stockbrokers on the streets crying: "Apples!, Buy an apple, buy an apple! . . ." Meanwhile the gangsters extended their largesse wherever necessary. They went into the poor neighborhoods of Chicago and Detroit. They cleared out and razed the gloomy hovels and Hoovervilles of Pittsburgh and San Francisco. They created shelters for the unemployed on the docks of New York. They rescued thousands of freezing old folks from beneath bridges. While the infamous ranks of Christian Scientists and the Salvation Army were swollen with a whole generation of youth whose able bodies were withered by hunger.*

A sudden urge to cry was only prevented by an even stronger surge of rage in the silence:

It has been said, and it is still said, that a gangster's charity is worthless, since his generosity really costs him nothing. What does money mean to their kind? Treating money with unbridled caprice, as though it has no value, isn't that the very essence of crime? But these are empty diatribes. Calumnies! But that's not how things really are. The real crime we all fear resides in the general misery of mankind, exploited and maintained by the parasitic urban plug of punks, hustlers, and opportunists who hoard power and privilege. Whereas real justice resides in one's liberation from that sorrow and pain, in the relief from its penury, thanks to the resolution of a precious few. So how can anyone say it doesn't cost them anything?! . . . Danger, risk, and cold critical decisions bear the highest price tag because they often cost one's life. Granted that, when considering the embarrassing paucity of the magnate's grasping avarice, how they scheme to get rich through the postal service, risking little more than the cost of mailings and circulars, telegrams, headlines, and radio ads, it's obvious that gangsters offer such a fine example of dignity! How superlative is the moral splendor of their actions! How the soul of humanity swells with joy to see itself reflected in the virile mirror of their exploits!

Katanga had abstracted himself to the point, now, that his whole being, abstracted, vibrated with emotion.

One always loves those tantalizing achievements, just out of reach!

Vibrating all the while, Katanga's eyes clouded over. Moving in procession through his memory, he saw Joe Aiello's funeral. All the humble eyes of North America crying as he passed by. And in sumptuous hearses, the five carloads of flowers delivered from Florida to perfume his cadaver . . .

Oh, to be mourned like that! To live and die that way! To glorify life with an even more glorious death!

Yes, one always loves those achievements just out of reach! Heroism can't be inherited; it doesn't get passed along automatically from fathers to sons. It leaps, skipping over generations, the way monkeys do, through the branches and foliage of family trees. Sometimes it lands on the slightest of branches. And they bear the fruit of great and mighty deeds, while the strongest boughs weaken and wither. Katanga knew it very well. On a hundred different occasions he had fallen into the flagrant misfortune of taking his own frailty by surprise. And deploring his lack of courage, he could only console himself with his complementary gift of overcoming that same weakness through cunning . . .

But that still wasn't the same thing! Intimidated and discouraged, sniffling up your own dripping snot, pondering possible alibis and getaways . . . all that couldn't be nearly as elegant and persuasive as firing a Colt .45. Flattening your tailbone in a police station to prevent your comrades being persecuted just wasn't as stunning and respectable a feat as saving your ass while driving a speeding armored car equipped with a modern machine gun.

His chest swelled up to let out a moan.

A moan that would have to wait . . .

One.

Two.

Three.

Four explosions, almost simultaneous, left Katanga breathless.

The detective sat bolt upright.

The proximity of the last blast rattled the windowpanes.

Both of them scampered terrified out into the street.

Everything was confusion and panic. Police whistles. Car horns. People running away.

As soon as the detective was able to gather his wits, he began to run, too. At his side, with equal velocity, sprinted Katanga, the two running wildly, propelled by the sudden danger in the streets. But authority reared its ugly head:

"Where're you going? Go back! You're being held incommunicado."

"Let me come . . . There's nobody left at the station. They

might need help."

They took off again, their feet smacking loudly against the pavement. Then, stopping abruptly, panting, the detective spat at him:

"Go back, that's an order!"

"Alone. . . ?"

The detective was struck with a frantic spasm of irony. Faced with the conflicting urgency of his two clear duties, he was unsure which one to follow. He felt a kind of grim annoyance. Finally, he nodded:

"Fine, come on. But act like a man. Don't try to escape."

"Not on your life, Detective. Nothing interests me more than the honor of remaining incommunicado . . ."

With the pandemonium came further catastrophe.

When the two sprinters reached the scene of the blast—two and a half blocks from the police station—enormous, dazzling flames were already dancing amid the dust clouds of the destroyed building.

The vestibule of the future Rural Credit Bank was a smoking pile of ruins. Ceilings collapsed. Partitions riddled with holes. Walls gaping with the snaggled teeth of shattered masonry.

The scaffolding hung down, crazily disjointed. The frame legs, girders, and putlog holes crackled in suspension between the fire and the ground like a hundred ghostly skeletons locked in a macabre battle.

The blast had also shattered the adjoining building which housed a religious icons shop: SANTERÍA SAINT TERESA OF THE BABY JESUS.

The evening breeze soon propelled the fire's saraband into this store with a Dionysian furor. Don Ezekiel Leibowich's mystical backstock crackled within a sour, curdling resplendent hecatomb of colors and odors of which Julian the Apostate would have certainly approved.

A haggard, seasoned newspaper reporter with yellowed eyes quipped:

"What a bunch of lucky sacred pricks! They've already been burned alive once, not they'll be double martyrs in this inferno . . ."

But the gambling crony to which he addressed this witticism was barely able to hear it over the shrieking of the icon shop's owner, as he rended the souls of the crowd now gathered.

Astonished by the fire, the Jewish owner's increasing desperation exacerbated the wildness of gestures, imprecations, and wails. He ran. He leaped into action. He tried dashing into the shop but then retreated before the squadron of flames. He tried to climb over one of the collapsed walls but recoiled, choking and coughing. His grotesque, antic motion was stopped short on each attempt by the roaring of shattering glass, the red-hot iron shutters, or the infernal reeking smoke.

"Noooooooo! For God's sake, neighbors! Don't jus' stand there! Help me protect my saints! Th' holy ship's goin' down in flames! Nooooooooo! Help me, brothers! Help! Help!"

But it seemed there wasn't a single fireman in the whole city.

A brigade of vigilantes and neighbors skeptically passed along the meager water buckets of their good will. A garden hose, proffered from the corner hardware store, spouted a laughable arc about as forceful as a boy peeing. Adding further absurdity to the pathetic scene, the Andalusian from the service station trotted over with his portable car fire extinguisher. Its weak, fragmented stream was also like piss, but this time more like the flow from a dog with impending kidney failure. The peals of laughter from the crowd shot holes through the Andalusian's sense of altruism:

"Goddamn it! Now tha's normally a pretty good gizmo. See, but what it is, it's got no pull an' pressure cuz' of a lack o' sulphuric acid. C'mon! Don't jus' laugh now!"

Meanwhile, Don Ezekiel kept shouting in alarm. Coming and going, back and forth, made into an automaton by his terror. Much as circus clowns will pretend to help their colleagues, and so sabotage the work at hand, the shop owner just got in the way, left and right. At the very moment that the detective and Katanga had picked up a fallen beam to use as a battering ram, trying to knock down the shop's back door, Don Ezekiel jumped right in front of them, trying to stop them, wailing worse than ever:

"Pogrom! Pogrom! Watch th' relics! Butchers! You'll kill lil' Saint Teresa!"

They paid him no mind. But as they backed up again to gain momentum, the reporter's voice paralyzed Katanga:

"Don't worry. This fucking Muscovite's a phony. He's fully insured. Let it all burn! The spectacle alone is worth our time. As it says in the classic text: *'Un beau désordre est un grand effet d'art...'*"

Then, with a disconcerting brio, Katanga rushed forward anyway, almost dragging the detective along, too. To do exactly the opposite of what was expected in that situation was worth just as much to him as winning the policeman's trust. Esteem—he knew—is frequently a corollary of embarking upon a doomed strategy ... and he didn't waste his opportunity.

Even still, foolish pride caused him to misjudge his maneuver. First, because the beam not only battered down the door, but also smashed into tiny fragments a still-intact display case filled with pious devotional images, triptychs, sculpted tablets, cameos, enamel virgins, rosaries, and miniatures. And, second, because a shipment of cheap trinkets—medals, candles, scapulars, missals, prints, stocked for the festivals of various patron saints—tripped him up so that he fell flat on his face an instant before a shelf rained down upon him a whole row of devotional niches featuring Saint Roch, his festering sore, and his dog.

Foolish pride caused him to misjudge his maneuver. But it's in precisely these moments of crisis that our inward estimation of our potential to act is eclipsed, leaving what is truly counter-intuitive shining like pure, classical heroism. When Katanga, now reeking of seared flesh, was extracted from the smoldering rubble, with half his back torn open and bruised, they could all still hear him cursing. His litany was an extended denunciation of all the saints of all the liturgical lists preserved in all the cathedrals, against all the saints of every martyrology, and against all the saints listed in the papal bulls of canonization. Saint Roch was singled out for particular attention . . .

Stretched out on the sidewalk in front of the shop, gasping and sweaty, Katanga was the first to be alarmed by the crowd's sympathy. Their pity even seeped down into his pitted back. His bruises were anointed with disinfectants and congratulations.

When he noticed that he was being ministered to, and with much solicitude, by the detective and the police doctor he began to exaggerate his agony, expressing it stoically in mute contortions. But having instantly become a living legend, Katanga knew he now had to consolidate his position. He forced himself to stand and listen to the crowd tell him how "fantastic!" his bravery had been. And he received new bruises from the crowd's hearty congratulatory embraces.

Don Ezekiel Leibowich also approached him, muttering and bumbling his way through a disconsolate consolation. As he was persisting in his plaintive lamentations all the while, Katanga said to him:

"Thanks, friend. But why are you crying so much if the shop's insured?"

"Because I could've taken out more coverage! But I only bought just enough!"

The clock on the parish church struck four.

At that moment the Chief Investigator and the Inspector General had reached the scene of the fire.

Their search had turned up nothing! They'd scoured the bordellos, the late night rotisseries, the taverns. The presumed Soviet agent, the distributor of Red gold, was nowhere to be found. They'd consulted various strikebreakers, questioned the hidden scabs and informers pullulating inside the unions, checked in with the organizers of the construction workers' Pro-Strike Committee itself but . . . absolutely nothing!

The four explosions had convulsed them like four colossal hiccups. They were eating dinner in the Criollo grill next door to "The French Embassy"—an elegant euphemism for the city's most highly regarded bordello—when they heard the blasts. The instantaneous contraction of their diaphragms and the violent interruption of their breathing caused chunks of the roulade they were eating to become lodged in their throats. Gagging and choking it down, they abandoned the rotisserie ipso facto.

Their guesswork began in the suburbs. Approaching the city center, they found their suspicions confirmed by three impressive scenes of havoc. As they reached the ruined edifice of the Rural Credit Bank, all the amazement built up on the way into town now escaped through their bewildered faces and gaping mouths.

But there was more. Not puzzlement but astonishment. As they broke through the ring of onlookers, they saw a man stripped to the waist, riddled with contusions. The crowd poured its praise on him like an unguent. As they recognized Katanga their astonishment changed to stupor:

"What . . . detective . . . What's the meaning . . . this man . . . here?"

"I'll explain later. For the moment it's enough that I can verify his heroism. Listen to what all these people are saying. I've never in my life seen a man more willing to sacrifice himself for the public good."

The young detective—professional skeptic—stood stock-still, blinking, as if beginning to grasp his error.

Katanga, meanwhile, lowered his eyes in smug satisfaction.

His heart was beating happily inside him—like a crazy bird. A hero at last! But his joy soon clouded over. He still needed to proceed carefully. Oftentimes it's the bravest and boldest who, crowned with glory for surviving a thousand vicissitudes, die from a simple, careless slip on a banana peel . . . While the coward, who cloaks his infamy in fiction, is showered with praise for simply picking up that peel . . .

He ruminated on his situation:

No! It's a ruse. I can't accept this "triumph." My personal code of conduct rejects it. How depressing. But I must maintain my pride, for obvious reasons. It's my pride that conceals me and protects me.

And so, seemingly submissive, buried beneath the "glory" he'd achieved, he fettered his sensations, to hide from himself.

Now the fire had lost value as a spectacle. The people began to wander away.

In profile, supported by a prie-dieu saved from the bonfire, Katanga turned back to the reporter, trying to hear what he was saying. With the perverse delight people find in newfound fame, he craned his neck toward the newsman shamelessly, as if tacitly claiming his attention. But the reporter ignored him. That alone set the standard for Katanga's worth, he thought. Indifference is the greatest stock symbol on the trading floor of life. The more something is disdained, the more avidly it will be sought and possessed.

The reporter was speaking to his crony. Sluggishly, but continuously. Muttering, chewing his way through his sentences. A voice almost fierce for being so thick and lazy.

Katanga now found himself won over by the man's emaciated face, bulging eyes, and seasoned aplomb: a strong man conspicuously afflicted with blemishes and defects always elicits more sympathy than one who's simply handsome.

Unperturbed by the reporter's disdain, Katanga gave up on him. Still, his inner self, impermeable to the stifling heat of this unified front of injustice, picked up such interesting remarks as:

"Yes. Imagine that. Fifty-four volumes. I leafed through the *Acta Sanctorum* in the main library at the University of Córdoba. Begun by the Jesuit Jean Bolland, the work is a kind of *Almanach de Gotha* of the celestial court and annexes. Imagine the Buenos Aires telephone directory with miracles and portents instead of numbers and addresses. As a nomenclature of saints, it's a wonder. But in terms of vital essence, a sticky-sweet extravagance. Nothing is so boring as the exemplary vir-

tue that church dignitaries slyly slather upon themselves. As far
as they're concerned, none of those poor bastards from heav-
en was ever really forced to slog through this vale of tears with
the rest of us . . . no, they were just passing through — doing us
a *favor* by landing here and suffering for our redemption! . . .
In Baronius's great *Martyrologium Romanum*, you can also read
the catalog of the saints who were 'taken care of' by the pagans.
But, really, they got off easy, strictly speaking, if we were to
compare them, say — not to put too fine a point on it — with
the hundreds of young men who were tormented by *dehydra-
tion* and hunger in the Chaco War, also known as 'The War of
Thirst' . . . But the friars know how to make themselves sound
good. For example, congregations are still showering Sedulius,
the fifth-century poet-priest who composed the hymn 'A solis
ortus cardine,' with lauds and hosannas even today . . . and our
mid-twentieth-century congregations like nothing more than
to hold up some holy nymphomaniac from the fifteenth century who could only see God through the peephole of sex —
Saint Teresa, for example — as the quintessence of blessedness!
. . . Man, what an easy con. When I think of how the Coun-
cils of Nicaea and Trent restored the worship of images, I laugh
at mankind's flexibility. Iconography is something horrible: a
real cacophonoyance, an icono-caca-phony. People don't even
know what they're worshiping. And the liturgy is just a fan-
dango in which primitive totems have been exchanged for little froggy figurines . . . Let's begin at the beginning: *Benedica-
mus Domino*. Christ, who was represented beardless until the
eleventh century, appears afterward, like a good Jew, with a
full beard . . . The statues and figures of the saints come later,
carved, incrusted with jewels, or painted in portals, retrochoirs,
altarpieces, friezes, euchologies, and antiphonaries. A tremendous invasion! Each artisan, each artist, in the throes of expression, making his habitually depraved models look imbecilic.
Why? The anthropomorphic variety of the saints is thus unified in a merengue of idiotic facial expressions and ecstatic postures. The heretical Byzantine Iconoclasts did well to reject this

particular artistic inheritance. They didn't want their congregation to develop into a pleiad of eunochoids, narcissists, and
paranoiacs ... Prayer is a serious thing. It's the spiritual vehi-
cle by which the *misericordia* of a favor is invoked, demanded, and supplicated. In other words: this method of adulating
one's chosen saint, or the saint of the day, so that it performs a
kind favor for us ... You have to understand, these fetishes that
Don Ezekiel sells ..."

"Used to sell."

"... at retail ... you can't beg any favors from them. Their
faces are of such repellently low artistic quality. As soon as any
faithful, cultured person—if a cultured person can even be
very faithful—sees the face of one of those monstrosities, he
breaks out laughing. And his prayers don't make it past the ceil-
ing ... The correct thing would be for Catholics, like Muslims
or some Protestants, to put a ban on all images, and so forge
their pictures of piety and worship out of real devotion. There's
no better sculptor than the imagination itself when sublimat-
ed by the ideal. Clearly it's necessary to purify the technique
of prayer. The 'presto chango' of divine grace must be pulled
off in silence, hidden away from everyone, even from oneself;
nothing pisses off our betters more than scrounging for favors
without first delivering up an entreaty absolutely dripping with
self-abnegation. So, a few good works wouldn't go amiss, as far
as sweetening the pot: why not glorify the divine name by ded-
icating schools, hospitals, swimming pools, and power plants
to it into the bargain ... Works superior, certainly, to the *Te
Deum* composed by Saint Ambrose and Saint Augustine to cel-
ebrate the hogwash of the latter's baptism. Catholics these days
are like little baby goats."

"Like baby goats? How?"

"Yes: like baby goats, like little kids. They gather around on
their knees, jostling one another so they can suckle ... they refuse to allow the exhausting burden of faith to remain inside
of themselves. They never gather up their skirts or roll up their
pant-legs unless they see some profit in it. They don't get *flex-*

is genibus unless there's a reasonable likelihood of its affecting their odds at the polls. Repugnant bargain hunters, the lot of them! And woe betide the saint that doesn't come through for them! They'll boycott him without the least hesitation. Hence the continuous need for the provision of new intercessors. The Pope knows the score. And as Administrator General of Indulgences, he's always setting newly minted martyrs, lay brothers, virgins, and confessors loose on the world, icons who capture our prayers in the net of fashion. After all, certain saints are supplicated only at certain times. Just like organdy, *albène* crepe, taffeta cellophane ... So, the Jewish idol factories can't keep pace with all the canonizations. The plaster casters in the suburbs quickly exhaust their stock of idols. And the saint shops like Ezekiel Leibowich's get rich before our eyes."

"Nevertheless, Leibowich has gone bust twice."

"Once."

"Twice."

"One bust and one conspiracy. Hardly the same thing. When SANTERÍA VIRGEN OF LUJÁN got auctioned off, he purchased all the existing stock himself through a third party. That was a good, underhanded day's work for him. He got to keep the saints ... and the dividends. Years later, when he took over proprietorship of SANTERÍA DON BOSCO, the contract he signed with them awarded him the usufruct of any saints included in the liturgical calendar for only ten percent of their going value ..."

"So it's a business that pays dividends both in heaven and on earth: as above, so below."

"No doubt about it. But then, everything that pertains to Western religion has always been in the hands of the Jews, above and below, in heaven and on earth ... Jehovah and Moses ..."

"God and Jesus."

"Exactly. There are no Hungarian gods, no French, Italian, or Yankee gods. Mere amanuenses, mere peons at best ... Which is why I suspect that this fire ... this fire ... I'd bet my life that it was set on purpose ... it's just more business."

At that moment, the Chief Investigator passed by. As he heard the reporter's last sentence, he made a face, then shook it in denial:

"No. No. You're mistaken."

"Mistaken? What are you trying to tell me? The guy is a faker, that shitty little Muscovite. He's got more than enough insurance."

"Oh, yes ... you reporters from *La Verdad* know it all ... Just not enough to keep your mouths shut, this time."

There was a heavy silence.

The reporter—actually, editor of the opposition newspaper—stood looking at the cop petulantly. As if trying to figure out what angle the latter was trying to play. Then he laughed to himself, three nasal snorts, and, turning to his companion, called:

"Come on, let's get out of here. The fix is already in. It's their thing. Wrong, wrong, wrong—that's me!"

The Chief couldn't tolerate the man's scornful mockery:

"Yes, sir! You're completely mistaken! Ask anyone you like! There were four explosions! Four bombs! Yes, sir! Four criminal attacks! Right here! And at Doctor Perea Muñon's home! And at Carminatti's! And the site where they were building the new cold-storage plant! Building projects under construction! Goddamn it! You go and find out! Don't talk nonsense! Yes, sir! Four explosions! Four terrorist attacks! Yes, sir! You reporters from *La Verdad* print nothing but distortions! But this time you're dead wrong! Yes, sir! Ask whomever you like! This is the work of anarchists! Of agitators! Who knows! It'll all become clear! But you're really wrong! Get all the facts straight for once! Four attacks! Four big explosions! The whole town heard them!"

The reporter was dumbstruck. His haggard face turned livid. His bilious eyes seemed to leave their sockets. The equivalent of a cold sweat ran right through his insides, viscerally, while his ears burned as though his every thought were struggling to come surging out through them.

Controlling his breathing and heartbeat, he began to reflect. The aggressive punctuation in the Chief Investigator's angry outburst indicated a sincere spontaneity.

Well, I really got his goat this time, he realized.

And, smiling, he recovered his sluggish calm:

"Hey, listen fella, I'm sorry! I can see by how angry you are that you're serious. I'll take your word for it. But I didn't hear the explosions."

"You didn't hear the explosions? Where were you?"

"At the club."

"And you didn't hear the explosions? . . . Really, you didn't hear the explosions?"

"No. I told you, no."

Exasperated, the Chief was about to launch into another tirade but the reporter's gambling crony interceded:

"It's entirely possible, Chief. We couldn't hear a thing with all the racket they were making at that poker game!"

It was a few minutes after twelve when the newspaper boys broke the silence in the streets with their cries:

"*La Verdad . . .*"

"*La Verdad* with all the latest news about the terrorist attacks . . ."

"*La Verdad . . .*"

The detective, who from the early morning on had been overseeing the compilation of the summary report of the day's events, stood up heavily. His thighs and buttocks felt hard as blocks. He flexed his joints. And accepted a newspaper through the iron bars of the station window.

Katanga, who had just finished making his sworn statement, saw the detective plunge into its pages. He read with a grim scowl. He growled. Nervously manipulated the newspaper. Settled down as still as a pool of water. And at last smiled.

He didn't understand a thing.

Between the Chief Investigator and the detective there existed many silent, unspoken grievances. Discrepancies due to some kickbacks from bets on soccer pools. Quarrels about certain bordello connections. As a result, knowing about his superior's altercation with the reporter, the detective overlooked the niceties of the article in order to savor the inevitable fiery obscenities that it would provoke. He was completely absorbed in imagining one right now. He was tasting it in sips of irony, delightedly, as if he were drinking *curaçao*. Then, suddenly serious, his face took on a disgruntled expression.

"It's a very thin joke for such a boring idiot," he said, tossing the paper away.

By sheer coincidence, the issue of *La Verdad* hit the floor in front of Katanga.

"It couldn't be any other way. Always *la verdad*, the 'truth' at my feet . . ." he mused.

Hunched over like Rodin's Thinker, he read the paper's slogan:

FERVENTLY ILLUMINATING THE PUBLIC CONSCIENCE: *LA VERDAD* IS PUBLISHED EVERY DAY AT 12:00 P.M. SHARP, EXCEPT MONDAYS,

He couldn't help but comment:

"What delicious nonsense! If only every day were Monday!"

And feeling sickened by the smell of the carbolic soap rising from his body, without lifting either his head or the newspaper, he immersed himself in the column printed in ten-point boldface type:

FIRE

Fire, as a work of art, is a theme that urgently needs an illustrious lyricist. Just as Thomas de Quincey wrote an ungainly essay about the aesthetic aspects of murder, we fail to see why one shouldn't also study the beauty of arson. Indeed, besides the advantage of having its own god assigned to it—Pluto—and a magnificent origin myth

to boot—the Prometheus affair—a dazzling collection
of fires adorns "the black night of history": from Sardanapalus's great funeral pyre through to the burning of
the Library of Alexandria, from the positively incendi-
ary "sketch" about Rome performed by that magnificent
ham, Nero, to the stupendous rotisserie spits of Jan Huss
and Joan of Arc, through to the Nazi combustion of the
Reichstag, all the way down to Don Ezekiel Leibowich's
auto-da-fé, staged for the devotees of Saint Theresa.

Our city is home to a Plutonic cult worthy of the
highest respect. Given our situation—that we have
nothing remotely resembling a fire brigade—one may
pay homage here to the king of Hades with a devotion
sure to favorably impress all the pagans in the vicinity.
Such infernos, it is true, almost always involve properties that happen to be heavily insured; but that ought
not diminish the generous attitude with which gasoline
is spilled nor the heroic disdain with which matches are
flung about.

Fire, as a spectacle, admits all adjectives. Suffice to say
that it surpasses in rhetorical grandiosity any parliamen-
tary discourse or the lamentation of any suffering Jew.
Suffice to say that we may judge its importance from the
anguish of the spectators it summons and the sad whistles for help that it elicits from our gendarmes. All civic activity ceases in the face of fire's arbitrary, consuming
advance. There arises a kind of ecstasy, a loud vainglorious ecstasy, wherein the most worthless exclamations
become mingled with the collective indifference refusing
to contribute even one single, shallow, hero-manqué's
washbasin worth of water.

From the decorative point of view, a few tongues of
fire dance a lovely, Dantesque divertissement in the
night, comparable only to the display of the thousand
tongues of our townspeople, who themselves dance a

rather wild, improvised set of steps, full of "What do I care?" intrigue: a "ballet" of cruel mistrust. The burning hot coals, meanwhile, crackle and snap into the air, amid thick curtains of smoke, veritable swarms of igneous bees. These bees, in truth, also give honey; but they have a tragic calling: to drift away to burn down the house of a trusted neighbor (or the straw hats of the impertinent and inquisitive). In any event, those motes only add to the fire's overall grace, just as sequins decorate a gypsy ballerina's slender figure.

Frankly, after having enjoyed the catastrophic beauty of last night's fire and of other recent occurrences, we are tortured by the news that any day now a squad of fire-fighters is due to be installed here in the city. Such an attack upon a work of art, so near to perfection, is sure to have fatal consequences for our citizens' peace of mind, not to mention the finances of all our local "pyrophiles." Thus, we venture to guess that such measures will never actually materialize; the powers that be preferring, at all costs, to keep their police-spies tooting their little whistles for aid ... Thus we will always have the consolation of ignoring those who call for help and the satisfaction of knowing that no help will ever come.

At last Katanga straightened up, half crippled. A ray of sunlight rested comfortably upon his bald patch—holy ground of his diabolical ideas—reflecting this way and that.

He didn't know what to think.

A slight, bitter, secret suspicion had been eating at him since morning:

It's fine that I ignored the reporter and broke down the door. It's all right. Everyone has their own tactics. But among educated men, intentions are what speak. No language can compete with the subtlety of intention. A simple fluid glance, meeting the eyes of another, is enough to infiltrate the most unlikely confidence. A token smile, accentuated by a knowing wink, is sufficient to veri-

*fy the falsity of the most respectable attitudes. I tried to broach the
subject with the reporter... But if I reached out to him it was to
get his attention, not because he'd inspired my little heroic charade.
The presence of such a lordly spirit as his filled me with joy. I tried
to make contact to vindicate myself, to explicate my own exquisite
farce. But it was a clumsy gesture. I couldn't gain any leverage. Superior in his indifference, he left me to bear the false cross of glory
that the crowd placed on my shoulders ...*

A great racket of footsteps and voices.

The detective got up again and went to the door to the hallway.

There were new people to question.

Returning to the desk, he retrieved *La Verdad* from the floor.
He'd not yet put it away when the Chief Investigator, the In-
spector General, and the Examining Magistrate all appeared.
Ahead of schedule. An intimidating surprise.

"I've always told you, Detective: There are no real papers
published in this city, only tabloids! What passes for a local
press is little more than a farcical clutch of garish broadsheets
and satirical rags. Especially that one! Remember that! And
turning to the Magistrate, he added:

"It's a pity that our city has no photoengraving studio, either. At least if the newspapers had some pictures in them—
replete with clichés though they'd be!—there wouldn't be room
on their pages for quite so much idiocy."

An ambiguous smile or perhaps only a slight torsion of the
carmine-colored burr that was his lower lip was the Magistrate's response. He was what was called a *pituco*, an ignorant
upper-class snob. Beardless, bespectacled, smelling of Narcisse
Noir perfume. Bluish temples and very fine, oiled hair, his elegance clashing with his office. Having gained his post through
political connections, he was sustained by religious ones. President of the "Pious Union of Saint Jerome," his chosen reading
material was the Parish Bulletin.

"Indeed," he added scornfully. "Reporters are the vermin of
the mind. You'll have noticed that they don't work out their

ideas properly as do ecclesiastics in their deep meditations. No, they just whip themselves up into a frenzy at their typewriters and shred them all into one awful goulash. They're masters of simplifying things by mixing them all up. Ignoramuses, they mutilate order and morality. Louts, they deliver nothing but false ideals and sham sentiments. Newspaper offices are dens of iniquity. In their zeal to inform, to propagate sensationalism, they spew out lies, abuses, and calumnies. They're not interested in the reputation of a decent man. They shake it. They crush it. And, of course, we all lose because of it. Yes, I agree with you. The press is the god Moloch of the abominable times in which we must live. Daily it devours its sacrifice of innocent victims."

"You're telling me! That's why I can't stand it that these local rags never have any pictures! Oh, just imagine—with only five or six soccer photos per issue, why, I'd be home free!"

At the mention of soccer, the Magistrate frowned:

"And why soccer, precisely? Any sport would do, surely . . ."

As president of the Pious Union of Saint Jerome, he had, several times, captained the "veterans' team" to victory . . . but there was a famous local anecdote about "the opposing teams being filled with ex-cons," who, when the great man advanced with the ball, moved aside, crying "Watch out! The Examining Magistrate!" Thanks to the fear, complacency, and sloppiness, so called, of those old crooks and parolees, he was able to reach the line and score goals . . .

The Chief noticed his annoyance:

"Fine. Any sport you like . . . or religious ceremonies, crimes, weddings . . . But, photographs. Photographs!"

The carmine burr that was the Judge's lip stretched out into a rabid grimace. He was about to answer:

A rugby match is not the same as extreme unction, nor a wedding night the same as hyperdulia!

But he restrained himself. And twisting his face in disdain, opted instead for barking an order at the detective:

"Bring those men in here."

Presently, they began to enter.

Skilled at eliciting the compassion of others, Fortunato and Viejo Amor came in first. Better to say: they slid in. It was a drifting-in, really, full of rags and fearful glances. The former: fat, soft, square-headed, puffy-faced, bleary dishonest eyes, a bulbous nose overgrown with vinous tubercles. The latter: deformed, Socratically bald, billy-goat curls in his sideburns and beard, with thick rings of fat rimming his gut and neck. There they stood, in the middle of the room, as if petrified. Animal lethargy. Passive as idiots.

The Examining Magistrate was instantly furious:

"What a fiasco!"

And then spotting Longines's plucked eagle's head, his flabby, drooping skin — bumpy and red — and his one healthy eye spying sideways, the other weeping pus, he wasted no more time:

"That's enough. Outside! They're bums . . . Beggars . . ."

"Aren't you going to question them, Your Honor?" prompted the detective.

"No. You can see from a mile away that they're just some poor devils. They'd be better off at the St. Vincent de Paul shelter."

"That's what I think: drifters . . ." agreed the Chief Investigator. "I told you."

"Nevertheless   . . ."

"Nevertheless what? Take better aim, friend. Don't waste my time with such ridiculous suspects. They're practically wearing scapulars. Communists are atheists, young and active. When have you ever met an agitator who looked like those wrecks? How exactly do you figure that they could afford to be giving away money if they spend all their time begging? You've got to be more logical, got to use your head. Where did you get the idea that these people, who don't even look the part, could be terrorists? Come on. Show a little common sense in your work."

"Nevertheless . . . I have my doubts."

"What doubts do you have? Let's hear them!"

"A cot. In their campsite, under the bridge, there was an extra cot."

"That's it? That's all? That's enough to make you believe that the one individual who happened to be missing, and who's almost certainly cut from the same cloth as the rest of that miserable crew, is the one and only person who delivered the money, who planted the bombs, et cetera, et cetera?"

The detective nodded categorically.

There was a moment of queasy discomfort. Stepping aside, the Examining Magistrate summed things up:

"Do me a favor, Chief. Tell your junior detective to go find this cot, lie down on it, and sleep off his idiocy."

As the detective left, herding the vagabonds along with him, Katanga looked up from the floor with a brilliantly malicious squint. And he extended it towards them. Longines caught it as he and the others went out. A look of intelligence and wit. A furtive and amiable indication that everything was resolved.

The two of them shared such a unified perspicacity that even the slightest trifle, even the most tenuous confidential intimation, was always perceived. Leaders of the group, each was a master of confidence and self-restraint. They could get out of any fix, no matter how difficult, by intuition alone. The one frugal, the other garrulous, each was the other's perfect complement. Longines brought his will to power to their cause, while Katanga brought his genius for persuasion. The former was pure calculation in action—the latter, pure calculation in inaction. The first man conquered; the second convinced. In this way, no matter what the situation, while one was suffering the secret shame of doing, the other was enjoying the shamelessness of pretending.

"We'll go very far, this way," Aparicio used to say. "You, Longines, are the very embodiment of audacious precision; you, Katanga, the epitome of ingenuity. While I . . . well, what is there to say?"

Recalling his companion's praise, Katanga's eyes filled with laughter. In his mind he contemplated the amusing spectacle of Aparicio dancing a wildly contorted *malambo*. Like some drunken preacher, his anathemas against the fabric of society had turned into obscene caterwauling. And across the distance that, in actuality, separated them—which he could see stretching out behind the immediacy of his eyelids—his absent comrade's voice called to him.

"Yes, yes!" Katanga answered him, under his breath. "We'll see each other soon. Our business here is concluded!"

When he refocused his attention on the police station, he could still feel his heart swelling with triumph, the sensation slightly diminished for his still being in the precinct. Through the net of his eyelashes he scrutinized the men assembled there. Seeing the Examining Magistrate approach him, he shrank inwards like a turtle, lowering his head, and dampening his excitement, wincing from the smell of the carbolic soap.

"Allow me, sir, to express to you my pleasure and satisfaction. The Chief Investigator and the detective have just informed me of your extraordinary valor yesterday evening. Your actions at the fire have erased even the slightest suspicion we might have harbored for you. You're free to go. Civic heroism is all too rare in these impious days of profit and vice. You are free. Although, if you like, we can try to find you some employment, locally . . ."

The opportune moment. Katanga knew that he had to make full use of the mask of humility and suffering that he had so arrogantly concocted. He tried to stand up, to thank the Magistrate. In doing so, he deliberately dropped a small notebook onto the floor.

Feigning sharp pains, Katanga made it clear that he was unable to retrieve his property, so the Chief himself crouched down to pick up the scattered papers and cards. He was astonished.

"What! You belong to the Conservative Party of Buenos Aires?"

Katanga nodded shyly.

"Oh! I should've guessed. I'm so sorry . . . !"

The Magistrate peered at some of the other items, curious. And after reading a certificate of good conduct from the Bishop of Paraná, his bluish temples as well as the smooth gloss of his oiled hair wrinkled in bewilderment. Filled with a sudden mounting enthusiasm, he continued:

"I say again: if you'd like to stay here, we'll do whatever it takes to find you a job, say as a watchman. These documents and your good deed are precious credentials. If you should decide ..."

Katanga sighed lamentably.

"Thanks ... Infinite thanks ... But that's a job I could never do ... I'm not my own man, you see ... The courage that you attribute to me isn't really mine ... It's a mysterious impulse that flows into me in the face of horror or misery. I'm unable to explain even to myself where it comes from ... God, perhaps! ... Many times I've thought about the moral strength that inspired the Good Samaritan ..."

Touched by these ideas, the Magistrate insisted, with even more vehemence:

"It's your choice. But you can count on my most earnest aid. I can promise you a peaceful and most dignified position at the Pious Union of St. Jerome."

"Thanks ... Infinite thanks ... I'll think it over ... Allow me time to think and pray ... I need to seek comfort in prayer ... Life has been so hard for me that I'm accustomed to rejecting the feather pillow of kindness ..."

Spurred on by the situation, the Chief piped up:

"Accept the offer. You won't have to worry about your future anymore. With the help of the Examining Magistrate, the change of government won't affect you in the least."

"Thanks ... Infinite thanks ... What consolation to find an oasis of men such as yourselves along the road of life! Oh, what a balm to my fatigue is the shade of comprehension! How my thirst is quenched by the wellspring of noble hearts!"

Simulating a sob, Katanga wiped his eyes. Moved, the Magistrate patted him on the shoulder. And let fall his pity:

"Weep!"

"Yes . . . let me . . . I can't hold back my tears . . . I weep with joy!"

Immersed in the fiction, sniveling, Katanga sniffled up nonexistent mucous.

The others gathered in a knot, standing apart from him.

"A true philosopher! A stoic!"

"I've known more than my share of intelligent drifters, but this one . . . !"

"What do you think . . . should we give him a few pesos to help him get healthy, get something to eat and find some shelter?"

"Agreed."

"It's painful to see men in such shape, punished by cruel fate . . ."

At that moment, the detective reappeared, fierce and fiery with the Treasurer of the Pro-Strike Committee in tow, as well as various construction workers who'd been arrested. On seeing him, the three officials exuded a rather unpleasant wave of hostility.

"Just a moment! Wait!"

"We'll be right with you."

Moving back to the threshold, the detective bit his lip in rage. From there he observed the men hand over the alms they'd pooled together, and heard the Examining Magistrate's touching farewell:

"Go, my good man. You're free now. No one will bother you. May God be with you!"

As Katanga passed in front of him, the Chief's look seemed to wrap the bum in a mantle of tenderness.

Indignant, the detective almost exploded with scorn. He could barely contain himself. Stammering, he finally vomited out a whisper:

"Go on, only watch out, you lousy fucker. No one'll bother you! . . . Hah, if it was up to me, I'd send you off on a third class ticket to hell."

....

RÍO CUARTO (NORTH)—ESPINILLO:

Dawn.

Before the freight train pulled out, Dijunto, Fortunato, and Viejo Amor were ordered to carry and arrange the bundles. Meanwhile, Longines and Katanga went out with Lon Chaney to finish a difficult mission.

Daylight broke over the horizon with the locomotive's whistle. They boarded the train.

They were riding in an empty cattle car, their temporary home as they headed out to a ranch in the country.

Annoyance all around.

First, because all their gear had been tossed in and arranged carelessly. Second, because Lon Chaney—delayed for some reason none could guess—had been unable to reach the train on time.

The car smelled just as bad as they felt, a stink to match their collective anxiety; in the same way that discomfort and bad odors produce the same grimace of fastidious concentration.

Katanga, his nose feeling quite sensitive, grudgingly stressed:

"Always in the shit wagon. You could've picked a different car."

"There weren't any . . ."

"Then clean it up a little. You've tossed our stuff around everywhere. We'll get all smeared with shit, even our faces."

"Patience! Just a little patience. It's a short ride."

"Always the same! Mr. Tolerance. You'll put up with anything."

Longines looked at him sideways, the way parrots do. He sucked in his right cheek. And pointed out:

"No. You know perfectly well I don't put up with everything! You've already commented upon how a lack of punctuality absolutely infuriates me. Look what happened with Lon Chaney?"

And they sank down again into a still pool of silence.

Viejo Amor was heating water for coffee. The fumes from the canned heat, mixed with the ammoniac waves rising from the sticky paste of manure on the floor, made Katanga's stomach turn somersaults. He gagged as if he'd just stepped into a patch of drunkard's vomit. He fumbled for his bag. A slug of cognac and a handkerchief soaked in eau de cologne set him at peace with himself once again.

The sun! A carbuncle in the rosy face of dawn. Each ray of sunlight floated just above the ground, in a sharp striated spoke. Then the full morning sun shot through the horizontal slats that composed the train wagon's wall, each beam spinning with dust motes and flies, painting the floor with stripes of light. Bands of purple shadow upon the dried yellow manure. Bands of light upon the noisy green buzzing of the cow pies.

"What filth! At the first station we come to I'm climbing into the wagon ahead."

"Fine. And good riddance!"

Nothing resembling actual and implacable antagonisms. Only feints. Threats. They liked to disagree simply "to test the waters." The pleated curtains of self-love artfully conceal all the dubious craft of personality. But those tricks and traps collapse once we reach the true self behind the mask. Thereafter it may be possible to establish the level playing field of true friendship, upon which the players can achieve that harmonious equilibrium which stabilizes relationships, shoos away all hints of gaucherie and malice, and proscribes any pointless struggles for supremacy.

Katanga never did clamber up to the next wagon. With his irritation diverted in contemplation of the pampas, the pampas seeped into him. And flattened him. The vast expanses pried open his psyche, as if were a pair of forceps wielded by two titans: North and South. Absorbed by the countless images hurtling past, he took in the rustic drama of the land, the distant mists of the sun on the planted soil and the spermy smell of dew among the nearby furrows.

....

BAIGORRIA-GIGENA:

The station at Espinillo was shrunken, almost buried, by the distance. Barely visible the stiff arm of the signa . . . Barely visible the zinc daisy of the windmill . . .

The iron rails stretched toward them from the distant horizon, as if trying to lasso our five adventurers. But the train is an indomitable modern dragon that huffs and puffs along its mighty way. And ensconced within its panting motion, the five escaped into time—marked by the tac-tac of the passing rail joints—and into space—measured by the kilometer posts.

Viejo Amor took a sip from the coffee jar and passed it on.

"Speak of the devil. Your turn. Here, help yourself, Lon Chaney".

"What? Lon Chaney!"

Their general stupefaction was followed by a Homeric laugh. Unhooking himself from the outside railing, none other than Lon Chaney spidered along towards the wagon's door. This was, for him, a simple operation, gifted as he was with exceptional dexterity. He laughed at vertigo, could squeeze out of any kind of tight spot, and never shied from danger.

"It's fine for you all to laugh. It's been very amusing. Look at the state I'm in. Almost naked. Too bad they didn't get the whole episode on film . . . I managed to deliver the message myself, but there happened to be two detectives there, and they started chasing me. But I managed to outrun them. Around the corner, behind the wall of an empty lot, I threw away most of my clothes. In a flash! And then I came heading back the same way . . . I went limping along so naturally that they didn't suspect me for a second. One of them zeroed in on me and asked: *Did you see some guy go running by?* Since I was sticking out my jaw like it was dislocated, I answered him like some simpleton: *A-ha . . . Yah . . . Tha' way . . . He cuh-limbed into the milk-man's wah-gon . . . Tha' way . . .* Afterwards, a truck dropped me off at the railroad crossing. And here I am. *Voilá tout!*"

Laughter was still burbling among them.

That's why they called him Lon Chaney: because he possessed the same protean capabilities as the film star. The most surprising "types," the strangest characterizations, the most contrasting temperaments, were all contained within his exemplary talent for mimicry.

He was French. Fifty-two years old, and though his face looked timid and embarrassed he was forever cursing the typical life of the bourgeois family. All in all, an enigma. It wasn't that he was worn down with age but rather the shame of his wife and children; he was afflicted not with poor health but with the tragedy of being a cuckold, the father of two kept women and a pederast.

From the confusion and disorder of his home he'd salvaged only his cunning voice and his clownish forelock. He left his wife in the arms of her lovers, his daughters to their libertine lives, and his son to his anomaly. And he went out into the world, wandering here and there, willy-nilly, as indeed he'd done while still a bachelor, before settling down. This was how the old kitchen boy from the Restaurant Pharamond, 24 Rue de la Grande Truanderie, Paris, drifting from Marseille to Beirut, from Liverpool to Sydney, first came to know the ravages of solitude; now, a defector from marriage, he enjoyed the happiness of submerging his inclination toward love and domesticity within the tribulations of comradely solidarity.

He knew a hundred trades but practiced none. A man only reaches Lon Chaney's exalted levels of disdain when he masters that greatest of skills: living without working. He'd been an itinerant photographer in Haiti, a partner in a mining business in Colombia, a local party boss and luxuriant freeloader in Ecuador, and a boatman on Lake Titicaca; he'd wandered from country to country, traveling all the roads of well-being and ruin. Until in the end, after being a Chilean spy in Peru and a Peruvian spy in Chile, he learned that success in life resides in conquering one's desires with the resources of imagination.

But we need not point out, one by one, each step that his indifference scaled, even as his reputation descended them four at a time. The point is that "some people you meet" suffer very badly from collective disorientation.

Since then, however, Lon Chaney had become conscious of the true facts of life. He no longer wasted time on the filigrees of honor or the frivolities of duty. He strove to achieve a state of fictiveness, the antithesis of reality. And with that mask in place, he was able to come into direct contact with the harshness and crudity of his appetites and instincts, while inside, his true self remained safely stupefied in a fantasy, a mixture of reverie and monstrosity.

He dyed his obstinate gray hairs and worried at his face with cosmetics to smooth over his inevitable wrinkles, trying to lend some truth to the essential lie of his adult life. And now, cut off from love and enthusiasm both, his main pleasure consisted in mocking others — starting, logically, with himself.

Essentially a man of cosmopolitan spirit, his narrow reddish, eyes and violet complexion were adequate mediums for even the most unusual modifications and modalities. In his tireless pursuit of whatever profit or advantage, he had become, variously, Canadian, Chinese, Lapp, Hindu, or Lithuanian, as the occasion required. Likewise crippled, hunchbacked, one-eyed, or knock-kneed when he wanted to exploit the pity the sight of him elicited — making a mockery of teratology.

He enjoyed a superb, easy command of feelings and sensations, his own and others'; he was a master of making gullible unsuspecting strangers shiver with horror while simultaneously feeding their greedy appetite to look openly on the grotesque circumstances of human misery. It was a talent that never deserted him — like some faithful phantom hound — on his long travels across seas and deserts, through cities and countryside. He experienced difficulties and disasters. He found himself stranded in the suburbs of London and the saloons of Vancouver, in the sewers of Paris and the underworld of Singapore. But he always managed to find some way to escape from these dire straits and keep moving.

Having wandered the globe he returned to France where he secured a permanent anchorage in the berth of loathing. Jaded and bitter, having known too much of people's strange selfish behaviors, including his own, he renounced any ambitions he'd ever had, but this led to his renouncing nearly everything else as well and withdrawing into a stubborn, proud asceticism.

But this bitter bankrupt Proteus still loved enacting the despicable amusements of his malleable myth. Pushing back his curling clownish cowlick, he spoke in a clear cunning voice, articulating, with a mathematician's cold logic, the terms of his personal equation composed of unknown variables, setting them out with the precise crystalline articulation of a frieze.

$$\frac{Family}{Love} + X \text{ tedium} + X \text{ hatred} + X \text{ loathing} = 0 \text{ illusion}$$

They rolled along in silence

The coffee jar circulated in its geometric round.

Following a kind of ritual, each man first silently inhaled the rich smell wafting up from the jar.

They politely allowed each other to enjoy such moments uninterrupted. Coffee was their nepenthes. Elixir and balsam. Almost unanimously, they'd resolved, to eschew any other decoction. Despite having recited Okakura Kakuzo's aphorism in his own defense: "Tea is free of the arrogance of wine, the conscious individualism of coffee, and the smiling innocence of cacao," Fortunato, who preferred drinking tea, was outvoted thanks to Lon Chaney's personal postulate: "Long live the mindful individualism of the black nectar!" And Aparicio, who dauntlessly defended *yerba mate*, referencing countless legends of hearth and tradition, was forced to yield before the aggressive energy of countless arguments about the hygienic hazards implied in sharing the same straw.

The coffee jar circulated in its geometric round.

The silence of each man waiting his turn matched the liturgical silence of the one sipping.

A long whistle from the locomotive announced their imminent arrival to the next town.

"Which station is coming up?" demanded Fortunato.

"Helena. Don't you know? You should've known that . . ."

"Yes, Longines. But my eyesight's getting bad. The lettering in the guidebook is small as hell!"

"Always with your lousy excuses!"

"Lousy excuses . . . lousy excuses . . ." Fortunato grumbled.

"And Aparicio's cot? Why isn't it here?"

"What! Were we supposed to bring it?"

"Of course. Come on, let's hear some more lousy excuses."

"Lousy excuses . . . lousy excuses . . ."

Seeing Fortunato crestfallen and contrite, Katanga intervened:

"One excuse is just as lousy as another. Don't argue over trivial matters. Just consider the cot as a memento left behind . . ."

"For the detectives, right? How nice. Compliments of "*El Tigre* Resort" . . . Don't you remember that the theft was reported. Don't you remember every cot was branded with the *El Tigre* insignia?"

"Not that one, not anymore," said Katanga. "I scraped off the brand with my knife . . ."

Longines and Katanga laughed and smiled at each other with reciprocal admiration. The others laughed, too.

Delightful camaraderie! For a moment they all shared a general satisfaction at their mutual zeal and collective wisdom.

Three short whistles announced the approaching road crossing.

"Crouch down" ordered Katanga.

As they obeyed him, each man peered out the right hand side of the wagon, searching for the prearranged signal.

Nothing.

They were now passing the town cemetery: a hectare of death with rows of corn planted right up to the very foot of the enclosing wall.

As if responding to a countersign, they reverently doffed

their hats, caps, and berets, suddenly exposing half a dozen bare heads.

"These new settlers are incorrigible. They don't plant a single tree, not on their farms nor in the cemetery. Their only plan for the future is to sow more and more grain . . . And all, for what? So they can groan their lives away, complaining about bugs, rodents, blight, droughts, and speculators . . . And to smell, even once they're dead, the breeze that worships the fresh ears of wheat and corn . . ."

....

HELENA:

Lengthy maneuvers in the station yard.

The train uncoupled at various junctions and sidings. Couplings and uncouplings. The livestock car where they were hiding, crouching in the shadows, stood for five long minutes near the cattle chute.

"As long as they don't decide to load any more cattle in here . . ."

But the dumb joke fell on deaf ears.

Like a python, the train slithered along, swallowing up four carloads of hogs, fifteen flatcars of wheat, and two Hamburg cars of flax. Slowed down by digestion, it twisted heavily upon the rails. And with its segments reunited, shaking the rattling caboose, it set out in a straight line north.

Feeling like a miracle worker, the switchman stood at the platform's edge and mopped his brow as he watched the train disappear, satisfied at having successfully accomplished such a feat.

A sun-dappled morning. Standing atop the earthen embankment or among the harrowed fields sliced into black bread, the cows' pale underbellies seemed anointed with liquid gold.

Gleaming in the sun, the distant mountains formed a delicate, rose-colored embellishment. Closer to the tracks the landscape offered an abrupt confusion of rough rocky ground and stark precipices.

The sight of the land, so fresh and beautiful in the morning light, loosened their tired tongues:

"Such a smooth porcelain sky! In Prague I once . . ."

"That rock formation over there, smooth as enamel, reminds me of the mountains around St. Moritz . . ."

"I like that grove of poplar trees, not much else . . ."

"I just find the pampas annoying."

"Me too: so desolate and lonely . . ."

They all murmured their approval at Dijunto's comment. And that encouraged him:

"I was a dirt farmer, twenty years, in General Pico. I've cleared thousands and thousands of acres. My harrow has sliced millions and millions of clods of sod. My sweat has watered the land of many aristocrats. What do I have to show for it . . . ? Nothing. All my backbreaking work worth about as much as a fart. A holy reverend fucking fart. Good for nothing. What have I got to show for it? Eyes half-blind from all the red dust, a face like a dirt clod sprouting wild grass, and dirty crusty overalls that look like the ground itself."

His voice sank, his head drooped in despair.

"Evidently," one of them said. "All that hard work didn't exactly turn you into a muscleman. You're so skinny that if your back itches you can probably just scratch your chest."

"Forget the jokes," grunted Dijunto. "When you've worked as much as I have, without rest, always and forever tired, the days turn into nights into months into years, why should the only reward for all that effort be still more hunger? No, goddammit! Where's the justice in that? Why should an honest man's labor sowing the earth, especially when it brings a good harvest, be stolen away and devoured by a few little rich dandies? If that's how it is, then to hell with work and whoever invented it!"

"Yes, it's sad but true. And the rich men on the other hand shout: *Long live luxury and those who hoard it!*"

Katanga realized they'd misunderstood his sarcasm. He felt the need to explain his remark. While the others remained focused on Dijunto's anger, he swallowed and cleared his throat, then said:

"Yes, old man. Humanity is like that. The poor cry out: *To hell with work and whoever made it!* and the rich respond: *Long live luxury and those who hoard it!* Justice is a night owl, a bird of ill-omen; it winks its eyes, alternately, to the left and to the right. Winks of hope for the miserable man ... Complicit, knowing winks for the potentate ... Engrave it deep in your memory. Justice is a whoring old night owl. It winks its eyes, alternately, to the left and to the right. It promises consolation for the poor. And, with despicable irony, hands everything over to the rich!"

Bull's-eye.

The analogy pierced the heart of their small company.

Lon Chaney and Dijunto nodded their heads in affirmation.

Their lower lips were still stuck out pensively as Katanga continued:

"Yes, old man. Justice is a bird of ill omen. Humanity is composed of two sorts of creatures: those who have good reason to complain, and those who don't. Those who have grounds for complaining do whatever they can to advocate change to whatever state of affairs currently afflicts them. Those who lack a reason to complain on that particular subject do whatever they can to ensure that those same things stay the same. For the former, their suffering constitutes a flagrant violation of the charters of social equity. For the latter, social equality is itself nothing more than some old rigmarole that doesn't show their comfort and privilege the respect they are owed. In such a way, while the former fight to erase inequalities, the latter entrench themselves within the gratifications of their luxury. Thus, the left and the right of humanity. And ... justice is a bird of ill omen. It winks every which way. Hopeful winks for the miserable ... Winks of complicity for the powerful ..."

Longines, with his back to the others, was carefully searching through his valise. He pretended not to listen, to be absorbed in his task. But, from time to time, swiveling his plucked eagle's head, he caught, with his suppurating eye, a glimpse of the huddled group. When Katanga finished, he declared:

"Humanity will always remain just as you describe it. Lamennais predicted it: 'All of society is founded on resignation.'"

"That's the false hope of a bygone era! In other times and ages! Resignation was an anesthetic invented by Christ. A heinous innovation invented to perpetuate class inequality. Happily, we've evolved beyond that. The *Komintern* . . ."

"You think communism is the answer to everything. I hate that multitudinous beast. Yes, 'multitudinous,' in the broadest sense of the word. Honestly, if the masses can't be broken up, disintegrated through culture into an individualistic form of anarchism that will nonetheless coordinate its every interaction perfectly, like clockwork, to mark the hour of its destiny, I'd prefer that it go on flagellating itself, that it continue to drag itself along and humiliate itself in the worst slavery imaginable. It may be that, forced to comprehend the ignominy of their fate, the masses will rise up out of sheer impotence. And once they've become steeped in the truth of individual effort, not in the reformist chatter of devious, so-called leaders, they will stage an insurrection, rebelling against and exterminating all the satraps and tyrants who live fanning themselves in the midst of the people's ignorance."

"Then, according to you, the serf . . .?"

"*Serf* is a very hackneyed term. Find another."

"So then, according to you, THE SERF must keep suffering?"

"Naturally. Until he can shed the appalling condition of being poor."

This led to a rather amusing general consternation.

Each man briefly recapitulated their own motivations regarding the enterprise they had carried out in Río Cuarto. Such similar arguments! . . . Were they considered opinions or wild outbursts? . . . Regardless, each of them was now forced to consider their own varieties of disenchantment:

"It's not possible, Longines, that you really believe all that . . ."

"How else to explain this little adventure that we're on? Does it not demonstrate the contrary?"

"If that's the case, we might as well have split the money among ourselves . . . and *tableau*."

"Oh, no one could be less deserving than ourselves—penny-ante beggars, handing out pesos . . ."

"Well then, our solidarity is absurd!"

"Our morbidity runs too deep for it to be possible to cure our open sores with the money we stole from Freya. If the poor old woman found out that the sixty-three thousand pesos she was hiding inside that loaf of stale bread had gone into the pockets of her old unemployed friends from Villa Desocupación, she'd die of heartbreak on the spot. We must spare her this shame . . . if for no other reason than to be sure that she has the strength to continue begging for a living . . . For us, it's too late—the money couldn't do us any good. Our bodies and souls alike have been gnawed by the desperation of life and the despair of death. Therefore, we do well by putting the money back into circulation, along with our sorrow. To galvanize our decadence so that it shines in a sunset of promises. To make the money serve as an agent of redemption. Because without money, *hic et nunc*, you can neither buy private justice nor foster the conscience of social justice."

"For that, ideas are more than enough."

"Forget your ideas, Katanga. The importance of ideas has dissipated completely. The Encyclopedists were only able to bring about the propitious climate of the French Revolution because their ideas had been sown into millions of oppressed souls, and when these finally sprouted, it was in a population carrying a garrote in each hand. The storming of the Bastille was possible thanks to the simple fact that the strength of the rabble was superior to the monarchy's. Facing every one of the king's henchmen—armed with muzzle-loading Moorish muskets—the peasants rushed forward wielding twenty axe handles, ten pitchforks, five daggers, and a pistol. Now, facing a machine gun, ten thousand men in equal conditions are scared shitless. Ideas … ideas … what the hell are ideas good for? What the people need is money. Money. Nothing more than money! Money to get educated about the revolution that must begin in the heart of each person standing up to a reality that's let him down. Money to stare down the elite armed with weapons similar to its own—the same ones that it's deprived us of thanks to its sinister manipulations of the class structure. Money to dynamite the juridical hulk we are currently forced to endure. Money. Money. Nothing more than money!"

Only Fortunato assented: mechanically swaying his head. Or tinkling the small coins in his pocket.

Katanga spluttered:

"I agree that money must be made to serve a noble cause. But money isn't everything!"

"True: it's not everything. But it's the only thing of value. The only thing with the power to bring people to their knees. Ecclesiastes says so: 'Money answereth all things.' It's the master of the world. We rebels—we who abjure it, who work it till it sweats blood at the grindstone of tragedy—we are the only ones it cannot dominate. Although it seems laughable, we will conquer money with the strength of our condemnation. And by giving it away, by wasting it, without wringing the least selfish advantage from it, we will carry out that most profitable form of sabotage, giving our faith and devotion free reign within the brilliant, antiseptic clarity of a heaven free from all that festering pus about God."

Longines had never before spoken with such vehemence. He blushed slightly. He almost apologized. Too much effusiveness tends to discredit those whose temperaments otherwise tend toward concision. This obliged Longines to recapitulate, concentrating his arguments:

"Without money we could never have provided for hun-

dreds of hungry masons, builders, workers and peons ...
Without money we wouldn't have been able to escape the police's suspicion ..."

"You're wrong. Katanga pulled that off himself by sheer cunning," ventured Viejo Amor.

"Pulled what off? It was the money! Money answers all questions. It's the universal retort in this debtor's civilization where
we live. Cleverness you say? An illusion! Maybe you've forgotten what sort of decisive response actually gets results ... What
were the explosions? The fire? Those were our answers. Replies
made with Melinite purchased in Pergamino ... Purchased.
Purchased. Did you hear me?"

As the train sped onward, rocking softly, the small coins in
Fortunato's pocket tinkled with insolent jubilation.

They stopped talking.

Each one looked out between the wooden slats, keeping an
eye out for the agreed upon signal.

Nothing.

Slipping sidewise, the train changed tracks, panting like a
dog.

....

LOS CÓNDORES:

When the dust cloud from the railroad crossing dissipated,
Fortunato did not reassume his former posture as did the others. He stood up from the huddle. He stretched his stiff, creaking legs. And, transferring his handful of small coins from one
palm to the other, he took to walking around the car like an
old ox ruminating upon the iniquity of not being a bull, and so
being incapable of making a sudden, unexpected charge.

A sad, restless, tiresome forward march. The march of a
conquered man with two invisible, leaden talons crushing his
shoulders. The march of a beggar continuously forced, profes-
sionally speaking, to bow his head and offer his neck. A pari-

ah's progress, just the sort of woeful march that the right *impromptu* might transform into the furious goose-stepping of the Führer's storm troopers.

And then he stopped. He raised his fists. His eyes shone. He spun around with an incomprehensible curse that was accompanied by a nasal scoff of derision.

"Which bug bit you in the ass?" Katanga asked him.

No answer.

Fortunato was a man of few words. Not dull-witted but economical: he knew the uselessness of all persuasive zeal. He knew from experience that in order to convince, one must discover within the interlocutor an open willingness to listen, a kind of reverse charity. The charity to listen quietly to your unconvincing argument. A submissive, permeable charity that doesn't respond with hermetic dogmatism. A logical charity, which abdicates its light in order to offer the "convincer" the glorious nimbus of conviction.

By the same token, he hated the ironclad self-confidence of those who scorn the delight that perfumes the faces of those poor devils who can't help but stubbornly argue and polemicize. They fail to see that the imbecile's delight is actually irrationality's tribute to our superiority!

For Fortunato, nothing was so agreeable as to offer one or another fatuous conceit the lavish applause that would inevitably only encourage further presumption on its part. He took delight in punishing with praise. Because it's when an individual has reached the captious age of reason that the tragic metamorphosis occurs. His countenance clouds over. His interior sun disappears. And instead of becoming conceited about his "triumphant" thesis, whatever it might be, a mysterious and opaque irritation begins, instilling him with a sense of his own ignorance and stupidity. All for no other reason than that the man most likely to attempt to convince another of his correctness has almost never convinced himself . . .

The pause, being so long, had become thick with tension.

But, suddenly, it ceased. Fortunato was going to speak.

There was no room for doubt. He squared himself off in front of the group with an attitude of haughty conviction. And cupping both his hands, while his small coins clinked in a cupped hollow of nerves and veins, burst out:

"You're the bugs. You: the ones arguing. I sympathize with nothing. Neither with communism nor fascism nor anarchism. Modern prejudices. Bah! When you least expect it, I'm going to annihilate all your 'ideals' with the fervor of the bazaar worker who goes crazy and destroys all the merchandise *with his bare hands*. Stupidities! This is what money is good for: to stroke the ego and whet the appetite. For pampering the eyes and the brain. Money achieves its full potential when one receives it, not when it's used. I, who've gone from being a financial expert to a beggar, can affirm that alms are the great gospel of this world. There is nothing like the happiness of giving—giving greetings, giving excuses, giving way—unless it be the happiness of receiving—a credit, an offering, homage. To receive! That is the supreme desire. No wonder God monopolizes the adventure of being the supreme recipient! I know what I'm talking about. I was once a bank manager in Prague."

His incoherence wasn't especially alarming. It amused some and worried others. He was the oldest man in the group. A *raté*. True enough, his confused thoughts did contain some lucid points, but these were stars in a murky lagoon. What nobody understood was his final affirmation: *I know what I'm talking about. I was once a bank manager in Prague*, his imagined authority served as the ultimate proof of his delirium.

Katanga tried to keep him talking:

"You lying mule ... you were once a bank manager in Prague as much as I was a monkey castrator in the Peloponnesus. You've lived on handouts your whole life. Borrowing money when you still had some credit or begging for handouts now that you're ruined ... You've obviously got that idea stuck in your head because some bank manager sent you packing when you came begging for credit. You're nothing but a vulgar, provincial, street-corner charity case."

Fortunato stretched out his stiff, creaking legs. He puffed up his chest to straighten his back. And arching his right eyebrow wildly, exclaimed:

"I'll permit no insolence. I'm a former loan officer — an *expert* almoner! I refuse to stoop to your level!"

"Nevertheless, you stooped so low as to become our informer. First you betrayed Mr. Burnt Fruitcake Face ... then it was the Russian Sow's turn ... and finally there was Freya ..."

Fortunato's face flushed purple. He was a small man, and small men seem much more likely to give way to shameful displays of opprobrium. Short people, as Rabelais said, are particularly irritable because they keep their shit so close to their heart ... though, in this case, it was already circulating torrentially through Fortunato's veins. It even infiltrated his respiration. He sweated it out in a rage. At last he exploded in displeasure, a malodorous foot-stomping tantrum, terminating with:

"The accuser is never as high and mighty as he imagines, and the one he condemns never quite so low. You, on the other hand ..."

He was a burning coal of indignation.

The scene might have had serious repercussions if not for the opportune intervention of Lon Chaney. At the critical moment, his goodness poured out its pacifying balm:

"No, no, no. This is bad. You shouldn't carry on like this, Katanga. I demand a retraction. Be loyal. You know that our *modus operandi* is never to ask anyone for anything. None of us begs. We stretch out our arms but confine ourselves to receiving. Hardly idle, street-corner beggars. We're hypocritical gods in miniature. Nothing more. A man gives alms because he is trying to escape some regret, to overcome some humiliation, to conceal some theft. Consequently, your scorn is excessive. If Fortunato says that he went from being a bank manager to a beggar, it's because no word that exists is adequate to describe those of us who industrialize others' compassion by presenting ourselves as vivid copies of the general infamy of the world."

He'd pulled that speech out of his ass ... Katanga didn't even move. With his face obscured by the smoke of this absurd fracas, he contemplated the best manner of expunging his irritation. He forced himself to remain calm a few moments more. And little by little, his perturbation transformed itself into something resembling the supernatural tenderness that glosses the face of certain paralytics.

"Judas Priest, man! It was a joke! Deep down inside we're all blameless. We dress like beggars purely for the sake of our farcical vocation. To avoid the well-dressed filth that migrates over to our side ... To fool death, that hellhound that always goes sniffing after the daintiest morsels ... I've not tolerated, nor will I tolerate, the suspicion of offensive purposes on Fortunato's part. The fact is that I've always found his allusion curious: *I know what I'm talking about. I was once a bank manager in Prague* ... and I wanted to try to cut through to its real meaning. Unfortunately, I spoke before really thinking it through. I'll certainly admit to that, if it's what you want. As for the rest, it delights me to recognize that in the business with Freya, Fortunato carried out Longines's instructions to the letter. A foray of mechanical exactitude and, therefore, of mechanical austerity. Because the theft, or better yet, the appropriation of sixty-three thousand pesos from the old woman, continues to be for me a *capolavoro* in which each one of us was nothing more than a cog in a precision calculating machine. Let's move on, now. Let's shake hands, Fortunato."

There was a very slight, very brief pause. Ideal for containing the anxiety of a passing sigh. And suddenly, as if driven by this same appeal to friendship, they were joined then by a trembling current that climbed up their arms, perforated their skulls, and made the hair on the backs of both their necks stand up,

Longines smiled smugly like an ecstatic buffoon.

....

ALMAFUERTE:

Their little skirmish blew away with the dust billowing along the tracks.

Each one of them began to put his things in order.

Everyone except Fortunato. He rode along, abstracted in memories he stubbornly kept to himself. He was thinking:

Nobody, never, will know anything about me. In reality, Jaroslav Kopecky doesn't exist. Nonetheless, he lives. He lives like symbols do, without a visible existence. This flesh that I endure, which once belonged to him, is only a kind of lichen. It lives; not because of me, but thanks to others ... My lips will never again speak of its true via crucis. *Jaroslav Kopecky shut down his life like a failed business. One day he lowered the shutters of his soul and departed. Now silent forever. How ridiculous to pretend that it can still speak! And it will remain silent everywhere, even beyond the walls of "forever." I no longer have the keys to its voice. They were flung away into the ocean of an empty conscience. In reality, Jaroslav Kopecky doesn't exist. Nonetheless, he lives. He lives by sheer force of habit. Only those who've already marched through half their lives, always on the double, always in the faithful company of fortune, can know the tragedy of being condemned to hobble through its remainder, walking the paths of past triumphs on crutches of memory. That is your* via crucis, *Jaroslav Kopecky! ... Oh, in those days you walked joyfully through the city and life smelled sweet! You'd leave your house, not far from the Cathedral of San Vito, in the elegant* faubourg *of Hradčany, and happiness lightened your step, tickling your heels. You'd cross the Charles Bridge, with greetings and salaams for its thirty effigies, and happiness wrapped itself voluptuously around your legs. From the Old Town Tower on the far side, you saw a vision of the crestwork atop the Royal Palace reflected in the river, and you tingled with happiness right down to your balls. That's how you entered the An-*

cient City, in the paradoxical vertigo of your beloved Prague, and the happiness spun your heart like a whirligig. The local office of the Zemska Bank then swam into your vision, and the happiness of having been promoted to the demigod status of branch manager intoxicated your senses like a blazing pyre . . . Poor Jaroslav Kopecky! Through my eyes your forlorn body must now contemplate the Calvary of a once-rich man. You learned late—far too late— that from Midas to Rockefeller, from Croesus to Mister Insull, all opulence is relative. That fortune's felicity harbors a weevil always eating away at it. A weevil named "Even More" . . . Ah, if only, instead of making yourself unhappy with that little spinster who lived in Vinohrady, you'd spent your leisure in that library in the Premonstratensian Convent! Ah, if only instead of piling up silver coins, you might've felt compelled to kneel down and pray before the massive silver Tomb of Saint John Nepomuk! . . . Poor Jaroslav Kopecky! Excessive frugality, which in the poor is perhaps a beneficial vice, becomes among the potentates of this world an outlandish greed. You see? Magnates are closer to misery than the most miserable themselves. How much better for you if you'd mortgaged your time to young ladies on the park-islands of Moldova; if you'd performed your calculations in the geometric gymnasium of the Sokols; if you'd counted, one by one, the seven hundred and eleven rooms of the Royal Palace, instead of tallying up your debtors' due dates! Poor Jaroslav Kopecky! You see? Pluto's greed and Harpagon's stinginess alike destroy the meaning of wealth. Nihil nimis! *If not, say otherwise! Observe yourself in me, see me as your own bitter decline. Observe yourself in this ruined piece of flotsam, through the ruined escarpments of the world, you, who drifted through your sleepy Sundays along the Legion Bridge, and snuck your anxieties by the joyous dockside; you, who breathed the cool fresh air along Myslíkova Street and, in the lighted roadstead along Žitná Street, facing the statue of Saint Wenceslas, used to lay your thirst to rest upon the foamy mattress of a beer stein. Observe yourself.*

"There! There!"

"The sign!"

"The sign!"

Various peremptory voices broke into Fortunato's soliloquy.

His gaze, still absent, soaring in his delirium, suddenly fixed on the top rail of the cattle car. But, even this sensorial confusion could not slow his streaming reverie. And the silent, confident voice that had been addressing his inner world, became a voice speaking aloud:

". . . in me, Jaroslav Kopecky. And if you're still crying over your old lost wealth, shedding tears for your youth long rusted away . . . then cry . . . cry. . . so that your exhausted flesh turns to dust . . . turns to nothing . . . little clay figurine . . . in a vortex of harsh winds . . ."

Guffaws and derision.

Their sudden excitement after a long quiet stretch swallowed his words.

"Did you see it clearly? Where?"

"White or brown?" Rag or paper?"

"On a signal box. White rag."

"Good. Then check out the corner fence post in front of the station."

A minute went by.

"White rag!"

"White rag!"

"Good. Split up into pairs. Be discreet. In an hour and a half we'll meet as usual."

In order to encourage him with his solicitude, Katanga was disposed to disembark with Fortunato. They were the last ones off. He lent him a hand. He took his baggage. And showed him the way.

Katanga felt guilty for losing his temper at Fortunato and wanted to set things right between them. He wanted to vindicate himself. But vindicate himself in secret, earnestly, applying just the right remedy to the older man's wounded self-esteem. But no. He knew how difficult it is to enter into another's loneliness, at the most propitious moment, to unite our offering of thanks and consolation with the emptiness of a soul in need!

Longines and Dijunto walked directly to the corner post.

While Dijunto put his boot up on the fence wire and pretended to tie the lace, Longines copied down the following letters,
written in pencil on the rag: **iauaoauuieeuiuioiiauuaioiaeuee**.

"Ready. Let's go."

Beneath the shade of an acacia, seated on the edge of the
gutter, he extracted a square of celluloid from his pocket:

	a	e	i	o	u
a	v	b	t	q	m
e	c	h	p	f	t
i	u	a	k	o	w
o	i	g	e	j	y
u	s	x	r	z	n

Jotting the result, he read:

"usina two km south."

Dijunto observed the task of decryption with a curiosity
tinged with contempt. Flattered by his interest, not noticing
his disdain, Longines explained:

"It's very simple. It's a code, a substitution cipher. The five
vowels repeated in a horizontal and vertical line, serve as indicators of twenty-five squares that contain, in random order,
the principal letters of the alphabet. Each letter is designated
by the vowels at the beginning of the vertical and horizontal
line that passes through each respective box. To make the puz-
zle more difficult, Aparicio, Katanga, and I have agreed to not
separate the words. The coded sentence thus seems, always, like
the transcription of some Gypsy wailing a flamenco tune . . .
iauaoauuieeuiuioiiauuaioiaeuee . . . You see? Other people use
numbers instead of vowels. That's a better system, but this 'vo-
calization' of thought sounds nicer . . ."

"Well, see: for me this kind of alphabet soup is just absurd."

"No, Dijunto. Tactics, that's what matters in life. Not asking
anyone for anything shows you have an independence of character. Not letting the next person's errors or opinions affect you
signifies having the courage to accept your own. That's why we

use this rigmarole, which protects us from insidious suspicions. If they saw us all together, working out Aparicio's whereabouts, figure for yourself what would happen, when there's a warrant out for his arrest right now . . ."

"Dammit, you're right!"

"Your surprise is understandable. The farmer cultivates that sector of his mind which relates to crop yields: grains, plants, legumes. His notion of the world hinges upon the practical predictability of nature. A watchmaker, a horologist like me, born to contemplate the ever- changing phenomena that emerge within the fields of time, is obligated to calculate the remotest contingencies of chance. We differ, in other words. But let's not discuss this further. Viejo Amor and Lon Chaney were in charge of buying the groceries to prepare today's lunch. We'll wait for them here. It's gratifying to me to see how we continue to understand one another, without sentiment, conscious of partaking in a destiny greater than any one of us alone; and how each man's duty intermeshes so sweetly with the others' as far as the mechanics of our little tour of the country."

Dijunto wrinkled his brow. No sooner did he hear an allusion to "duty" than his rough, earthy skin was immediately plowed with deep furrows. Next, the matted thicket of his eyebrows and mustache quivered and shuddered. And, like a startled covey of partridges, suddenly rocketed upwards.

Duty jabbed him in the heart like a cattle prod. He had worked so hard, tightened his belt so much beneath the iron rule of duty, that at the mere sound of its name, he hunched his back, submissive, ready to hop aboard the next flight to anywhere:

"It ought to be obvious to you by now, Longines: what I *should* do, I'll do. I've never been afraid of work, however hard and dangerous. No, it was the useless sacrifice of the work I did that put me off. Skinny and hunched over as I am, my arms are still just waiting for their orders, nothing more. I'm made for work—but *duty* pisses me off. Give me orders, that's all. But don't get me stuck in these quagmires of words. I'm a sim-

ple man. The only philosophy I understand is the one misery
taught me. So tell me to push and I'll push. But don't tell me
to think it through. Judges, attorneys, and those middlemen
who leased fields to me . . . whenever I had to talk to them, everything always went wrong. I don't know how to think things
through. I don't know how to express anything or speak from
the heart. That's why, whenever I've signed my name on a lease
I only did it because I had to, because so-called 'duty' demanded it. That's why signing my name, for the landlord's benefit,
always made me ache more than plowing a hundred hectares,
always hurt me more than losing three harvests in a row."

Seated on the curb, leaning back, Longines listened to him
with penetrating sympathy.

When Dijunto stopped speaking, the watchmaker put his
valise under his neck as a pillow. He preferred listening to his
suffering dreamer of a comrade while staring up at the sky.

His purulent eye seemed to be purified in the blueness.

Stubbornly welded to the earth, Dijunto kept quiet, only
perforating the silence with memory.

And he dove deep into his heart as into the water of a cistern.

Viejo Amor and Lon Chaney strode along, their footsteps out
of sync.

Walking through town in search of a butcher shop, the former paused to stare after every passing female, tracing their
shapes with his lewd lazy eyes. Neither face nor age mattered
to him. A whittler of obscene bone and wood talismans—in
which the vulva or virile member was always carved with tumescent deformities—Viejo Amor had reached a stage of sexual perversion to match his name, in which eroticism, now
wholly fetishistic, becomes a visual experience, and the optic
nerve opens the glandular floodgates, making the poor old fool
piss his pants and drool with desire. In truth, it wasn't really any particular woman he was attracted to, in and of herself,
as an agent of pleasure; rather, he used them to stimulate the

enjoyment of far less tangible delights. He had a lively memory—and there, in the basement of his brain, a woman's presence served as a lantern to illuminate his past exploits. Women lit up his lasciviousness. And as it was revived, his lust took
on new and anomalous forms. What better emblem of his ardor than the fabrication of these ribald dolls and libertine figurines? What better indicators of these priapic stretches of his irredeemable sexual decline?

Lon Chaney, who was standing and waiting for Viejo Amor
to catch up, for the fifth time in a row, could brook no further delay. Diligent as ever, he retraced his steps half a block
to demand, and imperatively, a little haste. Ensconced in the
vestibule of a photographer's shop, Viejo Amor was gloating
with gusto, chatting up a maid. One of those women who've
been so unlucky in love that they'll suffer any offense whatsoever coming from a man. Viejo Amor was already holding the
diminutive "sarcophagus of Tut-Ank-Amon" in his hand; seeing that he was about to trip the infamous spring release on
the lid, which caused a phenomenal penis, almost as big as the
"mummy" itself, to pop up and begin oscillating wildly, Lon
Chaney broke in:

"Give me that! Have you no shame? Get out of there. Let's
go!"

A look of tearful frustration flooded Viejo Amor's face. It
might as well have been a case of *coitus interruptus*, given how
deeply it rattled him. He sighed desolately. And softening his
expression, said:

"I'm coming. But ... give me back the sarcophagus. I can't
leave her like this, with her curiosity unsatisfied ... Isn't that
right?"

"Of course," she replied. "Why do you have to get in the
way?"

"See?"

Lon Chaney was magnanimous. Just like that famous country constable who surprised a couple coupling in the park and,
patting the fellow on the back, urged him to "Finish up now,

pal, so I can take you to jail," he handed the small toy back and made himself scarce. He was as certain of Viejo Amor's jubilation as of the maid's bashful surprise.

Ten yards down the street his ears caught a faun-like cackle and the wicked thread of her laugh. Turning to look, he saw that Viejo Amor had moved away from the vestibule while the maid remained on the threshold with a cloying look on her face, trying not to let him get away.

"Didn't I tell you?" Viejo Amor asked. "It's all set. I'll be screwing her tomorrow morning, bright and early . . ."

Lon Chaney smiled:

"Bright and early . . . you're obviously all washed up. A true Don Juan practices his devotions at night, upon the altars of shadow, braving the thousands of risks it conceals. Sunrise sours love. It's the hour for love between decrepit spouses, whose organs only gradually get moist and erect, respectively, now thanks to a warm bed, now from the pressure of a full bladder . . . In the light of morning, everything is sour and fetid. The dew is nothing more than nature's sweat after the nocturnal orgasm. I'm disgusted by those early-morning Casanovas who, while their little maidens' parents and patrons are still sleeping, steal a march on the milkmen to try and deliver first . . ."

"Don't be stupid."

"Exactly like that, just because they've got some readily available product they think they've got to unload it . . . Because, what you are . . ."

"I'm telling you, don't be stupid. I'm far from being one of those *hors d'oeuvre* types, I go for the full four courses. Love presents itself in a thousand forms, it possesses a thousand liturgies. That's precisely why the people who insist on never varying their repertoires are the ones whose appetite atrophies first. I, on the other hand . . ."

Given the evident delight with which the other man rambled on, his words lewdly malicious, Lon Chaney could not help but recognize Viejo Amor's authentic, deep-rooted depravity. The viscous virus of vice was oozing out through his pores, pumped by a concupiscent heart. It banished all passion and all sense of shame, an ominous leering mask.

Lon Chaney felt nauseated. He quickened his step. But he could no longer evade himself. The scene awoke bitter memories: his family driven mad by the misconduct of his wife, of his children . . . Then, like a flash of lightning there appeared in his mind: Eglantine, his youngest daughter. Her purity had not yet been contaminated. He vividly remembered bouncing her on his knees when she was a child, young, bright, and tender, pretending she was riding a horse. He could do no more. He snatched off his hat. And sweeping back his clownish curling forelock, he so quickened his long bandy stride that he seemed to be fleeing the abominable presence of his companion. It was the last thing he could call his own within the scope of his disaster! The tenderness of Eglantine! What deep joy, to protect her memory!

Fifteen paces farther, his chest swelled and deflated. Sighs. The labored breathing of someone about to faint. An unprecedented punishing anguish. He felt a terrible hammering at his temples. Floating behind the soothing hand of memory, in the black vault of his past, he glimpsed a pure, innocent prayer, clear as a shining light. The prayer he had once uttered so fervently—uselessly!—in the imminence of his total ruin:

TOI QUI PORTES LA TROUBLE EN PLUS D'UNE FAMILLE
JE TE DEMANDS, AMOUR, LE BONHEUR DE MA FILLE!

He advanced. But his steps were blind, unsteady.

"*Che*, are you nuts? You're walking right past a butcher shop!"

When Viejo Amor's cry resounded behind him, Lon Chaney's bleary eyes were red with tears. He tasted them. And he affected, involuntarily—as he'd done so often deliberately—the air of an ungainly simpleton.

Turning around, each additional footstep made the desolate plea reverberate in his cranium:

TOI QUI PORTES LA TROUBLE EN PLUS D'UNE FAMILLE
JE TE DEMANDS, AMOUR, LE BONHEUR DE MA FILLE!

Now in the shop's doorway, he flung his belongings to the
ground. He leaned on the window sill. And he sank a raw and
bloody look into the greasy odor of the meat.

After ten minutes of resting in the shadow of the platform,
panting like a dog, the train disappeared over the horizon.
Hanging in the sharp northern air, shivering as it dispersed: a
proud plume of smoke silvered by the sun.

Katanga and Fortunato avoided the uproar at the station.

They slipped between train cars, heading in the direction of
the railway signal. Trudging through the sand, gravel, and ash
was slow going. They persisted, not so much silent as simply
shriveled.

Small gusts of wind erased their footprints.

Always on the alert, Katanga made a mental note of certain
mysterious, seemingly spiritual connections:

Blow: dust :: soul: body.

Ash: shadow :: body: death.

Perfume: rose :: tenderness: love.

He could have gone on. But on second thought the game
was a bit too simple for him. What he was really interested
in was nothing more than penetrating Fortunato's reticence.
In drawing back the bolt that barred the man's thoughts and
mouth. To find the hidden door into his his confidence.

He tried his best. Banal remarks. Skeleton-key phrases. In vain.
Finally, fed up with his unanswered questions, he ventured:

"You walk like the Indians from the altiplano: with your
whole body leaning forward. With them there's an explanation: it's an atavism. They inherited that way of walking, which
seems ascensional in nature, ideal for scaling peaks and slopes,
from their ancestors, mountain dwellers. But you're Czechoslo-
vakian…"

"Bohemian."

"... you've done, perhaps, excursions in the Sokols. You should walk with rhythmic muscular tension, an athletic march ..."

"Impossible, Katanga, impossible! My heart isn't like one of those Innovation-brand briefcases, with a separate little compartment for each different emotion ... Oh, when you ran from the Hunger Wall to the Powder Tower! Do you remember, Jaroslav Kopecky? What hope I had then, Katanga! It's a trunk full of memories! One of these days I'll dive right in to rummage through it, with my legs hanging out ... Oh, the sensation of waking up in strange cities, when the dreams that one dreams actually come true! And, then, pulling them inside, I'll saw them off ... What good are my legs anymore! I know what I'm talking about. I was once a bank manager in Prague ..."

"Obviously, you're absolutely right," Katanga replied with slow, ineffable bonhomie.

But Fortunato was as impenetrable as ever.

This last barb hurled at his spirit having glanced off, Katanga began whistling to distract his comrade.

A masterful whistler. He knew how to draw the air from his lungs with the same melodious dexterity as Woodrow Wilson, illustrious scheming windbag. Every bit as eccentric—though not to the extreme of founding another League of Nations—Katanga's musical eccentricity dated from his adolescence. Not for him the fripperies of instrumentation or fioritura. Neither Pan's flageolet nor the aulos of Marsyas. To pipe with his lips alone! His most notable ability consisted of imitating the one-stringed "Chinese violin." It delighted him—puffing out his cheeks, holding the air in his mouth. Such was his innate appreciation for those ancient *auletes*! And spoiled by having such a clever tongue, he curled it softly, subtly, polishing the melodious nuances of a *lied* or an *aria* to a fine filigree.

"What did you prefer, the Meditation of Thaïs or Cardillo's 'Core 'ngrato'? A difficult choice, eh? Now listen to this: the 'Improviso' from master Giordano's opera *Andrea Chénier*."

"No. Whistle something ... how shall I say ...?"

"Right, right. Something closer to you. Delighted. What do you prefer: 'Blue Danube' by Strauss, or the 'Pizzicato Polka' by Krull, or perhaps *The Gipsy Princess . . .*"

"That's it."

Katanga filled his lungs. And he attacked Kálmán's imposing *intrade* with brio. Then, in a lower tone, duplicating the melody with near perfect fidelity, he unwound the underlying thread of half the operetta. He whistled the tune almost perfectly but meanwhile his thoughts were elsewhere. And along with the sonorous thread, his train of thought finely embroidered the following analysis upon the canvas of his experience:

His mind was wandering all over the place. Yet Fortunato isn't the sort to fall prey to incoherency of any kind. Those phrases of his are cabalistic incantations meant for a secret interlocutor. Who? Who knows? It's the same as with those somniloquists, those of us who surprise ourselves with sudden random locutions while we sleep, who can hardly be said to be raving. The fact is that, awake, it's difficult to simultaneously dialogue with oneself and converse with others. Your responses to your friends get mixed with your responses to yourself. Threads tangled. Ecco il imbroglio!

They were now in front of the signal. Katanga crossed the wire barrier. He read: **iauaoauuieeuiuioiiauuaioiaeuee.**

"We're fine. Look, over there by the path to the right of the tracks, here come Lon Chaney and Viejo Amor. Let's go."

They walked limp and withered more than silent.

A strange impulse then led Katanga to tromp through the loosest drifts of sand. Kicking up the dust, his walk combined the sadism of a child with the masochism of an old man. He didn't think too hard about whatever peculiarity of his nature had led him to behave in this way: whether it was the itch to annoy or the pleasure of meting out punishment. Whether it was a secret penitence or just a deeper depth of humiliation. Whether it was a delight in donning sackcloth or the pain of being taught a terrible lesson. He simply surrendered to his impulses for several minutes, after which his voice came out in what sounded like a ragged G major:

One must arrive
through the discipline of indifference
to the great wisdom of abandonment.
One must conquer
through the discipline of abandonment
the great tribulation of misery.
One must surrender
through the discipline of misery
to the great fortress of death.
One must surpass
through the discipline of death
the great indifference of life.

He spoke no more. He had composed—half-unconsciously—the ill-fated summary of yet another chapter in the story of their *caterva*.

The main road ran along the opposite side of the rail line. Trying to reach it, Fortunato snagged his clothes on the barbed wire. Suddenly agitated, he tried clumsily to free himself.

"Be patient for a second. Don't force it. You're going to hurt yourself."

It would have been easy to step down on the wire, apply pressure, and yank him through. But Katanga didn't let minutiae slow him down. He took a pair of pliers from his case, and with two snips opened the way. Cursing, he blurted out:

"Just think how this country's character would change if each citizen made free use of a pair of pliers ... And went about without worrying over scruples. Cut here. Cut anywhere. It's ridiculous to believe that all it takes is five steel wires to hold back the right of all mankind to the land. Nothing more than guitar strings ... In Europe, you know, privileges are confined by walls, ditches, or civic groves. Veritable fortresses! Going from La Valeta to Città Vecchia, in Malta, I saw how the island's tiny estates were securely parceled out to each and every person. A labyrinth of walls and barley fields. Here, you see, it's a trivial matter. One, two, three: a few snips, and all the prop-

erty spills out into the roads! ... Five hundred thousand pli-
er-wielding comrades, within a plan of premeditated commu-
nization, could raze all these wire borders in ten minutes flat.
Nothing but guitar strings ... The big estates would be abolished. Fear and confusion would be the order of the day. Tan-
gles of wires. Fence posts on pyres. Mountains of turnbuckles.
And then, with the entire agricultural and fishing industries in
chaos, the *gratissima rerum possesio comunis* will follow naturally ... Ah, if only someone could develop a theory on how to
conduct a revolution with nothing more than pliers!"

"*Gratissima rerum possesio comunis* ... ! Bah! Impossible!
Someone has to give. That's what! Give, not share. Alms are the
true gospel of this world. I know what I'm talking about. I was
once a bank manager in Prague."

Katanga swallowed his reply. Why get him worked up all
over again? Three blocks further south their big surprise appeared:

"Aparicio!"

"Aparicio!"

They were at an intersection. As always. Their recurring
theme.

"Over here," he said. "The others have already arrived. We're
staying at that little house."

He seemed unaffected by his adventure of the last few days.
His bumpy and protuberant face—a pockmarked mix of
wrinkles and reliefs—showed no anxiety.

"I can only presume you have no idea what's been going
on. Haven't they filled you in on the mess we've been dealing
with?"

Aparicio clucked his tongue: "Don't start in talking nonsense."

"Something more than nonsense ... Four bombs ... and
one hero."

"You're the hero. That goes without saying ..."

"Seriously, *che*. They saw through you right away. As well as
that idiot Treasurer from the union on strike! They came this

close to throwing us all in the slammer. Longines cooked up four simultaneous explosions, all by himself. I was already in jail when it happened. And when one of those buildings under construction collapsed, I played the hero in the fire. They just about promoted me from prisoner ... to watchman!"

"You should've accepted ... You watch everything anyway ..."

Katanga immediately changed his expression. Aparicio's lightly disrespectful tone was enough for him to validate a certain unjustified grudge he'd been nursing. He only asked:

"At that house, did you say?"

"Aha!"

And Katanga set out walking with unusual energy, carrying his own gear and Fortunato's bundle.

When he arrived, he drew Longines aside:

"You need to have a talk with Aparicio. About complicating everything, about why he permits himself the luxury of insolence ... I'm not disposed to tolerate abuse from him. Of any kind."

"Whoa, whoa! It can't be all that bad. Let me take care of it. You get busy making sure this house gets cleaned up. If not, you'll like it even less ..."

Longines knew what he meant.

The hostility between Aparicio and Katanga was coming to a boil. Mutual dislike. Bitter competition. Since they had all first gathered together in the encampment of the homeless and unemployed near Buenos Aires known as "Villa Desocupación," the former man's snide remarks had cut the latter to the quick. A typical situation: when two individuals with similar skills and temperaments live together, the least intelligent of them always comes to see it as a struggle for dominance. And at times he does dominate, because years of being browbeaten in school tends to encourage a certain submissiveness; a problem at the root of so many tragic marriages ... So while Aparicio and Katanga fought one another with the same weapon—dialectical cunning—it was with this enormous difference: one spoke with emphasis, the other with sagacity. Broadsword versus stiletto. The latter will inevitably win out — that much is obvious. But the battle tends to be so dramatic and exhausting that the defeated one is usually able to usurp the victor's triumph . . .

In any situation, faced with anyone at all, and with a verbal fluency bordering on delirium, Aparicio liked to extoll his role as political messiah. Although shrunken somewhat by age, his neat, handsome figure would swell up with pretension. His olive-green face became flushed. And then, shaking out his head of long, sloe-colored hair, his opinions would gallop spontaneously out of his mouth, as if it were the gate to a paddock of unbroken colts. But soon Aparicio would get lost. He'd get all tangled up in his own oratory. And on he'd go, albeit with difficulty, until he was entirely spent, rambling between the prudent and the incongruent, between daring and defiance, between history and vainglory.

On this occasion, however, Longines did not permit him to perorate: "Let's avoid too much chatter. I'm convinced by facts, discipline, duty."

"So what? Maybe you're saying I didn't do my part?"

"No."

"No?"

"No!"

And while the Swiss laid out charge after charge, reproach after reproach against Aparicio, the latter bowed his head beneath these accusations, lowering it to the very nadir of his failure, feeling once again the bite of a distant, mournful melancholy.

When Longines finished his vehement Catilinarian discourse, the Uruguayan resumed: "From the looks of it, Katanga's the only one who can do anything right. I might as well quit this outfit."

"Never, Aparicio, never. You're the only South American in our gang. That's a great honor. You've just got to restrain yourself a little. Act more like the rest of us. Sweep the stupidities of this stupid continent out of your spirit. We're heroism on the march, after all, not a mule train."

Aparicio grunted.

"Bah. I wish I'd stayed in the freight car! Hiding inside my stack of logs, a cloister of fetal darkness. Maybe that's where I'd have seen the light. I can't see it anywhere living this awful life with you people."

His face exhibited the sadness that weighs down all redeemers. He straightened himself up and walked off.

Though it remained fixed and staring, Longines's suppurating eye clouded over. Though this was due more to the shadow cast by an approaching thought than the pall created by Aparicio's departure.

What a perfect charlatan, with his disgusting elastic conscience! He's so coarse and tiresome, a complete drag from start to finish. He lacks all sense of solidarity. His apparent revolutionary zeal is a mere fraud. He screws up everything he sets out to do. There's no true dignity anywhere in his personality, only inferiority complexes. Withered leaves, not hummus.

But he reacted coolly. It was imperative to prevent any more quarreling. He followed Aparicio. And patting his shoulder fraternally, reinstated the deserter:

"Come on! Stop kidding around. You're a good guy. But your goodness isn't doing anyone any good. All it does is bug you. It weighs on you. It's like a spoiled daughter. And the horrible thing is, since you can't keep her quiet, you're taking it out on us . . ."

"And you punish her just for fun!"

"Well then, why not try a little restraint, as far as she's concerned . . . A little discipline . . . Goodness is a quality that has to be repressed, regulated, administered with caution — otherwise, it makes you stupid. Excuse the word, but that's how it is. And you're always slipping down that slope. Katanga is quite right to point at you and say: *Look, you're an idiot, Aparicio!*"

"Sure . . . after all, when is Katanga not in the right!"

Ninety-eight point six degrees in the shade.

The sun swooped down on the flat, open countryside like a

bird of prey. A talon of fire. Dragon's breath.

While Lon Chaney and Viejo Amor prepared lunch, Longines, Aparicio, Fortunato, and Dijunto descended the cliffs to the river. They were heading down for a swim. Abrupt declivities. Rough terrain and prickly pear cacti.

Now almost undressed, Katanga shouted to them:

"Come over here: to the canal that feeds the turbine. It's better."

"For drowning. There's a ferocious current."

The voice sounded with Dijunto's broken inflection.

A northern breeze weighed upon the backs of the company, like a heavy, unwelcome hand.

Naked, they slipped into a quiet bend of the stream, a sandy bed surrounded by granitic masses. The water came up to their groins. They were embarrassed by the ripples that kissed them there. And silently, to elude that scandalous voluptuousness, they slipped under the surface.

The pleasure produced by nature left them speechless. They turned their heads in slow, lingering delight. They drank it in. Perfumes of spearmint and peppermint. Warm exhalations from the nearby cliffs. They noticed how certain recondite pulmonary cells felt revitalized. And in the full apogee of their enthusiasm, the light seemed to enter their spirit in wide beams, illuminating areas infected by the sensorial overload of the cities.

They remained silent. The sun penetrated their lymph nodes. Its catalytic action—subtle as the needle which perforates the coin through the cork—pierced their flesh, reaching down to their cells. They looked at one another, astonished. They experienced an inexplicable heartache. A mysterious euphoria. As if they had suddenly flushed all the toxins from their bodies. As if the anemia, the atrophies, the profound morbidities, were dissolved by the kiss of the cosmic elements.

Longines murmured: "Water, sun, air, light! How wonderful! Man is more plant than animal. He is revived in his confluence with nature. In this moment, my soul moves in harmony with those venerable willow trees. My body identifies with the vigor of those poplars. My blood feels as fresh as this watercress."

They got dressed.

As they gradually covered up, the feeling of clothes upon their skin saddened them. The complicated dialysis, which had infused the vital juice in their organisms with an unexpectedly fresh, healthy vigor, suddenly ceased. Animalized once more, they set out to ascend the steep slopes, over the rough terrain and prickly pear cacti.

Once above, the view from the edge pulled them together in collective delectation. A hundred meters away, a small irrigation dike combed the river's course into the thousand curving spouts of a cascade. The water splashed and bounded among the rocks, turning to foam, slipping away in woolly clouds, spun into tulle and misty rainbows.

But something caught their attention. It was not the weak profile of the power plant silhouetted in the ochre of the distance. Nor the energetic noise of the streams diverted by the electrical generators. At the edge of the canal, erect like a caryatid, the naked body of Katanga!

He was a nudist by nature, garmented only by necessity. Clothed in nothing more than a ruffle of air, in a mantle of sunbeams, in the tunic of the moonlight, he felt a thousand times better in his own skin than outfitted in the best-cut suit of the most distinguished London tailor. Between his hatred of clothing and the heartwarming simplicity of his skin in the open air, he never vacillated. He opted imperiously for the latter, the pristine charm of paradisiacal happiness.

As his companions approached, Katanga performed a series of downward flexes. Without bending his legs, he folded his body over until his fingers touched the water. He showed no fatigue. On the contrary: his movements mimicked the beauty of the Muslim liturgy; each rhythmic motion was accompanied by the monotonous chant of his anthem:

"The abdominal muscles are the muscles of health. The abdominal muscles are the muscles of health. The abdominal muscles are the muscles of health."

Straightening up, he showed no haste in dressing. He walked about, from one side to the other, chatting. Without any scruples. Without a touch of shame. With the ingenuous *sans façon* of a little boy. His hands were occupied in braiding a handful of aromatic wild herbs, resolving, in a simple way, the tricky issue of "where to put them," which obsesses the garden-variety nudist. This also offered him, as an added benefit, an elegant way of avoiding the impulse to illustrate his words with hand gestures:

"You will have observed: I wear my nakedness with absolute naturalness. It is a much more difficult thing than it appears. People in the West have become accustomed to covering up with hypocrisy, the vulgar loincloth of sin. To conceal the body, better yet; because clothing constitutes the most ruinous concealment, perpetuated over the centuries. In its purity the body displays the most decorous and dignified haughtiness. It has no need of secretive coverings. Disguised as it walks, then, each body is an ill-fated lie, monstrous and lascivious. We need to react, react! So that nudity may shine forth in its splendor of health, beauty, and equilibrium."

They spotted a small-sized man with a large, elongated skull, edging his way along the top of the canal wall, timidly approaching their circle. His self-conscious manners, like his lustrous, peeled, unwrinkled face, caught their attention.

Without any preambles, he stated:

"Can't swim here."

Aparicio found this injunction most annoying:

"Why not, you little double-yolk egghead, why not?"

"Sign over there. Orders from electrical supervisor."

"The order is suspended whenever I feel like it," said Katanga, and dove back into the current."

Tranquil, softly, gently, the guard turned his steps back toward the power station.

"OK, I telephone police."

Longines sensed the danger. He beckoned the man over. He attempted a dialogue in German. Unsuccessful because the egghead was Estonian. But softened up now, perhaps because of the phonetic affinity or some private resonance, he acceded:

"Yeah. Here no swim. Here go away."

"Katanga: come out! Get dressed."

Longines's peremptory tone hastened Katanga's obedience.

As Katanga dressed, an affront to his body, his memory lit up. The sudden flash was transformed into an inkling of nostalgia. He was in Barcelona. Ah, Barcelona! When his previous incarnation as Doctor Inhell—three tricks in one: Thurston, Houdini, Fregoli—had to be packed up in the off-season, leaving him with himself once again—a man, no more, no less. That man could often be seen walking out in the countryside stark naked, accompanied by various friends. Oh, those delicious days as a member of the Gymnos Club! Oh, the victory of superimposing organic full-frontal nudity, with neither briefs nor *maillot*, upon the mockery of well-catalogued social perversions! Now, pulling on his undershirt, he raised his arms to the sky, and accompanied his pose with a hearty curse. And he saw in his mind's eye the Manes, the ghost of Joaquín Valldaura, the erudite comrade who had been instrumental in the clergy's first sudden reversals of fortune. Katanga smiled in his remembrance. The initial debate, backed by Hippocrates, Galen, and Paracelsus; by Priessnitz, Kühne, Kniep, Rikli, and Souza; by Fletcher, Hanisch, Pascault, Carton, and Duliu, was a disaster: the Christian journalist dogmatically denied the mental hierarchy of such subjects! ... The second controversy, with the professor from the Catholic Lyceum, was another disaster. With both contenders installed in their respective corners—Rousseau, Michelet, Reclus versus Duns Scotus, Saint Francis, Saint Thomas—healing for the body and soul through communion with nature, *di frate Sole,* was discarded offhand. "*Altissimu onnipotente, bon Signore—per sor' Acqua—la quale è multo utile et humile et pretiosa et casta—y de nostra matre Terra—la quale sustenta el gouerna, et produce diversi fructi con coloriti fiore et herba ...*" The final polemic was the greatest disaster. The adversary, an apoplectic priest, justified his admonition against

nude bodybuilding, citing the Bible and the Holy Doctors of
the Church. Valldaura followed suit. He was no dunce. And
he used the cleric's own weapons against him! To chapter eigh-
teen of Leviticus, which abominates nakedness, he responded with the versicles of the Song of Songs that exalt it. And
so they mixed it up, trading an endless volley of punches:

*"I advise you to purchase gold tested by the fire, in order that
you may be rich, and that you be CLOTHED in white garments,
so that the shame of your nakedness be not discovered."* REVELA-
TIONS III, 18.

*"NAKED I came from my mother's womb, and NAKED will I
return there."* JOB I, 21.

*"Happy is the man who keeps his vigil and does not cast off
his GARMENTS, so that he does not go out naked and expose his
shame."* REVELATIONS XVI, 15.

*"Do not give your bodily members over to sin as instruments
of iniquity; instead, offer yourselves up to God, NAKED, as dead
men brought back to life, and your members to God as instruments of justice."* SAINT PAUL, ROMANS VI, 13.

*"You shall not go up to my altar by steps so that your nakedness
BE NOT DISCOVERED."* EXODUS XX, 26.

*"Now both of them were NAKED, Adam and his wife, but they
felt no shame in front of each other."* GENESIS II, 25.

From the little cabin, Lon Chaney and Viejo Amor were
calling to them. Lunch was ready.

Katanga, his left foot poised on a rock, stayed bent over.
Pensive. His vision firmly fixed upon a frieze of memories. Absorbed. Repeating to himself that phrase of St. Augustine with
which Valldaura had left the cleric dumbfounded:

"A time will come when we will delight in beauty alone, in
our mutual beauty, without impure desire."

Aparicio was getting impatient:

"Let's go, hurry it up, man! How long does it take you to tie
your shoes?"

Nomads luxuriate in darkness. To build, on the scaffolding of the bright midday, a space that transforms the empty dream into an oasis of voluptuous reverie. To mold the shade until it becomes a transparency of obsidian and fresh cavern coolness. To work the dry, black matter of the confined air, until impregnating it with a lunar humidity. It's an art! A delicious art.

Katanga knew it.

And he had worked carefully.

While Lon Chaney and Viejo Amor had been toiling away at the lunch preparations, he had taken measures of his own for their repast. He removed the unnecessary junk from the little house. He swept and dampened the earthen floor. He threw several buckets of water on the rough thatched roof. He cut the pineapple into thick slices. He excitedly rubbed together the rinds of two melons. He hung up the ripe bunch of bananas. He set the bottles of wine to cool in an earthenware jar. He blocked the crack in the window with a damp, rolled-up towel. He shut the door tightly. And, conscious of the pleasant effect of his preparations, he had gone outside for a swim.

Returning, coming into the cabin, he found the normal hullabaloo of voices smothered in surprise. What a nebulous symphony of calm and fragrance! What a condensation of happy blessings from simple resources! What a delicate bouquet of harmonious fruits! What a rustic poem of home-baked bread! Their pupils sparkled with the unexpected pleasure. And now seated, each man believed himself to be sinking down into the darkness.

Yes. Sinking into darkness. Settling down into it. To feel that life advanced its legions with statuary slowness. The gentle sound of relaxation, floating flat on your back over deep currents. Swimming in oneself. Upon the penumbra. In the perfume and gentleness. It's a delight! An artistic delight.

Katanga knew it.

Nomads luxuriate in darkness.

And hearing the inner-complacency of their hearts sunk deep in comfort, he smiled within, Buddha-like, with an ironic gaze beneath his lowered eyelashes.

"It's pointless to get your hopes up too much. I see that now. The whole dream of life drifts away the moment you feel a toothache or receive notice of an unpaid bill. I know what I'm talking about. I was once a bank manager in Prague. The search for eternity within the confines of daily existence is a luxury reserved for rich people who never suffer hunger or for poor devils who suddenly inherit a fortune in their old age."

"Health is achieved by keeping the soul free of worries and protecting the body from the embarrassing compromises that can result from youthful indiscretions. With that, a good dosage of altruism, a pair of beach sandals, a deep flow of love in the heart, and a bit of spinach each day, the noblest longevity may crown the sweet fatigue of enthusiasm and the graceful disquiet of ideals."

"Sweet ... Pleasing ... I'd sell my soul to the devil in order to be reborn for love. What bothers me about old age is that once-virile strength is forced to content itself with fraudulent platonic love. A swindle! The worst filthy rubbish! Platonic love is the vegetarian form of physical love ..."

"Why don't we become old men like we should? Let's enjoy the kindly old age which Horace dreamed of in his "Secular Hymn" or which Zola manifested through his hero Abbe Pierre Froment. And let's forget about silly ideas: of monkey glands, revitalizing serums, Fountains of Youth ... The philosopher already said it: nothing is more calamitous for the human being than anxiety about the future."

Lon Chaney's last words foundered in the general somnolence.

Five cots squeezed together in the cabin.

How lovely it is, when one is sleepy, to sleep well ... and snore like a Subchanter!

Defying the drowsiness of siesta time, Longines and Aparicio had gone outside. They had much to talk about.

"I suppose that you've followed through with the plan."

"Partially."

"What do you mean partially? This is a temporary stopover."

"Yes. This evening we'll move on to the house of a man named Rufo Pereyra. He's coming to pick us up in a truck they've lent him. He's a loyal, solitary compatriot and it's a large, comfortable farm house. We'll be able to spend several days there. The owners won't be back until the end of next month. It's just about six miles from the lake at the dam. Completely hidden from view. The only thing I regret is that I'll have to leave you all . . . "

"Leave? Are you thinking of ditching us?"

"Not that, exactly. Just for a few nights in Almafuerte. I've found a . . ."

They stopped talking.

Dijunto came walking by, headed for the line of Carolina poplars. He felt uncomfortable in the overcrowded cabin, but the humid air and dazzling sunlight didn't bother him in the least. In hot, muggy weather he liked to sit out beneath the trees. Finding a comfortable spot, he settled down in the damp shade of the foliage, lulled by the murmur of the water in the irrigation ditch.

There, he was content to relax, at peace with himself.

He stretched out on the grass.

Soon, the afternoon breeze brought him familiar aromas. Hemp. Broom. Fennel. He heard the lowing of the cows. The bell of the lead mare. And the sounds drifted away as his eyes began to close . . . The heavy drowsiness mingled with the water's lullaby. Distant stench of manure. The flute of the canebrakes. The fine dust of freshly threshed straw. And his eyes closed . . . Asleep, like a hummock upon the lawn, like an acacia among the grass, his face was transfigured. He dreamed . . . Perhaps of the house he would never own. Perhaps of the productive, profitable plot of land that would never be his. Perhaps of the model farm that he'd always aspired to cultivate. Perhaps of the fine country house where he wished to spend his old age. Perhaps . . . Maybe . . . And diminishing, diminishing, he turned, effectively, into a lump of earth and an acacia tree rising up out of the exuberance of the dream and the field.

Angelus.

Upon the lectern of the mountain, the sunset opened his book of hours. Hours illuminated by masterful monks. Hours disintegrated in the fugacity of changing minutes. Pastoral, in gray tones of silence. In lowing brown. In the bell-bronze reds of the countryside.

The tiny church of El Quebracho sat next to the road like an old invalid woman, humiliated by truck's burping, farting motor.

The shadows of the sunset stretched out their quiet melodies.

The open road was filled with a breviary of moans and scolding. Of distant dogs. Of blood-curdling screams. But only for a short while because then the moon came out. The moon which completes the night with its polished, finishing touch. The moon! Pure sonority. A bell of crystalline timbre. A voice of Argentine liquidity which brings everything into harmony: the owl's eyes, and the wind's sacred song; the phosphorescent sky and the effervescent mud; the fever of hell transmuted into life's pleasant essence.

A cattle gate.

The truck passed through, then went bumping along the rugged road.

Another cattle gate.

The truck began snorting its way up steep hills. Sharp turns.

Suddenly: the reservoir at the dam! Dazzling. A clear copy of the night, right down to the atoms of carbon dioxide. Each star, an asterisk in the blue sea. Each cloud, a silver fish scale ... majestic bays. Translucent roadsteads of tranquil dreams. Shapely coves penetrating the belly of the mountain. Steep hilltops like the prows of ghostly galleons.

"There, take a good look, the Tercero River dam. It's quite a construction."

"Is it yours?"

"How could it be mine ... ?"

"Then skip the propaganda."

This brief exchange between Dijunto and Don Rufo Perey-ra was merely an aside. Everyone, except Aparicio, had their necks twisted around, observing the white line bordering the body of water—the upper portion of the dam, an audacious arc, the mouth of the spillway, the cylindrical intake tower.

Aparicio hated the word "dam" which continued vibrating in his mind.

Dam: dike, wall, brake, limit, censure. Artificia barrier. Authoritarian bridle. Obtuse delineation. Censure a priori. Don't talk to me about dams! Whatever kind they might be. Their sole purpose is to industrialize the natural instincts of the world. And of men! To carry them along urban channels! To boil them down in mystical millponds . . . All false. False! Society should not employ dams to hold back the currents of being. The law should not confine nature within stone walls of narrow conventions. Religion should not abase itself in the putrid stagnation of asceticism. All the dams must be blown up! Raze them from existence. So that human forces can roll along torrentially to their destiny. Without walls of "defense." Without contentious containment walls. To something else: social dams . . . urban canals . . . mystic millponds . . . . Bah!

And he clucked his tongue.

He sat there in bitter silence, invisible to the others. He'd worked himself into a rage. Persuaded by his own arguments. His eggplant-colored lips trembling within the despotic rigidness of his bruised and dented thug's face.

The truck staggered and shambled through a series of jolting bumps.

"We must be getting close," ventured Katanga.

"You're, right. How did you know?"

"It's the Argentine way of doing things. The worst roads are the ones nearest towns. You just can't believe how you rattle and shake entering and leaving town! But look who's in charge, the *criollos*."

"That's right."

By the time the truck pulled up and stopped in front of the

house, the water was boiling and hissing in the radiator.

"Just go on inside, you lot. Those are your rooms."

Viejo Amor got down first. An enormous dog rushed out at him, barking furiously. A farmhand intervened.

"Don't be frightened. He's fixed. Doesn't bite. Go on inside. Don't be afraid. He's fixed."

"Why do you keep saying he's fixed? I'm afraid he's going to bite me, not screw me!"

The two rooms opened onto a verandah adorned with honeysuckle and geraniums. In the front garden, three loquats and a magnolia tree. Beyond, a cypress. Right and left, two battalions of poplars. They were all quite impressed. Clean, well-swept floors and rooms. Fragrant flowerpots. One noted a careful, almost feminine touch.

"Leave your things. Gather round here, then."

In the kitchen they were greeted by the aromatic hospitality of meat roasting over the coals and fresh baked bread, hot out of the oven.

They felt an exciting, boisterous happiness. But they ate supper without talking. They loved an adventure that did not exhaust, a discovery without disappointment. And they were content, nestled in the lap of nature, allowing themselves to be soothed by the tenderness of the breeze and the kindness of Don Rufo.

"This is precisely what we needed. A peaceful refuge . . ."

"Refuge?" piped up Longines.

". . . a tranquil asylum amid the sweet rustic surroundings."

Don Rufo stopped to listen to the pretty phrasing. It was his weakness. Better yet: it had once been. Since childhood, he had felt an invincible attraction to the delicacies of speech. As a young man he'd planted a lovely garden of words. He cared for it with a zeal incongruous with his rank in life. And he became so famous that the whole town gathered round him to delight in his gracious displays of language. He shared out its flowers generously. On any occasion, for any reason, he created bouquets of words. For the illiterate farmhand unable to declare his love for a girl. For the young blushing nursemaid in love. For a friend overstepping his bounds in conquest. For the relative afflicted by disgrace. For settlers facing hardships, their crops destroyed by hailstorms or their son's departure for military service. Opportune flowers. Sentimental bouquets. The delicate wild honey of expression.

Eventually his ears started to ache from so much praise:

"What a polished lad that Rufo Pereyra!"

"You won't find his equal for three hundred miles."

"Nobody so expert at stringin' thoughts t'gether."

Now a grown man, life had taken it upon itself to ruin his garden. Weeds of impulses. Scrubby thickets of passion . . . his father and mother passed away, fell from the family tree. Hailstorms and blizzards poured down from the skies. Migrating to new pastures through small farms and towns he came to know homelessness and loneliness. Searing droughts and scorching sun. Thus the garden and orchard were transformed into barren wastelands. Bitter winds. Disappointments.

Then, in a respite of luck he felt his flesh grow anew. A woman came his way. There were sprouts of lyricism. Boughs of fruitful happiness. He married. He fathered a child . . .

But destiny lashed him again. And then it froze him completely. His wife died. He'd been a widower now for four months.

An annoying wail, persistent and monotonous, came from his room.

He paid it no mind. He continued feigning interest in the conversation, pretended to ignore the insipid unease of his tragedy. If luck had not been so treasonous, perhaps he would now be the elite and elegant *gaucho* he'd dreamed of becoming. The elegant sort of *gaucho* who grafts his fame onto eternity. Not some small time *gaucho* minstrel . . . An austere country singer, upholder of *criollo* traditions. Not a performer at horse races . . . An authentic bard of the servant and the farmhand's grandeur and misery. Not a cemetery singer on All Saints' Day and the Day of the Dead . . .

His servant appeared to tell to him:

"Don Rufo: the baby is crying."

He knew it. He sketched an impatient gesture. It bothered him to be reminded. Excusing himself profusely, he left the gathering.

"Why don't you take care of the kid?" Aparicio reprimanded the servant.

"God save an' protect me. He don't let anybody touch that baby. Rumor say that baby got a umbil'cal hernia. That's why he take care of him all by himself. Poor Don Rufo! Every day he look worse and worse."

Indeed. He seemed weary of body and mind. Barely thirty years old, Rufo Pereyra had been aged before his time by anguish, malaise and mourning. The burden of desperation which makes one unsociable. And, at times, in his moments of introspection, dwelling on his misfortune, the senile calm which sweetens the face of those whom hardship visits early.

"Let's step outside a while."

They went out.

The night shone and shimmered with wondrous transparency. Silver poplars. Bronze cypresses. A shy, hesitant night, without exaggerated displays of clouds nor parades of stately trees. A warm night, rocked to sleep by gusts of perfume. Magnolias and loquats. Geraniums and honeysuckle.

They took a stroll together. From one end of the property to the other. In pantheistic silence. In cosmic communion.

Lon Chaney, shyly, made his way over to Katanga and Longines. They thought he might want to share something in confidence. It was nothing surreptitious, however. Lon Chaney merely muttered languidly:

Le vent d été souffle et caresse
La nature et le firmament
On dirait un souffle d'amant
Qui craint d éveiller sa maîtresse.

The scene had a perfect charm, an ineffable rhythm. Easy and soulful harmony. Their faces shone with grateful satisfaction.

Longines didn't feel like turning on the radio.

Viejo Amor did not head out to spy on the night with his lascivious satyr's eyes.

Fortunato abstained from stacking his peso coins in little columns.

Katanga did not read, as was his custom.

Dijunto did not unravel his usual thread of complaints.

Lon Chaney skipped his habitual tale of the habitual adventure.

Aparicio failed to deliver his layman's sermon before turning in.

A tacit unanimity led them to the spacious bedrooms. Each one set up his cot. And, with everything in place, each one stretched out to lay euphorically in the darkness with eyes open.

Aparicio, Katanga, and Fortunato occupied the room next to Rufo Pereyra.

Mute rhetoric.

Blind reading.

Immaterial finance.

Impossible evasion! They couldn't break free from their customs, as familiar as clothing. Aparicio listened, spellbound, to his own discourse:

How bitterly we must accept the state's phobia of those who honor the prestige of nationality. Why are my preachings pushed directly into exile? Why must I travel in such a disordered fashion through strange lands? Perfidy! The riffraff of the current political machine pursue ideas that feed the fanaticism of the baser instincts. The future, as the new postulates reveal it, is farther than ever from the snub-nosed bourgeois and the plebian rear ends. When I return to Uruguay I will be the messiah of the final revolution. Traitors will quake! There will be freedom from all oppression and salvation from secular disgrace. The purest of insults will be epically raised on high! How noble the closed fist that becomes a finger to point the way!

Rapt in thought, Katanga heard these lines:

When culture becomes pervasive, reading is reduced to a simple optical activity, a whim. Habitual perspectives are viewed from the intellectual pedestal upon which the subject sits. And grazing in the valleys of the mind and on the hillsides of the sentiments, the livestock of ideas and emotions are branded with ambition. Then, boredom emerges from the familiarity of concepts and perceptions. One longs to smash the monotony and tedium with incursions of novelty. But novelty does not come. It gets bogged down in the exhausted will. And the internal devastation of culture continues in an unending dialogue between mountain and cloud.

Fortunato constructed his chrematistic castle in the air:

Heroes are those individuals who push all their chips to the center of the gaming table, who risk themselves completely by betting against destiny, and win! Lindbergh, placing his Atlantic bet against universal fear. Byrd tossing his polar chips at the borderland. The crew of the Explorer II hurling their aerial chips into the atmosphere. Guynemer, Amundsen, etcetera. Bad winners are those types like Nobile who vociferate against luck instead of plunging into the silence of the afterlife. I need a lot of coins to buy the big stack of chips I desire. I know what I'm talking about. I was once a bank manager in Prague.

Annoying and persistent, the child's wailing continued in the next room. They were wide awake.

Aparicio then remembered Longines's admonition of his attitude towards Katanga. His opportunity to make amends had arrived. He decided to test the waters:

"Are you asleep, Katanga?"

"Not at all."

He did not know how to begin. The Swiss man's reprimand lingered in his spirit, inhibiting him. A soldier always seeks vindication but when he recognizes that he has disobeyed direct orders, the rebellious momentum is halted. And it becomes worse the more he dwells; because emotion stubbornly floats to the surface and responsibility must be accepted. He pondered a while more; pride can be hard to swallow. And he found the pretext:

"I can't get any sleep in this cot. What a shame mine was left behind in Río Cuarto!"

"Circumstances required it."

He took a deep breath. Pure living pleasure. No longer mired in hesitation. He could set sail towards his apology:

"So. Longines has mentioned your hero's journey to me. This morning, when you yourself wanted to explain it, I don't know why it interested me so little. Forgive me. Through him I've learned many juicy details. If you're not sleepy, tell me how it turned out in the end."

Katanga took the bait immediately. Ingenuously.

"Something amusing. But delicate. Like Anatole France . . . After the fire at the SANTERIA SAINT TERESA, the Inspector General, the Chief Investigator, and the Examining Magistrate stepped into the snare. Amateurs! They believed my heroic pantomime, my comedy of necessity. And they honored me with courteous observances. First, they offered me a job as a watchman . . . Second, I collected, by right, twenty-three pesos . . ."

"By what right?"

"Copyright. For my exquisite fiction . . . Compassion touched their conscience and their pockets . . . Poor fools! I've always been disgusted by the piety of idiots. It lacks moral fiber. It's a kind of suppuration . . . No doubt about it: amateurs are the rabble of the world. Too bad they swarm under heaven like bedbugs beneath a quilt at an inn!"

"Speaking of bedbugs. It seems to me . . . These loaner cots! . . ."

On that tangent, Aparicio drifted away. His inferiority complex was satisfied. He had "complied" upon retracting before his companion. Without doing so very openly, it's true; but very much to his taste: with the slyness which synchronizes pride and baseness. And he fell asleep.

Annoying and persistent, the wailing continued in the next room.

Katanga heard Don Rufo's efforts to quiet the little child. Walking back and forth preparing the bottle. His eagerness to conquer, the refusal to accept. His distraught attempts to incite sleep.

Nothing. The tense resistance of screams from the nursery seemed to exasperate him.

Then he remembered the image of the baby provided by the farmhand:

"He's a skinny little monkey, earth-colored, with a hernia, tremendous eyes and two ears as big as fans."

But he couldn't help envision him as a fragile puppy, hollow from hunger, dirty from orphanhood and neglect.

Two hours of sinking anxiety.

Rocked by the ebb and flow of the wails, Katanga finally got used to it. He laid down flat on his back and philosophized . . . But the father's worry pained him, tirelessly courageous in his insistence to lull the baby to sleep. He was moved by the man's stubbornness in foregoing a nursemaid to care for the baby. Suddenly, he detected the presence of ulterior motives. And, laying aside his sympathy, he waded into an ideation of the passionate chaos which certain men arrogantly conceal.

A brief intermission. More suffocation than calm. The child was now croaking, quavering, gurgling with drool. Sweating. Writhing. His pupils sunken in a sea of tears.

Katanga thought he heard a furious curse from Don Rufo. He pricked up his ears. The silence became so light, so nervous, that instead of hearing, he saw. Yes. His clairvoyance perceived the father's ginger-brown face, sharp gaze, and aquiline grimace. A strange shudder ran through his body. Why that hard menacing air? Why that evil shadow on his face? Why that cold nakedness of disconsolation in his soul?

Turning toward another supposition, he discarded the notion that the boy was a bastard, born of a sinful coupling, or that the father had made himself a widower through murder. It couldn't be! ... however, vindictive beings are found the world over, annihilating not the enemy but instead punishing their own cowardice with constant self-harm ... Was Don Rufo waiting to find some convenient cliff? Was he that kind of a masochist? Who knew! A kind thought, as a counterweight, then occurred to him:

If in each ejaculation man secretes between two-hundred and five-hundred-fifty million spermatozoids, the fact that only one of them procreates is positively an extraordinary privilege. What this valley of tears might be if, after sexual orgasm in copulation, every s eed reached the goal of manifesting itself as an individual! ...

Aparicio's and Fortunato's snores had synched up in a mournful rise and fall. For a moment, the insomniac imagined they were pulling some sarcastic mocking ruse. And he went wandering away in his mind, down along clear passages. Through illuminated mansions. He seemed to flee from the night as from a lair of wild beasts. The dawn! He was desperate for the virginity of dawn. To tear off her gown. To possess her. To bathe afterward in the lustrous torrent of those first rays.

His eyelids fought to slide down. They closed at last. But sleep would not be captured. Behind the curtains of his eyelashes, his pupils — swaying pendulums — continued to scrutinize their cloistered darkness.

He was interested in sleeping. He knew that sleeping and dreaming nurtures the womb of death. And that one is reborn from it each day. But, now, Rufo Pereyra's anxiety had him chained to his vigil. He could not leave the man alone. A morbid solidarity incited him to accompany Rufo through his torturous endurance of the wailing. The sad, weary grating of the cry in the muted silence of the night.

A mosquito's whine made him open his eyes.

The trees were beginning to sharpen their branches into silhouettes. To break their foliage loose from the claws of shadow. And he smiled. He confirmed the irony of an old rule of child rearing: "The well-disciplined child must sleep and let his parents sleep, between nine at night and six in the morning ..."

Suddenly, the sound of a cooing lullaby startled him. He
lay frozen in suspense. The cooing conquered the crying, now
barely a nasal moan. The voice, racked with melancholy, became clear. It pushed the annoyance aside and sank into the
heart of the cradle. Katanga sat up halfway on his cot. Never had a more lugubrious inflection struck his ears. More groggy, drunken daybreak than tenderness. More fast-flowing power than prayer:

Sleep softly you shitty
little snot-nosed brat:
Here comes the dawn
Painting the mountain,
May the bellowing beasts
rupture your tiny ears:
Sleep softly you shitty
little snot-nose brat:

The whole long night
Awake by candlelight
your little ass a purple rash
from urine and diarrhea.
Who has the courage
to clean up your slop?
The whole long night
Awake by candlelight!

With so much bitterness
I'll go out of my mind:
Your fucking crying
drives me insane; no truce
My life is pure pain
Without peace or desire
With so much bitterness
I'll go out of my mind!

My dead wife told me
"Love him, Pereyra!"
That's fine, but then
You better shut your mouth
Because I'm half crazy
from lack of sleep and pain
But my dead wife told me
"Love him, Pereyra!"

If I was a settler
With cash and a car
You'd have it all
Miserable little baby boy
A plump little wet-nurse . . .
And diapers of silk . . .
If I was a settler
With cash and a car!

Sleep softly you shitty
little snot-nosed brat:
Sleep so I can cry
Shedding tears for her
Because she cries on, seeing you,
Orphan boy here on earth.
Sleep softly you shitty
little snot-nosed brat!

The monotonous song faded out as the child drifted to sleep.
There was a sigh of relief. But the little lullaby had screwed its
way into Katanga's acoustic soul. The words of the psalmody
depressed him. That mix of insults and tenderness! That into-
nation of both prayer and diatribe! The spiral was now drilling
into his subconscious. In a whisper.

Half asleep he heard a peremptory shout on the patio:

"C'mon! Enough *mate!* Go fetch the horses. We've got to get
plowing."

It was Don Rufo.
Full of rage.
Dead tired.

It was a quarter to twelve when Katanga woke up. Realizing that the others had left in the truck, driven by Longines, he was astonished to the point of stupefaction. In the hidden slot in his valise he found a scrap of newspaper: oiouoiuaueeeuioi-eu.

He translated in his head:

"Eyes . . . X h . . . ret. Keep watch, ten hours, we'll return."

His pupils shone anew:

"Nice prank. How much trouble would it have been for them to wake me up? This disorder . . . It's already midday. We've agreed that the disorder among us is over and done with. That it shouldn't be provoked. Why such conduct, then? I'm not some scarecrow you can just push around."

He'd added the last phrase unconsciously, some non sequitur plucked out of the thin air. Someone was repeating it out on the patio.

He stuck his head out the window. It was the farmhand, arguing with Don Rufo:

"I'm not some scarecrow you can just push around."

"Fine, don't be stubborn. If you don't like it, beat it."

"Pay me, first. What d'you think? I'm sick of puttin' up with your bad moods."

"Fine. Go on inside."

"Don't screw around! Pay me right here. I don't got no screws loose so you can make fun o' me."

"Don't shout, dammit. Come on."

"I don't care. Pay me right here and we're all finished."

Unexpectedly, with surprising energy, the baby began howling again. An icy moment of desperation and teeth-rattling uncertainty. Don Rufo did not know what to do. He looked back and forth from the farmhand to the baby's room. He gnashed his teeth. He clenched his fists. Finally, he went to his son.

Katanga spoke up suddenly, his voice full of arrogance and authority:

"How much do I owe you?"

"A month an' a half, forty-five pesos the month."

"Sixty-seven and fifty, right?"

"Let's see . . . Half of . . . Yeah, that's about right."

"Good. Here you go. Now leave, immediately!"

The farmhand looked at Katanga, stupefied. Unsure of what to do or say, he stood holding the two fifty-peso bills in his hand.

"What are you waiting for? . . . You're nobody's scarecrow to get pushed around. Beat it!"

The man slipped away with a look of misgiving, holding the bills up to the light. He hoisted his bundle. And exiting through the patio door, he vacillated between contentment and compunction:

"Holy shit! One guy rips you off, th' other pays too much. Everybody roun' here got their saddle on sideways."

Longines spoke several different languages, but he preferred to keep quiet in all of them.

When the truck got stuck, slipping in the muddy ditch, he clenched his teeth, fiercely. And he swallowed saliva. Obscenities always being the first words learned, if he were someone else, he would have cursed in German, French, Italian, Spanish, and Esperanto.

They had been stuck for forty minutes in the middle of a road that was slowly turning into a creek.

None of them wanted to remove his shoes and wade through the big puddle to the neighboring farm to ask for help.

"If one of you could drive, I'd happily go," Longines boasted.

His comment received no answer.

"We catch your drift and grasp your intention," said Viejo Amor, pointedly, scornfully.

"Well, fine, we'll just stay here until someone passes by. What surprises me is that you, Dijunto . . ."

"Me . . . Me . . . Always me . . . You're all really cruel with me. You're all talk, 'lotta big talk. But the only one who really deals with anything is me. Always me."

In a heartbeat he had taken off his shoes and rolled up his pants.

His legs—two withered posts with big knots instead of knees—sank into the muddy water that reached halfway up his thighs.

He evaluated the situation.

"Three yoke of oxen won't pull this truck out of here."

"Look: over there, under that carob tree. There's some workers with horses and plows, taking a rest."

Submissive, struggling to extract his legs, and sweating as he slopped through the sucking mud, Dijunto went off to procure some help.

The sun beat straight down. It shimmered off the spinning zinc daisy of the distant windmill and the wings of hovering dragonflies. It danced upon the turbid muddy water and bubbled inside the rotting roadkill.

"It's good that Katanga didn't come. The putrid smell would choke him to death."

"Bah. Solitude chokes him much more. I can hear his insults right now."

Skimming the surface of the water, a swarm of mosquitoes hovered, seemingly transfixed, above the thick rainbow sheen of the spreading oil slick. On the horizon, haloed by a tenuous luminosity, three haystacks raised their house-like silhouettes.

Aparicio sat contemplating them for a long while. They presented a familiar outline: the silhouette of his childhood home, out there somewhere in the distance, beyond the knife-edged mountain ridges of Paysandú. Easily ensnared by enchantment, he felt his body turning to air. And entering the presumed gate to the haystack's supposed yard, nostalgia instantly filled him with thoughts and affections. But perhaps harried by some remorse, he returned to himself, and he said:

"Look. There. The house is nothing more than the outline of a haystack. Its astral form. Inside it, the hours pile up like sheaves of wheat harvested from years of disappointments. The haystack is no more than a compact, inhospitable house, where greed lives. Flesh of clay. Soul of straw."

None of them really understood his remark.

The heavy truck kept tipping little by little. Lon Chaney tried to neutralize the imbalance. He clung to the left-side railings and jerked his upper body backward. The sliding stopped. Next he climbed right over the rails, set the brake, and sat down on the front fender.

"You, too, Fortunato. Sit on the back one."

A sulky came spinning along, driven by an Italian couple, heading in the opposite direction. Its thin wheels conquered the puddle, smoothly, with the elegance of a marsh bird.

The cart passed them by without a word.

His face red with indignation, Aparicio expressed their disappointment with an admonition:

"*Carajo!* Stop! You got no shame, you jackasses!? Can't you even ask: *Do you need a hand or anything?*"

"Eh, we're in a hurry, we are," the driver said. To which the girl added:

"*E non somo caraco, sabe?* An' we ain't no jackets, y'know?!"

Clucking his tongue, Aparicio climbed up on the side rails, and retorted:

"Jackasses! ... not jackets. Not jackasses? Jackass bastards a thousand times over, and the whore who bore you. This is why these Italians come here. To pay with ingratitude. To refuse a small favor. Here, they can fill their bellies; they make something out of themselves: for what? For this. So these settlers can come walk all over our generosity."

The driver cracked his whip to resume his course, when a mellifluous Italian voice stopped them. It was Viejo Amor. His cloying, affected charm worked like an eraser. The reproaches disappeared. He said he understood their haste in getting to town. And he begged their pardon for their wasted time. Less fluent in Italian, Longines and Lon Chaney, supported him in the same spirit.

Now taking their leave, the settler commented:

"Ma por qué non diqueron qu'eranno paisano? In veche, avría achutato. Alora non posso."

"Sará in altra volta."

"E boeno: de pasar non ha pasato niente. Addio."

Triumphant, thanks to the proffered explanations, the Italian woman fixed her gaze on Aparicio. And sputtered:

"Grandíssimo belinún: non somo caraco, sabe? You great big stupid little prick: we not jackets, got it?"

Two sounds simultaneously. The crack of the whip which made both the water and the horse shiver. And Aparicio's usual clucking of the tongue, now fuming from the insult.

They sat for several long minutes, disturbed by the encounter.

"Well, I did the right thing. You never know who you're dealing with."

"Perfectly. You should arouse neither dislike nor suspicion."

"Of course! They're peasants . . . pears for them are tops for spinning and bladders become lanterns . . . You've got to recognize, nevertheless, they behaved badly. Horridly."

"The same as you."

Watch in hand, Longines cut the dialogue short:

"One thirty-five! We've been stuck here for two hours and twenty minutes." He almost failed to see him coming. Sitting on the rump of an old bay nag, their "emissary" had returned. The drover leading the horse stared with haughtiness at the travelers stuck fast in their truck:

"Y'all made a pretty mess of it! The road goes through on t'other side."

From the other side of the puddle, Dijunto explained, shouting directions:

"They want twenty pesos to pull us out. Pay in advance. They'll bring five horses and everything necessary. Not a cent less. Seems outrageous to me. A jacked-up price for this little mess. But, if not, nothing doing. We'll be stuck in the mud. Decide."

They accepted.

The drover took off at a gallop to give the news.

They weren't peasants. Nor were they plowmen heading out to the fields to hitch up their teams. Nor were they on a break. They were three workers from the reservoir, freelancing.

When they arrived and caught sight of them stuck in the mud, they exchanged a meaningful glance. To be sure, while they went through the motions of arranging harnesses and teams of horses, they ordered the drover to collect the money. And with the money pocketed they set right to work. Steel cables, chains, guy lines, ropes, straps. They seemed to know exactly what they were doing.

"Now! Giddyup! Let him have it! Aiee! Yip yip!"

There was a flurry of whip cracks and interjections. And shuddering and rocking violently, the truck lurched up to the side of the road.

Now on dry ground, everyone let loose. In a big hurry. They were possessed by a strange, almost infantile joy, and they wanted to display it. Thus, the merry roistering overshadowed the light misfortune of having been prisoners of the mud for three hours.

Aparicio struck up a friendly conversation with the foreman of the "rescue crew." A skinny, muscled *criollo* with clear blue eyes, sun-colored skin, built tough as an acacia. His movements, gestures, and expressions displayed an arrogant, swaying grace. He treated the foreman with excessive familiarity. He stared at him enviously, the most human form of admiration. It pained him that, being just as scrawny and lean as he was, he lacked the man's style and grace. A wicked streak, some buried sarcasm, must have overcome the Uruguayan, because he began to question the man tauntingly.

"From the looks of it, around here, a man can harvest 'milk and honey' from the bogs, isn't that right?"

"That's right."

"For our part, if you demanded a hundred pesos, we'd pay up, one hundred pesos. Appearances are deceiving, sharecropper."

"That's right!"

"Good thing there are always some folks who're 'generous' in lending help."

"That's right."

The falsity of the dialogue made them explode into an equally false burst of laughter. They shook their heads. They studied each other, first with derision, then with respect. And each understood the other to the core.

"Don't worry, friend, we won't report you. We're very grateful. You do well to dig holes, to make big messy puddles, to destroy the roads. After all: the poor victim either rides a horse or drives a sulky ..."

"That's right ... if the peasant had a field, a house of his own ... But what can he expect to have! Children and chiggers! ... The only thing we're good for is towing cars! It's the only job that them gringos have left us."

"It must pay, however."

"I'm tellin' you ... it used to. Now'days, with that issue of the highway administration, far as I understand it's an issue of foreign auto dealers, the situation's getting really tough. Totally smooth roads everywhere you look. You can't dig out mud puddles in the cement! Forget it. That's why we've had to come out to the country roads, to hope some Peruvian, tourist, or *porteño* happens along ..."

" ... !"

"Turns out they don't even try these roads. Car clubs are just killin' our profits with all their reports and guides. They register everything, right down to when a magpie takes a shit! And there's nothing you can do about it: we had to jack up the price just to get by. But there's no traffic anymore!"

"Well, looks like you do all right with this little job ... Don't try to fool me."

"You're wrong. I been workin' this seven months now. The most? Two hundred pesos a month. There's all these schemin' road planners, see, believe me, they stitch up all the roads, like new. No business in this anymore. I'm leaving this spot to my nephew. I got my eye on a washed out road between Almafuerte and Rio Tercero, marvelous, real muddy. In two weeks I'm movin'. Y'know: stop by sometime if you feel like it . . ."

The motor and the peals of laughter bubbled up in unison . . .

Aparicio enfolded the *criollo* in an embrace.

As they moved apart they raised their hands in the air, waving to one another.

Fickle fate made sure they didn't go too long without another mishap. Far from reliable, the truck soon had another breakdown. Repeated *pannes*. They came lurching and rattling into a country store with a gasoline pump out front. Four small rooms with zinc roofs, three squalid willow trees and a bocce ball pitch. Luckily there was a mechanic and spare parts. Longines laconically handed the repair work over to a professional. There was a more pressing matter: killing their hunger.

Lon Chaney—former scullion of the Restaurant Pharamond, 24, Rue de la Grande Truanderie, Paris—composed the menu with confidence and skill. He stepped behind the counter. He gathered from the shelves an arsenal of canned food, fresh fruit and vegetables. To inspire confidence, he paid the owner in cash up front. And while the others sipped a vermouth— placating their thirst more than their appetites— Lon Chaney, making splendid use of a dozen onions and tomatoes, prepared a magnificent first course of cold salmon salad and some well-garnished sausages.

Proud of his ability, he showed it off with the sarcastic haughtiness of a *maître d'*. He was irrepressibly witty and talkative:

"Please be seated. In addition to the main dish, we'll be having a succulent *ragoût* of beans with pork ribs which I have set to warm in a *bain-marie*. And a generous fruit salad."

"Outstanding, *che*. I applaud you."

The late lunch progressed smoothly with much playful banter.

"Serve yourself. Do me the honor."

"I can't wait! You first."

"I'll pass. I'm saving my appetite for the tagliarini."

"My dear Viejo Amor, I regret to inform you that they are not on the menu. Besides, tagliarini are worms made from semolina; they twist up inside your intestines. They're not good for you. I tell you, I who was once a waiter . . ."

"Me, too . . ."

". . . a waiter in a hotel. Hotel waiters are the only people I know with good stomachs. They know exactly what they're eating! If they possessed any altruism at all they'd be able to establish an International Organization of Culinary Hygiene . . ."

"Perhaps. But the only International Culinary Organization that I know of, more prevalent than the international organizations of Marx, Sorel, and Lenin, is the one belonging to fava beans: found everywhere . . ."

"Ugh! Give Aparicio a spritz of that Flit bug spray so he'll flit on out of here! The only one? How? And what about the Rotary? . . . Oh, the Rotary Club's International Gastronomic Organization! Oh, such sweet charm, such imposing ingenuity, swapping over dessert those little emblems that you affix to car radiators!"

Lon Chaney solemnly presented the fruit salad. Pears, peaches, and apricots from Mendoza. A syrupy babel of slices served up on a round platter.

"*Pour* dessert, Monsieur? This phrase lives always in my memory. As a chef in Lima, I used to utter it hundreds of times a day. One night there was a simple, rich dessert: Rice Condé, *c'est á dire*, the ermine pelt of rice pudding with the black motes of various prunes in compote. I offered it to a grouchy customer, one of those who leave miserable tips:

Rice Condé, sir?

Bring it. With D, with X, with Z: it's all the same to me.

Sir, it is not the same. If you like, I can bring it with wild mushrooms . . .

Just bring it.

There happened to be a rice with wild mushrooms dish that

night. As I placed it on the table, the man made a gesture of disgust:

What kind of slop is this?

Rice with mushrooms: choice wild mushrooms cut in small wedges. Rice Condé is not the same as rice with mushrooms, sir ..."

Aparicio interrupted the story:

"I'd like to know, what kind of a tip did you get out of him?"

"Exactly the same as the tip I'm going to get out of you all right now ..."

Their faces were flushed rosy red from the claret they'd been swallowing. An amiable joy illuminated their retinas. Now they killed the time with jokes—the red wine sparked laughter. And they laughed. They tried out a few songs ... sang a few snatches ...

The mechanic let them know that the truck was ready but no one paid any attention, except for Longines who asked to speak with him, disdainfully, to be sure. They weren't ready to leave, they wanted the fun to continue. They paid no attention when, scurrying from behind the counter, the mechanic started talking with a local fellow: a grain buyer, Jewish by his looks and by how he pronounced his R's. Nor did they take notice, later, of the arrival of two farmers, lamenting the state of their crops. They were lost in their own jabbering. Soon, however, they pricked up their ears when the conversation, in a general tone of pessimism and disappointment, turned technical. And, discreetly, they chose to listen:

" ... "

"You've seen it, amigo. What a monstrous thing! That new blight on the wheat has ruined thirty percent of my crop."

"If it were only that! ... The recent wind and heat have been so disastrous you've got to figure another fifty percent loss."

"The way I see it, the settlers are to blame for everything. When the Ministry of Agriculture advised them to plow deep, none of them took it seriously. That's why, any profits, if they even exist, will be twenty-five percent less than what's calculated."

"And now, look, it seems a devilish thing: the weather turns against itself. All of a sudden tremendous heat. Then all of a sudden a scorching cold. The plantings look pitiful with these abrupt changes. I estimate another forty percent of the harvest has gone up in smoke."

"Yes; now add thirty-two percent lost due to poor seed ... You forget the main cause of it all."

"You're right: but it's also fair to figure fifteen percent, at least, is affected by blight, and ten percent by coal dust in the air."

"It's a disaster!"

"You're telling me: a real disaster!"

Longines could stand no more. He was curiously restless:

"Come on. Come on. This conclave of pitiful alarmists bothers me. I don't know anything about country life; but I've never heard so much exaggeration in one place. Have you no mathematical shame! If anyone actually counted, your losses would add up to more than two hundred percent ... Let's say, this year's harvest, next year, and something more still ... Come on. Come on."

Dijunto pulled him aside. He was gloomy. His broken voice straightened Longines out:

"You're partially right. Regarding unfounded alarms which some men deliberately exaggerate and spread for their exclusive benefit, to the detriment of agriculture and the settlers. But not about the other things. No. You don't lose just one single harvest when the harvest is lost. You lose several. Many. Outside and inside. On the land and in the soul. The grain harvests and the dream harvests. The harvest of sterile effort. Of spent health. Of useless hope. Let me tell you, Longines, I've wasted my life crying ... over hail ... locusts ... weak shoots ... corn that doesn't grow or ripen ..."

"Listen, Don Rufo, since you fired that farmhand, if you don't mind, I'd like to help you out this afternoon."

"All right."

Katanga was interested in studying the enigma of how Don

Rufo had become a widower. A condition he suspected was the result of a complex and mysterious passion. But he recognized that his hypotheses tended towards the absurd. Perhaps the most logical explanation was that Don Rufo was actively avoiding any new dealings with women ... But he aspired to know something more. To inquire into the secret causes of the man's attitude.

The plenitude of conjugal felicity is so difficult to recreate, and happiness so incompatible with certain phases of life, that anguish is exacerbated and becomes a prolonged desperation! Married life rarely achieves a balance of love, because love feeds on restlessness. And all kinds of restlessness are the same: the imaginary anxiety of jealousy, and real worries over disloyalty; because with equal force they stir up the innermost lake of tranquility. How do you manage to make the miracle repeat itself! *Amour: ce que jamais on verra deux fois!* ...

Skepticism is inevitable. Katanga was a skeptic by nature. His intellect won out time and again when faced with life's events. He posed the problem to himself:

Was Don Rufo's marriage just like any other? A miserable mishmash of spite and tenderness. A balance in continuous vacillation between hatred and love. Never a truce in which to weigh the happiness enjoyed. Without even a respite from the assiduous, sinking anxiety. Might he have confirmed for himself—poor fellow!—that happiness is a primitive thing? Might he have learned too late that love is an imperfect harmony, unless found in two innocent hearts without any control over their reason? ... The anguish and rage of his lullaby still resound within me. It's what intrigues me. How to explain, therefore, his adhesion to the memory of his wife, refusing even the indispensable service of any other woman? What spiritual conflict compels him to care for his little baby son, alone, in the most solitary solitude?

They set to work.

Each one led his worries by the bridle. And three horses.

There was only one stretch left to plow, alongside a row of apple trees.

Under the nearest thick foliage they attached the teams and plow lines. Don Rufo grasped the plow handle. And somber as always, he took up his task with the driving crack of a whip.

Filled with curiosity about the labor now underway, Katanga said nothing. From afar, from the train, he had many times seen the living vignette of men plowing the fields. How different close up! The crude sketch stripped the memory of all charm. His vision drifted away from the open furrows. He observed foreshortenings and long perspectives. He brought it back. He compared the imperturbable appearance of Don Rufo with the muscular, plastic movement of the beasts. Afterward, letting them go, he framed the scene on the landscape. To the left, a backdrop of cumulous clouds draped in sunlight. To the right, an opaque immobile border of foliage. And he returned. He smelled the hot stink of the fresh-turned earth. The sour perspiration of the animal's flanks. The . . .

"You call this helping me? What kind of dirty trick is this?"

"Easy. Don't jump to conclusions. First things first, I'm looking for the poetry in the action. So much fuss has been made over farming, the action of plowing so highly allegorized, that I'm trying to connect with it. Argentina has even issued some postage stamps with a picture of the plowman! Just like you in this very moment. Honestly, apart from sweat and rhythm, from the tense volition which drives your horses forward, from your pain and their suffering, I perceive nothing that really deserves deference. Pretensions, allegory, they're just fireside stories, invented by wholesalers and grain merchants."

"That's right. The people who talk poetically about farming are the ones who exploit us. If they hitched up from sunup to sundown, day after day . . . There was even a minister who reeled off a few countryside verses, by a certain Virgil, to motivate us . . ."

"Ah, yes, I knew it!"

"What a pretty little idiot! Go figure . . ."

He figured. Ruminating on such a ridiculous delivery of the *Georgics*, Katanga turned aside, mute. And he began to speak to himself in his mind:

It must have been in a rapture of perverse good humor ... Driven by a refined malignity ... To offend the illiteracy of the country folk ... No other way to explain it. The immeasurable fatigue of this country's farmers deserves sympathy. And their ignorance, more efficient tutors than Dante's Cicerone set to wander the pampas.

The weather-beaten farmer, who prefers to work twenty-five acres of land to having the bloodless work of DRAWING his signature; the migrant worker, who lives out his dreams of gold swaying on the golden sprigs of every wheat field; the humble criollo, *cloistered between his goats' paddock and the impassable barrier of his cane liquor, they will never be able to grasp the beauty of* Publius Vergilius Maro.

What do they know of the chariots of Potnia, of the hard Eurystheus, and the sacred groves of Malorco? Not a fucking thing. What can interest him about the Orphic chant, the love of Alcaeus and the Bacchantes of Laconia? Absolutely nothing. If it were the chorus from a good tango, 'Los amores de Giacumina' *and the lack of hands on the threshing machines ...*

The joke even shows the terrible filth of its derision. The Argentine countryside, a hive of landowners, offers no similarity to the fields of Lazzio nor the perfumed hillsides of La Campagna. Here, the great estate extends its flat expanse, barren or exuberant, without greater charms for the eyes, offering nothing more than inequality.

Poleaxed by unfair contracts, plundered by all manner of abuses, the rural worker lacks both the sufficient spiritual serenity and the necessary intelligence to delight in the sweet, lofty cantor of Aeneas. After the copious sweat of his labors, his slaughtered spirit finds no other palliative than the pious peace of his ignorance.

It must have been in a rapture of perverse ill humor ... Driven by a refined malignity ... To offend the illiteracy of the country folk ... Nothing more typical of a Ministry of Agriculture. Nor nothing more appropriate for the foreign Italian brute and the uneducated countryman. It's his destiny: suffering. But making fun of them, offering their rough cracked lips the glory of an unapprecia-

ble nectar, instead of red wine or grappa, is an acerbic and pain-
ful sarcasm.

Sensitized as he was after such a long sleepless night, and now in the confused dream of the morning, Katanga found that this reflective self-absorption pained him. A strange stupor, a kind of diathermy of psychic origin, began to churn inside him. He felt it flow through his body in a bloody, visceral flood.

Unexpectedly, and for his own good, Don Rufo Pereyra pulled him from his reverie:

"Well then: when are you going to help?"

"Right now. Let me take the plow."

The sudden jolt back to reality restored, in the act, the dominance of his willpower over his languid flesh. He shook the plow lines. He breathed heavily. He was splattered with sweat and dust. And in a rapid mental flight, believed himself to be the charioteer of an ancient carriage, circling the stadium, delighting in glory like an epic hero.

By now he had gone more rounds than his strength would permit. But he didn't yield. He feared the farmer's pithy, wounding words:

"These city people! Not even good for answering the door . . ."

Tough, inwardly intrepid, he continued following the plow handle, passing with a light step over the turves sheared cleanly by the plowshare. He plowed two more furrows. FOUR MORE ROWS! SIX MORE ROWS TO GO! He was about to give up. He was completely spent, when Don Rufo spoke up:

"Stop, my friend. You've done all right. We'll do the last strip after sundown."

"We'll do it," Katanga mused, cowed.

Fingers, handkerchiefs, forearms, were not much good for wetting his face, neck, underarms. In the palm of both hands, a vague mixture of tickling pain was beginning to burn and sting. He ignored it. His imagination forged ahead, not an Olympic chariot race but the sad opposite, the bitter outline of the man who plows.

"How about a drink of *mate*? Under the trees."

"Wonderful. Let's go."

He preferred any other kind of tea. But this time he felt no disgust. The important thing for him was to lie down. To stretch out on the ground. Because the fatigue of those who never perform hard labor, more than provoking weariness, prompts sleep.

They sat sharing the *mate* for a long while, one gourdful after another. Don Rufo steeped the leaves and prepared the tea with an almost liturgical precision. Every five servings he changed the leaves. He knew from experience that after steeping for too long, the *yerba mate* loses its succulence. He took care that the water did not boil. The *mate*, a source of vitamins for the country farmer nourished on roasted meat and coarse bread, shone in his clean white teeth, a clear sign of its antiscurvy properties. After repeated rounds, gentle, relaxed, Katanga found the opportune opening through which to penetrate Don Rufo's privacy:

"Last night I was awake all night. Not because I was bothered by your child's crying. But out of solidarity with you. For me, nothing is more impressive than a man alone with a nursing child. Suffocating anguish. What can you do!"

"Right. What can you do?"

"A man's hands are hard and angular. Clumsy for the delicate needs required by the baby. The prickly beard, mustache, are not made for caressing. They rasp the baby's silky skin. And even the man's voice itself can offend its tiny tympanum, requiring the tenderness of cotton. The mother, friend, the mother!"

"True. A man ain't worth shit without the child's mother!"

"This morning I heard you singing to him. I paid attention. Believe me: I've never heard in my life a song more laced with sorrow and . . ."

"Say it . . . with curses. What do you want? I've become sour and dirty. Before I got married I was a polished guy, the most splendid singer . . . Since Jacinta died I don't enjoy anything.

I'm going backwards. Soiling myself. Turning into a brute on purpose. And I'm afraid I'll end up, God forbid, wallowing in the worst kind of filth ... It's the only thing that attracts me, the only thing that consoles me ... Might sound like a lie, but that's how it is. Don't even understand it myself."

He said it all with progressive disillusionment. His psyche slunk around his ankles. Ecstasy and annulment. Confusion of the senses and perturbation of the conscience. Growing increasingly wan, he took Katanga by the arm. He drew close to his ear. Ardent and humbled, in his morbid rapture, prickling with passion and pain, he shared his secret:

My pretty girl, was really nothing special
but she was happy and clever
She behaved like ...
A good wife should.
Today I sit and cry by her grave
For my lousy rotten evil luck,
And I'm going with the flock
of memories of my lost wife.

Since Jacinta went and died
My pleasure is withered and dry!

Beneath the harshest sun
On two stray potbelly nags
To ride ... among the pricking cactus
We went together often.
Other times through the raw
Shivering snowfall
After a good one ...

"Please, my friend, enough" Katanga interrupted him, embarrassed.

Rufo Pereyra didn't obey him. His voice rose from the putrid depths of his affliction, escaping his lips like poison sap oozing from a broken stem. And he carried on, ardent and humbled in the apogee of his morbid rapture. Katanga begged repeatedly. But his pleas ran up against the scatological continuity of his poem, barely interrupted by the inconsolable sigh of the refrain:

> Since Jacinta went and died
> My pleasure is withered and dry!

By now he had rasped through seven *espinellas*. He seemed exhausted. Languid, languishing, he had enough strength, nevertheless, to pronounce *sotto voce*:

> Today sunk down in bitterness
> I'm a fine saddle horse gone astray
> Condemned to the . . .
> For the lack of her . . .
> Never was exactly pure
> My sweet beloved wife
> But never any . . . comparable
> With that . . . of my lost wife

> Since Jacinta went and died
> My pleasure is withered and dry!

An extraordinary commotion shook Katanga's soul. His shock didn't escape from his open mouth; the stupor seemed fixed in his eyes. It wasn't the obscene elegy, fraught with lewdness, which perturbed him. It was the man who stood before him, in full melancholic rapture, crumbling to pieces in a vulgar and repulsive charade. It was his voice, once firm with sobriety, prostituted now by the plaintive moan of a raging spirit. It was the hyperbole of Don Rufo Pereyra, undone by the calamity of a moral crisis.

Katanga stood a long while gazing at him affectionately, as one observes a person who is ill. Don Rufo lay stretched out on the ground, veiled by a flood of tears, suffering a vascular spasm. His pulse beat weakly below the shroud of his internal chaos. Immersed in the perverse delight of satisfied instinct. Katanga's sympathy was good for him. It reanimated him, like a miraculous balm. In the wake of this reverie his understanding visibly returned from dream zones deep inside the mind. And he settled back into the tangible reality of the countryside.

There are people who retire into the silence of the flesh and the desperation of misery. People whose souls are stitched together; who accept all of life's reparations. To whom nothing matters any longer, not even dying; because their existence survives on offerings of compassion and pity; because it is a long agony which fights to sever the unbreakable bonds! But there are other people, avid for love, thirsty for joy, who refuse to surrender. They are beings of an upstanding inner-self, mysterious on the outside, who don't tolerate the oppression of sentiments. They are the ones who have the definitive mark of an ill-fated destiny engraved on their soul.

Rufo Pereyra.

At last he understood! The delight of having discovered the key to Don Rufo's mystery filled Katanga with gentleness and good humor. Nothing like comprehension to erase embarrassment! From this new vantage point everything became clear. Spread out before him was the psychological state of an emotionally introverted man, actively concealing his outcroppings of passion, his nooks of nostalgia, his springs of intimate pride, examining his own agreeable but inaccessible tranquility, the strange inflows chilled by his pessimism. Conquering his nervous exhaustion, Don Rufo took careful control of all his actions, sidestepping his infected chasms, his brambles of anguish, the monsters of his erotic fantasy, and the fervor of his hidden religiosity. Nothing like sympathy to drown oneself in tenderness!

The sunset lit its transparent fires along the hills. Soon the crepuscular coals would crackle in the sweeping close of evening.

Katanga stood up. In each hand, where his fingers joined the palm, a string of blisters had formed. Painful as it was, duty ordered him to come through in an emergency:

"All right, Don Rufo: let's plow."

He nodded his head. And, agile, suddenly, as if shooing a kettle of vultures circling about him, he traced a series of windmill gestures. Then he tied the horses and, directly, with a crazed impetus, he launched into work, cracking the whip, as if trying to escape himself through the violence of the effort.

"Come on, let me do it. I think I like this work."

Don Rufo knew Katanga was just being kind. His eyes showed gratitude above a tired, gaping smile. But stubbornness tightened his jaw. And he remained at the plow as in the air above his head, the whip snapped and cracked like the sound of shattered dreams.

He'd been working for an hour when he finally acceded:

"Go on, take the reins. I'm goin' to gather up the things."

Pastoral hour. Austere silence. The vast asylums of foliage palpitating with the beat of wings.

Beneath an apple tree, Don Rufo's profile cut through the mystery of an incipient mist.

Katanga saw him. Philosophically. And he kept on plowing, joyful to incarnate the preeminence of a biblical role before his friend, tiny in the distance, reduced, looking like a figure by Millet:

Man is the wood-cutter in his forest of symbols. He impedes his own ascension toward the light. He thoughtlessly fells enigmas, which stretch out along the branches of the blood. He destroys seeds that would have germinated in eternity. He disobeys the command to be slow and majestic. One longing absorbs him: pleasure. In pursuit of it, desire bites and stings. Vermin themselves become frightened. And when he believes he has arrived at the source of beauty, he finds only dejection, desolation, vice. Then, it pains him to witness the sap of youth exhausted in banal trivialities. And with the humus of his dreams now sapped of nutrients, he falls with his rotten trunk into the peat bog, alongside the very axe of his sex.

A great racket, erupting from the direction of the farmhouse, cut short his meandering thoughts.

Liberated at last from the truck's *pannes*, his comrades advanced toward him, hazy among the first shadows, like a troop of scarecrows.

They had mistaken him for Don Rufo.

Hilarity gave way to astonishment!

"You . . . Katanga . . . plowing!"

"Who would have thought?!"

"Katanga . . . plowing? It can't be!"

"Oh, Katanga, plowing!"

"Yes, yes: he's plowing! How amazing!"

"You . . . Katanga! It's incredible!"

There was one furrow left to plow. He finished it. And joining his companions, spent, drenched in sweat, he showed them his palms, now running with blood:

"I'm not plowing. I'm not plowing. I'm just working up some callouses. In case some idiot detective forces me again to show him my hands . . ."

It was eleven o'clock. A morning the color of honey. The sun shone bright, the insects buzzed and whined.

Fat, spongy, splayed out in a wicker armchair, Fortunato was enjoying the tinkling of his beloved coins. Suddenly he had an idea. He moved to the table. He raised four little columns of ten-*centavo* coins. Then, very carefully he began to pile five-*centavo* and twenty-*centavo* pieces upon beams fashioned from toothpicks, raising a kind of façade.

Viejo Amor arrived in that moment.

"What a pigheaded obsession with your coins. Leave them alone for once. You're like those stubborn dominoes players, who, having no opponents, play architect with the pieces."

He was now stacking three five-*centavo* coins along the triangular peak.

"It makes me furious seeing you like this, so fascinated with your money. It looks bad. It leads to ridiculous extremes . . . In Rosario, I knew a *criollo* miser who was a monarchist. Imagine: a monarchist! . . . He knew by heart the names and faces of an endless succession of kings. He spoke of them affectionate-ly. As a citizen of a democratic republic, such political regres-sion repelled me. One day I learned the source of his faith, see-ing him play as I always see you. He was a monarchist for love of the kings on his golden coins! . . ."

Absorbed in his work, Fortunato was not paying attention. He sat back in his chair. The same rounded folds of fat that weighed his belly down were now repeated in the softness of his nape. And he was smiling. Smiling.

"But, dammit: are you deaf?" Viejo Amor accused him, giv-ing the table a shove.

In the face of disaster, Fortunato did not complain. He ig-nored the malice, hurrying to gather up his coins. And then he spat:

"Brute! Cretin! Didn't you see that it was a Greek temple? Doric columns, with striated shafts. Proto-Doric, not Dor-ic. The Parthenon, now demolished. Moron! Didn't you go to school? Is that how you were brought up? Why don't you show some respect? Jackass! You're a vile, stinking, cranky old goat. A degenerate old man. Just last night, I saw you sneak out to screw that jenny out in the shed. Why do you have to bother me? Have I said anything to you? My poor Parthenon! Don't you see that I was building a bridge between art and finance? A pleasure to the eye as well as security for the future? Brute! Brute! I know what I'm talking about. I was once a bank man-ager in Prague."

"Psssst. You already broke the agreement . . ."

Startled by his anathema, Aparicio and Katanga stuck their heads out onto the verandah.

"Come on: silence! We're dealing with some serious topics," urged the first.

Viejo Amor was angered by their reprimand. And it induced him to reply to Fortunato's shouting, which he'd been prepared to ignore:

"I also have serious business to air out. I'm not a rotten old goat. Not a degenerate old man."

"Yes you are. Last night you screwed that female donkey out in the shed."

"Don't you see? Why do you offend me? Didn't Jupiter turn into a swan to seduce Leda? Didn't Jupiter take the form of a bull to seduce Europa?"

They stood staring, awestruck by his sudden erudition. Prudently approaching the circle, Katanga dished it out to him:

"Depraved men indulge themselves by making literary justifications for their aberrations. They absorb myths, legends, tales, novels, fragments propitious to their respective psychosexual pathologies. They exalt their own idiosyncrasies. They boast about them. And the vice appears so exalted to these types of people, that everyday life starts to seem to them nothing more than an insulting inanity. I know pederasts who wear their aberration like some kind of medal. But I didn't realize that Viejo Amor also had such arguments to justify his bestiality . . . That's great! . . . In truth, bestiality is a human thing with a divine genealogy. Zeus was an inveterate rascal, he had no fear of de-anthropomorphizing himself . . ."

"Into what?"

"Into what?"

" . . . into losing his own form . . . So he turned into rain of gold to ravish Danae and he disguised himself as Amphitryon to sweet-talk Alcmene. He resorted to any means of the lowest animalism. It's true that he turned into a swan to yoke up with Tyndareus's wife. True that he became a bull to lay down with the nymph Europa. Certain that he changed into an eagle, a serpent, etcetera. But, you, Viejo Amor, you are not Jupiter . . ."

"Exactly. That's why I don't transform. It's Jupiter who seduces me, him transformed into a beast! That's why I slide straight in, smooth and plain, right into a mare; rough and torturous with a nanny goat. What's the particular problem, then, if I get right up close, rim to rim, with a little jenny like Don Rufo's, so full of divine attractions? . . ."

"You're shameless!"

The unexpected paradox led to hilarity.

Half-convinced, Aparicio pointed out:

"And what if, you animal, you produce some monstrous child?"

Viejo Amor hesitated, turning pale with lewd craftiness. He was almost going to admit defeat, closing his mouth, when Katanga intervened:

"Bah! Wasn't Pegasus the child of Poseidon and Medusa? If the winged horse that carried Bellerophon to annihilate Chimera was the child of a god become human, why can't Viejo Amor take great pride in begetting a mythical animal child?"

"It's the father who's the animal!"

"Fine, Fortunato: enough! Let's not stir up a scandal. We're in a beautiful place where deference must be both the setting and the script."

Muffled echoes of galloping hooves.

Soon, from behind the houses, dogs barking.

Then a creaking of rusty hinges. Someone was entering through the patio gate.

Two men, dismounted from their horses, appeared. One, lean, with bilious eyes and bandy legs. The other, chubby, cautious, with a drooping mustache.

The first man openly inspected the four of them.

Snapping his whip sharply against his boots, he inquired:

"Where's Don Rufo? What're you all doing here?"

He was nervous, evidently. Viejo Amor didn't hesitate to answer:

"He'll be back soon. He went off to clear out a blocked culvert. It couldn't wait."

"Good! But, you bunch, what're you doing here?"

"We're spending a few days resting."

"Resting! That's nice . . . And what're you resting from?"

Aparicio was starting to develop a serious dislike for these men. Such an interrogation at close range . . . Dispensing with any legal formalities . . . He was going to offer a vehement reply when the figure of Rufo Pereyra caught their attention instead. They went straight for him.

"Good thing you're here," Aparicio stammered. "I've already had enough of this bowlegged creep with his balls in parenthesis. What's needed is insolence!"

"Don't get heated up over a bit of nonsense. Let's go back to the room. I'm interested in the case of the *Juventud Obrera*, the Youth Labor Party in Almafuerte . . ."

The recent arrivals were none other than the Police Captain of Amboy and the Justice of the Peace from the district of La Cruz. They were on the hunt for a fugitive delinquent. One Ruperto Alaniz, alias *"El Yuyero"*—the herbalist—perpetrator of assault and robbery against Don Bonaventura Venturi. They made no attempt to conceal their indignation. Each man in his own way: one shooting sparks from his eyes; the other restlessly smoothing his mustache.

"Escaped from right under my mustache," the Captain commented angrily. "These selfish rogues have got no respect anymore. They've got no consideration for authority. Before, remember? You gave an order and everybody just lay down. Now! . . . What offends me most is how he did it. Such a devilish thing, Don Rufo! I was bringing him in, revolver in hand. No way's he gonna get away from me!"

"Of course. You shoot well."

"Don't flatter me. I was bringing him to La Cruz, to write up the relevant indictment, when a beautiful partridge landed right there, in the middle o' the highway. You know how I like to hunt. Letting myself get carried away by temptation, and also to show the aforementioned criminal my deadly aim, I tied my horse, aimed, and by the Holy Virgin . . . listen to this! . . . the gun didn't fire! . . . Bugger me, I aimed again, pulled the trigger . . . and, click! The gun didn't fire! I was 'bout ready to give up. Then . . . to top it off! Ruperto Alaniz, who's been a shameless rogue his whole life, took advantage of the circumstance and says to me:

Well, Captain. I see you've got a faulty revolver there. So, bye-bye, baby, no?

And he struck spurs to the sides of his tobiano. No way I was

gonna catch up with him! You know, Don Rufo, I don't travel easy, with my bad liver, and that lazy crackpot was the most
wanted man riding the highways around San Bartolomé ...
They've assured me he's been seen out round these fields. You
swear you ain't seen him. Right ..."

"Of course."

"You'll let me know. If it were just something small, amen.
But he gave that Italian, Venturi, such a whippin', and to top it
off, stole his billfold."

"With money in it?"

"Um ... I'm ... not very ... sure. Had some papers ... important ones, they say; but the victim still hasn't declared their
worth, like he's supposed to."

Turning away from the horses, the Justice of the Peace,
who'd not yet opened his mouth, asked:

"Tell me, Don Rufo: who are those men?"

"*Hombre*, they asked me if they could put up here for a few
days. They're not drifters. They paid me in advance. They've
brought everything they need, all kinds of stuff. But they're not
tourists either. You've just got to look at them. From what I
understand, they've come to fulfill the bequest of some dead
man."

"A dead man's last wishes? Is that their story? Watch out!
They're swindlers."

"Hmmm ... I'd like to take a closer look at them," added
the Captain.

"That's fine! Stay for lunch. We'll eat together. You'll see
how good they pull it together."

"Pull what together?"

"The cooking. They prepare everything. And with real class!"

The Captain and the Justice of the Peace exchanged a knowing glance as if itching to have their suspicions confirmed.
Grateful for Don Rufo's kindness, they followed him to the
kitchen. No one was there. Nothing. Already on the alert,
Aparicio started buttering them up:

"Such a lovely day, we'll have a picnic, there, by the irrigation canal, beneath the apple trees. Let's go. The food is almost ready."

"Uh, well, see, I invited these friends of mine ..."

"Like I said, let's go. No fuss. Your friends are my friends."

The Justice of the Peace felt a bit stymied. He was a comfortably wealthy peasant. What is derisively called a "solvent peasant." With a haughty air of stupidity and vanity. Protected by the rustic lineage of a colonial family name, sheltered by his time in the seminary, an oddball who believed himself a superior kind of being. He walked disdainfully. Possessing a distrustful ignorance, one of those men who squint and scrutinize in silence, emitting the occasional phrase, as powerful as a proverb; all the people in the surrounding countryside feared him. For this reason, Aparicio's breezy familiarity annoyed him. To be spoken to like that, him, a judge, whom the professional politicians babied as "the most distinguished personage" in La Cruz!

When they reached the spot, the two representatives of authority were bewildered, pursing their lips in disbelief and disapproval. A large cloth was stretched smooth upon the grass, surrounded by four folding canvas stools. A brilliant collection of glasses, plates and utensils. Fruit, breads, cheeses, bottles, and tinned foods. The turkey cooking on a tripod over a tin of canned heat. And crackling on the Primus stove, tended by Fortunato and Viejo Amor, two aromatic chickens slathered in good-quality olive oil, surrounded by tomatoes, onions and peppers.

Nearby, in the small pool by the floodgate, Katanga was swimming.

Don Rufo led them to the spot:

"I present to you, here, my friend. He's skilled at everything. You've got to see how he handles the plow!"

Katanga emerged from the water. He greeted them and shook hands. His nakedness clashed visibly with the visitors' false modesty. In an attempt to improve their impression of him he stated:

"Swimming, like this, is a blessing from God ..."

"From God . . . like that . . . stark naked? By the Holy Mother Church . . ."

"One is fully connubial with nature. Air, sun and water gravitate to the body, infusing it with health, strength, grace. Take a swim. I'm going to stay in a while more. Why don't you all jump in? The water is wonderful."

He failed to convince them. Rufo Pereyra and the Judge whispered back and forth about who knows what. Splashing around in the water, Katanga reiterated his offer to the Captain:

"Come on, dive in! It's a magnificent swim!"

"Me? . . . Not on your life! You think I'm some kind of athlete?"

The Captain's answer made Katanga want to laugh out loud. To avoid cracking up hysterically, he ducked his head under the surface where his laughter exploded in a large uprush of bubbles. He stayed under water as long as he could. Back on the surface, he was greeted by the Justice of the Peace's bilious sidelong gaze and the surly Cordovan accent of the Captain from Amboy:

"Me? . . . Not on your life! You think I'm some kind of athlete?"

Longines, Dijunto, and Lon Chaney had gone hunting that morning. They were carrying two rifles, a pick-axe, and provisions for their outing.

"I can't figure out how you hunt with this tool," grumbled Dijunto, intrigued.

"You'll see . . . you'll see . . ."

They clambered through steep, rugged ravines and tangled, woodsy thickets.

Bald stones and shaggy willows. Formations of pudding-stone, pebbles, sandstone. Shadows of pepper trees, coconut palms, poplars. Hillsides of biblical sterility and fecund mounds of watercress and mint. They crossed different landscapes. Now a series of rough hills, hostile to the foot and the view; now a barren fragment of wild reeds, carob trees, local buckthorns; now a valley offering the stenciled image of a grove along the banks of a rushing river.

They went along happily, but quiet. Their eyes watchful, their ears alert. The mica shining and sparkling everywhere between flat, layered sandstone and rocky outcroppings. Partridges appeared then scattered. The pick and the rifles . . . They used none of them. Why bother?

Leaving the farm houses behind, Longines had the intention of doing some prospecting. He knew that the local geology around Córdoba was rich in tungsten, vanadium, lead, etcetera. That the veins come to the surface, inviting the lazy inhabitants to gather those riches, with no more effort than it takes to reach down and grab your cock or the rope of a bucket in a well. But he yielded to indifference. Why further mortify the flesh of the Earth? Why pierce the already-wounded pulp of our solid sphere? He would sooner pierce his own skin:

Ego: anagram of geo! The Self: mere transposition of the Earth! The flesh: telluric catenation of man! Ego, geo!

Sinking down into the philosophy of his own existence, he arrived theoretically to the central fire of Descartes. The heart? He passed through the cortex of the antipode. Instinct? And now in the immense void, he connected with the celestial mechanics of Laplace. Thought? He could not confirm his suppositions. He sensed the artificiality of the false tenants of cosmology. He floated in a trance, contemplating man's geocentric and egocentric errors. But he held back. Geo and ego in equal measure. And he returned from the abyss, elastically, to the level of common sense. No prospecting after all. Why? For what purpose?

Lon Chaney confidently hoped to hunt the stupendous birds forged by his imagination. He shot projectiles outside of time and space. And his fantasy came undone, fluttering to earth in heaps of feathers . . . He felt a bitter sensation of guilt. Cured of his evil fowl hunting dreams, he set about gathering small pebbles. To take delight in their granular, scoriaceous whimsy. To see in them what is not there. To feel the weight of the wolfram and asbestos. To console himself in the wingless death of minerals.

Only Dijunto was not doing or thinking anything. He was walking through the countryside with ancient familiarity. The way one must walk in nature. Encrusted in the earth, threading through the air. Breathing with his own cosmic lungs. Feeling like one stone more, one plant more. Never a man! Because man always conspires against the integrity of nature.

"All right, then, show me how you hunt with the pick."

By way of reply came a jeering duet:

"The pick is for hunting gullible fools."

"The pick is for hunting gullible fools."

"If it's for that, then to hell with it. I've fought enough with sticks and picks! The pick is the anchor which the desperate man throws into the earth. He buries it fast in her. And as soon as the excitement passes, the anchor turns into a grappling hook. My guts are broken from swinging a pick, again and again."

"Well deserved. That's what happens to all those who dig for self-interest and profit. To those who venture to Atlantis and Lemuria. To those who came to search for El Dorado and the City of the Caesars. The pick-anchor turns into a grappling hook! Absolutely correct, Dijunto."

"Well deserved. The birds of paradise, the golden orioles, the sumptuous herons, are like Maeterlinck's blue bird which on *cherche par tous places et . . . demeure dans la propre maison . . .*"

"Precisely, Lon Chaney. Why the pick? Why the rifle? The only thing that matters is to overcome the pride of comfort and satisfaction through the power of intelligence. That's how one achieves transcendence. Man, an animal that emerged from the earth, has a fixed period of existence: X number of millennia; because the duration of any species through the geological epochs has always been limited. Accordingly, the life insurance that man's legacy will collect, will be the memory of his intelligence. Nothing more. Why fortune? Why love? What good are they?"

"That's right, Longines!"

"That's right, Longines!"

They ate their picnic in peace.

And serenely, they lay down to sleep their *siesta*.

When they awoke, they anxiously noted that the afternoon had gone floating away on the current. Nothing remained but the backdrop of the sky and the line of the river. The riverbank was no more than a smear of deep greens, rusted shadows.

"Let's go, quick. It's easy to get turned around in the dark."

Before they had walked three hundred yards they saw, in a bend of the stream, a man with bare legs and his sleeves rolled up, gathering reeds and tying them into bundles. Upon seeing them, he froze. The rifles frightened him greatly. His sullen, liver-red face wrinkled with alarm.

"Don't be frightened, friend. No need . . ."

"Ah! I thought . . ."

The tobiano that was grazing along the riverbank, started up, nervous. Holding it by its loose reins, Dijunto patted its neck, coaxingly:

"Easy, frisky, easy. I like you because you're the same as your master. He shies and you shy. But there's no reason . . . On the contrary. You'll see."

Extracting several lumps of sugar from his knapsack, he pressed them up to the horse's muzzle:

"Didn't I tell you? Are we friends or not?"

The horse quivered voluptuously in a shockwave of gratitude.

Seeing this, the owner's face smoothed out. He breathed in the unimaginable sweetness of relief. Country folk unerringly measure another man's goodness by how effusively he shows his love for animals. In even the purest love between two human beings, many things are always still guarded, unknown. An animal's affection, on the other hand, implies a complete surrender, free from haggling. The country man's arms cordially embraced a bundle of mint. His gesture not only captured the clump of plants; but Dijunto's sympathy as well, mingling with the minty fragrance.

As the man came up out of the river, the new friends met alongside the tobiano. The horse's playfulness made them playful too. But, as soon as Dijunto pulled out more sugar, the horse's owner repressed an imminent sob. Distraught, struggling to control himself, he pleaded in a low voice:

"Couldn't you . . . spare a little for me?"

"Of course. Here. Here you go."

"Three days now since I ate . . ."

"Three days? Here. Take it all."

"I been in jail. Cowards beat the crap outta me. Goddammit! They didn't even offer me a crust of bread. Sonsabitches!"

"Explain later. Eat! Eat!"

The provisions spread out upon the horse blanket, Dijunto moved away to confer with his companions. The spectacle of the famished man touched and saddened him. He had seen it before. The hungry drifters who passed through his farm had stamped upon his mind, from temple to temple, a frieze of suffering faces. He saw it again in that instant. No grimace so pathetic as the one that cries out from need! A mute, frozen cry, a grimace of the enormous yet diminutive agony of every cell. Multiple agonies channeled into one single desperation.

Nourished with dried meat and bread, comforted with fruits and wine, the man came over to them:

"From the looks of it, they got a bit carried away . . ."

"I thought so, too . . . They must be after me. To lasso me in, y'know? Yesterday I slipped away from the Amboy Police Captain when he was taking me to court."

"It must have been for something. But at least they haven't caught on to you yet. Guess they don't cotton to you. You caught-on, yet, man?"

"Yeah. You need some cotton . . . and arnica?"

The joke cheered him up. His eyes sparkled knavishly and his response was ready:

"That's right. Cotton for the cuts and arnica for the bruises. They beat the crap out of me for beating the crap out of Bonaventura Venturi, an Italian more full of villainy than the lying devil Mandinga himself. He was partners with me and a Galician that 'bout a month ago went to Brazil, where, as they tell me, he used to be a nurse. The three of us was just getting by selling medicine herbs, barely had enough to eat. And then the business took a nosedive when the Galician left. He was the smartest one of us three. Knew how to make a fortune preparing *carqueja*, khaki weed root, *rica-rica*, mallow, *botón de oro*, peppermint, nine-herb tea. A hell of a Galician! It was nice hearin' him brag about the prop'ties of the gentian, *ipeca-cuanha*, and stone-beard lichen. We had a carriage, got it for a song from Serafín's widow, the chicken farmer, and we scoured the country selling herbs from here then bringing back herbs from other provinces. We boxed up ones from the North to sell in the South, ones from the East to take to the West."

"You put them in the wrong boxes, what for?"

"No: they sold them that way on purpose."

"Tha's right. We sold the herbs from the North in the South and vice inversa. But the business went belly-burp. That Italian, Venturi, with more of a taste for *zio vino rosso* than working, managed to come out on top. He wanted to keep all the profits for himself. Twenty times I asked him for the horse registration certificates that were owing to me and twenty times he went nuts on me. Ran into him three days ago. I spoke to him real nice, friendly. He blew up on me, again. I'll never work with him again! What was I gonna do? I cracked his ribs good, knocked some sense into his gourd. I took those papers off him. But the police arrested me, beat the shit outta me, no mercy, and according to the Police Captain, those very same papers are the main crime. Imagine that! Turns out I fucked myself just tryin' to get some justice . . ."

"Justice is a sublime hoax," pronounced Longines.

"Justice is as arbitrary as any fashion," added Lon Chaney. "I share Voltaire's opinion on this. As for the rest, you surely know the anecdote about Roca and Bismarck. No? They say that Bismarck was a man who loved justice. In *La Vie Littérai-re*, Anatole France affirms it and he adds that the statesman ate and drank enough for a whole fire department ... What's certain is that in his old age, because he was a just man, Bismarck was tortured by the pain of all the crimes that he had promoted. On one occasion, Bismarck asked General Roca if in the grand nation of Argentina, which he had just described as overflowing with greatness, there was that thing called justice. The 'old fox', astuteness shining in his glassy eyes, answered immediately:

And how! Our Constitution of 1853 establishes justice from the preamble to the last article: and from the tail ... of the tumbril to the prick ... of the prod. What did you expect?

"Convinced of the sincerity of Roca's response, the Iron Chancellor did not insist. And he had the courtesy to believe that this is a civilized country, with justice and everything ... Thank goodness the protagonists of that anecdote have died! Your particular case, friend, piled high with hunger and onslaught, would really do them in. The injustices you've suffered are only matched by the ignorance of your abusers. If I were you, I'd seek out some spiritualist who can communicate with the dead. And I'd have her send a message to the formidable Chancellor of Prussia. It would smack of such panache that, from the *main bier hallen* of hell, he would deliver Roca the ultimatum of a mustard-slathered sandwich and yum! Yum! *Nein! Nein!*"

The red background of the sunset turned opalescent purple streaked with deeply fluted black-green clouds floating on the horizon.

Dark now, the stars and lightning bugs began to wink.

The panorama was reduced to a single line. They spoke anxiously:

"Now we're really fucked."

"Don' be scared. Where you headed?"

"To Rufo Pereyra's place."

"To Don Rufo's! What a coincidence! I was waitin' for nightfall to go to his house. He's the most honest, helpful man around. He'll tell you who Ruperto Alaniz is. Follow me. I know this area like the back of my hand."

He led the horse by the bridle. Two bulging sacks hung across its back like panniers.

"With these herbs I'll be able to earn a few silver dollars. Then ... I'll swear I don' remember never seeing you before ... nobody locks me up, no matter what authority they got. Less they rattle me with bullets ..."

They arrived at the very moment that Fortunato, Viejo Amor, Katanga and Don Rufo were sitting down to eat dinner.

Viejo Amor, with the euphoria of the one posing a picaresque riddle, demanded:

"So, can you guess who Aparicio went to Almafuerte with?"

" ... !"

" ... "

" ... "

"With the Police Captain from Amboy and the Justice of the Peace from La Cruz. Oh, the friendships we entertain!"

Ruperto Alaniz stood stiff and pallid as a freshly dipped candle.

"Holy Virgin of my soul! The vultures are on my trail!"

As they looked at him sidelong, Katanga moistened his lips, licking and re-licking one with the other. Such an attitude, ironically reflexive, was typical in him when his self-interest was secretly weighing the possibility of a good human specimen. In reality, he was a prospector of souls. Thousands had slipped through the gold pan of his consciousness. But, how few pieces of pyrite stayed in the pan! When he had begun to enjoy some clear success in his career as Doctor Inhell—three tricks in one: Thurston, Houdini, Fregoli—his perspicacity always tended to seek, to feel for throughout the show, that authentic, twenty-four carat curiosity. Nothing! Quartz, sand ... he found nothing more than the stupid skepticism of the crowd, which devalued its applause with an ironic smile, as if saying:

"Nobody's gonna pull one over on me!"

Or the total absence of enthusiasm, which suddenly cries out disdainfully:

"I came here to be entertained, not to learn anything."

For Katanga, the only thing that got him fervently excited was that unique skill by which those who are never fooled could allow themselves to be fooled. Rustic folk, for example, from the countryside or the mountains. Their ingenuous astuteness allows them to give in to the power of enchantment. Those who possess the capacity for being amazed by the dazzling glare of the spotlighted spectacle have a perception sharper than any X-ray machine, able to reveal the most serious lies and the very mechanism of illusion. The rustic man is a crafty diviner and a mind reader. Speaking with Alexander Hermann the Great, with Harry Keller, and with Howard Thurston himself, he had reached the conclusion that the dangerous decline of popular culture wreaks far more havoc on society than any magic show. The country bumpkin's innocent vision is so cunningly sharp and sly that it penetrates far deeper than the diplomat's contemptuous glance or the writer's tired eye. Katanga must have noticed something in Ruperto Alaniz that made him moisten his lips, repeatedly licking one with the other. But he didn't hurry. He allowed Don Rufo to give him assurances, to offer him his heart and his house. And, once installed in the confidence of them all, to take a seat at the crowded table.

A little bit embarrassed, Longines tried to give explanations about why they'd been delayed.

"Pardon. Unforeseen motives . . . I realized we were going to arrive late . . ."

"Never late when it's a matter of good luck. It's no small thing to share the company of a brave adventurer like Ruperto, who has pulverized the ribcage of a really annoying Italian. Don't you agree?"

"An annoying Italian? You mean there's another one besides Viejo Amor?"

Viejo Amor didn't take it personally. He continued nibbling daintily at the chicken wing he was holding between his fingers. The tendons of the porous, succulent flesh, caught between the two small bones, made him work even more carefully. Already feeling right at home amid their noisy mirth, Ruperto followed his messmates' jibes with laughter on his lips. And also ventured his own:

"He really holds back onna food, seems he needs some remedy . . . t'whet his appetite. Just in case: I sell herbs."

Neither dim-witted nor lazy, Viejo Amor responded to the scurrilous mirth:

"So here you are then, made to order, you'll fit me like a ring on a finger. Or like a finger in the ass, if you prefer . . ."

"I prefer the ring . . ."

"Seriously, friend. I'm exceedingly interested in herbs for love . . ."

". . . and love among the alfalfa."

"Don't get tangled up with him again, Fortunato. Why don't you tell us what you've got, Ruperto, one by one."

"For love herbs, which is to say, for a roll in the hay, you've got to look for the one called *mina*. Of course that means a mine, y'know, but it also means a spring, and it means a girl. I'm no miner . . . As for herbs of love I've got the famous shining clubmoss right here in my knapsack. You make a decoction from this and you'll see the vitality it gives you. It's marvelous!"

"Marvelous? No way, man. I drank it once . . . nothing. Drink two cups of tea made from *baila bien* and you'll snort like a bull."

"Fine, which one is it? Shining clubmoss or *baila bien*? I need a good concoction, of proven efficiency: because the same thing is happening to me as that countryman of mine who so rancorously sang the swan song for his flaccid member: 'Gia non se me para piu: se me ne'hincha!'"

Their breezy banter did not please Katanga nearly so much as that inner whisper which carefully pronounced decoction as de-cock-shun. The effort the herbalist had made to isolate the word between two brief pauses, in order to emphasize the force of the k-sh combination, made it clear that Ruperto had some expertise in preparing the medicinal flora. And the distinction between infusion and decoction, well and truly a simple one, is tremendously important. The former is prepared with boiling water. The latter, slow brewed in cold water. The former involves buds, shoots, leaves, flowers. The latter, roots, seeds, husks, plant dust. Friend as he was of natural cures, of herbivorous methods, of the modern dietetic regimen that recommends nourishment itself be medicine, Katanga poured out a copious stream of understanding on the herbalist:

"Friend, you don't know how much it pleases me to meet someone who understand herbs."

"Not so much as all that. A Galician associate of mine, who took off for Brazil, he really knew how to find them! I never saw a guy more skilled at curing suffering!"

"When I happened to be in Brazil, where the mighty jungle surges impetuously from inland, nearly leaping into the sea, there, in Rio de Janeiro, I met Doctor Monteiro da Silva, a true sage of plant therapy. Through him I learned about *porangaba cha* which provides an excellent tonic for the heart; the powerful diuretic goodness of bristly star burr; the invigorating *raspa de juá* which refreshes the capillary bulb; and the valuable *catinga de bode*, a plant which exudes an 'odor of goat' (no offense to anyone present) ... whose aromatic and sweat-inducing virtue cuts through flu, catarrh, colds. His passion for, and his faith in, plants like land cress, *rasura de ipé preto*, pink *ipê*, *cogonha de bugre*, and slap root was something to see."

"Slap root? Does it give you a slap in the face?"

"It's not what you think ... *sapucainha unguent*, *pepira em pó*, passionflower leaves, *sacco-sacco,* and a thousand more plants. Fervent supporter of the empirical method, he defended the tribal witch doctor and the *curandero* of the *sertão*. Science, he declared, owes many of its official triumphs to those backcountry healers. In Paris, I myself have seen two supposed 'discoverers' of quinine enjoying the prestige of their false merits ... when in fact, the use of cinchona bark to treat paludic fevers was common among the Incas! The witch doctor and the curandero were and are pioneers of medicine. Forced to survive on their own, they employed their cunning to extract nature's secrets. Did Hippocrates and Paracelsus do anything different? Obdurate experience brought about the discovery of medicines that, otherwise, would perhaps still be shrouded in mystery. Since then, I never blaspheme against the witch doctor or the *curandero*. I see in the far off past how much balsam, how much relief, how much healing they brought thanks to their love of plants. And I surrender to the rude, rough pain that they soothed, the reverence offered up, by catharsis, to the forces that taught the gods and titans a lesson. I'm one who is convinced that pain and suffering are the great seasoning of the world. Almost indispensable. So, why persecute those who manipulate those spices with wisdom and gentle intention? Why accuse those who add zest to life, who enable happier souls to live and work, or attenuate the excess of those unable to care for themselves? Rest assured, friend: I'd never denounce an herbalist for practicing medicine illegally."

"You ... 'course not. You're a good man, educated. An' you 'ppreciate us. But catch a ride with us and you'll find out how humble folk like us are really mistreated. There's no doctor or pharmacist that doesn't denounce us. A quick example, on my last trip to Sumampa we barely missed being gutted by an ignorant brute. Turns out there was a native from Santiago whose wife was on death's doorstep. The sister-in-law had brought her a medicine from the pharmacy. We examined her, and naturally gave her a different remedy. They say it was hilarious to see how angry the pharmacist got when the sick woman herself, all better, showed up at the pharmacy: *Here, I'm returning the medicine Regina brought me. For what it's worth ... I cured myself using Quebracho leaves, what the people call bull's shadow. Now, give me back my three pesos eighty* centavos!"

They celebrated the efficacy of the bull's shadow with rowdy shrieks of laughter. All of them, except Don Rufo. His sad demeanor barely lent the sketch of a smile to their merriment. More moderate inside than out, he hated hilarity because its cat's-paw wind caused ripples in his interior; a place where he was comfortable, curled up inside his familiar lugubriousness, stoically bearing the pressures of his abnegation.

Seeing him so withdrawn, Katanga tried to snap him out of it:

"Let's see, Ruperto: you who perform so many miracles: why don't you brew up some potion to lift Don Rufo's spirits? Yes, that's right: but nothing with *baila bien* or bull's shadow."

The two Argentines glanced at one another with sweet comprehension. And both of them shook their heads:

"Who's gonna raise his spirits? Rufo can't be cured by herbs, only by words. He's like a horse with worms. Nobody'll cure him with ointments or theories. Only with words, with words: isn't that right?"

"That's . . . just . . . about . . . the sum of it."

It wasn't prudent to insist. Don Rufo's discontentment, more implied than palpable, kept them from tossing any more jokes about. Embarrassed as well, he sank down. Then, feigning interest, he stood up and took the herbalist by the arm:

"Though they may inflict the worst punishments on you, you mustn't ever stop spreading the virtues of herbal medicine. Plants carry life to the sick organism. Their sap is blood; their essence is soul. Every true seed bears the fruit of health! Don't give up. Minerals, on the contrary, are heavy, opaque death. Synthetic, chemical pharmacopeia is mere labeling. Fabricated by . . . Packaged by . . . A formula and a signature. It's all clear! . . . God—yes, let's say God—has given man two openings: through which all nourishment must enter or leave. Injections are invasion! Synthetic pharmacopeia is a force that attacks from the antechamber of hell. Believe me: the syringe is a weapon as deadly as the machine gun . . ."

Ruperto barely grasped the meaning of Rufo's speech. But he roundly affirmed his agreement:

"Of course! That's right!"

The night was a diaphanous blue portent. The waxing moon, resplendent among the trees, blooming in the branches, one magnolia flower more.

All of them now in the patio, their chatter became disjoint-ed whispers, clacking, and yawning articulations. Prompted by the baby's wailing, Don Rufo disappeared into his room. In that moment, as if compelled by some tacit signal, they all gathered around Ruperto Alaniz.

"All right, amigo: don't be a fool: hightail it out of here!"

"Wha' for? This here's a safe place to hide. Besides, I need to fix me up some money."

"You'll have all the money you want."

"We'll give you what you need."

"Slow down! I won't accept charity."

"It's not charity. It's solidarity."

"What'd you say? Y'can still find that, these days?"

Longines had a wad of bills in his hand. He insisted:

"Take it. Don't be an idiot: run away!"

"It's jus' that . . . I'm offended by freedom offered for pity's sake . . ."

"C'mon, pal!" interceded Katanga. "You think that we're ca-pable of such sloppy disgusting behavior? Our sensibility bris-tles against any sort of restraints; we reject any and all authori-ty. That's all. Accept it!"

Ruperto remained undecided. Until Viejo Amor intervened with a persuasive ruse:

"Gimme the money, Longines. Good. Now, listen, you: I need ten kilos of *cola de quirquincho*, that love herb you recom-mended. I won't haggle for prices. Take it: I'm paying upfront. When you've got the product ready, send it to Don Rufo, wherever you happen to be. He'll get it to me."

The herbalist grabbed the wad of cash. Without looking, he stuck it into the pocket of his shirt. And stammered:

"Ten kilos! That's crazy! That'll put some lead in your pen-cil!"

They all said good night.

Now in the bunkhouse, stretched out on his pile of gear, Ru-perto was curious. He lit a match. It was a ton of money! He counted feverishly:

I'll be damned! Three hundred pesos! I'm gettin' the hell out-ta here!

Muffling his breathing, flustered and overwhelmed, he stealthily dressed to ride. He saddled his tobiano. And leaving the two bags of herbs as a testament of his gratitude, disappeared like an idea in the brain of the night.

Since their shared meal, Aparicio and the Police Captain from Amboy seemed to have reached a mutual understanding. Both equally astute, they got on well together, despite many underlying disparities. Each man—an ox without yoke or field—crossed the other's wire fence. And they grazed unmolested in their mutual confidence.

The only one suspicious of their sudden friendship was the Justice of the Peace from La Cruz. Bound by his solemn status as a wealthy churl, stooping to be friends with a drifter like Aparicio would have been degrading. He bowed to no one, and permitted nobody to put themselves above him!

Aparicio sensed this characteristic immediately. His own adventurous, transhumant life had brought him face to face with many such individuals, who "don't back down from anything, who are on top of everyone." Pure nonsense! Lacking any legitimate titles, they forge their own name, a custom fit. True enough, they deceive many people. But those who understand such self-valuations as a kind of camouflage, laugh delightedly. Who hasn't seen those poor devils, saturated with self-importance, who, having climbed the government ladder in some small city or nameless little town, make their first official act the purchase of an automobile to show off license plate No. 1?

Riding on horseback along the road to Almafuerte the three of them found no room for conversation. They'd chatted, perhaps excessively, as the *mate* was passed around after their picnic beneath the trees. But now the road unspooled its panoramic scenes more in the manner of the old silent films than an edition of *Travel Talk*.

In an instantaneous naturalization for convenience's sake, Uruguayan Aparicio had become an honorary Argentine. Typical skeleton key. Habitual strategy. Thus he achieved entree into the favor of his "compatriots"; the *chuncanos*—Argentina's rustic mountaineers—are terrified and must make the sign of the cross at the mere mention of their neighbors to the east, the dreaded Uruguayans. They are haunted by the memory of the few Uruguayans who moved about or settled in the sierras of Argentina. Indecent people. Every one of them. Shitty, sneaky, cheating horseflies. Not one of them would hesitate to commit deliberate outrages against the submissive, though vindictive, humility of the true citizens.

The Judge, a torpid, obtuse hinny of a man, had now made up his mind. Neither Aparicio nor any of his companions were con artists. He'd seen for himself the two thousand pesos representing the dead man's bequest, all the cash fully displayed. It wasn't the old swindler's trick of a wad of newsprint with one authentic bill wrapped around it to make it look like a real roll of cash. No. He was well dissuaded. The Police Captain, however . . . had also seen the loose bills displayed; and he wanted to get his hands on them . . . to take a closer look. And biting his mustache with his lower teeth, he envisioned the road ahead, calculating the distance remaining for them to ride, and hypocritically plotting, as he trotted along, a way of keeping the money for himself.

They only needed to combine stratagems.

Halfway along their route, within a ravine carpeted in clover and kidney-leaf mudplantain, also known as duck salad, they dismounted. They feigned the need to answer the call of nature, while Aparicio watered the horses. Seeing them return, he sniffed out something foul: the pretext, not the other thing. The pretext that impregnated their features with the worst filth of fiction. Suddenly the confidence between Aparicio and the Captain was transformed into a field of brambles and caltrops. And the road ahead, a trail bristling with inquisitions and mistrust.

Aparicio privately celebrated this turn of events. It favored his strategy. His plan called for him to "buy off" the authorities, so he could carry out, with impunity, certain clandestine activities. That morning, Katanga had advised him:

"The true, proper manner of screwing over authority is by imitating the one who screws you. You've got to act like a turkey, always. Playing a role, some invented character—but for real, handing out cash instead of newspaper clippings—rewards to whoever pretends to show such openhearted kindness, such uncommon innocence; earning the title of idiot procures you the ability to later carry out, surreptitiously, the most subtle, intricate misdeeds . . ."

Together the three of them rode past the property of Gumersindo Páez. A small farmhouse built on a hillside. A steep, stone corral. Just over an acre of corn. And a locust tree bored stiff from staring at so much misery.

They drew near. Barking dogs plagued with ticks. Greetings shouted by a disheveled woman, two filthy children tugging at her skirts:

"G'd afternun, compagre. Long time no see. We're so happy. C'mon you: dontcha know the gourdfather? What're you two doin'? Ask his blessin', then."

Peeking out from behind the woman's rear-end, a tiny, sullen voice piped up:

"Blessing, gourdfather."

And the Justice of the Peace's response fell solemnly on him:

"May God make you a saint, young man."

"Ain't you gonna dismount there now? Gumersindo's out back."

"No, Romualda. We're on official business. And it's getting late, it'll be nighttime soon."

"But, gourdfather, don' be like that."

They did not accede. It was all a setup, calculated, to be able to ask the question he now recited:

"Tell me: around here you ever hear tell of a man named Domitilo Sayavedra?"

"Sayavedra . . . Tha' name's not from round here."

"Doesn't sound familiar to me either . . ."

"Me neither!"

They both fixed their gaze on him. Their eyes seemed to

warn him against even attempting a lie, letting him know that they would not be easily fooled . . .

They galloped on for a good stretch.

Coming in sight of FLOWER OF DAMASCUS, GENERAL STORE, POST OFFICE, NASSIN FLORES, PROPRIETOR, they were drawn in by the trapezoid of light given off by the carbide lamp.

They dismounted. Inside, many locals stood drinking or buying *yerba mate* or twine, though it was not clear exactly who was doing what. The store was a jumble of merchandise, with a single counter dispensing sugar, bacon, grappa, and sateen . . . As they came through the door the Captain placed his order:

"Serve us up three gins, dirty."

"Just two. I'll have aguardiente."

"Three dirty gins. I'm ordering and I'm paying!"

"You can drink whatever hogwash you like," replied Aparicio, slightly annoyed. "But *I'm* having what *I* like."

"All right, fine . . ."

The Syrian proprietor dribbled a few drops of *fernet* into two glasses of gin. The turbid brown *fernet* oozed slowly through the clear liquor, the thick nectar dissolving exactly like a squirt of mud. Remembering the Argentine's fanaticism for the dark, bitter *fernet*, the Uruguayan realized his blunder. And to erase his haughty misstep, he quickly tried to set things straight:

"You know, that's a really nice-looking drink! How they serve it with *fernet* . . . Why don't you give me a dirty gin, too."

But now the Police Captain from Amboy could no longer contain his dislike. He swallowed his drink all in one gulp. Then loudly asked:

"Let's see: which one of you from around these parts, in about the last twenty years, has ever heard of a fellow by the name of Domitilio Sayavedra?"

The question fell into a void of empty silence.

Then, turning on his heels and slapping his boot with his whip, he chided:

"Have you seen . . . Sa-ya-ve-dra . . ."

He muttered to Aparicio in a low voice:

"Now I've caught you telling stories, you."

Back on their horses, Aparicio noticed the Captain whispering something to the Judge, his foot already in the stirrup. At that, the Judge, his legs splayed over the horse's back, smiled a great big pompous showy smile, randy, dandy, and pandering. Aparicio felt a prick of humiliation. It was painful to contain his anger. But he held back. And soon after they had started out again, he asked the Judge point blank:

"Don't try to evade my question. Tell me: what are you smiling about .... that way ... so ... smugly?"

"Hombre ... to tell you the truth ... about ... Romualda! Yes: about Romualda."

"Get out, that's bullshit!"

"Yes. I swear ... about Romualda. She used to be my cook, y'know? She was the mother of four bastard children, from different fathers, when one day Gumersindo comes to see me: *Beg pardon, your honor. You see, I've gotten married with Romualda.*

With Romualda! That's odd! Have you really thought about this? Haven't you noticed she's got a pack of kids already?

Yes, your honor. That's why. She's so good at giving birth that it's going to be easy!"

He'd evaded the question.

The tale—as unbelievable as it sounded—caught him off guard like a kick from behind. He took it out on the horse, lashing it to a gallop. His face tightened into a grimace. His fist clenched on the riding crop. The breeze, to spite him and mock him further, threw his companions' taunting laughter back into his face. He knew by now what was going on. And he became taciturn:

It's sad to be taken for a total idiot. But there's no other way around it. Now the money will never reach the Youth Labor Party of Almafuerte. They can smell it ... They'll confiscate it from me because of its fine smell ... They've already forgotten the herbalist, he's escaped their clutches. Not a thought for him now ... Instead, I'll be the one to pay for his salvation. But it pains me to play the

fool when I could whip them both into shape. Be patient. Be re-
signed. Act stupider, still. It's a great truth: the most correct way of
fucking with authority is to pretend it's fucking with you.

Dwelling on the herbalist compromised his composure.
Carried away by his somewhat exalted imagination, Aparicio
went rolling through the declivities of fatality until he had persuaded himself that the true criminal had safely slipped away
and he would now be tried in his place. The night and the silence muddled his emotions. Bringing up the rear, stern and
fierce, the Captain and the Judge were polishing up their cunning plan. They had cast off any and all pretense of friendliness. And now Aparicio—forgotten friend of the afternoon—
rode along like any king or criminal: with an escort.

Unconsciously, his annoyance made his tongue sputter between his teeth. It was the hissing of a red-hot iron plunged
into a bucket of water. And he returned to reality. But the
thought was launched. What to do? To lose hope, be demoral-
ized? No. It kindly led him along the line of thought which began to uncoil in his mind:

What a discovery! Kings and criminals, among the many iden-
tical qualities they possess, coincide most precisely in the escorts that
shadow them ... The subtlety of protocol twists the meaning of
things and does whatever possible to dignify the monarchy. Thus,
the little knot of henchmen who act as the guardians of the integrity
of majesties and highnesses is called an "honor guard," ... A simi-
lar logic would oblige one to apply the title of "entourage" to the de-
spicable guards who keep the criminal in custody ... But that's not
possible because logic adapts to the taste of its many consumers ...

An ironic little cough reinforced his reticence. Not for nothing. When one believes that widespread justice has been achieved, a period in which one's natural rights cannot be undone by
convenient sophistry, then all euphemism becomes repugnant,
and all wily, exaggerated praise simply causes annoyance.

They must have spied a sarcastic expression, resulting from
that curious confirmation. They must have glimpsed the little smile that decorated his face. They must have intuited some

scoffing allusion in his cough. Because a riding crop instantly
cut into his back like a striking snake followed by a hard punch
that nailed the back of his neck.

"What the hell are you thinking about?"

"You're not gonna laugh at us, no way!"

And the cruel treatment continued, the Captain's cutting
whip and the Judge's fist, raining down on him from left and
right in a staggering series of blows.

Stupefied, full of bruises and anxiety, Aparicio didn't know
what to think. He used his own riding crop to block as many blows
as he could, and several curses to stem the persistent beating.

"You've got no right, goddammit! You shouldn't assault
someone like that, you cowards! I'm a peaceful man, I'm unarmed. Why this shameless treatment, dammit? I'm going to
send a telegram to the government!"

The Judge calmed down, his expression friendly once more.
Following the gratifying punishment, his excited satisfaction
gave him a jocund air. He breathed happily. His arrogant authority vanished, his face radiated a luxuriant light of sadistic
fulfillment. Flush with the Dominican beatitude of inquisitors
standing before a pyre of immolated heretics. His eyes were no
longer folded in deceit; his happy harmony allowed them to
shine without any falsity.

"No right, goddammit!" Aparicio continued. "It's brute ignorance and ignorant brutality to suppose truth can be annihilated by blows and whips. Any day now. You'll see, goddammit!"

Master of himself, with direct simplicity and cold, revealing
viciousness, the Police Captain laid a formidable blow across
Aparicio's neck with his riding crop.

"Here: scratch yourself with that! And keep swearing, you'll
see."

Aparicio cut his insults short, burning now with shame.
A stinging, more psychic than epidermal, reduced him to a
moaning sob. A moaning that became a broken protest. It was
not their thorough abuse of power that piqued him so much as

his humiliation.

Belicose by nature, he could not remain passive much longer. He suddenly recalled his incursions in the Uruguayan civil wars. What was one beating more upon a back hardened by machete blows? What were a few slaps and punches to his dented bully's face? A wind of rebellion blew through his spirit, gusting hot from his eyes and mouth. But his fists did not curl and rise with their old impetus. It was now the expired rebellion of the young fighter grown old and crafty. And he growled:

"It's brute ignorance and ignorant brutality to suppose the truth can be annihilated by blows and whips . . . Conviction, a conscious sense of duty, cannot be unwittingly snuffed out . . . Those who unjustly grant themselves authority swindle everyone, conferring themselves with a power to judge that does not rightfully belong to them . . . Ideals, like vital strength, do not experience anxiety, nor can they concern themselves with anyone's perverse fetishes . . . They fulfill their mission impersonally. That's why this ridiculous situation is really laughable . . . When a reason offends you there's usually a reason and usually it's because its truth is undeniable. Fine, I'll accept the insult . . . But look at the public consensus. My truth blazes up with my every loyal thought . . . Upon the effusion of each feeling, one with my duty . . . The rest matters little . . . Let the beatings continue . . . Let the quarrel of the inept continue . . . Let egotism continue to bask in satisfaction . . . I, as always, will come, come what may . . . With my conscience ready for fairness and my face open to the ignorance of all brutes and the brutality of all the ignorant who suppose that the truth can be annihilated by whips and blows . . ."

Satisfied with the speech delivered by Aparicio, the Judge and the Captain let his peroration slip by with disdainful indifference. There had been no heavy words to make one cover their ears. The insistent, hammering phrases didn't bother them. And they carried on as if nothing had happened.

They could already see the lights of Almafuerte in the distance.

Aparicio rode along lax as a lasso. Like one more garment slung across the saddle. Listless. He was mute with scorn and the vehemence of his declamation had left him exhausted. And he had just surrendered to failure! All the gabble he'd reeled off had been committed to memory after a similar experience in Paysandú. Having received a black eye from a politician, the very same rant had bought him two feasts, in reparation. Now, here, nothing. Not even an explanation. The ridiculousness of having repeated the speech — with slight variations — made him feel such shame that his only consolation was to hide beneath the cloak of darkness.

They had not gone half a mile when they entered an alley of poplars. The dense shade cast by the foliage allowed only a few splinters of moonlight to pass through the narrow gaps between the trees.

The predetermined spot.

A quick gallop was all it took to bring the Police Captain alongside Aparicio's horse whose reins he now grabbed. In an instant the Judge had flanked him as well, and in a brusque tone he spat:

"Come on: hand over the cash."

"What do you mean, hand over? That money is to pay off the debts of Domitilo Sayavedra. It's a mandated bequest of his last will and testament."

"Sa-ya-ve-dra ... really? Am I supposed to believe that! You're nothing more than a shameless grifter. You came along with us just to try and carry out a typical old swindle. That money is counterfeit."

"Counterfeit? You've already wished you had your hands on it ..."

"Of course we want it. As proof! Let's see: bring it out for once. If not, you don't know what's coming to you."

"It's just ..."

"Hand it over, that's an order. It's the *corpus delicti.*"

"The only criminals around here are ..."

Aparicio instantly stopped speaking. Blocking him from

both sides, their brusque search forewarned more extreme violence. Suddenly he longed for his bygone days of knife, blun-
derbuss, and Mauser. The epic of Aparicio Saravia. The furious skirmishes of Tres Árboles, Hervidero, Arbolito, Masaller
and Tupambay. And the massacres of prisoners: slit throats, de-
capitations. How he would have delighted in lopping off the
heads of these two henchmen he was forced to suffer! With
such pleasure, grasping them by the hair, he would have given
them the good old knee to the backside, sending their decapitated bodies off on that last macabre march, arms flapping like
wings until they fell forward, burying the stump of their necks
in the dust of the road. What pleasure! Lip-smacking pleasure!
But there was no way he could. His role was to let himself be
the butt of the joke. And he lowered his hands and face, offering himself meekly to their pillaging.

They struggled to pull the money from his trouser pocket.
Their haste made them clumsy. Seeing that they were going to
rob him of everything, he settled on the best solution: to help
them.

"Fine. Help yourselves. But keep in mind that it's real money, authentic legal tender. I've got the serial numbers of all the
bills. You won't fool me, swapping them for newspaper clippings to try and ruin me."

"No; don't worry."

"We'll give you a receipt for it."

"That's good. But the money's for the debts of Domitilo . . .

". . . Sa-ya-ve-dra . . ."

". . . you'll have to suck it up."

"Maybe not!"

They didn't go to the police station, as was normal. They
headed straight for the house of the Captain's crony: the Police Captain of Almafuerte. The place was already dark. All the
better for their objectives. The master of the house turned on
a light in a little drawing room crammed with tacky knick-
knacks. They introduced Aparicio as a friend of the most absolute confidence, worthy of the finest respect. They recom-

mended him earnestly. They explained that they needed to close a business deal, and asked for paper and ink.

The air hung heavy with sarcasm. A comedic atmosphere. A hasty, specious courtesy. With tidy, elegant gestures, the Judge rolled up his sleeves to write.

"I'll draw you up a private receipt that the court will recognize. State clearly your first and last names."

"Put down: Juan Aparicio."

He wrote up the document. He signed his name with a tacky flourish. He blew on it to dry the ink.

Now in his hands, the Uruguayan tried to interpret it. Impossible. He struggled to decipher the scribbled letters of the nonsensical text. He read it word for word without capturing the overall meaning. As he skimmed over it once more he was able to make out the text's unusual qualities:

Being of sound mind the Justice of the Peace of La Cruz surtifies to the effecks which taken place when in the place of his districk he found the indivijewel Juan Aparition, an unknown person in the zone, with billes which looking like two thousand pesos total (that is 2,000$) that accordion to him are to foofeel the order of a desist subjeck and since this smells like a lie and as a crime is completely open and shut and said and done so accordion to law I must contravene and proceeded to seize the money ut supra in order to see if it is money with value or is the evidence of the crime in standing in effeck for the crime and the suspeck on horseback to the point of having disclobbered the pertaining confirmations.

Aparicio bit his lips to keep from laughing out loud. Nevertheless, he permitted himself a joke:

"You said that this was a private document?"

"Uh-huh."

"More like a privation document: deprived of a date, of spelling, of punctuation, and even of a signature."

"Well! So what?"

"Ah! Permit me."

He took the pen and wrote at the foot of the page: Illegible signature.

"That's good enough for me. I have the list of serial numbers on the bills. I'll be back to have them returned to me. Meanwhile, do me a favor: I don't have a penny left. If I were a con man I would've asked you for a certificate of deposit. But I'm not. And I want us to remain friends."

The Judge and the Captain looked at each other. At the same time they searched their pockets. They gave him two pesos eighty *centavos*.

"Fine. Thanks. Until next time."

From the threshold of the entryway they both watched him turn the corner. He walked along, tranquil and dashing. Smiling. And they murmured, crestfallen:

"There's still that bit about the serial numbers . . ."

"Maybe we've stepped in shit . . ."

It was too late to make it to the office of the Youth Labor Party. It would have been imprudent to try to schedule an interview with some member of the Pro-prisoners Committee at that hour. He opted instead to search for somewhere to spend the night. He'd stayed in one of the local inns before but the filthy room, the portrait of the Italian royal family over the bed, and the dining room saturated with the rancid odor of fried garlic induced him to try a different one. What a coincidence! There, gathered with three other comrades—a deck of cards and counting beans as a cover—he found none other than the Secretary of the Party, in the flesh. He did not present himself. Turning away, he whistled for the waiter:

"Che, come over here."

"What d'you want? . . ."

"You to come here. Bring me a *completo* with two rolls, plenty of butter, and several *fetas* of ham."

"Sorry. No *jetas*, no ugly faces round here."

"*Fetas*: slices, slabs, strips."

"Oh! Well, talk straight old man. Why dontcha make sense like everybody else?"

Sliding down in his chair, Aparicio laid his neck against the backrest. The Secretary was speaking. He had the man's face etched in his mind. It was as if he could see him! His expression was unforgettable. Firm features. A direct, icy stare. The son of parents from Palermo, he seemed to have inherited the hard and violent looks of "The Condottiero" by Antonello di Messina. The Secretary was speaking. And his voice struck Aparicio like a thousand tiny sparks. His illation carried shades of persuasion so penetrating that they made Aparicio forget everything else. An anxious, roving, peripatetic mind. Swindles and counter-swindles. He liked the cutting intimacy of such oratory, in which reason whispers and wounds. The Secretary was speaking:

"It's an ignominy. When one observes the eternal carnival of our politics, the ridicule suffered by our democracy becomes evident!

"Our three-ring legislative circus reenacts in each province the same little farce put on by the national parliament.

"Histrionic postures, shameless actions, these men gabble right through the heart of our principles.

"Everything they do is contaminated with the virus of the basest incivility, rights are infringed, both reason and faith in the republic trampled.

"He who observes the noisy game of administrative bedsprings, listens with disgust to the strident shouting from all sides. Bribery clouds our democracy like a permanent miasma, to asphyxiate and put good character to flight.

"Verbiage, phraseology, a crisis of ideals, because people's ears are filled with mud, hearing only the chant of ambition.

"One senses imminent disaster, because progress is degraded with the renunciation of past advances.

"There are such great failures in civility and community spirit that, for many, nationality matters little.

"Thus they stare unblinking at the neighboring tyrannies

and even long for our liberty to become the putty of satrapies and the shuffled little poker deck of merchants.

"Democracy is sick and it needs a cure. Let's have no talk of 'hygienic dictatorships.' No such thing exists. They use the poultices of fear and the opium of ignorance.

"It would only take a few decisive citizens of strong moral fiber to tear off the blindfold of depravation and imperialism, to dry our putrid open sores in the bright sunshine.

"All that's required is the rebirth of that ancient noble fervor: at once serene and tumultuous, brandishing the dashing elegance of the old swords.

"And especially that every flock of professional politicians be violently ostracized, with neither disgust nor piety, just as old sandals are tossed onto the rubbish heap."

Aparicio could not hold back. Some days before, in a long meeting, he'd become convinced of the Secretary's great leadership qualities, forged with strokes of audacity and kindness. By his standards, the militant politician must be that way, nothing more: a romantic amalgam to serve the homeland. Drunk with enthusiasm, he turned his head and exclaimed:

"Very good, friend. That's talking! It's the pure truth. We've got to save democracy, taking on half the world with gunpowder and bayonet. The ignorant people of South America have no need of Engels and Marx, Sorel and Lenin. They're irrelevant, as are all politicians who betray their country. Pimps of sovereignty! Con men of popular will! Hunger, the ferule which drives home the lesson of inequality, doesn't exist here. Here, the land is not entirely fenced off by impenetrable barricades, like in Europe. Here, anyone can slaughter a stray sheep. Here, no judge will condemn Jean Valjean for stealing bread. Here we have so much money that we let ourselves be consciously swindled . . . But watch out for professional politicians! Con men of popular will! Pimps of sovereignty! They gather up the votes of each country in the parliament, like sheep in corrals . . . For what? To be led to the slaughter: to the slaughterhouse, led by traitors. Into servitude for the English or to be fleeced by the Yankees. Do you realize? . . ."

Wildly, almost incoherent, he outdid himself in the diatribe.

In the blink of an eye, the five of them stood up together. The Secretary's fixed, frozen stare stood at odds with Aparicio's dreamy flight.

They made an appointment to meet the next morning.

Bidding one another good night, their firm handshake produced a magical effect. The Secretary, imprisoned by an instantaneous inspiration, hardened his facial muscles. An image flashed in his mind. And with philosophical inflection, he began to pontificate:

"In the past, the two hands emblazoned on our nation's shield shook in a friendly manner, like fellow compatriots at the general store counter. Now they wrestle with hatred, desperate to become unbound. One hand rises up empty, gesticulating a curse upon the other; the other hand shakes its clenched fist, threatening. Now the two hands upon the shield do battle! They fight, ultimately, to see who will control the symbol of liberty. They fight for the pike, the symbol of liberty! For the pike; for one of them it will serve as a rod with which to smite; for the other, as the pole on which to raise their banner. Let the sun of May illumine their consciences! Let the overwrought fumbling between right and left cease! Let the laurels of the past and the olive branches of the future keep both hands united! So that they never separate! It would be ruin, friend!"

"That's right. Let them never separate! It would be ruin, friend!"

Aparicio was headed toward the meeting place set by the Secretary. He was crossing the town plaza when a great hullabaloo stopped him dead in his tracks. Dirty, ragged kids: newspaper sellers, shoeshine boys, etcetera. Drifting along slowly, he followed them without realizing it to the front of the church. Then, a bench in the plaza beckoned him to sit. He accepted. And from there, displaced in time, exonerated from himself, he began to contemplate the arrival of a wedding procession, the curiosity of the envious young single women and the hopeless longings of the older single women.

Then . . .

He fell down the well of self-absorption. And he was talking to himself, plummeting ever deeper:

Oh, how many childhood memories that stentorian chant brings me: "Throw me some money, groomsman!" . . . I also played at that boy's game of chasing coins after weddings. We ran toward the parish church behind the wedding carriages shouting with delight for the coins tossed out, culminating in the atrium of white stones, when the best man cast his final offering to the wind's discretion. I can still hear the copper coins ringing in the bowl of both hands, like an ineffable song of happiness. Perhaps those far-off newlyweds still hear it, that musical clangor as a prelude to a romance of caresses . . .

But now he was no longer seated in front of the church, enjoying the boys' racket. He was now among them, in two places at once, spectral. And as the caravan departed he was shouting too:

"Throw me some money, groomsman!"

The best man, a full-blooded native of Piedmont, did not even await their exhortation for money: "Give it up, groomsman!" Like a sower of seeds, sure of his harvest, decidedly uncomfortable in his special clothes for the occasion, cast out the bright nickel seed which fertilizes so much delight in young boys.

Then followed the customary whirlwind of arms and legs. The cars all honked their horns in vain. All the boys were down on their knees in a loquacious mass, trying to procure the sonorous communion wafers that rolled in circles on the asphalt. The liveliest ones took communion many times, showing off their harvest of coins to the less skilled. So the fools and the greedy raised the cry again:

"Throw me some money, groomsman!"

"Coins, coins! Give it up, groomsman!"

Fruitlessly. The whole retinue had installed itself in the queue of autos along the sidewalk. The boldest of the boys climbed

up onto the "latest model" Ford at the front of the line. Aparicio, too. The bride was smiling like a rose in the flesh. Her husband, cruelly laced into a necktie, hid his settler's virginal ti-
midity behind his white shirtfront and in his boutonniere of
orange blossoms. And they insisted:

"Give it up! Moneyyyyyyyyyyyyyy!"

Automatically, the bride and groom blushed. But the groom
overcame it. And generously tossed out a single peso "for everyone"...

The car started up with a sudden violent rumble. The little
begging urchins stumbled. He could almost hear them. Their
balance regained, the boys ran to carry out the distribution of
coins at the corner shop. He returned to his bench. He felt like
he'd recovered a bit of the youthful optimism wrung out of
him by his long years of wandering. And he sat there, thinking about the couple's excitement, the sweetness of the bride's
smile and her beloved's open-hearted gaze as the prodigious
chant still jingled in his heart ...

He sighed.

Chimeric memory!

Days gone by!

And he clucked his tongue with brio to bring himself back
again to the reality of the morning.

A blonde went strolling past, returning from the church, all
dolled up with pastel blue eyes.

"What a woman!" he murmured, dazzled by her beauty.

An exclamation of animal instinct. Very odd. He was a rene-
gade from love. He detested it. His nomadic life had inculcated
in him something like the Muslim indifference to women. He
preferred to dream of her as a houri than to tolerate what was
present. Passion over feminine grace was something unknown
to him. However hard and rocky the heart there is always a
crack through which love flows but his heart very rarely poured
out sympathy or tenderness for the opposite sex. All his ardor
and vehemence was spent on the fire of the guerilla and in the
outbursts of the marauder. Fighting gave him a secret, perverse

delight. Fighting, he became polluted. And through those pol-
lutions he calculated the mystical superiority of conquering the
flesh. That was why, when all the women from the farms were
rounded up and raped, all the men plunging brutally into the
outrage, he held back. He sunk down into solitude, and from
there he gave voice to his nausea:

Ugh! What filthy rottenness! What meanness! Vile groping!

The painted blonde, with her pastel blue eyes, continued
to arouse his attention. Without knowing by what mysterious
means, he obeyed the impulse to follow her. *Turpis senilis amor-
is?* Fading ember of an unextinguished coal? He didn't find out.
He had followed her for fifty yards when a light flashed in his
mind: the meeting with the Secretary! Then everything seemed
ridiculous to him. He blushed on the inside. But the appointment's location coincided with the blonde's trajectory . . .

As soon as he rounded the second corner, he spied the Secretary waiting for him, standing in the threshold of the appointed shop. Striding across the street with a certain graceful
charm, Aparicio passed by without looking at him. The Secretary's frown turned dour. Imperatively he hissed:

"Pssst. Hey, friend . . ."

"Sorry. I hadn't seen you. What beautiful women there are
around here!"

"Forget screwing! The ideal is what mandates. Let's go. The
car is waiting."

Off they went.

Aparicio's eyes stared ahead in a vacant stupor.

Metempsychosis: what strange destiny had placed before
him the fresh copy of his past?

Avatar: what enigmatic power was at play in the risible liberation of his imprisoned spirit?

Ananke: what extraordinary *fatum* repeated the remote echo
of his words?

The *voiturette* penetrated the familiar landscape with monstrous impetus. It pierced the crystal of morning, cracking her
to splinters. Pitilessly, it perforated the passive vegetable silence. The air pressure induced by the car's tremendous veloci-

ty thrust them back against their seats and made it impossible for them to converse. The wind tore their words away, whipping them up into a confused trail like papers fluttering in the ruts of the road. Aparicio hoped that the approaching curves in the road would allow him to disgorge his now tumescent loquacity. No chance. The Secretary tore into each bend with such skill that the earth itself was drawn along by the physics of the car. On he drove, on and on! Passing vehicles with mocking horn toots and lampooning columns of dust. Zipping out in front of oncoming traffic and whipping safely back.

The Secretary drove with proud self-assurance, as if drunk on power. The barking of dogs, the disdain of the *paisanos* on horseback, and the curses of the farmers in their sulkies, did not alter his pace. Because he pulsed with the automobile's screaming, shifting, raging fever. Blurred by velocity, the surrounding countryside ceded before his direct, frozen gaze. Only the human panorama commanded his interest:

"What do we get from this lovely arrangement of trees and stones? Nothing. Leave that for the contemplatives who adore dully pondering infinity . . . What do we gain from the play of the sun on the waters? Nothing! Leave that for the aesthetes who cower in admiration . . . I love concrete and vertigo. Suffice to say: mankind!"

They reached Don Rufo's place not long after their company had quit the breakfast table.

Still reeling from the dizzying drive, Aparicio was unable to peel his neck off the headrest:

"You know you're ridiculous? I can't figure out why you drive so damn fast. It's just over the top . . ."

Katanga approached:

"Allow me to introduce the Secretary of J.O.D.A."

"*Joda!* What the fuck is that all about?"

"*Juventud Obrera de Almafuerte*, the Youth Labor Party of Almafuerte: don't play the fool. He's shaken me to bits, completely. He's hell on wheels! Do you know how fast we drove here?"

"Ummm . . . what do I know? In the truck it took us close to two hours."

"Twenty-five minutes. Can you believe it?!"

He didn't answer. Measuring the Secretary's stout, angular shape up and down, Katanga advanced to offer his hand. The exchange of impressions favored the Secretary because the energy he exuded through every pore demanded approval. Katanga's cunning complacency produced in the stranger a phobia that set the calm waters of his mirror-smooth inner lake boiling.

The contrast became even more violent when the Secretary began to reveal his convictions:

"This Aparicio is a chicken-hearted fellow. The virtue of the automobile resides casually in its nervous rumble and constant velocity. That compensates for the failings of man: slow to decide, slow to act . . ."

(I adore the luxury of slowness.)

". . . Just as the microscope relieves us from the human eye's inadequacy, the automobile engrains in the individual the rhythm of the times in which we live. It is imperious, definitive, rapid . . ."

(I prefer my full leisure to empty hardship.)

". . . The auto, additionally, serves humanity's social interest by signaling the imperative of converting each individual conscience into a combustion engine . . ."

(I aspire to humanize the machine, not to mechanize my humanity.)

". . . Man's salvation is now possible thanks to the influence of the automobile. When power is channeled into unanimous effort. When ideas are fueled with gregarious generosity. When the crank of the heart is exalted in the most impersonal optimism . . ."

(I know no other optimism than an active pessimism.)

Courtesy had taught Katanga to listen without responding. Thus, his objections were purely subjective. Murmured between the parentheses of chest and back. Astuteness pressed him, now, to calibrate the Secretary's fervor, not through muted counterpoint, but rather by means of some small nails, to blow out his tires:

"Nevertheless, friend, the automobile is one of the calamities of the universe. One single aspect: the problem of traffic brings consequences more terrible than cancer, tuberculosis and uremia all put together. Last year in the United States there were eight hundred and twenty-seven thousand automobile accidents; in which thirty-seven thousand people were killed, one hundred and five thousand permanently maimed or crippled, and more than one million injured. The total damage to property is estimated—if my memory does not fail me—at one billion six hundred million dollars. Four times the Argentine national budget!"

"Impossible, you're inventing this . . ."

"That's what the statistics say."

"I don't believe in superstitions."

"Statistics are history frozen in time."

"Rubbish! It's been said that there are three kinds of lies: lies, damned lies, and statistics. Give me a break! Please!"

Katanga had already settled his score. He assigned a splendid surplus of affection for the Secretary. He'd sized him up and seen right through him: a young man of brains and solid constitution. Just like a watermelon, he thought, considering the young man's rosy well-fed flesh, and his soft, watery ideas. Longines and Dijunto approached.

"Here you have him. Allow me to introduce the Secretary of J.O.D.A."

"*Joda!* Fuckin' A!"

"Oof!" Don't you understand that J.O.D.A. stands for the Juventud Obrera de Almafuerte? The Almafuerte Youth Labor Party, not, as you imagine, the imperative form of the verb 'fuck.'"

The man in question extended his hand with ill humor. The repetition of the "joke" bothered him. He was not especially proud of the unfortunate acronym:

"We usually just say: Youth Labor. This habit of using initials . . ."

"Letters."

". . . is becoming abusive. Abbreviations are not always propitious."

"Certainly not. Some letters are terrible. In Buenos Aires I was surprised to stumble across the C.A.P.O.N.; that's the "Committee of Argentine Pro-Orientation Nativists." But you imagine a castrated committee, an orientation of plumped-up eunuchs! . . . Letters matter when they sum up not only a name but also a defining characteristic. For example: STD: State Treasury Department; NUTS: National Union of Teachers and Scholars; DOA: Delegation of Accountants. Or when they point out some intention, like the formidable S.A.C.A. in Buenos Aires, whose Directory persists in publishing that it stands for Sociedad Anónima Capitalizadora Argentina, the 'Argentine Capital Corporation,' while the public translates it as 'Schemers And Con Artists' because, of course, *saca* can mean 'he extorts' . . ."

Laughing, they approached the verandah.

"That reminds me of the Justice of the Peace of la Cruz . . ."

"Ouch!"

" . . . !"

" . . . one of the biggest brutes in this whole region. One time the local neighbors asked him to sign an application authorizing repair work for a ford in the river. He didn't know the accepted abbreviation of S.E. for the town of Santiago del Estero. So at the meeting he began reading: *'To the Honorable Minister of Public Works of the South East . . .'*"

The mention of the Justice of the Peace produced a general interest and delight, except in the Uruguayan. Katanga had just been describing both the magistrate and the Police Captain from Amboy. And he repeated:

"I've never seen such pure, undiluted stupidity. Their presumed seriousness is a sublime characteristic, simply because it's so laughable. During our picnic yesterday, Don Rufo, who is a silent, bitter man, could not repress his hysterics at their idiocy. Every being is a drawing sketched out with the words it speaks. Thus excessive reticence or loquacity derives in a soul

like a deformed caricature. Don Rufo being so sober and reserved, the Judge often comes here to consult him. And he told
me about the enormous blunders the man commits with official records and documents."

"Notorious."

"I don't know if you heard that bit about him mistakenly
calling the Interdict of *Habeas Corpus* the 'Interdict of Corpus
Christi' ... And there was another matter, a settler accused of
getting caught in 'second nuptials' with a woman who worked
the fields ... And then that *chuncano* detained for '*cattle rustling* a Tilbury carriage' ..."

"Yes. Of course! Hundreds of examples. A blunder for the
ages was the one where he recorded a complaint lodged by the
madam of a bordello: ... *appearing before the magistrate at such
and such an hour, Doña X of French sex, thirty-some-odd years of
age, performing professional duties appropriate to her nationality,
being as she is the madam of a brothel ...*"

As the shrieks of laughter died down, he continued:

"And what can you tell me about the reports from the Amboy Police Captain?"

" ... "

"What! You've never heard about the Captain's reports?
These fellows are two peas in a pod! You've never heard the
likes of ... *forthwith, for never having a doctor in the locality, I
proceeded to check the wounded. He displayed an agronomy in the
head: he seemed to've been stonied ... then the horse thieves commiserated for the mountain and we also commiserated with ourselves. And then the shootout begun. In the end there were no bun-
dled surprises: just a shot in the horns of the Mayan rustler and a
leg broken on his 'complice ...* Funny, isn't it? Nevertheless, this
one takes the cake; while he was dictating a report: ... *the cadaver was completely naked except for his purple pantyhose ...*

"*What do you mean, purple pantyhose?* asked the scribe.

"*Don't interrupt ... He had purple pantyhose from the cold,
right up to his balls. At the altitude of his haunches ...*"

After more shouts of laughter, they all quieted down. There

was a sort of muggy, collective embarrassment. The same as in the cinema, when the lights go up after a comedy, the audience looks around in shame, eyeing each other, as if embarrassed at having enjoyed such stupid humor. As the cloudy obfuscation of mirth passed, they felt the chastening call of duty.

Aparicio indicated that they should convene immediately to deliberate over a pressing matter.

"I have a document from this very judge that may be worth a lot."

"Two thousand pesos," estimated Longines.

"Two thousand pesos minus two pesos eighty *centavos*: nineteen hundred ninety-seven pesos and twenty *centavos*."

They went inside.

In their small conclave, the Secretary's well-cut figure stood out like an insult. His stout, dashing juvenescence contrasted with their extreme decrepitude. An emphatic contrast, which might belie more than one impending disaster. But despite the contrast, there were elements of solidarity which deserved consideration and stimulation.

Aparicio read the 'receipt' out loud. The incredulity that it would have awakened under normal conditions, was lessened by their prior knowledge of the author. Nobody laughed. They showed generic grimaces of hatred, disgust, spite, and disquiet. The note was the handiwork of a cynic masquerading as an honorable man: a beatified swine.

"The two thousand pesos I had were for the Pro-prisoners Committee. To hand them over to you," he explained to the Secretary. "Forced by circumstances, I had to ride with the Judge and the Captain. They'd already learned about the deceased's bequest, by way of Don Rufo. I sensed something in their rapacious, birds-of-prey instinct. I said so, here, to Katanga. We foresaw the coming plunder. And so, to gain the upper hand and assure our peace of mind, we resolved 'to buy off the authorities.' How? By swindling them with the truth itself. By letting them rip me off. I wish to God they could have done it with a little delicacy! They beat me like a thousand demons. And afterward, they brought out their genteel parlor manners; covering up the injustice with simulated legality, they produced this document. A real gem, if it weren't sad for being so jocose. I think we've run across a good deal. If they would just focus on the herbalist, we'll be able to rest easy. I can predict their tactics. They won't show themselves. The threat of our reclaiming the money will keep them hidden in their respective hovels. As for the rest, the precaution I took of writing down the serial numbers, as soon as I told them, really caught them off guard. Neither they nor the police in Almafuerte will dare cross me, even though there's a warrant out for my arrest. They won't cross us either. They won't dare; because we've shackled them with this trick about the bills. Perhaps this seems absurd to you. A paradox. But no. The procedure is curious: to con them while letting yourself be fleeced. But it's the only viable way to deal with these malignant riffraff, all dressed up in the 'respectable' suit of law. Allow me to confirm the absolute soundness of Katanga's advice: the most correct way of fucking with authority is to pretend that they're fucking you . . . You've got to pass yourself off as a turkey, always . . . When you can't act like a hero, like him . . . Being dubbed as a stupid boor enables you later on, to surreptitiously carry out the subtlest of misdeeds . . ."

The pause which followed his explication was filled with two kinds of silence. One, distracted; the other, concentrated. For the first time, Aparicio had paid homage to Katanga's sagacity. This seemingly insignificant fact consolidated the unity of their small faction. Each man celebrated it inwardly; because the praise we value the most highly is always the one most remiss. Even Longines himself looked up from his perplexed examination of the "receipt" to extend to Katanga, wrapped in a bubbling joy, the wink of his purulent eye.

The Secretary bulged with an irascible expression:

"I beg to differ. You will say: why must I involve myself in others' affairs. But let me speak. This matter no longer belongs to others alone. It concerns me as much as you. Perhaps even more than you. When I learned from a comrade in Río Cuarto that the construction workers' strike was saved thanks to help fallen directly from heaven, I refused to believe it. Heaven does not reach down to help the working man ... When I learned the next day that the four explosions had incited the acceptance of their petition, I refused to believe that either; because bombs cannot fall from heaven, only rise from hell. And the unions never get along easily, neither with God nor the devil ... I categorically reject miracles. But I recognize that my accidental meeting with Aparicio, who was already up to date on these events, was miraculous. It came in the tensest moment for me. Everyone was close to desperation. I do not wish to speak at length. You must know how much that confiscated money could have helped. How urgently we need those two thousand pesos. And so. Your stratagem, which reverses the fate of those two thousand pesos, may be as fully ingenious as you say. But it is malfeasance. A moral misappropriation. It is I who have suffered the true fraud. Or rather, those friends arrested, faced with deportation. It's a betrayal. For me, their freedom, utterly compromised, is worth more than your freedom; you are merely suspected, not imprisoned. And so. Good-bye! I have nothing more to say!"

Amid the general stupefaction, the Secretary stood up and shoved his chair back with his foot. And walked straight toward the door.

With equal celerity, Longines and Lon Chaney blocked his way:

"One moment."

"Hold on, friend!"

He was pressed, almost forced, to sit back down. Lon Chaney took over:

"There are some people who have the courage to heroically overcome the spirit. You, *verbi gratia*. Our thoughts are diametrically opposed. And we have the courage to overcome valor with cowardice. This explains our mutual position ... Your exasperated protest is logical, from your personal point of view;

but contemptible, in so far as it concerns us. We, the same as the six arrested men facing deportation, are sick men cured only by one single remedy: money. If therein lies salvation, why are we going to spare the life of others while killing ourselves? *Malheureux l'homme qui fonde sur les autres son appui . . .*

"Stop talking nonsense! Speak so I can understand! Aparicio told me you had more than enough money."

"Yes, yes! We have money to spare! But we don't accept your criticism for doing what is necessary to protect our well-being. Our liberty is as sacred as anyone else's. But despite your denouncement — making the exception that Racine is no charlatan — I myself propose that we dedicate anew two thousand pesos for the benefit of the detainees . . ."

"Approved."

"Seconded."

". . . and that we deliver them this instant, to our friend."

"Well done, Lon Chaney."

The Secretary was moved by their unanimous agreement. He was overwhelmed and sweaty. Stricken. Deep inside he felt the stinging lesson, the pleasure of the objective achieved, and the excitement of the imminent good fortune. All mixed up in the same confused and tremulous emotion. When Longines, coming in from the next room, handed him the appointed sum, he could not contain his emotion. And it was translated into a vibrant sobbing of gratitude and tears. He could not utter a word. As Longines, Aparicio, and Lon Chaney all patted him on the back, the Secretary at last burst forth in broken staccato:

"This will pay their bail! . . . They'll get out! . . . It's a tremendous battle . . . Greedy imperialist squids . . . They do whatever they like . . . They've got the reins of the country . . . Out of jail! . . . They'll get out! . . . They're not communists! . . . We're not communists, despite what they say! . . . Merely settlers trying to defend our harvest . . . Advising others not to sell at starvation prices . . . Let them await justice for the spilled sweat . . . Be gone! . . . They'll get out! . . . Their families . . . Their children . . . Oh!"

As if suddenly waking up from a lethargy, the Secretary's expeditious zeal was reborn. He quickly stretched out his hand to
each of them. Then he rushed to his car. He gunned the motor.
And he was lost in the whirling dust cloud of his haste.

Katanga was the only one still out on the verandah. Slowly,
calmly, he sat down in the rocking chair. He rested his head
on his interlaced hands. He pressed his eyelids tightly together
to squeeze out the vivid memory of the past hour. And quiet,
from the secular quietism of his philosophy, he found pleasure
in the gushing spout in the fountain of his heart:

*Youth is a lucid expectation exacerbated by the restriction of im-
pulse. It is pure clairvoyance in the act of rebellion. It always symbolizes truth. Each idea contains a rosy mental aurora of faith and
generosity. And an impetuous, cordial rhythm, at times broken in
the very effusion of the design.*

*Youth is always discontent. The reaction which represses its anx-
ieties can misinterpret the game of its vocation and the work of its
inner euphoria. Love, the supreme magnanimity, does not adapt
itself to the foolish shapes of its censors. And because it is love, it
crushes the wounding glass shards of evil . . .*

*When youth protests, it's because the health of its ideal is in dan-
ger. For the young, the ideal is not something that quells interest,
critiques sophistry, or spreads insidiousness. Its refusal is the revived
ritual of an ancient hymn. And its faith, the total devotion of sacrifice.*

*One must always side with youth: light and energy, flower and
fire, style and perfume of life. Although it shreds and tramples.
Although it bears the absurdity of the oriflamme. Because all is
vindicated in the Claudeline amplitude of its breath. Because all
things are clarified in the fervor of its vehemence.*

*Oh, when youth, flush with impulses, crosses over the horizon
encircled by its hope!*

At dusk they announced to Don Rufo that they were leaving.

But the rain extended their stay by two more days.

The past week had been so pleasant to their lungs, so full of favorable auras for their spirits, the air so populated by benevolent muses, that they nearly delayed their departure even further. Don Rufo's place was a blessing. Hills. Brooks. Idyllic vales. And the river, such a river! They soared on wings at rarefied heights. Almost free of terrestrial contaminations. In communion with elves and sylphs. Floating. Agile. Far removed from all that is ordinary, burdensome, or binding.

That sensation seized them while they were packing their bundles to go. They bowed their heads and their humility; but the ascending helix spun vertiginously within their chests. Only the ballast of duty held them fixed on the task ahead.

The day's humidity obliged them to eat inside. In the bunkhouse. Fortunato and Lon Chaney were in charge of the first dishes on the menu. A tapioca soup and a Lyonnaise omelet. These were their respective specialties. For his part, Don Rufo chose the two best kids from his herd of goats. He butchered and dressed them himself in order collect the succulent juices. He skewered the pieces of meat on thin branches peeled from a felled tree. And he placed them on the spit in such a way that they would be fanned by the infernal vapors of a constantly smoking pile of red-hot corncob embers.

It was the saddest lunch of any they'd shared. They seemed to swallow without tasting, to be chewing burlap. The white mucilaginous soup, despite emitting perfumes worthy of the Grand Hotel, despite the exquisite halo of steam that floated above each plate, slipped down their throats without leaving a trace. They swallowed mechanically. They yearned for their days of peaceful pleasure. The fragrant green onion omelet, made with eggs fresh from the nest and crumbles of deliciously rich pork and veal sausages, elicited no comments. They were absent, displaced, looking back on the ineffable moments of their recent respite. And, getting ahead of themselves, they already felt nostalgic for the melancholy scene of this good-bye lunch.

Don Rufo tried to shake them out of it:

"All right, amigos. The roast is jus' done. Cut the pieces you like."

Careful without being fastidious, tranquil without affectation, he'd seen to every detail. While the others worked on their food, he tasted each dish thoughtfully, then pierced the golden tenderloin, fanned the fire, or basted the ribs with the marinade brush. He took pride in his mastery of the art of roasting baby goats. And so their slowness in responding irritated him:

"C'mon, dig in, dammit. What're you waitin' for? You want it overcooked?"

They gathered round, cutlery in hand.

Longines pulled out his combination penknife-fork-spoon-punch-canopener-corkscrew-awl-screwdriver-glasscutter-scissors. "The Ten Commandments" sparkled and glittered. Slow, meticulous, mouthful after mouthful, he devoured the little kidneys, the neighboring offal, and in small fillets, the crunchy flanks of meat and toasted cracklings. Viejo Amor hastened to eat all he could. His lips and pupils glazed over from gluttony. Dijunto, latched onto a side of ribs, extracted every last bit of meat with his incisors, ripping off the gristle and sucking out the marrow with a serious, conscientious sound before tossing away the little bones. Aparicio asked for, and received, all for himself, the two neck pieces. He knew quite well what a plentiful cut it was. He accurately located the cervical joints, sunk his knife in, applied a bit of pressure, and the parts he wanted were speared by his fork.

The tense silence of the first course was followed by a more sumptuous hush, filled with the murmur of chewing teeth and smacks of delectation. Katanga, enjoying the delicious roasted kid, had followed Don Rufo's attentive precautions and vigilant cares with interest. He understood the man's admirable vocation. And he praised it without mincing words, praise that brought forth an approving murmur, but nothing more, because they continued eating. It didn't matter to him. His praise remained concrete, like Juvenal's words, formulated in the Roman countryside, facing the *pinguissimus haedulus*. He knew

that the cook is taught, while the *rotissier* is born. The fact had
just been corroborated. He'd never before observed such a meticulous ritual of vigilance, and seasoning, and the thousand
little culinary solicitudes necessary to glorify the beast. In a
century of electric stoves, Taylorized ovens, and pressure-cook-
ers fitted with manometers, how wonderful to confirm the efficacy of intuition, touch, and grace! What a pleasure to certi-
fy the existence of these innate qualities! How flattering to see
Don Rufo triumph in the succulent minutiae of his art! In risible contrast, his imagination conjured the vision of a group of
cuisiniéres brevetées in a French culinary institute. Unbearable.
He scattered the vision with a convulsive shake of his head.
And in a transcendent anger which none of them understood,
he sent the figments off to fry asparagus . . .

"What's wrong, Katanga?" asked Don Rufo kindly.

"Nothing. I was just lost in my thoughts of praise for your
expert preparation of this delicious food."

"Exactly: delicious food."

"A true delicacy!"

". . . the delicious morsels you've gifted us with, brought to
my imagination a clutch of disgraceful cooks, the kind who
stuff the magazines with extravagant recipes that only provoke
indigestion. Their intrusive presence irritated me. So I gave
them a thrashing! That's all . . ."

"Oh, I was thinkin' maybe . . ."

"Not at all!"

"The way that you fight with ghosts. That's good . . ."

"Of course. And now I'm going to quarrel with you, for
that very reason: for not having stuffed us before, every day,
with roasted goat. When one possesses the expertise that you
demonstrate in slaughtering them, dressing them, and roasting them, it's a crime to have allowed us to subsist on blended, compounded, canned foods, and the like. I'm a frugivorous
vegetarian. Not exclusively. Not fanatical. It's true that I prefer
the diminutive brains of a walnut to the brains of a heifer. It's
true that for me there is no egg comparable to an orange: the

stupendous egg of the orchard! But set me in front of a turtle soup, Chicken Marengo, English cured beef, or baby goat, the way Rufo roasts it . . . and you'll see! This is my struggle. To reclaim the pleasures which have been stolen from us. You are a wonder . . ."

"Exactly!"

"A true portentous wonder!"

". . .You've beguiled our palate like the Judge and Captain bamboozled our pockets."

Don Rufo caught the general smile on everyone's face. He turned pale. He remained absorbed for a moment, as if meditatively auscultating the resonance of those concepts. Yes. He understood. Those scoundrels were capable of anything. And he rose to the surface from the depths of suspicion, dragging with him the evidence:

"Swindled! What? How? How much?"

Aparicio and Viejo Amor intervened to soften his surprise. And to dissuade him:

"Don't worry . . ."

"After all . . ."

"After all, nothing! Who introduced you to those men? I did! Then I'm guilty by association. Maybe they'll take me for an accomplice. I've got to clarify the situation. Explain everything!"

"Impossible. What for? . . ."

"Within two hours, they'll be here to pick us up, so we can resume our journey . . ."

The baby was crying. His screams drilling through the walls, piercing the afternoon quiet. There was an indecisive pause. Don Rufo was simultaneously halted by his sense of shame and compelled by his paternal instinct. The double anguish, inhibiting him, showed on his face as his expression moved from opprobrium to desperation. The cries turned harsh, braying. The baby was choking. What to do? He was choking, too.

Aparicio took him by the elbow:

"Don't worry," he repeated. "Please, go: take care of your little boy!"

Don Rufo ran as if drunk. Staggering in his ignominy. Frightened. Anxious to return. Terrified that they might all leave without explaining.

When he entered the baby's room, the wailing resounded in his ear like a gunshot. He stumbled. Tormented with nightmares the baby flailed between the sheets. Then he lay still for a few moments, apathetic. It wasn't feeding time yet and so the baby was soon soothed by the rocking of the cradle. And as the outburst ceased, the two sat exhausted, motionless, like a flat-bottomed scow and a rowboat tossed up on the beach of desolation.

He had no idea how drained he really was. Then an intolerable smell forced him to regain his wits. The room stank. The odor of fresh excrement. The heavy stench of dirty rags soaked with urine. Valerian odors of soiled booties and mattress. Plagued by the thought of the swindle, he carelessly unwrapped the baby. He soiled his hands. With the corners of the diaper he dabbed at the child's flaccid buttocks. He rocked it to sleep in his arms. And then he left the room, his normally kind disposition throbbing with anger, the hand that had caressed the baby's yellowy flesh was now a clenched fist.

He found no one on the verandah.

His fellow diners were walking or resting, leaning in the shadows of the hallway. Nonchalantly. Thinking of nothing. With the casual carelessness they had agreed to project; because, in the interim, they had resolved a way to repay Don Rufo and, for his own good, had decided not to mention the matter of the swindle.

There are some men who remain mild until the tongues of hatred turn them wild. Until their passion becomes confused by their hidden, innermost voices. Don Rufo was transfigured. Katanga had seen him this way in another formidable scene: when he had unleashed the pain of being a widower in the lewd furor of that obscene elegy to Jacinta. Love and honor confuse the senses, perturb the conscience, and provoke, in equal measure, groans and paroxysms. Perhaps the same kind of jealousy is present in the knowledge of impending loss. He gathered the men in his gaze. He noticed an air of artifice about them. Something not quite sincere. And he harshly reprimanded them:

"I demand that you tell me how, and for how much, you were swindled by the Judge and the Captain. You won't be leaving here until I know. It's unavoidable. Don't try to trick me."

Longines had the job of answering. His pithy words drove the point home:

"Before anything else, I want to point out three things to you: First, that we lack adjectives to thank you for your hospitality. Second, that we have spent such beautiful days in your company that it would be very difficult to repeat them anywhere else on our tour. And third, that our departure is not forced, but spontaneous, free of reproach; because our longing to spend a week among the mountains has been fulfilled."

"No! You're leaving because of the dirty tricks you've suffered."

"I beg you, not to mention the subject anymore."

"How much did they take you for? I need to know. Tell me . . ."

"But, Don Rufo . . . For what it's worth, it doesn't matter to us at all. To show you that it doesn't make a dent in our wallet, here, help yourself. It's a poor retribution, a mere token of our satisfaction.

He mechanically reached for the roll of bills. But reacting on contact, as if he'd grabbed a bunch of stinging nettles, shoved it back at them:

"Poor retribution! . . . Are you crazy? A big fat wad of cash? . . . Never!"

"Do us the favor."

"No! No! You've been swindled in my house. That's disgraceful. Really despicable. Never!"

Longines beckoned to Aparicio, pleading for him to intercede:

"Allow me, Don Rufo. I'm going to be frank with you. We've not been ripped off inside your house. It happened on the road to Almafuerte. You know that we brought two thousand pesos to pay off the debts of Domitilo Sayavedra. Cash money, like this, go on, take it."

"But, my friend . . ."

". . . look, look, it's legal tender, no lie. Do you remember how those two behaved in your presence? Good. You should've seen how they beat the hell out of me. What hurts most is that they wrested the money from me with their high-handed arrogance. Sacred money, Don Rufo. Money for debts that exist in this area; one only has to look for them, no more. If you agree to engage yourself in this matter, I'll give you the receipt that they handed me and even the serial numbers of the bills that they took from me illicitly. And if you get the money back . . ."

"If I get it? . . . Not a shadow of a doubt. They'll pay it back to the last *centavo*."

". . . I'll leave you our address in case they do. Agreed?"

"Goes without saying. I'm very sorry this happened to you. Be sure."

They were delighted with the arrangement. It was the height of irony. They had succeeded with their counter-swindle and the money was now going to be recovered. They were assured by the powerful moral influence and probity of Don Rufo's character. The others observed their two friends setting him up to take the bait, sarcasm crouched in wait behind each pupil. And they laughed, smiled, teasingly.

Now they just had to make it official. After a perfunctory meeting Katanga drafted the agreement transferring ownership from Juan Aparicio to Don Rufo so that he would hold the power to demand repayment. He copied the Justice of the Peace's "receipt." He transcribed the serial numbers of all the bills. And then he handed over the document:

Don Rufo:

If the money returned to you by those two rascals—the Police Captain of Amboy and the Justice of the Peace of La Cruz—is not sufficient to pay off Domitilio Sayavedra's debts—and it won't be—please resign yourself to accepting it as a donation, from all of us, so that you may be able to afford your little boy's hernia operation as soon as possible.

The cars had now been waiting for a while.

Upon handing him the papers, Katanga pointed to the sealed envelope:

"Don't open it yet. It contains instructions, addresses, etcetera."

"Must be secret orders, eh? Like the ones they give to sailors, to open when they're out on the high seas? Hmmm . . . you're up to something."

"Yes, Don Rufo. As you say . . . out on the high seas. When your memory of us sinks into the depths."

"That's good. I congratulate you for making such a sweetheart out of me . . ."

Their farewell turned into a seditious riot that was intended to dispel the emotions they were choking back. Each man's face was a mirror, deliberately fogged to obscure the kind of sadness in which laughter quickly turns to wailing.

Wishing him well, Lon Chaney could only say:

"Believe me: I got so wonderfully used to this tranquil, ancestral environment that I lament leaving."

"Nice of you to see it that way. When a fine horse is fond of a place, it misses even the thistles . . ."

Katanga tried, in vain, to hide himself behind a smokescreen of phlegm. His unflappable nature failed the test. His grimaces, his hands, nervously gave him away. When it was his turn, they embraced. Nothing more. But there was a bitter smile in each throat, as it swallowed the furtive tears which slid down inside.

They pulled out onto the road, the riotous motors shredding the rustic miracle of the well-ripened afternoon.

A beating of rainbow-hued wings above the divinities of the countryside.

Don Rufo slipped down a well of crystalline silence.

And so the *caterva* departed, both sad and happy, like seven flickering flames.

It was then, in that critical, delicate moment—when the former reality becomes remembrance—that a whispering voice was heard:

Alles in der Welt lässt sich ertragen,
Nur nicht eine Reihe von schönen Tagen.

It was Longines, carefully reciting Goethe's verse:

All may be endured in this world,
Except a series of beautiful days.

....

RUMIPAL:

As they drove up to the boarding house in Rumipal, the land-scape resembled a Japanese painting. Moiré of watered silk. The hills like silken corduroy. Silken lamé the firmament. They grew quiet, admiring it while the drivers carried in their lug-gage. Without exchanging words, they found their tired indi-vidual wills unified by the natural beauty. And they bathed in it, idealistically. They'd travelled tired and uncomfortable, car-ried along dusty routes, heads and stomachs unsettled, spin-ning with emotion and the excess of the midday meal with Don Rufo.

They were standing there gazing at the scenery when the landlady approached. She scrutinized them from behind, backlit and silhouetted. And casting an eye on the drivers she seemed to recriminate them for the look of the guests they had delivered. She was a fifty-something woman, a meager thing, with a clear expression and languid smile. One of those women punished by experience who, after countless disappointments suffered, become suspicious of their own shadow. Attenuating her antipathy and lack of confidence for business's sake, she did what she could to put on a friendly face:

"If it's a view you want, you've come to the right place."

"Certainly. The picture is good, not to mention the frame."

"And the glass? Where did you hide the glass?"

"Indeed. Even the glassy water is beautiful; because the landscape is inverted in the lake."

Following the way she pointed, they turned around. Hills. Coves. Meadows. Chalets. Yachts. Beaches made for swimming. The retaining walls of the dam. Here, there, everywhere, the view inspired one to discover some new unexpected grace. To bask in nature's manifold charms.

Afterward, she herded them along to their rooms with subtle skill.

"We don't offer too many comforts. But I see that you've brought your own folding cots. Congratulations. Here, three of you can stay in this room. That's right, but in your case, since you've got no baggage, you pay upfront for the room."

"No baggage! And what about the cots?"

"Don't get upset. They don't count. Besides, it's the house rule."

"Fine. Here. We'll pay you right now."

Dinner was soon ready. But no one was hungry for it. Seated on the patio, a few steps from the kitchen, the heavy smells from the food and spices cooked in lard made them gag. Everything they'd eaten at lunch, not perfectly digested thanks to the hustle and bustle of the trip, had left them with little appetite. All except Dijunto and Viejo Amor, the only ones who weren't suffering from cramps, gas, heaviness, nausea, rumbling in the guts, flatulence, or a whole mess of discomforts at once. They simply had no interest in eating. When the maid arrived, announcing that dinner was served, their reluctance spiraled down into laconic negativity:

"We're not eating."

"Bring us some tea . . ."

". . . Well steeped . . ."

". . . with lemon."

"Peppermint tea for me."

"Me, too."

The landlady came right away to see what was wrong. She was incredulous. Tired of kicking out guests who ate without paying, she couldn't now believe that there were men who paid without eating:

"What! You're not having dinner? But you've already paid!"

"That's right, ma'am. Tea. Nothing else."

She was amazed to discover that such people even existed. Feigning the annoyance of a hostess scorned, she teased them:

"Oh, what a shame. Y'see, I'd prepared a chicken stew for you all, and some squid paella, a nice stuffed roast, caramel flan . . ."

Longines and Fortunato nudged one another. It was a scandalous lie and they knew it. She recognized the moment as a splendid opportunity to show off her boarding house; to offer a token gesture of friendliness; and she took full advantage of it with perfect, premeditated perfidy.

While she was talking, Aparicio leaned back in his seat, trying to scrape the chair legs on the rough mosaic floor. He had an explosive fart ready to let fly out the gates . . . And he found no other solution than to let it out while making noise with the chair. Katanga perceived his intention . . . and then the fetid smell. He shot him a sidewise glance. And shook his head, unbelieving. But, as he did so, Katanga suddenly felt his own insides seize up. He sat bolt upright. Bubbles of acid were rising from his stomach, ascending up his throat, the acrid taste threatening to make him retch. He made a sort of hiccup. The sour burning passed. He firmly tensed his core, auscultating the insides of his gut, a yogi uneasily contemplating his navel.

The tea soothed and relieved their indigestion, and they soon felt better. All except Katanga. His intestines whistled continuously. Food and juices now emulsified, new spurts of acrid gas were unleashed whenever he moved, sonorously wounding the intestinal plumbing as they expanded. And he stammered:

"All this gas rumbling in my guts is killing me. It sounds like

I swallowed a syrinx, and an abdominal demon is blowing a
Stravinskian rhapsody . . . It's useless, always the same: the price
of pleasure is the loss of contentment. (*This sentence sounded so
nice to him that he progressively augmented his voice.*) Since time
immemorial, man has kept up a heated feud with nature. Instead of obeying its precepts, we jokingly skirt them. Worse
yet, we mockingly contradict nature, setting up our most foolish caprices in opposition to its wisdom. (*His peroration now
stretched out into robust affirmations.*) Thus we also pay. The human lifespan is increasingly limited, to the point where any day
now we're going to end up being born dead . . . Ancient philosophy, deep in its conceptual opulence, understood the science of life. It awarded the key of happiness to simplicity and
prudence. It charted the course, leading the way with the blazon of its actions. But we humans are giddy ne'er-do-wells. To
the Greeks' *méden ágan*, to the Latins' *nihil nimis*, to the *nothing in excess* of temperance, we offer the formidable apothegm:
'Better to burst than to leave a scrap uneaten.' And instead of
learning to discover the natural comforts provided by the sun,
the air, and the tutelary gods, instead of enjoying nature, we
give it a saucy nod and wink, dizzy with drugs and cocktails;
cloistered and benumbed with comfort, we commit a whole series of heresies against nature . . . heresies in the purest sense of
the word. (*He smiled at Viejo Amor and continued on his verbal
jag.*) Considering all this, it isn't strange that many hygienists
and physiologists scream themselves hoarse proclaiming that
we must cast our minds back to the past in order to cast a new
die for our existence. That we must return to primitivism and
isolate ourselves completely from the deleterious flattery of the
present life. Charles Richet is one of them. In 1913 he was already trumpeting the so-called 'caveman diet' so that we might
save the body from the many evils that enter through our eager, open mouths."

So speaking, Katanga's speech ended abruptly in a loud, throaty burp. He demurely raised his napkin to his lips, but when
he tried to continue, Longines had co-opted the conversation:

"As you can see: the evils that beset us invade through the mouth ... So of course it makes sense that sometime later they conveniently slide out in sealed, cylindrical 'cans' ... Nudist cans, vegetarian cans, dietetic cans ... Authentic, natural tins of putrid preserves. It's all the same if you wish to dedicate your time to canning up the 'caveman diet.'"

In spite of their collective languor, the sap of humor began to flow in each mouth.

Aparicio made the most of the moment:

"Bull's-eye. Ten points. The thing is, Longines speaks in installments. Slow and terse. But when he speaks: he settles it."

Katanga was, indeed, settled, the thread of his truncated discourse snipped and tied.

They went to bed early amid orders shouted at the servant and the clatter of silverware and dishes. They trusted that a good night's sleep would restore the normality of their functions and the function of their normality. But the house beds were rickety and filthy. The rooms foul and stifling. Mosquitoes everywhere. If they closed the door to the patio they choked on the fetid legacy of a thousand previous travelers. If they left them open, they suffered from the dazzling glare of the exterior lights. Unanimous in their annoyance, each man fretted impatiently to himself. No wonder. After a long busy day, the mind remains alert in the night, like an anxious spectator at a movie theater, awaiting the tame, amiable unfolding of the scheduled programming of dreams. When the show begins badly, the temper is strained. It moves out to pace the hall of wakefulness with its multitudinous nerve endings. It protests against the light, the noises, the mosquitoes. And, protesting, the same nerves founder in the deep disappointment of the sleepless night.

Dijunto—who lay spread-eagled, trying to identify the regional tone of the landlady's Spanish—gave a sudden, violent shaking. His sheets flew up like a skittish ghost. And he sat, half-naked, on the foot of the bed, investigating with his flashlight the folds and tiny buttons of the bed-ticking, the loops and grooves of the rubber mattress. The evidence sent chills crawling up and down his spine. His folding cot was out in the corridor. He took up his pillow and blanket. Without saying a word, he crossed the patio and the garden and went to the small lakefront beach a short distance from the boarding house. There he set up the cot, spread out his blanket, and lay down to sleep.

Lying next to Aparicio, Fortunato was a fat lazy poltroon of implacable bonhomie. He was already on the verge of sleep when a sudden request awoke him completely.

"*Che:* hand me Dijunto's flashlight."

Adiós implacable bonhomie!

"Come find it yourself," he responded, justifiably angered at being awoken.

Aparicio got up. He vengefully pointed the sudden bright light right at Fortunato's face, lighting up his bulbous nose threaded with wine-dark tubercles. Moving the cone of electric light across Dijunto's abandoned mattress he noticed a swarm of bedbugs. Startled, he ran back to his own bed. Lifting up the pillow, the skin of his neck, back and thorax automatically recoiled and tingled.

"Get up! This is disgusting! They're going to eat us alive!"

The alarm was raised and they got up immediately. Lights on, they carefully inspected the lamentable lack of housekeeping. Sputtering with indignation they marched out of the room, each man with his folding cot tucked under his arm.

The landlady watched the procession from her chair on the patio where she sat rocking away her menopause.

Indifferent.

Married to a miner in Santander, they had moved from the Immigrant's Hotel to settle in Córdoba. Disappointment! It was a different kind of mining, the procedures were unfamiliar, the miners hard to deal with. They couldn't tolerate the foremen or the rough conditions in the quarries. Calera, Yocsina, Malagueño: *adiós!* They resolved to start their own operation. Partnered with another couple, amid the teeming chaos of broken stone, they grappled with excavations of mica, asbestos, calcium carbonate. Without any financial success. Oh, the costs—freight, storage, and middlemen! Someone lured them away from that with a plan to prospect for tungsten and magnesium in Calamuchita. Bust! The only payoff from that operation was striking a unexpected vein of limestone in Los Cóndores. Working with the owner of the estate, they began to save money. But she'd grown weary of their grinding life in miserable tents, ramshackle tin-roof cabins, and adobe huts with thatched roofs. So they set up a boarding house in El Quebracho. He remained faithful to her. But working with stone makes a man's life multifaceted; hardens it, files it down until it's all sharp edges and needlelike points. It makes the scab of civilization lift and crack like the appalling surface of a slag pond. Until the miner is mimetically transformed. Turned into stone as well. With geological flesh. With a telluric soul. And with a stony spirit, impenetrable amid the solitude of the petrified desert and its environs.

The landlady watched the parade from her chair where she sat rocking away her menopause. She was not terribly concerned by their midnight exodus. She knew about the bedbugs; but she also knew that when folks are truly tired there are no bedbugs:

Lazy drifters are always the worst: the picky, demanding ones! If they'd ever experienced the fatigue of walking among the craggy broken scrub lands, of working them, of burning out there in the sun like my husband and I did, they'd sleep all right, yes, right back inside on my beds.

Their attitude smacked of insolence. And, firm in her loathing, instead of feeling any embarrassment about the bedbugs, she simply let them do what they liked. She was not one for noble gestures. Life had stolen from her the essential motives which justify the hard work required to live it: wifely voluptuousness, motherly tenderness. Why toil so much, then? Why bend over backwards for the sake of living? Business, if prosperous, did nothing more than pave the way to a death she did not fear. If it went badly, perhaps it would hasten the outcome already planted in her *melancholia menstruatio-suppressa*: to do away with herself. Why, then, bend over backwards just for the sake of living? Her clear unwavering eyes searched for the men. They were camping on the beach.

"Now that'll sure teach them a lesson . . ." she spluttered. "Idiots!"

And her usual hypocrisy compounded with genuine spite, her withered lips twisted into a scornful grin.

How did their seven cots, arrayed along the lakeshore, come to be transformed into airships? None of them knew. They perceived the motorized nature of their enigma only after they were already spin-sliding vertiginously along, crewed by Medusas, Gorgons, and Erinyes. The turquoise water turned to violet blood and the night-time sky became a purulent dawn. There, within a vaporous nest of noisy swallows, the Vortex opened its mouth and raised its hand. Hand or candelabra? The number of the apocalypse: from atop each one of its seven fingernails a muezzin enthralled their hearts like a magnet. And then the mother-of-pearl windows slid closed. The glaze of each pane visible in the reflected light. Neo-lux arteries. Viscera of flexible glass. And in the background, behind a phosphorescent nimbus: the Magnetic Titan, the Benevolent Monster, the Devilish God. Three in one: mercurial body; spectral soul; larval volition. The hand tensed into a cataclysm of waves, stars, and celestial bodies, and wrung out the taut silken lake and the stained velvet air. Whisk and froth. Quirt and saddle. And they fell into the vacuum of a deep box canyon, next to the frou-frou of the foam, the stars that pricked the verisimilitude of the senses . . . They spun headlong, stunned, blinded by panoptic vision. Like a slew of sleepwalkers. Expeditious sleepwalkers. Sliding along on seven starry wheels. Upon seven exhalations from strange sleeping bodies.

To where? To where the where becomes tangled in the abstruse qualities of Goodness. Until when? Until the when is condensed in the diaphaneity of Evil. They had grown. Homo septuplex. *Im-*

possible to discern the seven dimensions of the spirit! Each one of them was seven times the stature of his Virtue and his Vice: breath; fever; pendulum; scepter; saber; impulse; flame. What better way to become intimate with phantom dignity? They were gigantic. Cro-Magnon. Super-anthropomorphized. The viscous, carbuncular pituitary gland truculently preserved in the nonexistent serenity of the forehead . . . "This way. This way." A roguish interpreter carrying on with a negotiator's exaggerated pomp. A witch brandishing a witch's talisman. They shouted panaceas and exorcisms. For what? Dissolved potions . . . Shapeless martingales . . . Forward! And forward flew the mast with its weathervane of golden oriole wings. The erect lighthouse phallus with its aerodynamic glans and its luminous meatuses. The pergola-gallows where sighs are hanged. And the roster of eloquent orators trained in Satan's schoolhouse . . . Seeing them arrive they emerged from their lairs: Arcturus of Krakatoa. Canopus of Vesuvius. Betelgeuse of Pelée. Pollux of Etna. Columba of Hekla. Regulus of Mauna Loa. And Pisces of Cotopaxi. Frenetic, after the monastic pleasures of solitude. Enfeebled, after ruminating shadows on their palate of fire. And each one brandished his ebony cane, to lead them through the ghost towns of death. To tighten the springs with prizes from the carnival of the dead. To walk among philomuses who crack open the rarefied atmosphere with arpeggios, dense with emptiness, concealing incoercible symbols in the same way the desert sands bury mastabas . . . "Psstt! Don't you hear us calling?" They couldn't have heard a thing. When it came to feigning death, they were nothing but rank amateurs. There in the great beyond, they possessed the deaf-mute brains of newborn babies. The strident booming voices merely ruffled the plumed torches that now replaced their hair. An insignificant detail. Then, the last resort: a blow to their weak, translucent bellies. The macabre gong released its packs of ululating hounds. And the phantasmal horde drove them to the very mouth of the Vortex . . . Only then did they begin to wither and fall away! And that was the final episode of their first karmic odyssey: because the life of death begins there, flush with agony, at the very parapet of mystery . . . They could never have imagined the

*abject lavishness of their reception in the Great Receptacle. It was a
superstructure of plague and morbidity. Carved from the living
rock of all cadavers, boasting the altitude of the future and the amplitude of the centuries. Upon carpets of rotting chancres and
brains; between walls festering with death rattles, screams of madmen, groans of women in labor; upon the great table where worn-
out crimes pant in exhaustion and epidemics spread wide their legs
like prostitutes: there! . . . Oh, there! Caresses of scorpion and leper.
Embraces of cobra and tetanus. Hyena laughter and cackling para-
noia. Confections of hepatic secretions and bonbons of gangrenous
arthritis. Such kindly hecatombs! "Help yourselves to a cocktail of
hemoptysis." Such deferential Cataclysms! "Taste this vermouth of
septicemia with some hor d'oeuvres of prepyloric cancer." They tasted it all. It was the will of the Magnetic Titan, the Benevolent
Monster, the Devilish God . . . Immediately the air was populated
with a tremendous dissonance. Schoenberg's baton raised to the
Nth power. Then the Sun rose vibrating its yellow E. Venus its D
flat. Saturn its G flat. Mercury its F sharp. Jupiter its G. The
moon its D. And Mars its G flat. They staggered on drunkenly.
Singing like Italian bricklayers on payday. Warbling phlegmatical-
ly. The disorder became sublime. The stellar harmonies nestled in
shamefully, like a faithful husband slumming in a whorehouse.
They slowly sauntered in, quite unruffled. Bringing up the rear,
the Earth's F natural . . . In one chromatic sweep, the baton
launched it. The missing note! Thus began the great crazy saraband of the scruffy stars, of the celluloid asteroids hurtling headlong! The angelic choirs which heard Pythagoras before the angels
bawled and tore at themselves like a frenetic jazz band. They were
playing the "Seven Last Words" from Haydn's Oratorio with hints
of Gershwin. And the faun's festival erupted just as it always did.
The Seven Sorrows of Mary began to fence in the Seven Infants of
Lara. Jealous, the Seven Against Thebes attacked the Seven Sleepers
of Ephesus, who were making sweet love to Persephone. Their bellies burst open mystically, and they were forced to dance a decapitated ballet with the Seven Deacons of Jerusalem. And they continued thus, magnificoes of macabre insolence . . . The Theban street*

gang were bragging loudly when, in full hurly-burly, they crashed into the Seven Deadly Sins. Say good-bye to the spear of Ajax, son of Telamon, the shield of embattled Pelion Achilles, and the sharp-edged astuteness of Odysseus! They made seven grimaces, seven swaggers, seven winks. And all the heavenly drag queens gave in to their charm, setting aside weapons and battle armor. Hermaphrodites dressed as men with women's names. Genuine Afro-machos. Unbelievable she-members. And then the most scabrous Olympian saturnalia—solar, martial, hermetic, lunar, and Venusian—ever known! Pride with the iron of Mars. Lechery with the copper of Venus. Wrath with the mercury of Hermes. Envy with the silver of the moon. Gluttony with the tin of Jupiter. Sloth with the lead of Saturn. Avarice with the gold of the Sun . . . All of it melted down into the spasm of the Cosmos. In the heavenly orgasm. In the chilled astonishment of the soul. And there were rains of imprecations. Hailstorms of salutations. Blizzards of orations. Crotales, cytisus: Evohé! Soma, semen: Alleluia! Penis, opium: Hosanna! And to the victor of the antipode: Banzai! Banzai! . . . They were bewildered. Corrupted. Such seeming corruptorium corruptori had transformed their sense of shame into zeal: Bravo! Bravo! Bravísimo! And they were mixed into the various, gregarious, eccentrically slovenly Lupercalian lupanaria . . . Oh, the Jesuitical depravation of all things pure, spotless, and true! Now they were sardonic little hobgoblins. Sardanapalus rapt in his glazed silken hobgoblinopolis. Hobgobbleaningsardanappallingsadismindfully . . . Oh, the sharp elasticity of the honest dead who tell no tales! The chromatic symphony of the supposed dead! The rhythmic calligraphy of those who played dead! Yes: they observed it well, observing themselves. It was the critical moment. The dead consciences of the world were rotting away. Crimson crimes. Yellow betrayals. Mucilaginous miseries. Boiling here. Boiling there. Boiling, boiling everywhere. And they trooped in, one after another, alongside the Seven Deadly Sins, in immediate macabre succession, through the feverish secret entrance which runs between passion and vice: in the underlying agitation which displaces ruination in order to locate infamy . . . How glorious it would have been to remember! To *bathe in the memory of the vital course of time! But the amateur dead do not remember. They move about with stately step like strangely majestic plant-beings. With the lethargic steps of rheumatic poplars, in obsequious subjugation to irrigation canals. With the antediluvian sadness of elephants sick from phylloxera. How glorious it would have been to remember! ... Seven quivering javelins lancing the bull's-eye of seven memories. Liquid impact. In succession, their adventure brought them to the banks of seven rivers Styx, then seven lagoons. Then they heard the menacing voice: "We shall see! Who do you think you are? Get to work! Peel off the blood-encrusted forelocks and dust-choked rosettes from that suicide battalion ... Blue temples livid with purple forelocks! Lily white chests with gloomy rosettes! ... What? Tired? Overwhelmed? Good! That's better! Now remove the neckties from all those hanged men in the martyrology. Diadems of light turned into hempen slipknots. Rope neckties with the knots pointing up! Their lean, dry tongues swung like pendants! Uuuh! ... " Rasping effluvia. Virulent ecstasies. They were caught inside a malvaporous climate with emotions rising. And suddenly still, the mob! Like seven Heracleidae twisted into a terrifying marauding septenarium, legions of corrupting captains, obscene saints, and great cowardly leaders, they drove their capsules through the seven wonders of horror. What a strange anatomy of clouds, of stones, and creatures! Clouds, stones, and creatures impregnated by phantoms. Superfetation in the womb of death. Abominable abortions of slobbering laughter and tearful floods of formalin. Bearded sunsets in the beardless youth of high noon. And the lowbrow athlete with colossal loins plunging his sex organ to slurp up the soul of a flapper with delicate ankles and bouncy bangs ... What horrendous tasks they contemplated! A thousand archimandrites, their guts and hides rolled up, looting and skinning millions of skeletal corpses, assassinated, dried and salted. Putrid fumes of ancient soot and smoked carrion. A thousand bishops, resplendent in their miters and dalmatics, dressed the tumescent entrails of scrupulous scrofulous millions. A thousand Salvation Army generals enlivened the task with guitars and concertinas, singing: Alleluia, Alleluia, to* the Savior! ... And from amid the moaning and groaning emerged swarms of sparks, hornets, and horseflies. And amid the crash and clamor of that seething frenzy of death, the souls, oh! The souls were fleeing—diaphanous squirrels—from their skeletal cages ... How happy, blessed ceux qui meurent sans l'avouer! The only ones dignified and worthy. The only ones raised in the great vault of indifference. They knew it. And there they corroborated it. There, where all corroboration is the credential of definitive disappointment ... Oh, yes! One must revile the snobbery of death, always renewed by the feverfew of glory. Those who are truly resurrected are the ones who prefer the perfect oblivion offered by the illustrious vulgarity of death. The ones who go plunging into it, swimming submerged, without anyone noticing their movements, below the sticky waves of sloe, latrine, and dextrine. Intoxicated by their dismay, they complete their odyssey. A lugubrious odyssey of Oneiromantics. Of drunken hypnotists. Of the nymphs of Nephele, those cloud walkers who detonate clouds of liquid pitch, until discovering, below the most diminutive hem of the dream, the seed which will germinate destiny. And, meanwhile, they cry because they know that jocosity is the least absurd form of self-loathing ... The seven beasts of the fabulous monster called Endriago "made flesh" conquering their sentiments and resentments, thunderously huffed and puffed their sarcasm. The preemptory voice of the Magnetic Titan, the Benevolent Monster, the Devilish God was now a flaccid quaver, sinking down into itself, into the glug-glug-glug of pus. The infernal tumult was softened by hurricanes of somniferous ether. Downpours of bromodiethylacetylene. The horizon sank to ruin. Proximity became wasteland. And each curse, a swamp of dreams ... There were seven dreamlike swamps! ... Where are the metaphysical derricks? Where are the abyssal winches? Where are the everlasting life preservers? ... They kept their predawn watch in the swamp of their disaster. Conscience was a lucid viscera. They clutched it in hand, like a boomerang, to hurl it toward the eternal principles so that it might return, now dead from truth. But truth does not fly: it drags itself along. And weak from hunger they devoured the lucid viscera of their own conscience ... And they *continued to cultivate the horror just as orchids are cultivated. All was now winged and perplexing. An inoperative tenderness softened the heart and the trochanter of the dead bones. And they were compressed into a very soft paste like the adagio sostenuto—sustained D minor—of the "Clair de Lune." Because the Moon floated amidst their fright. Because the Moon remained in the permanence of the enigma. THE MOON! THE MOON! The Moon! . . . And they died and sank into the depths of space . . . But was there space? Yes! Space was time conquered. The abstract reality. The desolation of the Self . . . And there was a joyous sighing along the borders of silence!*

Dawn found them convulsed, peevish. Not fully awake but still sunk abysmally deep in their respective fragments of nightmare. A compact nightmare which assembled, in one single horror, the aliquot aspect of fear. An obtuse nightmare which even now kept the subconscious dozing upon the chilly terror of a mattress of mystery.

Their flesh was slow to awaken. They stretched lazily, their eyes still swollen with visions, almost blind to the dawning day. They were on the very edge of the sensorial slopes: on the summit of the isthmus which separates the psychic world from the material.

The sun, skating on the lake, slipped and crashed into their faces. It danced on their eyelids with feet of gold. Yet, fraught with such drowsy bewilderment they did not open their eyes!

They hung in that intermediate stage between subconscious and awareness. Without perceiving anything outside themselves. Clouded over by the horrendous inner-phantasmagoria. The bad humor broke out right away. The skeleton key of scintillating sunshine obfuscated their instincts. Reason, bedazzled, went up in flames. And Katanga, Aparicio, Viejo Amor, and Fortunato suddenly found themselves tangled up in a violent, dyspeptic brawl.

An eruptive instant. Inexplicable. Like the explosion of four tanks of compressed anguish. Like the blind obstinacy of four brute forces. Like the delirious fury of four mortal enemies. Luckily, immediate intervention from the others managed to absorb this reciprocal aggression. And the blows and punches got tangled up in the defensive commotion of pillows and blankets.

"Calm down, please, calm down!"

"What's going on? For God's sake!"

"Are you crazy? Have you no shame?"

They were drunk tired with restlessness. Trembling. Sullen. Still suffering the perturbations of the uncanny episode. With neither insanity nor shame. Excited. Still convulsed. Each now exploring the carnal reality of their internal world. Perforating the groggy torpor of their understanding. Slowly coming to, finding themselves on the lakeshore.

Little by little, the foggy memory of their nightmare vanished. Amnesia sponged off their dream-dusted brows. And their eyes looked out on the world.

They were bewildered, confused, forced to confront their mutual outrage. Each one tasted in his mouth the cloying paste of grease and wine. Nausea. Deep in his mind, each one felt the traces of some absurd illness. Sadness. And now calm, the illogical perspectives of incipient insanity, the clumsy excesses of sleep's inebriation, blew away with the cold north wind of morning.

The landlady had been crossing the patio outside the boarding house when the scuffle erupted. Her clear unwavering eyes looked through the tangled branches of the orchard. Reaching the beach itself, she was pleased to confirm the certainty of her prediction. Had she not, after all, foreseen the moon's curse? Hadn't she told herself?

Now that'll teach 'em a lesson. Idiots!

Well, all right: now they were properly chastened. And seeing them after the terrifying crisis, mired in the stagnant lagoons of apathy, her lank smile wrinkled into a puckered pout of mocking pity.

She'd known it. And in a soft, quiet voice said:

"The moon . . . last night . . . exactly the third day after the start of the full moon! . . . During the most violent period of its malign, poisonous influence . . . To sleep outside! . . . Fools! Idiots!"

Her guests went straggling back to their rooms. Mute. Listless. Their wan faces peaked and drawn. They put down their things and settled themselves on the verandah. Longines then called her over.

"We're hungry. Could you please serve us seven full breakfasts?"

"Right away. I've just brought some delicious butter from town. You've got to try it."

Indeed. It was the only really good thing in the house to eat. The block of butter had a creamy pureness, the fragrance of a fresh morning. They seemed to be spreading sunshine across the home-baked bread. They munched away with eager appetites. Little by little, the meal refreshed their bodies, providing them with warmth and energy. But, suddenly, as if they had all been hexed, they rushed for the toilets. Their urgency was brazenly comical but quickly resulted in a glorious relief.

At first there was a deliberately strangulated silence. Afterward, a kind of comfortable laxity. Why speak? Why dissect emotions?

When the landlady came to clear the table, they sat back and stretched out in smug, nonchalant satisfaction. Only Dijunto, Longines, and Aparicio showed a different spirit. Alert. Expectant.

"I've noticed. You've had a bad night. You, too! . . . Outside, the moon . . ."

"Inside, the bedbugs . . ."

"Between the bedbugs and the moon, always better to choose the bedbugs."

"No question, between a mild itching and a psychic disturbance . . ."

"Oh, you're fine!"

"How am I fine? Can't I speak for myself?" Katanga joined

the chatter, chiding Aparicio. "Our hostess is right. The moon's influence, especially when it's waxing and waning, is not some phony superstition. It's a proven fact. And I didn't realize it last night. Or I would've never been so stupid as to sleep out there. Out there in the open, where, in addition to being bathed in full, direct moonlight—basically, the electrical and magnetic discharges that disturb our cenesthesia—the moon, which prompts the rising and falling of the tides, creates a poisonous fog that enshrouds the sleeping body. Our hostess is right. Bedbugs are preferable to the moon."

"For my part, I think just the opposite."

"Obviously, Dijunto. You're accustomed to the open life in the countryside. You enjoy—how shall I say?—the moon's friendship. And instead of making you crazy, it swaddles you in its trust. But, to us, who see it differently, who offend the moon with our presumption . . . Didn't you used to put your hens to brood during the first quarter?"

"Exactly. So they incubate successfully: the new moon."

"And shouldn't you make your wine under the waning moon?"

"I wouldn't know. I've always bought it already made."

"If you had, you would've also discovered that, in that phase, the fermentation is marred by the moon's nefarious influence upon the yeast. It's a very well-known fact that in matters of planting, harvesting, fertilizing, and pruning, gardeners and ranchers are guided by the lunar almanac. Well, the same influence has repercussions upon human beings. Vertigo, hysteria, sleepwalking, are influenced by the effluvia of our great satellite. Science has not yet specifically stated its expert opinion. But the moon's influence is real. In the same way that a fisherman's catch will spoil faster in the moonlight than under the blazing sun, the nerves of both men and the sea catch fire more easily below the mantle of Selene. There is something magical in that which I've tried to elucidate through the concomitancy of my profession. In vain. It's a sublime occultism. Nobody discovers the trick. I've read everything I could get my hands on.

From some sixteenth century volumes—one: *On the Secrets of the Moon*, by the physician Antoine Mizauld, and another by Dr. Jouvert, from Montpellier—as well as other scientific authorities like Manuret and Bruce, up to even the most penetrating essays by physicists, astrologers, and psychiatrists. No luck. They just lump this vital enigma under the trite heading of folklore. And the worst thing is that you can't laugh at it . . ."

"You're right. Consider our own experience last night."

"Our experience, Longines, has a lunar depth but a somatic base. There were various underlying causes: gluttony, traveling, yesterday's indigestion. Our entire vegetative nervous system was thrown into confusion. The nightmare, as a consequence, was the product of a disturbance in the cerebral balance. A kind of delirium through intoxication, which brusquely awakens, in the full inertia of sleep, the force of terror. There's nothing inherently dangerous about a beach. But . . ."

Katanga stopped talking. The landlady was nodding her head gravely:

"I knew it . . . Oh, the moon! . . . And just last night! . . . Exactly the third day after the start of the full moon! . . . In the most virulent period of its malign, poisonous influence! . . . What folly to sleep outside!"

Aparicio and Viejo Amor suddenly stood up:

"We're leaving. If not, you two lunatics are going to ruin us, too."

Insidious, tenacious, the landlady pursued them with her words:

"Say what you please. But don't cut your hair or beard when the moon is waning; you'll end up bald and beardless. And make sure you don't trim your nails any other day besides Monday, which is the moon's day. That way you'll spare yourselves toothaches and headaches. And be sure not to . . ."

Forty minutes later they returned, beaming with delight.

"We've come to propose a fantastic outing for the day. We've found a boat and an excellent captain. For only thirty measly mangoes we'll get to see it all: the lake, the dams, the power plant. If you like, we can have lunch on board or on one of the islands. It's a great opportunity to disinfect our shaken collective memory."

Apathetic, they stood listening as Aparicio unrolled his proposition. But his final sentence made their eyes light up and mobilized their wills *ipso facto*. A splendid idea! A marvel of psychological marksmanship! Giddy with sudden enthusiasm they all clamored with approval:

"Splendid. Of course!"

"Right away. Say no more!"

"Longines should bring his valise, just in case . . ."

"We'll eat a light lunch on board."

"No doubt. It's a great opportunity. We've got to disinfect our memory!"

Buoyed by the unanimous sentiment, Aparicio led Lon Chaney and Viejo Amor off to buy the necessities.

The landlady was suspiciously disappointed to hear that they wouldn't be eating lunch there at twelve o'clock. She'd never met such an unbearable band of freewheeling spirits! With real misgivings she went ahead and prepared their picnic lunch of chicken, ham, bread, butter, and mineral water. She felt certain they were going to try to swindle her somehow, perhaps ask her for a partial refund. But no. Her cloud of doubt dissipated when they handed her the money:

"Here, take what we owe you. But we want some more fruit, too, the best you've got."

She went to fetch the fruit, and Lon Chaney saw her shoot a meaningful grimace to a local man who was reading one section of the newspaper, the rest tucked up under his left arm. He shot a concerned glance at Aparicio who boldly turned his head to inspect the man.

"Who? Mr. *Armpit Illustrated* over there? Bah! He doesn't look like anybody's flunkey."

The landlady returned with the fruit, and handed Aparicio

the change. In that moment, a newsboy skittered in, offering his papers for sale. Ragged. Skinny. Filthy. Yellow complexion and black eyes. Aparicio gave him a dose of tenderness, along with a few coins.

"No thanks, kid, don't harass me with newspapers. Educated people don't read papers."

The little boy looked anemic and exhausted. He ignored Aparicio's sarcasm. His black eyes simply opened wide like a cow's. And he stood staring at him, watching him.

"What? You think it's strange I gave you seventy cents? Bah! I work for my money. Reading papers turns people into imbeciles. They lose the habit of thinking for themselves. And that's a very high price to pay, *che!*"

All seven of them now present, they began to depart.

The local fellow with the newspaper, Don Baudilio Pérez, a pharmacist from Rumipal, fixed his eyes on them.

Crossing the threshold, Katanga and Longines turned round to scrutinize him in their turn. Unable to stand it any longer, he returned their contemptuous stares, muttering to himself:

"Insolent riffraff, no doubt about it! Who do they think they are? I'll teach them to show some respect."

And he nervously scratched at his smooth, bald head.

The newsboy was counting his coins.

"Ten ... Thirty ... Forty ... Fifty ... Seventy. Exactly! He wasn't shitting me. Seventy *centavos!*"

Late in the afternoon, the seven excursionists returned, wonderfully revitalized from the sunshine and fresh air. Their skin taut and red. Tingling inside and out, from head to toe.

"What a trip! What landscapes! What colors!"

Their boat tour had been a magnificent outing. Fortunato, especially, demonstrated an almost euphoric loquacity. His habitual concentration had mellowed, flowing out in praise, admiration, and expansive happiness. The afternoon spent sailing along sinuous shorelines, deep coves, and burnished bays had set his whole organism buzzing with intoxication. He felt the same light, carefree sense of accomplishment he'd once experienced in younger days, stirring within his arteries now temporarily de-sclerotized by the noisy merriment. Even his tongue, always curled up tight, now felt silky and free as he rediscovered the long-dead pleasure of laughing.

"What a trip! What landscapes! What colors!"

He carefully reviewed his memory of their outing, because it was necessary to preserve the scenes as a future remedy against lonely, gray, impenetrable days to come. The indigo of the distant waters. The emerald-green alfalfa fields. The violet, vespertine shadows. And those exquisite multicolored mountains, the snowy crepe slopes dissolving into dark scree, the wondrous misty gorges, the pearly gray sunset, and the opaline iridescence of the lake.

"What a trip! What landscapes! What colors!" I could never have imagined a more pleasant sight. So much graceful beauty, so wonderfully well-proportioned. I've just relived so many happy moments of my life. This outing has been a blessing for my senses. Oh, there's nothing like the water. Water in all its flowing glory. The calm composure of the foam. The shoreline reeds like eyelashes, the moss like beautiful hair. Oh, the serene water! Sundays, together with some of the junior employees at the bank, we'd sail a yacht down the Moldova. A yacht whose mainsail sported an enormous percentage sign. Inside a purple border, two zeroes separated by an oblique line. Our heraldic mark! You had to see the jubilant receptions the people staying on the resort islands gave us!"

"That's strange. I've never heard of people anywhere applauding usury."

"There they do. Because people there are raised right. Because a certain percentage isn't usury. Because the well-educated percentage demands it. Because decent lenders and borrowers do exist there. Not like here! Mortgageopolis! Bribeopolis! Not like here! Loanopolis! Usuropolis! Not like here! Debtopolis! Accountopolis! Not like here, where education and good upbringing merit such miserly percentages while usury rakes in such enormous dividends! I know what I'm talking about. I was once a bank manager in Prague."

Now his good mood was broken. Lost in his thoughts, he continued his rambling digression listlessly. His joyful glow snuffed out. Sunk in sullenness, the cadaver of his happiness drawn and quartered.

Viejo Amor tried to cheer him up.

"C'mon, don't be mad. Can't I joke around with you?"

When they reached the patio of the boarding house, Aparicio, who was leading the way, slowed down to wait for the others. Don Baudilio Pérez, the pharmacist, was still there. Pretending to read *La Prensa*. With another newspaper stuck fast beneath his arm. Waiting for something. They stared at him unabashedly. At his scrawny body which seemed to fold in upon itself, as if on hinges; at his round, perfectly bald head balanced nervously atop it. Aparicio paid the man the compliment of noticing him:

"Well, well, take a gander at that: *Mr. Armpit Illustrated* is still here . . ."

Furious, the pharmacist shot straight up out of his chair. His face seemed to boast an inexplicable plurality of prominent features, each one noticeable in its own right, all centered around the wide slash of his mouth, with its crooked, bucked, tobacco-blackened teeth clicking back and forth atop one another, the seeming prelude to some testy remark.

"Well, sir. If you cannot remain calm and explain yourself better . . ."

"I'll be damned! If I—I, A MAN OF BURGOS—have to explain myself to you!"

More than his mouth, his hands did the talking. Bony hands, with prominent knuckles and curved nails. They flitted about in a continuous rising and falling, marking time, punching the downbeat for emphasis. And they created a propitious atmosphere for insult, now folding together as if in prayer, now tracing curves, parallels, angles and spheres to illustrate, conduct and round out his periods.

"Don't get crusty, pal. We really don't get the gist of what you're saying, 'cause you're bein' such a pill. Can you be specific, even for a moment?"

"*Gander... crusty... gist ... pill* ... drunken libertine slang, that's what that is! Oh! The choking stench, I can't breathe!"

The grievous pharmacist crouched down, writhing in his wool jacket, the original black color now shimmered with a filthy green-brown patina. A thousand conjectures might attempt to shed light on his bitterness but there was no discernible explanation, it was really anybody's guess.

"You're angry for no reason. No one's insulted you, sir."

"What do you mean, you've not insulted me?! I'll swear you're up to no good, and may God curse you all to the depths of the everlasting bonfire! And this morning ... and today ... and just now ... with your crooked galley-slave slang?"

"Aaahhh! You're tuna-white mad *porque no chamuyamos comm'il faut*? Can you imagine that, angry at someone because they don't speak the way you do?"

Lon Chaney's franco-lunfardo mockery exasperated the man even more. His dull, pale, sky-blue eyes, with their eternally vague inward gaze, lit up. His switch had been tripped. His whole human machine was set in motion, as if impelled by cogs and wheels and pulleys. Creaking and gnashing, on edge, he broke out talking. Spewing. Holding forth. Dogmatically denouncing the general failure of education in teaching foreign languages, spurious semantics, and those barbarisms which destroy language.

His voice, high and fluty to begin with, gradually descended in tone until it became warm and vibrant. His words glowed with color and brilliance. His self-apotheosis bristled with arrows and sharp, jabbing cadences. None of them standing there listening to him tried to block him out. They respected his enthusiasm and his concepts as he rambled on, gushing forth tumultuously, fanning out, cooing, whispering or upbraiding, astonishing or tormenting.

They all felt some sweet relief as they began to understand

the workings of his mania. His Catilinarian oration even aroused interest. Never, until that moment, had they known it was possible for different people to speak the same language without any mutual understanding! . . . His cascade of pure, correct, antiquated words, *recherché* verbs, archaic adjectives, and strange interjections fell so thick and heavy on their ears that no one was able to get the gist of what he was saying. Instead, they could only respect—as happens in the theatre when one cannot understand the actors' language—the classic flair, the metallic sonority, the dignified inflection, and the haughty tone of his words.

Dijunto tried to understand something but didn't grasp very much. He blinked continuously, displaying the uneasiness he frequently suffered for his ignorance. Pained by his own lack of culture, his social inferiority, the man began to annoy him. And he turned to Aparicio, also fed up by now, so that he might rein in the orator:

"That's fine, old man: that's enough chatter out of you."

"Chatter? *You* be quiet! Scram! Shoo!"

"Exactly, chatter: you're all hot and bothered because I called you '*Armpit Illustrated.*' Because I said that an educated man doesn't read newspapers. Because I speak Lunfardo and enjoy it . . . So what. Why all this grousing? Go fuck yourself! Now you've really pissed us off, you know . . ."

Don Baudilio fell silent. Nothing like a crude shower of rude insults to cut off the piss-stream of presumption. Insults overwhelm and pillory magisterial dignity in such a way that the mouth slams shut as the brain cuts off its flow of thoughts. The pharmacist's pride was crushed; he slouched his shoulders. He seemed now to deplore his squandered lexicographic logorrhea. But he regained his bearing. Smoothing his old Serge jacket, disheveled during his wild harangue, he gently pulled it close around his neck as if it were some elegant cape.

All of them, including the landlady, watched him withdraw, his pomposity already beginning to resurface.

Katanga was the only one who felt sorry for him. Unnecessary pity, certainly; it was the pharmacist who abandoned the forum after his frustrated lecture, with the all the noble bearing of a wounded rhetorician.

"In Colombia and in Ecuador, I've met many of his stripe, infected with Gongoran psychosis. Great savants of our linguistic patrimony who understand precious little about the imperatives of the hour. Men who fail to understand that language is a living thing, not merely cold erudition. Men who speak Spanish with such a chaste, pure style that one is obliged to translate it . . . into modern, everyday language."

"Well, you've got that right . . . on the button," said the landlady. "Don Baudilio does all he can to complicate what's simple. You'll never hear him ask: *Give me half a pound of cheese*, but instead: *Secure for me in a paper and twine package eight ounces of lactic condensation*. He'll never tell you that he's the chief pharmacist, but rather: *I offer solace and consolation to those poor souls racked with grievous ailments* . . . Yesterday, he threw me off by asking for a *Medusan floorcloth*."

"Medusan floorcloth?"

"Yes, gentlemen: *'me-du-san floor-cloth'*. A bunch of nonsense which means, quite simply: a string mop . . ."

Their laughter cleared the way for Dijunto:

"I'm Spanish; we speak the same language, but I'll confess that I can't stand *paisanos* like him. One of them came to General Pico boasting of his family lineage. He'd bought a large estate next to the farm I leased. He came by recommendation from the Argentine Ambassador in Madrid. He began directing the settlement in that area. And that's when the real pain started. It was a total disaster. His workers didn't last. He mistreated them because they didn't understand him. How were they going to understand him? He used words like 'cob' instead of 'horse'; 'declivity' for 'gully'; 'offshoots' for 'branches'; 'beast of burden' for 'mule'; 'drip irrigation system' for a 'tree well' . . . just fine if the workers were all teachers . . . But they didn't even understand his insults! One winter afternoon he started threatening this guy from Piedmont: *Eh, poltroon, to your toil and travail! Enough solar soldering there, you mealworm!"*

"Translate."

"*Let's go, lazy, get to work. Enough sunbathing, you greedy loafer . . . !* The best part was that the kid just laughed. And then all hell broke loose because he was so furious. It goes without saying that the kid got a good walloping . . . The only solution he could come up with was to hire a *criollo* overseer, one of those foul-tempered assholes, the kind that get their point across without even talking . . ."

The landlady now made a culinary interruption:

"Excuse me: are you planning to eat dinner?"

"If you have the menu you rattled off yesterday, yes."

Astute, knowing how their guts had been suffering, she smoothly carried on Longines's joke with the appropriate straight face:

"Perhaps not quite such fine cooking as last night. But I'll try to please you. How does this sound: stuffed cardoons, bean stew with pig's ears, cured beef with oven-roasted potatoes, walnut cake, Camembert cheese?"

"Fantastical."

"What do you mean 'fantastical'? Do you think I'm teasing?"

"Yes . . . And the worst thing is that we can't confirm our suspicions by eating it . . ."

"Well then, tell me what you'd like," the landlady said. "I'm just not a fancy cook with a big imagination."

"All right. Something simple, without sauces or condiments or . . . imagination."

"Spinach omelet, mashed potatoes, macaroni and cheese?"

"Just right. As long as the butter you served this morning doesn't turn into sunflower margarine," said Aparicio. "The gringos are already selling that slop everywhere. It wouldn't surprise me if any day now we start instinctively craning our necks toward the rising sun . . ."

He shook his head ironically and walked away.

Thanks to the delicate good humor, this brief exchange erased the rough bitterness of pharmacist's tantrum. They sat a while, enjoying the silence. The landlady now delighted them with her vivacity. In no way a graceless woman, they suddenly recognized her as a kindred spirit who fit right in among their respective idiosyncrasies. She had more than enough of her own to go around!

The night was warm. Except for Fortunato and Viejo Amor, they all sat out on the patio. Placid breezes and smiles fluttered around them.

As always, however, the same thing happened in the end; *il ritornello!* Like an obligatory musical reprise to close the concert, the conversation circled back to focus on the pharmacist. Katanga took the issue back up and felt the need to deliver the resounding final note:

"As I was telling you, I've encountered men whose classical vulgarities actually cause sickness. In Bogotá there was a young professor who was famous for his irrepressible urge to speak with prissy affectation. One night, after the show, some acquaintances invited me to a party at the city's most elegant brothel. That's where I met him. What a phenomenon! He spoke with style, grace, and ringing sarcasm. When I asked him bluntly why he didn't go upstairs with one of the whores, listen to what he said:

Well, allow me to explain. Do you see that hussy over there? I know her well. She's a stuffed doll, all lissome and randy, and the truth is that she is boundlessly, hopelessly devoted to me. But, whenever I divest the steaming, missy trull of her gaudy adornments, when I strip away her frills and fripperies and all her cheap finery, that overheated concubine un-bewitches my medulla oblongata. Therefore, nothing doing, my friend, nothing at all!"

" . . . !"

"Well, nothing doing here, either. We don't get it. Translate."

"It's something ultra-smutty. Let the papal nuncio translate it for you. I don't take communion alongside such anachronisms."

"You're right. Authentic anachronisms," emphasized Aparicio. "But that correction is not correct. Language must translate people's natural modality, must suckle at the authentic nipple. Reject the dry love of those Spanish professors who seek to profit from their bad temper. And reject the local ersatz expressions of those presumptuous bombastic writers who want we should all sound like Galicians. They can fucking-well stop kidding themselves! One of these days they're going to require us to call the city hall 'the municipal intercourse'! Municipal intercourse . . . do you get it? Municipal: 'citizens taking privileges,' in this case, carnal copulation. So city hall becomes slutty hall. Nice job for those city councilmen!"

The Secretary had come to pick them up. He urged them to hurry by laying on the horn. He was anxious to present "the saviors" to the group of settlers who had been on the verge of deportation for unpaid debts. They had organized a festive dinner party at the farm of Saverio Di Noto, the man deepest in debt, situated in the nearby town of Río Tercero.

Since there was only room for three passengers in the Secretary's car, each man tried to excuse himself. They considered such lavish attention an excessive show of gratitude. Whatever their individual proclivities, the moral modesty which restrained them was authentic and shared by all.

"What they should really do is pay homage to the two thousand pesos . . ."

"Our bit of generosity has served them well. But, let's recognize something: it's cost us very little . . ."

"You go. And you."

"No. It's your job. You were the one . . ."

"Fine, Longines, I'll go, and Katanga, and whoever else wants to."

The horn brayed a long painful lament, sounding as if it meant to flush the quarry from the thicket and into the net. And off they went, in a gaggle, Aparicio, Katanga, and Viejo Amor, who fell into the car at the last moment. They looked as if they had been lassoed in and were being dragged along by the Secretary's urgency.

It has been said that tyrants have ears in their heels. Thus they hear nothing more than the voices of the humiliated and the clamor of those who are dragged along in shame. But there are also larynxes that sound like clarions! Temples engulfed in the pure oriflamme of combat!

From his steering-wheel pulpit, the Secretary was shouting the dry gloomy truth of the times at the top of his voice. The vile maneuvers of grain speculators. The collusion of authority. The trumped-up charges and trials levied against dignified settlers. The damning moniker of "communist" hung round the neck of anyone who dared raise their voice in protest. And seeing the imminent muzzle, brandished point blank at the lively, spirited meeting of the winds from every quarter, he hurled back furious anathemas against the plutocratic whitewash painted upon the moral backs of the people.

His clamorous voice echoed auspiciously in his companions' hearts. And as he lifted his head, bowed in shame at seeing so many Argentines disloyal to the their homeland in its hour of need, his voice trembled as he sharply reproached the stubborn apathy of its illegitimate children who exploit the nation's greatness. Then, transmuted into fire, his voice and his hair flamed like a torch.

Aparicio felt himself vibrate with a strange, adolescent turbulence. He wanted to raise his voice and hold forth, too. But he could not. So, almost with delight, he let the Secretary continue sinking the spurs of his rage into the imaginary flanks of the country's "traitors."

His horny head bent forward, Viejo Amor seemed to stir up the embers of a smothered rebellion. Suddenly, he melodramatically clasped his hands round the empty air in mock strangulation. A zealous pantomime of heroism that made him feel like the vindicator of civility, despised and trampled by widespread docility.

Deep in his thoughts, Katanga measured the radioactivity of ideas. He rode along tense and stiff. Listening and scrutinizing. Inside and outside. In spirit, he respected the Secretary's noble conduct, but not his passionate words. Unlike the others, Katanga preferred to prune the verbiage from his ideas. He quietly welcomed a just verdict in the dark night of injustice, magnanimously helping those oppressed avoid "the anguish of an unanswered call."

"According to . . ."

"Goddammit: wha' d'you mean, 'cording to? It's the truth what's proper. You can't flout the evidence just because."

"Listen to him! You keep goin' on that way pretty soon you'll be bragging that you taught the Tercero River how to flow."

The farmer's comment made the dinner guests roar with laughter. He was arguing with Saverio Di Noto's brother-in-law about the perennial rural theme of foreign influence on the country. And, naturally enough, they disagreed about the reality of the supposed benefit.

On the verandah, an enticing aroma rose from the heaping platters of pasta. With the men now seated at the table beneath the pergola, the housewives began serving. They dished out, Italian-style, *sans façon*, superb portions of food onto each plate. There was no ceremony in the attack. Accustomed to field work, the majority of them clutched their cutlery the way one clutches a pitchfork, and in the same way that one forks masses of cut grain into a threshing machine, they began stuffing their mouths.

Viejo Amor and Aparicio had no trouble enjoying themselves . . . or matching the rhythm of the other men's gluttony. The stewed meat with its hearty garnish of garlic and mushrooms, along with the pasta sauce, excited their sense of smell and regaled their palate. After fifteen days incommunicado in jail, the settlers' hunger justified their avidity and satisfaction. In the face of their unabashed voracity, restraint would have been a sin. Katanga tried his best to feign some interest in the food. He took a few modest bites from the appetizing heap of meat on his plate but then ignored it. And his contrast to the general feasting seemed deliberate, premeditated; because

while the others went straight for a second-helping of everything, he took his time, perplexedly twining a knot of noodles
onto his fork, then slurping them down with whistling epicu-
rean delight.

The discussion continued:

"Now, tell me something: did anyone ever used to serve *tagliarini nel paese* round these parts before?"

"No. But there weren't any foreigners here either. Every little
thing was happiness back then."

More laughter, rather forced this time in an attempt to buoy
up the joke. But the comment provoked resentment, too,
among the foreigners present, as they were all too familiar with
those unkind words. Courtesy, now out of fashion, gave way
to joking and mockery. Why argue, if the clash of ideas has
proved counterproductive, the debaters themselves grown sus-
ceptible, excitable, and restless?

Scorn was something which Saverio Di Noto understood
from experience. Thus he demanded greater kindness, greater understanding, greater tolerance. He was a robust Tuscan,
with an angular chin and prominent forehead. His mustache,
with drooping handlebars, skirted the edge of two hollow
cheeks. His ink-black eyes looked out at the world with velvety smoothness; but when he concentrated they sparkled with
the cold fire of composure and courage. For years he had struggled to raise the intellectual level of the local farmers. Tenacious in his efforts, his life was an example of innovation and
propaganda. The first farmer's cooperative had been founded
thanks to him. He also saw to it that production improved:
pedigree seeds; modern systems of sowing; practical tools; si-
los; grain elevators. Then came his motto: "Fair prices for quality grain." They were fed up with unjust exploitations, and resolved to not sell a single piece of wheat. They could resist!
They would resist. Local landowners Rey Fils and Ponce y Lord
had both tried to "reach out" to him. Naive fools! To bribe
him! A man like him, who arouses the sympathy of hearts and
minds; who recasts labor for the collective well-being in cruci-

bles of progress! Never! And so the war began. They withdrew
their agents, began to antagonize the local farmers. Business
slowed to a crawl, followed by terrible days of restricted credit. As this undermined the confidence of some of the less deter-
mined farmers, the first quarrels and disagreements broke out.
Their disunity facilitated disaster. Judges and police began to
get involved. And everything went downhill: trust in leadership, wheat storage, the settlers' dignity, fixed prices . . . Saverio
and five other men refused to give up. They took to the streets.
They organized meetings. They frequented protests. But this
provided little protection against harassment and dispersion,
only a small dike to stem the general dismay. And the same
thing happened again: the people's professed respect and admiration drug through the mud. And the farmers' spongy faith
and solidarity were conquered by the concentrated phobia of
a few capitalists . . . When Saverio finally realized the settlers'
true venal character, it was already too late. Man matters only
when he can help others to wake up and see the truth! Success is measured by attending to your neighbor's interests. Pure
egotistical folly! No one really sacrifices himself for anybody
else. No one esteems the effusion poured into an ideal. No one
values the fervor of hardened devotion. People sought exclusively to increase their own profits while disregarding the need
for others to earn something too! . . . Arrested and put on trial
thanks to vile betrayals by former friends turned enemies, Saverio and his companions in the cause saw the Law of Residence
swing the other way, not only over their foreign heads, but over
their Argentine homes, too. Deportation seemed imminent.
Once more the voracious squid stretched out its tentacles towards the wheat, corn, and peanuts, sucking up the lifeblood of
the earth and the sweat of men! Then . . . Saverio learned that
impotent suffering may, in fact, incite sympathy. Loyal friends
who endure through any adversity. Friends like the friends who
now sat before him at the table, serene, their serenity brought
on by exalted fatigue. Friends, like his newfound friends, who
arrive out of nowhere to extend their hand. Friends like the

ones who act anonymously, who think like him and thus defend him, believing that justice enforced by the rabble is not injustice, but true justice, a more pure, dignified justice, given that its outrage demonstrates the rejection of infamy.

Katanga did not avert his eyes from Saverio's strong, commanding expression, the face of a born leader, possessed as well of a spectral gaze that reached back to the Renaissance, to the slender figures of Il Bronzino. At the same time he noticed the opulent breasts of Saverio's wife. A benign opulence which would have tempted the brushes of Titian. And, sweetly, his imagination forced the husband's forehead, overcharged with pain and worry, to seek and cleave the tranquil gulf of the conjugal breast. And to lie there. To rest there, while his own words came falling down:

Saverio: it's no easy feat to inspire individuals to act with noble strength. This task requires insight into the sad, secret harmony which links all living beings—necessity—so that it might be guided by the rules of optimism and be founded upon orders of happiness.

It's not enough to know the old profession of manhood. Honesty, the clear mirror wherein one sees oneself is, for many, turbid quicksilver. It fails to convince. Each man believes himself better than another. And everything becomes wasteful disappointment. Because the people's prosperity is rooted in the equilibrium of their moral greatness and the efficacy of their effort. Because the effort of the majority is sub-moral, immoral, amoral.

In the life of society there are stages of disdain and neglect which fail to synchronize with the generosity of intentions. Achieving such generosity is the most beautiful apotheosis of altruism, and the mission of privileged beings. But, lamentably, the privilege that superiority confers also levies the accursed burden of disaster!

I'm sorry for your tragedy, my dear Saverio. Your incarnation of lofty virtues, of gallant examples, matters little if, down below, the flock mutters the prayers of the rosary handed down to them and accepts the meekness imposed upon them. In the opinion of the current public conscience, you will always reap a bitter deficit. What a tremendous crime that the hope of the disinherited is not rewarded with immediate benefits. But it is a great honor to have attempted it: because on the scales of history those deficits are reckoned among the propulsive forces of humanity. Allow my expansive sentiments, then, to be a foreshadowing of future gratitude, and thus pour a little healing balm on your wound. Because civilization has received a new spear-thrust in its symbolic, lacerated breast!

The servant's buttocks moved like two cheeks chewing food. She was a *chuncana*, a coarse young woman from the high mountains. Her undulating hindquarters lit up Viejo Amor like a candle. He looked for every excuse to call her over:

"Hey, girl: bring me some salt. This suckling pig is nicely marinated, but it needs a little more salt, for my taste."

The salt delivered, it then occurred to him that she should bring him a glass:

"I want to drink clear pure water. I don't like to mix it with my wine."

Diligent, helpful, the servant went to fetch it. And his roguish serpent's eyes slithered round her stout, shapely legs, coming to rest on her backside, jumping from one buttock to the other to caress their roundness. When she returned, he thanked her with some furtive pinches and flirtatious remarks. Promises of gifts: wondrous talismans and lockets. And again, as she moved away, his drooling sensual delight ogling her buttocks which flexed like two masticating jaws.

Meanwhile, the Secretary, unaware of the old Italian's lechery, was explaining to Aparicio how one managed to free prisoners who were already being processed for deportation.

"Don't think that I hesitated to act. I know how to manage those people. I went to see the local boss. Without any preamble, I laid the money on the table, right before his eyes. And I told him:

"*There's two thousand pesos; a thousand for you, a thousand for whoever is working on the case. You have evidence that what they're doing with Di Noto and the others is a lowdown dirty trick,* planned by the grain speculators. Your own father himself has been a victim of Rey Fils and Ponce y Lord.

"'It's true,' he replied. 'But the Minister is interested in snuffing out these movements. Imagine if they become widespread. The railroads won't be able to transport a damn thing and England will call in its debts on us. I'm going to make a call to Córdoba,' he said.

"'Do what you like,' I replied: 'but these people have got to be freed in forty-eight hours.'"

"And? Did he accept?"

"Partially. He displayed a very curious shame. People were already talking about the meddling influence of Russian gold. He didn't want to get his hands dirty. And, because of his doubts, he demanded a thousand pesos more, given the risk . . ."

"I don't understand. Is there a difference in the exchange rate between the national currency and this alleged Russian gold?"

"Nothing like that. He simply wanted the bigger share. You can't imagine the dirty tricks such men play, nor how scrupulously they manage their wicked dishonesty. And I had to pay him. Promise it to him, rather. Now that they've been freed, we'll find a way to raise the money. They're fully capable of arresting them again . . . for failure to pay."

The house cast a fifteen-meter carpet of shadow across the patio bedecked in geraniums, cranesbills, carnations, basil.

Through the trees, the fading fires of dusk flickered in the distance.

The lonely *pampas*.

Within the encompassing silence, bell mares clinking, the lowing of cows. Near the bunkhouse, the timid curiosity of a flock of sheep.

It was the hour of *mate* and coffee. The hour in which duties fulfilled are unsaddled and opinion dismounts to stand firm and upright in frank conversation.

The diners split up into various small groups. Cards. Phonograph. Pastries.

Viejo Amor and Saverio's brother-in-law opted for wine. Tasting it, the former boasted:

"They sure make some good wines back home, eh? Not this hog's piss made of tannin, sulphuric acid, red dye, and a thousand other things."

"Tell me about it: really lethal poison. *Tutto nell' Argentina é mistificazione. In veche, recoerda lei y vini di Frascati, Albano, Lanuvio, Velletri . . .*"

"Just remembering it makes me feel loaded drunk. Roaming through the Roman countryside, sitting at outdoor tables in country inns and roadside *trattorias*, how many liters of Frascati, Albano, Velletri have I poured into my gut!"

"Eh! The bes' thing y'can do:

Se lavora e se fatica
Per la panza e per la fica;
E quel poco que s'avanza
Peri il mánico della panza . . ."

"*Bravísimo!* To your health!"
"*Salute, mío caro.*"

"Yes, there, it's a real pleasure to drink. Wine is sacred. The very nectar of the earth where our dead ones lie! They make sure that the roots fulfill their duty. And above ground, out of respect for those below, we'll have no impostors. There, wine is the affectionate offering of the dead to the living. Here . . ."

"*Salute, mío caro.*"
"*Salud.*"

"So very true. I've drunk the blood of my own father. The cemetery is right next to my house."

"Here the wine is—*hiccup!*—an insult . . . It seems—*hic, hiccup*—the very scorn of the earth."

"*Salute, mío caro.*"

Their faces shone. The libations awoke in them the well-known Italian faculty for ironical understatement which rhetoricians call "litotes." Each one in his turn began to hum the old songs from their native land. When the song was familiar, the voice of one joined in with the other, in a rough but close-knit duo of happy remembrance. Thus, their souls relived the happy, innocent hours, of chaos or sadness, of love or nostalgia, according to what the song's lyrics or modulation demanded.

Eventually, their strident voices reached unacceptable limits. Approaching them with the Secretary in tow, Aparicio tugged on his companion's sleeve:

"*Che*, keep it down. There are ladies present."

His reprimand had no effect. They kept on singing. Half in a daze, they were about to separate when the servant girl walked by. Strapping and dusky, her buttocks still grinding away. Mesmerized, Viejo Amor quit singing and left the circle. He made a beeline for her derriere. And began unloosing his stream of seduction.

"C'mon. Don' run away. Show me where the toilet is. Why're you frightened? Of course I mean you, you're the prettiest lil' gal at this dinner. Goes without saying! . . . If it were those other sows, that's another story. But you . . ."

The girl stopped in her tracks. No man conquers a woman's sympathy more quickly than the one who speaks badly of other females. Especially if they're her friends or betters . . . Stretching out her arm toward a miserable little hut with a sackcloth curtain, she pointed:

"Over there."

"Thanks. As payment for your kind attentions, I'm going to give you a lil' present."

From his pocket he removed two objects: the wooden sarcophagus and a circular amulet tied with two pieces of twine. The *chuncana's* inexpressive eyes stared fixedly from beneath her thick eyebrows. Her nostrils flared and her chin, from which rose the curving line of her chubby cheeks, began to tremble. No man had ever praised her before. She was enthralled by embarrassment and curiosity. Viejo Amor urged her to accept his gift, his words dripping with lasciviousness:

"Take them . . . They're for you . . . A sincere token . . ."

Dazzled by their gleaming golden luster, she nodded and held out her hands. Confused but slightly suspicious. Feeling somehow inhibited, she scrutinized the giver's faun-like face.

"They're two precious objects, very interesting. Which one d'you want to see first? This one? Good. Let me show you. It's an amulet sailors use to guard 'gainst shipwrecks. See? On each side of the medallion there's a swimmer. Now, look. When the sailors are in danger they make it spin like this. And it summons the divine protection that'll save 'em. Come closer: you're going to see God's very providence!"

The maid drew closer. She fixed her gaze on the rapidly spinning disc and was instantly shocked by the lewd image. She backed up three steps and laid into him:

"You dirty old man! What're you thinking? You're a real filthy pig!"

She still had the sarcophagus in her hand. Accidentally, perhaps from a light pressure from her fingers, the cover popped open. She was alarmed to see the outstretched body of the priest:

"Take it back. I don't want anything from you."

"But, darling, that's a priest. It's a sin for you to reject him!"

"Well, then so be it."

Libidinous, brimming with lubricious liquor, he stepped closer to retrieve the charm then grasped her extended hand by surprise. With his right palm he stroked her flesh several times, from the wrist to the elbow. And to the girl's complete astonishment, he pressed the hidden spring that caused an enormous penis to pop up from the priest's robes and bob wildly in the air.

Nearly choking with fright, she wrenched herself away and ran off shouting:

"Pig! Throw this old pig out of here! It's Pedro Urdemales himself! Get out of here, you pig! Throw this dirty old swine out of here!"

Her buttocks seemed to be coming loose from her hips as she ran; a chimera of cantering dray horse and waggling goose.

The others had already said good night. Walking to the automobile with the Secretary and their host, Katanga was expounding on his theory:

"Well. Until next time. Thanks very much for everything. And don't worry, Saverio. You've got to take these things in stride. Like accidents on the job. The less seriously you seek a utopia and actual goodness, all the better. The road becomes less arduous. Remember how I mocked the magistrates and police in Río Cuarto. Like that. Proceed that way. The fire of the ideal must be maintained with a happy, active spirit. No gloomy insomniacs. Those who stubbornly persist in the schemes of the Carbonari snuff out the fire in the darkness. A mistake! In ancient times, fire was the exclusive privilege of the gods. We all know the high price Prometheus paid for his magnificent adventure of stealing the sun's fire from Phaeton, whom Zeus filled with the desire to drive his father's fiery chariot through the sky ... The Titan was lashed to a peak in the Caucasus, with heavy iron chains forged by Hephaestus. And in that uncomfortable position, an eagle was put in charge of greedily devouring his liver ... Take comfort, Saverio: this myth is nothing more than a tired old cliché, possibly due to the superiority of *paté de foie gras truffé*, or because people now prefer the vitamins in cod's liver oil ... But life is no more than a succession of myths. History, charged with complicating legends, does no more than change the names of their characters, settings, and the circumstances in which they unfold ... Why suggest, then, that I see in you a minor Prometheus, a 'clairvoyant precursor' according to the etymology of his name? You were filled with that most noble zeal of serving mankind's ideal, trying to procure for them all a divine gift: justice. But you had no tact: you've burned in your own passionate fire. A disaster? No! Push on! Stubbornness mans the helm of all heroic endeavors. But, let me tell you again, Saverio: abandon the austerity that hobbles your character. Get used to laughing instead of making your hatred crack like a whip. Pour out your private drama in comic prose ... And through the cloudy travails of the millennia, upon the altar of the future, all those who searched for the illusive trifecta of Goodness, Truth, and Beauty, will be identified and unified. And will have their own lighthearted myth, at odds with history and exalted by mankind. What more can we hope for?"

The Secretary was now at the wheel.

They got in the car.

Upon the blue profile of the mountain glowed a red sunset of tragedy.

He started the engine.

A halo of sunlight encircled the head of Saverio Di Noto.

RÍO TERCERO:

They arrived a little too early, perhaps, to the brothel. But such was Viejo Amor's urgency that Aparicio interceded to please him. The wine, the rich, well-seasoned food, the servant's buttocks, and various other excitations had gotten him so worked up that his very blood was as hot as a tincture made from the essence of the aphrodisiacal Spanish fly.

Katanga went along with them reluctantly. He lived in retreat from love and sex. Especially from sex. Many times, perforating his aplomb, he had examined the deepest, most hidden folds of his abysmal psychology, in search of his old libido. Without success. Now, weighed down by apathy, he explained it:

"During my career as an illusionist I enjoyed women in abundance. Thus, as Doctor Inhell, I've lived through the inferno of the feminine reality. Believe me: I'm so fed up with women that, naturally, I've become difficult for them. So much so that I remain celibate. I have the honor of saying it: I'm a confirmed bachelor. As far as love's concerned I've stopped at the *hors d'oeuvres* . . ."

"Well, that's fine; but don't worry, there's no danger here of them eating you alive," replied the Secretary. "I urged you to come along because this brothel is one of our true local wonders. Keep your eyes open, be observant, and you'll see what I mean . . ."

A large number of benches surrounded the rectangle of tiled patio. It was delightful to look up from the semidarkness and see the stars but miserable to look in at the prostitutes in the light.

The women were still all gathered in the bar. As if just passing the time. Gross. Indolent. Opaque. Blind to intimacy. In forcibly uncomfortable positions. As if seeking, in their contortions, something more than voluptuousness, some punishment for their sensuality. The tedium gnawed at their thickly painted faces. A profound, anatomical tedium that twisted their arms like snakes before slithering away through their abysmal yawns.

Aparicio broke the silence in brute fashion:

"So, what do whores and oysters have in common?"

And right away, without giving anyone time to respond, he answered his own riddle:

"They both die of boredom waiting to get eaten out of their shells."

Only Viejo Amor laughed at the dirty crack, yawping away like a baboon.

The Secretary and Katanga, on the other hand, began to deconstruct it:

"The prison of her oyster cell! The stinking wound that wounds and vexes, as Michelet described it! The vertical mouth through which the species speaks! The slotted shell where a man puts his coin to see life reflected in his son! Is it a jail cell? No, Aparicio. It's not a jail cell! It's a wound, a mouth, a slot that must be dignified. I may be romantic; but I disagree with you."

"I'm also a romantic. However, I agree. Oh, the prison of her oyster shell! The boredom of the flesh! The annoying friction without pleasure! The disgusting contact without marriage! What an inhuman prison! It's an apt phrase. Is it yours, Aparicio?"

"Of course . . . Who else's would it be? . . ."

The madam was making her way downstairs from her apartment. A crepuscular woman with a hooked nose, a spongy dou-

ble-chin, and a corseted belly cinched tight. Draped in a pro-
fusion of costume jewelry, she passed before them glittering,
clinking, rattling, jingling. *Aigrettes*, hoops and *strass* brooch-
es. Necklaces and Moorish glass bangles. Fastened to her waist,
on the left-hand side, a leather wallet. From the firmness of her
bearing and the authoritarian expression in her eyes, one could
read her experience as patroness of crapulous orgies, of bothersome clients, and drunken outbursts. It was nine o'clock.
She clapped her hands. And her bevy of whores fanned out
through the rooms.

They had, *ipso facto*, four before them.

The instant a chubby little Italian blonde opened her mouth
Viejo Amor fell under the spell of her rough, tubercular voice,
with touches of falsetto that made her *Cocoliche* accent comical. Just to confuse her, he feigned a bit of resistance. But when
her bloodless hands caressed the curls of his beard, when his
compatriot languidly grazed his erotic nerve, *arrivederci*: Viejo
Amor stood straight up at attention!

Triumphant, she began to recite for him a parody of the
Third Canto of the *Inferno*:

Per me si va nel luogo desiato
Che in general bordello bien chiamato
Per me si va tra la perduta gente.

Che di puttane ahn nome nel presente
Per me si va nell eterno amore
Dove si fotte sempre in tutte le ore . . .

I am the path to the place of corruption
So well known as the house of prostitution
Through me pass those with lives shattered.

If they call us whores nowadays, no matter
I am the path to love's eternal bower
Where it's nonstop fucking, hour after hour . . .

And, arm in arm, they walked off, holding each other up.

In her place appeared a slender *criollo* woman, with wide shoulders and narrow hips. Her hair, falling closely round her neck in shining waves, highlighted her features. Her eyes radiated the sad, dismayed splendor of the mulatto woman. She clearly had African ancestry in her blood. Aparicio asked her about it. And the answer came immediately, not so much spoken aloud as purring in his ears with feline caresses.

"A Uruguayan girl! Where from?"

"Let's go upstairs. I'll tell you there."

They stood up. She, lissome, flexible. He blushing, bashful.

"Well," said Katanga, "those two bandmates wasted no time banding together to get bandy and bandy it about . . ."

"So? Ideas need to be lubricated with love . . ."

"Lubricated with love? You mean here, of all places . . . in this service station? . . ."

"Do you have a personal problem with that?"

"No, nothing personal. But public, that's another matter."

"Oh! You . . . always the same. Lighten up, sweetheart."

Katanga smiled at the Secretary's reproach. He'd just confirmed, once again, desire's subconscious nationalism. In his long wanderings, whenever he ran across an Islamic woman, he put aside the beauty of other women, to wrap himself warmly in her breast, as if resting at some heaven-sent oasis. Since then, he knew that if love is a universal instinct, desire is an appetite conditioned along mysterious, inner frontiers. Each pilgrim, each outlaw, each one on the move to greener pastures; the more he wants to destroy those frontiers, the more he is an anxious antenna of his homeland. Imperceptible reasons persuade, attract, and bind. It's neither the tongue, nor race, nor idiosyncrasy of another being, but the common nostalgia and collective memory that sprouts in different hearts. Coming together, they come closer to this commonality. As they join together, they experience the same pulses and same effusions in the conjunction of their native sentiments.

"So then if you don't meet an Armenian . . ."

"That's right . . ."

Leaning out naked from various occupied rooms, the whores clapped their hands:

"Water."

"Quilmes White for room fifteen."

"Water, Doña Raquel."

Immediately a little old lady—a study in two curves: that of the scarf tied round her head and that of her shawl-draped back—came gliding across the floor, two glazed pitchers of hot water hanging from her arms, nearly even with the floor. She was followed by a swarthy, strapping boy in gray Oxford pants and an electric blue jersey, conceitedly carrying the bottle of *weissbier* and two glasses.

"Look! Look!"

"What?"

"The servant and the waiter."

"I'm looking. But I don't see anything of interest. What's unusual about them?"

"You'll find out later. Now let's go to the bar."

Heading that way they spotted the porter, a poor old man seated by the door. Each time the bell rang, he stood up from his chair. He pulled back the lace curtain. Sticking his nose against the glass, he peered out. Opening the door, he squinted his eyelids, scrutinizing the clients while the watchman on duty frisked them for weapons.

"Did you observe that little old man?"

"Yes. Bad job to have at his age."

"Bad and evil. C'mon. Let's go in. We can sit at that table."

The Secretary waved his hand. The bartender approached them, a fifty-year-old man in his shirt sleeves. He had a white complexion—softened by the late night—bilious eyes— shining with mistrust—and a sad mouth, his thick lower lip grimacing with resentment.

"What'll you have?" he demanded, scrunching up his bushy eyebrows.

"Coffee."

"Coffee. With some liqueur?" he added, as if complaining that they should spend so little.

"Just coffee for me. Let's see, one moment: you, too? Yes. Black. And two glasses of water."

The bartender walked away, annoyed with their order.

As soon as he left, the Secretary continued:

"I never drink at the brothel. I suppose the same is true for you. I've brought you here only so that you can observe."

"*Hombre*: your refrain there is quite intriguing, but . . . observe what?"

"The bartender. And wait: don't be hasty: there's still something more . . ."

The next room was supposed to be "by reservation only" but that night — raffle night — there were no distinguished clientele: businessmen, unfaithful husbands, authorities in transit, some salesmen throwing a bachelor's party for the bookkeeper in their department . . . There were young fellows, too. And youth is a sad age; an especially conspicuous fact from the vantage point of the bar. A young man's vehemence is mere fire, not happiness. Happiness is the private domain of the adult man, the one who has found himself, who has already achieved his dreams. From their table Katanga and the Secretary saw the crowd growing thicker by the minute but no happier. Noise. Shamelessness. Ostentation. Vanity. Every once in a while the radio broadcast some danceable piece, the reward for so many annoying ads interrupting the fun. When a tango played, the whole room, bucks and dams alike, ceased its noisy chatter. Unctuously intertwined, they danced to the song with the enthusiasm that was otherwise missing from their outward demeanor.

"Quick! Look! They just walked in. Look at that woman with the dark red hair, with the picaresque laugh and a ringlet above her left eye, walking with her pocketbook in her hand."

"The one with a black velvet ribbon round her neck and a matching black apron over a tight green dress?"

"Yes, her! It's Wenzi."

"Although she looks like an *apachinette*, by her face I'd swear she's Jewish."

"Polish."

"Polish-Jew, then. One of many! What's particularly special about our Wenzi?"

"Oh, a great deal. She's the pick of the harem. She's not lavish with her favors. She costs double. With her, the mystery is locked away. And I don't mean her whore-mongering, flesh-peddling, ruffian pimp of a brother who's in jail . . ."

"If you speak to me in Turkish, you're speaking one of the few dialects I don't understand . . ."

The "Rodríguez Peña" tango came pouring out of the radio. It formed an island of silence. Virulent passions flowed to an expectant rhythm. And grandiose carnality, which does not yield to mere temptation, stepped out onto the dance floor.

The Secretary and Katanga abandoned their table without touching the coffee. They'd seen Aparicio and Viejo Amor nosing around. And they went to nose around too.

When the dance finished, the radio announcer took over:

Dear listeners:

Tonight we are offering a concert of tangos chosen from the traditional repertoire.

By the time Jean Richepin had made his memorable defense of the tango in Paris, and the many rhythmical contortions of its cuts and breaks swept through the cabarets of the City of Light, our national dance, par droit de conquéte, *had already taken the world by storm.*

Waltzes, mazurkas, schottisches, lancers, and other dances were eclipsed by the tortured indolence of its movements and its plaintive, sensual harmonies.

As a dance, the tango enjoys a perfect relationship to its music, and carries in its rhythms a sweet, decadent melody. It lacks the brutal brio of the maxixe, or the dizziness of the waltz. A deep tenderness of longing, a weariness from pleasures enjoyed, a profound sadness of dead love, all vibrate through its notes in a soft exquisite amalgam.

*The pavanne and the minuet both lie dead in the golden cas-
ket of the Romantic age. The tarantella and the jota agonize in
the throes of a death-rattle as violent as their spinning. The furlana was born dead in the innocent soul of Pius X. The active frenzy of the one-steps and fox-trots are simply a vertiginous gallop toward oblivion. But the tango—only the tango!—persists. With its
genuine sentimental languidness enlivening the cadences of Euter-
pe and the rhythms of Terpsichore, crowning the former with sighs,
the latter with sobbing.*

*The shimmy made a vain attempt to displace it. Everything in
that dance was false and savage. From its stolen, syncopated, strident music to the spasmodic tremblings it copied from Hawaiian
dances.*

*Now the rumba seeks dominance. In vain. What matters is the
voluptuous emotion that filters the pain. Not the African excess of
desire. Its winnowing shake contains too much lubricity. And the
pantomime grossly suggests the act of copulation. Too much bodily reek in its animal sweat and jungle humidity. The desire to compare this apelike dance to the meritorious tango is more than an irreverent affront to its charged evocation of dreams, the ridiculous
proposition of affectedly scrupulous prudes and snobs.*

*When the inspirations of fashion run counter to the most intimate
facts of our idiosyncrasy, they must be proscribed with firm national
pride. And because we, bursting with affection, love our country's
own music, we hope that tonight's program might awaken in our
souls the ineffable delight sleeping in the beauty of the old tangos.*

Despite the stupidity implied by clapping, under any circumstances, for a radio broadcast, the majority of those present ap-
plauded.

Rejoining their companions, they were surprised to see Viejo Amor clapping, too.

"What! You, an Italian, also applauding? Didn't you hear
what he said about the tarantella and the furlana?"

"After making love, you always applaud the tango. The tango revives the memory of love!"

"Well, well! Looks like a little gallop now and then isn't bad for the old boy . . ."

"Hah, you don't even know!"

The first chords of "The Man from Entre Ríos" were sounding. The crowd drew back, opening the floor to the dancers. Wenzi was a voluptuous flame whipping around that circle of passions and desires, of timidities and self-assurances, of depravations and insatiable thirsts. And she knew it. From her ankle to the tip of her pinkie, her skin—a natural golden-rose tone like a tree-ripened peach—spoke to their sensual gluttony with the splendid promise of her thigh, her belly, her breast, her throat, and her mouth.

Aparicio wore a look of corrosive melancholy. Something was eating away at his inner equilibrium, beginning with his eyes, now sunken in by an unmistakable depression.

"What's the matter with you? Are you regretting it now? You've got to think beforehand. You know: an hour with Venus and the rest of your life with Mercury . . ."

"No, not that. It's the sheer quantity of nostalgia that tart has uncorked in me. She comes from a town near mine. She knows all my cousins."

"Bah! A fine thing, relatives, women, and all this. Shall we go hit the sack?"

"To sleep?! Right now?" The Secretary was alarmed. "Not on your life! They draw the raffle in ten minutes. Something very interesting. Observe."

"A raffle?"

Viejo Amor intervened:

"That must be what this is. I wasn't sure what it was for. When I paid for the bar tab up in the room, they gave me this coupon. Look."

Katanga read the paper. He was stupefied:

"You're not kidding! I've never seen anything like it!"

"Go ahead and read it."

He read:

LA ESTRELLA

Grand Raffle - Big Prizes - Compliments of the House
TUESDAYS, WEDNESDAYS, THURSDAYS (9 P.M. to
1:30 A.M.).

For each guest consuming $1 in drinks.

SERIES A. NO. 38. The holder of this ticket has the right
to participate in the raffle for the prizes described below:

1st **Prize:** ONE NIGHT IN BED AND A BOTTLE OF
CIDER. 2nd **Prize:** EIGHT BOTTLES OF BEER. 3rd
Prize: ONE UPSTAIRS VISIT AND ONE BEER. (See reverse side.) The drawing for this raffle will be held on the
premises at 24:00 hours on the Friday of the week corresponding to the distribution of the present ticket, and the
respective prizes for winning numbers will be awarded in
the order drawn.

NOTICE: Winners must claim their prizes within ten
minutes after the drawing: after this time they forfeit all
right to claim.

ALSO: The first prize winner can choose three bottles
of cider, or a case of beer, instead of the night in bed.

"Frankly, it's extraordinary. I'd like to keep this coupon. They
won't believe me when I explain it."

"I told you ... Look: they're already bringing out the basket."

Standing atop a table, Wenzi was vigorously ringing a little bell. The big midnight crowd of ticket holders—from that
night and earlier in the week—began gathering on the patio.
The group was largely made up of young fellows, shop workers, and humble laborers. The age of fury and dance. The age
of sex without brains. The age of unanimous onanism. Poor
men lacking funds, living the hard life. The eagerness to win
a prize was evident on every face. Each one of them speculat-
ed in secret. None of them would ever have twenty pesos to

spend the night *in baccho et veneris*, drinking cider and screwing a "*mina.*" Nighttime trips to the brothel, on foot, with various friends, to make out a while, to have some fun dancing and blow a little money, granting them the right to participate in the raffle, was all the fun they could afford. And it awoke in them the hunger to win the big first prize. Oh, to live the dream excited by privation! To escape, just once, from the well of solitude! To soothe with drool, sweat, and tears, the fever, fever, fever, fever of the flesh! Oh!

Suffused with pity, Katanga observed the thin, tormented faces of that youthful crowd. And wishing them good fortune in the fulfillment of their desire, he was filled with rage and disgust for himself. He'd been a stubborn offender against instinct. He'd participated in the sexual debut of many a virgin. He'd known the despotic longing of various old maids and the scrupulous depravity of countless housewives. Sickened and disdainful, he contemplated the plethora of women he'd encountered along the way, from the confines of adolescence to the very edge of menopause. And he suffered.

The growing din of the crowd had grown to an uproar when the clock struck midnight.

Wenzi, elevated by the feverish excitement, called for silence. She lifted the spinner basket above her head. The woven wire sphere spun in a blur. Then, amid mute expectation, she proclaimed:

"First prize, number thirty-eight. First prize, number thirty-eight."

"Me!" shouted Viejo Amor.

The crowd turned toward him, their eyes, at first, visibly aggressive, followed by a disdainful muttering which quickly cascaded into brutal, obscene, hostile diatribes. Soon, perhaps, their cheated passion would find an outlet in violence.

Katanga quickly sensed the possibility of some real danger, and compulsively intervened:

"What? You'd seriously consider spending the night here? Haven't you just been upstairs? Here, give that winning number to some young fellow!"

Viejo Amor swallowed hard. But he obeyed. Not so much because of the reprimand as for the crowd's menacing disappointment. Such good luck for a man of his age and appearance was simply disgraceful. They seemed to be letting him know that lovemaking is the exclusive domain of young men. That older, more mature creatures must content themselves with the memory of their erotic feats, and not compete with the urgent ardor of youth. Brimming with fear, he handed his winning ticket to a shabby young man in threadbare mourning clothes whose rancor threatened to block his way out:

"Here, kid. Go cheer yourself up."

The young fellow offered him no thanks. Instead, he whooped like a hyena and, elbowing his way through the crowd, made his way over to Wenzi:

"Here it is. I'm the winner!"

When the basket started spinning again, the Secretary said:

"Now we can go. Were you watching? Is this fascinating or not?"

"What I don't understand," interrupted Aparicio, "is the tradeoff between a night in bed and three bottles of cider or a case of beer. How much does it cost to spend the night here?"

"Fifteen pesos, I believe."

"Well, it's not fair then to swindle the lucky winner, supposing he might opt for the drinks. They're worth five pesos at the most! The owners must be Jews. That Uruguayan girl told me some incredible things."

As they passed through the doorway the porter stuck out his hand.

"Eh, mister: no tip? Help out a poor old man!"

Aparicio handed him a coin. The instant he did, the Secretary smiled:

"Now you've been swindled, too ... This entire place is a mechanism of exploitation. A collection of unbelievable relationships. For instance, that doorman is the madam's father and Wenzi's grandfather ..."

"What do you mean!" exclaimed Katanga, cutting him off.

"Just what you heard. And that's not all—that little old lady who carries the hot water to the girls upstairs is the bartender's mother-in-law and the serving boy's grandmother. He's the pimp for two whores, while the brother who's in jail is the pimp for three more. So, as you now see: it's all in the family . . ."

"Some family!"

"Some business!"

"Grandparents, parents, children . . . Three generations splattering their vice and misery around in a brothel . . . It's the most fantastic aberration I've ever seen in my life!"

"There was a reason I kept telling you to keep your eyes open . . ."

It was nine o'clock in the morning when they started the drive back to the boarding house in Rumipal. Too late. Their plan had been to meet by that time on the road that crossed atop the nearby dam: Longines had arranged a visit, and the power plant manager had agreed to give them all a tour of the installations.

They had barely left behind the town of Río Tercero, when the wheat fields began to aim their shafts at the horizon: a citadel of diaphanous walls. A thousand legions crouching in furrows. And millions of quivering arrows flew out against the enemies of the countryside and the settlements. Astute enemies. Strategists of hunger. So that their bank accounts would not be squeezed by any greedy hoarder, and no farmer profit from some embargo against the owner of a large estate.

Afterward came the corn battalions. With their soft green swords, machetes, and scimitars sprouting from the stalks. Awaiting the attack. Hidden in valleys and hollows. Under the command of bearded willows. And sentinel poplars with plumed steel morions. So that the line of their faith would not be pushed back by the onslaught of lucre and disorientation!

Further on, among the desolate plateaus, there appeared

the indigenous militia of spiny acacias and tall *altiplano* grass, with their despot-stems and their captain-carob trees. Ulula-tions of Indian raiders. Whoops from *gauchos*. And up above, wild foresters, the autochthonous guerrilla band of peppercorn trees and coconut palms, whose rough, hirsute chieftains — the locust trees — carried a *criollo* dagger in each sheath. So that the theodolite of the gringo settlers would not even attempt to break their ranks!

They sped along lightly. The Secretary gripped the wheel, chasing curves and dodging potholes. A herd of cattle stood motionless in the road, staring scornfully, but he made the car skitter around them like a frisky horse, leaving behind a hazy dust cloud that covered their retreat; dirt in the eyes of a whole civilization of happy, systematic predators.

Suddenly, an abrupt hairpin turn. An explosive crash, wrenching metal. The secretary hit the brakes and the car came to a sudden, shuddering stop. Imprecations. Insults.

But the driver of the other car, going in the opposite direc-tion, did not wait around, did not even show the common courtesy to assess the results of the accident. Instead he pressed the accelerator once more and, too late, made the horn growl. Then he was gone, speeding off wildly toward the town.

"That big sonofabitch! Did he blow his horn before that turn?"

"No. And you didn't either . . ."

The Secretary and Aparicio surveyed the damage: a blown tire, five twisted spokes, a dented radiator.

Katanga and Viejo Amor stood staring into the distance as the automobile raced away, now no more than a distant rumor among the hills. Barely a vibration. An almost imperceptible buzzing. They stood thus for a few brief moments. Rapt in hy-peraesthesia . . .

Coming to their senses after such an auditory assault, still listening for the distant, receding motor, they could hear the sound of their own hearts pounding like mad. Rapid, an-guished pulses. Tachycardia of tragic news!

They shot one another questioning glances. Rattled and ter-
rified. Mute. A tremendous anxiety overshadowed their faces.
Great chills and dreadful fright. An oppression in the throat.
An urge to cry . . .

Then they scrutinized each other more closely. They were
trembling. They saw their own melancholy written in each
other's faces. They understood. And without saying a word,
they drew near to one another and embraced.

And choked back a sob.

"What's wrong with some people?"

"Bah! Don't worry. Just a scare . . ."

"Good thing. Help me. We've got to change the tire. Go
pull out the jack out and the tools."

EMBALSE:

As they drove towards the dam they spied an unusual amount
of activity along the road. The Secretary thought it must be pay
day. True, it was the second Saturday of the month, but the faces they observed did not appear to be in a smiling mood. Katanga and Viejo Amor took that as a sign of something wrong.
Entering the roadway that crossed the top of the dam, they
saw many people lined up along the railing, looking down the
dam, and felt their presentiment confirmed.

"It's terrible," Katanga said. "There's been an accident!"

Aparicio turned his head:

"What do you mean?"

"Something terrible . . . people in mourning. Mourning.
There's been an accident . . . I'm sure of it. An hour ago this
strange feeling came over me. Viejo Amor also felt it . . . a premonition. It's telesthesia! Telesthetic messages! Grief. Mourning. Who can it be?"

As they got out of the car, right at the ladder that zigzagged
down to the power station, a policeman blocked the way.

Convulsed, raving deliriously, Katanga blurted out:

"It's my friend . . . let me by . . . He's already dead . . . No . . . I don't want him to die . . . He's got to see us . . . He's not dead yet . . . Let me go . . ."

Pushing desperately with his arms and words, he managed to get past the officer. And down he went, quickly, on a crazed, dangerous descent. Aparicio, Viejo Amor, and the Secretary followed. He spotted Longines, Dijunto, and Fortunato down below, and Lon Chaney laid out on a cot. In three leaps he was by his side, pale, exhausted. He couldn't muster the strength to speak; as if instead of descending, he'd just climbed a terrifying summit. He was shattered by his emotional fatigue and torn nerves.

"Lon Chaney!" he burst out, striking his own head with his fists. "Lon Chaney!"

The man's visible wounds had been cleaned. The emergency treatment did little more than disinfect them. Katanga fell to his knees. He took his hand. Cold! As if waking from his dream, he searched for Lon Chaney's pulse. Fading. He could hear his breath getting weaker. Tormented by the pitifully gentle fluttering of his eyelids, he shouted:

"Longines, this man is dying!"

"Yes. He's fractured the base of his skull."

"Lon Chaney's dying, he's dying!"

"It's fatal. We're waiting for the doctor."

"But it's not fair! Lon Chaney can't die! It's not fair! It's not fair! It's not fair!"

He was raving angrily, confusedly. Dijunto led him aside. He patted him on the back. His words of comfort poured out, pure and clear. Dry-eyed effusion. Stoic conformity. The dry sorrow of a wooden Christ:

"Patience, Katanga. It was the hand of fate. You've got to resign yourself. I know my words offer you little consolation. Calm yourself. Your mind will know how to convince your heart. Why be desperate? Come on. Stay by his side. He was most loyal to you of all. You know it. Lon Chaney loved you.

He loved you with his admiration. Don't cry. Go to his side. Your presence will comfort him more than anything."

They were soft words spoken in a rough voice. Unguent words meant to staunch the wounds of others without curing inner turmoil. Soothing words that can calm other pains but not personal anguish.

Katanga acceded. And was docilely led to the side of his dying friend. His spirit had changed. His face, too. He appeared softened, with the gentleness obtained through contemplation of the ineluctable.

Many times, philosophizing about the prospect of dying, Katanga had deplored the slow unraveling of his own *kismet* for not having offered him a death such as this, in the high, critical moment of his triumphs. A clean, secular death, without religious or medical complications, without prayers or patented medicines. Why was he so perturbed, then, in the face of Lon Chaney's imminent death? To surrender life tranquilly, as if it were a careless trifle; is that not the privilege of righteous beings?

Lon Chaney was transfigured.

If dying meant that the physical body's immaterial counterpart ascends, to be incorporated with the eternal fraternity of the great beyond, the flesh — bidding its beloved soul a fond farewell — painted its final anguish in a series of fleeting grimaces. And if it were not for the radiant morning, so blue and sunny, no one would have seen the luminous white aureole round his head, detaching in its turn to say good-bye forever.

Lon Chaney's spirit slipped away with sublime serenity. No stumbling blocks of suffering. The soul left the body, dissolving into light, becoming one with peace.

Katanga was profoundly gratified to see how the fluidic entity slowly abandoned its clay vessel. How death went gathering up the tulle of human configuration hidden within the intra-atomic spaces. And how, as if in a horror movie, Lon Chaney's spirit would soon be housed in the ghostly copy of his cadaver.

Illuminated by the splendor of life as it drifted away to live on in its illuminated future, Katanga mused:

The agony of good, honest, learned men must be so bitter when the heavy solace of rude friars, sinful pastors, and venal rabbis chokes up their smooth slide toward death with hooks and asperities!

His psychic equilibrium was now almost restored. Scruple by scruple, he had conquered the sentimental rebellion always provoked by the shock of death. He now contemplated its limits, naturally. He conversed with it. And he even permitted himself to say to it:

At last, I've satisfied a great yearning: to understand the centurions, who played at dice while Jesus was dying on Calvary!

Pregnant with funereal predictions, the surrounding silence was roiled by hope. A man was descending the narrow cement staircase, a small kit bag in hand. Behind him, walking in a slow stride, a quiet, serious man, his composure foiled by the steep descent. It was the doctor.

Opaque, frowning, without wasting time on greetings and questions, ignoring the others, he set himself to attend to Lon Chaney. He focused all his senses on him, including the clairvoyance possessed by those clinicians who wisely and fervently bow before their patients. He did what he could. Very little now. He gave him an injection to soothe his agony. And moving his head and his lips in a skeptical summary, he murmured:

"There's nothing to be done! Nothing to be done!"

Those present exhibited their remorseful disappointment. Throughout the doctor's examination, silent and withdrawn, they had been gathering and decanting all the moral strengths they would naturally need for such a difficult trial. Just as electricity and diathermy penetrate and sanitize bodily tissues, they all emitted waves of high-voltage love from the power plants of their stricken hearts. Waves meant to vivify the psyche, while the doctor persisted in trying to save the flesh. Waves which were, like all their hopes, wasted, thanks to the rupture of Lon Chaney's bi-corporeal nature and the final ataractic eclipse.

Faithful guardian of the silence, Katanga made a sign to Longines so that he might bear witness: Lon Chaney opened his eyes and mouth in a rictus of stupor. He seemed illuminated by the presence of a beloved being.

"Listen. He's saying something."

Longines crouched down low to listen, his ear brushing the dying man's lips. Indeed: he heard him whisper ever so lightly:

Pas ... grande ... choo-se ... É-glan-ti-ne ... Ma ... pe-ti-te ... É-glanti ...

Then his eyes stared straight ahead. He clenched his teeth.

There was a hemorrhage of light.

And he expired.

"The best tomb for the dead is in the heart of the living." They all felt that way. And they did not fret themselves about other, more earthbound, tombs. Lon Chaney was already enthroned in the heart of each one of them. Upon the true altar. Alongside his little Eglantine. Magnetic pole of his wandering and his desolation. Flower of his agony. And the flower of friendship was scattered in petals of tears. Tears of intimate cries. Tears of mute sobbing.

The doctor had already filled out the death certificate. Always helpful, the Secretary pulled them from their despair. In his judgment, they needed to comply with standard funereal practices for Lon Chaney. Enshroud him. Hold a wake for him. Bury him.

They'd never considered such a thing. Living in Buenos Aires, in the solitude populated by misery, they'd never witnessed or attended such rituals.

Longines said:

"When someone died in Villa Desocupación, a black van came, picked up the body, and that was it. Why such a fuss here? Lon Chaney's body doesn't interest us. We can throw it into the river. Let the current take it."

"What do you mean! You can't do that!"

"Fine. Then, do us the favor: take care of it yourself. Go back up the ladder, look around for any old box. Dig a hole up on the mountain. Spend whatever you need: take some money.

We'll bury him immediately."

"Impossible. There are cemeteries . . ."

"Which one is closest?"

"The one in Santa Rosa. Fifteen kilometers."

"Fine. I'll get the driver. You do your part. The sooner we finish this business, the better."

"Without wrapping the body? . . . Without a wake? . . ."

"Are the casualties of war ever shrouded and given a wake? Each dead soldier in the war cost twenty-five thousand dollars in war material. I've never heard of them spending ten cents on shrouds and candles. They dug enormous pits and stacked up the bodies in great big piles. Earth and fire. By the way: couldn't we simply cremate Lon Chaney?"

The Secretary left without answering. His mind was troubled by a feeling of sharp intemperance. And something else which he did not know how to define: tenderness overcome by rage. Fear of the body's ability to renounce life and simply perish. And the urgent need to avenge and placate—by refreshing it—the future thirst of his spirit.

Heading back up to the road, the Secretary ran into someone.

They recognized each other:

"You're the one from the accident . . ."

"Why, you big son-of-a-bitch!"

"Well, you could have honked the horn."

"And did you honk? What side were you driving on?"

" . . ."

"Say something, goddammit! We're going to settle this right now. Why the hit and run?"

"I wasn't running away. I was going to get the doctor . . ."

The Secretary felt the bottom drop out from under him. Defenseless. Now, understanding the man's wild driving, there was no way he could hold him responsible. He suddenly had many reasons to be grateful to this man.

"Yes, of course, that's right. Pardon me, friend."

"They gave me a hundred pesos to bring the doctor in an

hour. Understand ... the job was worth the trouble. If you like, I'll pay for the damage ..."

"No. I don't want anything. Forgive me, I've reconsidered."

"Sure ... just insults, like blows."

A little while later, they carried an almost cube-shaped crate down from the power plant's utility shed, made of spruce, covered with German writing. Longines, satisfied with its strength and place of origin, silently translated:

Siemens-Schuckert. Coil type M/. Turbine. Net weight 140 *kilograms.*

And he spoke out loud:

"Good. We'll place the Frenchman's remains here. He'll be a *Made in Germany* Frenchman for the worms."

Katanga felt the moral cruelty of the act. He knew the dead man's patriotic tenderness and he reacted. He had spotted a paint bucket nearby. He went to look for it. And while they folded and accommodated the not-yet stiff remains, he blotted out the German words and wrote in block letters on the lid of the crate:

CI GIT

PARCE QUE VIVRE AVILIT

L'AMI DIT

LON CHANEY

(MAURICE COUSCOI DE GONDRECOURT)

L' ÂME D'ÉGLANTINE

COMME UN SOURIRE DANS CES LÉVRES

The body fit perfectly inside, only the corners remained empty. Alongside a nearby shed, Katanga spotted some huge mounds of quicklime. He asked Dijunto to bring him several shovels of it. With all the little gaps filled in and the top nailed down, two sturdy workers set about carrying the crate back up to the road. Following behind, single file, came Lon Chaney's companions, the Secretary, the plant manager, the driver, and several others.

It was a taciturn expression breaking out in an artistically geometrical form. An ascending march of exhausted beings, up from depths of nightmare to the plane of indifference ... a ceremony touching in its pathetic simplicity. Worthy of the fune-real chisel of Leonardo Bistolfi. Worthy of being mimed by a Greek chorus . . .

At last they reached the road above the dam. The serenity of the reservoir seemed to wash away their anguish. The multi-spirited blue of the water, of the sky, and of their humbling pain. Overwhelmed by Lon Chaney's death, the loss of their respected companion, their faces were clouded. Only Longines growled. A voice like a broken bell, a voice defeated by emo-tion, announced:

"Everything is ready. Time to go."

And the cars slowly disappeared among the meandering mountain ridges.

SANTA ROSA:

The Secretary did not want to see the President of the Neigh-borhood Commission.

"I've had a quarrel with him. I can't stand him. He's an ig-norant peasant full of twists and turns. I took care of the death certificate. You go see him."

Katanga headed for an adobe house, whitewashed with pun-ishing bad taste. When he knocked, someone shouted from in-side:

"Office isn't open. Can't help you now."

He stood there in suspense, uncertain of how to state his business. A dirty, friendly little boy, with a small toasted ear of corn stuck between his teeth, was spying on him from the far end of the porch. Katanga took out a peso and handed it to him. Instantly, after disappearing into the inner rooms, the boy stuck his head out again alongside a man dressed in pajamas, who asked politely:

"Did you knock, sir?"

It was the same voice as before. Katanga nodded his head.

"It's something urgent: If you could please help me . . ."

While the man approached, Katanga pulled out the death certificate.

"I need permission to bury a dead man that we've brought from the dam. I know you're closed. I could pay the fine . . ."

"The fine for what?"

". . . the surcharge for making a request after hours."

"Ah! Well. Give me the certificate."

He went into his office. Two minutes later he returned with a receipt book. He tore out a slip:

"If you please. The fee is one peso fifty."

Katanga handed him ten pesos. With the money pocketed, the functionary's deference poured out artfully, covering up his informal conduct:

"Now, sir, you must go see the cemetery manager. I'm not sure if you'll be able to find the house. His name is Abel Cuimno."

"Abel what?"

"Abel Cuimno. The easiest thing would be for me to send the boy with you. Ceferino, come here. Accompany this gentleman over to Don Hangin' Ass's house. You'll have to excuse the expression, that's what the whole town calls him."

The boy climbed into the battered phaeton, which had the makeshift coffin tied securely to the rear luggage rack.

From the car behind, Katanga studied the crate with a certain professional mistrust. He'd performed thousands of escapes, before many savvy audiences, from similar boxes, tied, bagged, and sealed . . . Why didn't Lon Chaney escape? Death has its own tricks and intrigues. Perhaps, when the box thumped into the pit, the secret spring would be released. And thinking they were burying a cadaver, they'd find out they were really burying a dense joke of rocks and quicklime. Oh, Lon Chaney was capable of anything!

When they reached the cemetery gate, while Ceferino ran to call the manager, Katanga had the desire to get out of the car and, as his former *partenaires* once did, thump the box and ask the dead man if he was there. It was a ridiculous urge but, by association of ideas, absolutely logical. He was not ashamed to check and make sure. Those who can pull off impossible tricks and intriguing illusions, or who have done so, believe more than anyone else in the falsehood of eternity.

"Don Hangin' Ass says he's coming right away," the little boy informed them.

Only Katanga understood. The others raised their eyebrows inquisitively.

Aparicio spotted a man walking their way from a cluster of shacks in the distance, halting at intervals. He was carrying some tools hoisted on his shoulder. His strange bow-legged gait was rather intriguing. Aparicio's gaze and attention were transfixed. Whenever the man stopped, he also dropped his pick and shovel. He pulled on his suspenders with both hands then picked up his tools and continued his march. Closer now, Aparicio analyzed his bizarre appearance: a filthy straw hat dancing atop his skull. Mustard-colored short cotton trousers partially covering his shins. And a pair of new suspenders cinched as tight as possible.

He waddled clumsily past them. He set down his tools next to the cemetery gate post. He pulled on his suspenders. As he leaned forward to insert his key—his bowed-legs curved like a pitchfork, splayed wide as a gallows—everyone understood the aptness of his nickname. It was no joke.

"Hangin' Ass!"

"Hangin' Ass!"

Silent, the gravedigger stuck out his arm straight as a scarecrow's as he pushed the gate open. Then the cars entered the simple country burial ground enclosed in solid brick walls, a perfect square, a corral of death.

Aparicio couldn't restrain his anger:

"What kind of slob is this! Sure has one hell of a perfect nickname! I'm surprised Don Hangin' Ass doesn't have his tongue hanging out, too!"

No one laughed. The man's clumsy, indolent walk was somehow unnerving.

After asking for the required document, he began the work of digging the grave. His effort seemed mindless, lax. Now and then, he paused in his work. He'd mutter something, spitting out his words as if they were a plug of tobacco. He'd pull his suspenders again. And continue digging.

Then something strange happened. Perhaps an identical perception. Perhaps a psychic contagion. They all suddenly found themselves feeling a profound respect for how this man performed his task. What had made such an impression on them? The allegory of the shining wet mound of clay heaped up beside the open pit? The image of the daring man balancing on the edge of the grave? The habitual transhumance from the subtle isthmus which unites the present with the mysteries of the great beyond? The disdain with which the contents of life may plunge down to the continent of death? What was it? No one knew. It was an irrepressible feeling, a mixture of fear, admiration, and approval.

When the gravedigger instructed them to lower the crate, their faces were stony and their hands felt like sand. They obeyed, trembling. Dijunto asked to toss in the first few shovels of dirt but found himself unable to do it. He stammered a few disquieting words in a subterranean accent. Then he stood by in a kind of sensuous, mystical fervor as the grave was filled.

The job finished, Viejo Amor tipped the gravedigger. He pulled on his suspenders then tucked the money behind the leather band in his straw hat. And then ambled toward the gate, as if urging them to depart. Seeing him again from behind, each one remembered his nickname.

But no one dared to repeat it. Silent, taciturn, pale and discolored, they stood, languishing, their thoughts swaying and drooping like the gravedigger's waggling buttocks.

RUMIPAL:

They reached the boarding house at the very moment the pharmacist was leaving. As usual he was carrying a newspaper tucked under his arm, walking with the proper gentlemanly bearing of a man of good roots and status. Having already heard detailed accounts of Lon Chaney's fatal accident, he had come by to relate them to the landlady. Now he was heading back out.

This time there was no mockery or irony when they passed. Only a responsible, dignified silence.

Seated in a circle, they called out from the patio. The landlady, visibly affected, surveyed her guests. In her memory she imagined the one individual who was missing. She sighed. And, suddenly, remembering her role, she lamented:

"What a shame . . ."

"What's to be done!"

"It's a shame you've only just arrived. For lunch there was some roasted baby goats, delicious. Imagine: the kind you see roaming these hills! A perfect salad of tomatoes and beets. Also . . . Well . . . Food to make you lick your fingers."

"Don't talk to us about roasted goat. Nor menus . . . Imagine instead that we're actually hungry. Bring us some fresh-baked bread and fresh butter, ham and cheese, olives and fruit. Beer and Villavicencio water. Right away."

An empty chair.

All their gazes flowed together. And . . . the wonder of it! There sat Lon Chaney, reconstructed with echoes, tender feelings, memories, sympathies. He sat there with his clownish cowlick, his shy, embarrassed face, and his familiar anguish dissimulated by a veneer of *esprit*. Each one of them fondly recalled what he had admired most about their comrade. Katanga, skilled at hiding behind words, remembered Lon Chaney's protean capacity to disappear into his actions. Aparicio, loose-tongued and sneaky, recalled the wisdom of Lon Chaney's fictions. Longines, tidy and measured, noted the clarity and order of his ideas. Dijunto, shy and dexterious, admired the agility of Lon Chaney's heavy, sorrowful excellence. Viejo Amor, lustful, quarrelsome faun, the exquisite tenderness of his love for Eglantine. And Fortunato, grumbling miser, extolled Lon Chaney's skill at begging alms.

Lon Chaney sat there in their midst! Their self-absorption made their friend's presence a reality. And in silence they carried on six distinct and simultaneous dialogues with him.

More prone to abstraction, Fortunato drifted longer in his reverie. He went back in time with Lon Chaney to the saddest days of the crisis. Buenos Aires was tense, filled with beggars and workers without food or jobs. They went out begging together. They split up and wandered through the opulent streets, and at dusk they reconvened at Villa Desocupación, the encampment of the homeless and unemployed, to settle accounts in their newly formed cooperative.

"*Didn't the recounting of each day's odyssey amuse us, Lon Chaney?*"

"Evidentement! *Misery is a very entertaining thing. You often got angry and that increased my happiness. Your daily take was always less than mine. It's just that you stubbornly refused to be convinced. With your vision colored by your old job as bank manager in Prague, you blurred the distinction between the one who gives and the one who lends.*"

"*It's the same difference: giving or lending earns marvelous dividends in heaven.*"

"*Don't you see? You're still confusing charity with finance. You demanded alms instead of asking for them. And then you'd utter the typical thanks: May God repay you. An empty endorsement which no one accepts. The correct thing, I tell you again, is to feign situations of such penury that you seem to sink far beneath even the donors' worst suffering. It's the only way people will really dig into their pockets.*"

"*Perhaps. But I was repulsed by your theatrics. Makeup; artfully ragged jackets and pants; your sorrowful grimaces as you stretched out your hands which you never retracted empty; in a word, your lack of professional integrity. For me, charity is a business insured by God. For that reason, I don't sympathize with the nightmare that you played out on the street. Because the ungrateful person, the one who refuses the beggar his mite of money, doesn't know what he is missing.*"

"*Of course; because you wished to hierarchize the profession: making compassionate beings believe that your personal tragedy could have just as easily afflicted them. Therein lies your error and your disaster. No one wants to see themself reflected in the mirror of another person. Why did you allow your reason to hold you back? I, on the other hand . . ."*

"*Yes: you created the most abject, distorting mirrors. Out of sheer fright, no one dared to look. They tossed you a coin with a sidewise glance. And they walked off, happy to have eluded you.*"

"*Bravo! While they simply avoided you, sad and embarrassed by the encounter! . . .*"

The landlady brought the food and drink they'd ordered. She laid it out on two round tables while her face expressed a wordless grief.

"Thanks a lot. Everything looks good. Now, prepare our bill. At six o'clock we're leaving."

Disconcerted by the news, her expression changed subtly:

"What a shame! Guests like you don't come every day!"

Those who say that food assuages sorrow are simply spreading lies. Knowingly. Funeral meals, when a pure emotion predominates, are unapologetically sarcastic. The simple gesture of raising food to the mouth offends the pain that the lips mutter. Chewing is a corrupt, lascivious chore, dominated by sighs. And swallowing, a profanation that can only be cleansed with tears. They lie knowingly. The ones who eat heartily at funerals are the lucky heirs, who need to restrain their mourning with enough ballast to prevent them from suddenly taking off in a flight of joy.

They felt a generalized and profound inhibition. They tolerated food only to assuage their hunger and thirst. No appetite. No pleasure. On this occasion—lunch, of course, where Lon Chaney's exemplary *savoir faire* always shone brightest— a strong claw gripped their throats. They understood it very well. And they remained silent, gloomy. A long while. Sifting through everything. The fantasies of life and those of death. An hour of raw introspection. A bitter hour of detachment. An hour in which all disasters are recapitulated, disappointments tied up, pessimism sealed with sealing wax, and each one dispatches his message!

KATANGA:

Hey, Lon Chaney! You may not believe this but . . . your behavior has got me a little bit upset. I mean that swindling of common happiness which your death implies! . . . That peculiar peace achieved by accident! . . . Oh, yes: I harbor my doubts! Sickness, when's it's a passing episode, offers, at the worst, a gentle brush with death: a little sparring session with microbes. Natural defenses. Therapeutic counterattacks . . . but not an accident. That brings a definitive betrayal which stuns and upends good health. I prefer sickness a thousand times over! According to the opinion of Doctor Berryer, it must be le plus coûtex des luxes; *but at least you leave your friends and relations the chance at gentle adaptations and consolations in the face of destiny . . . I've always maintained that man shouldn't suffer anything more than senility. Now more so than ever. Seeing you so triumphantly peaceful and unruffled, wandering through the blue meadows beyond the grave, I'm accosted by bastardly passions: envy over death's automatic exculpation. And rage provoked by those who rush headlong toward eternal servitude . . . Yes: you can be vainglorious. You're free of worry. You show-off, enjoying the delightful contrast; because, while life is a sifted discernment of lies, death is a transparency of the truth discerned . . . You can boast! But that's wrong, dammit! It wasn't in the pact we made. Nobody was supposed to die. We left Buenos Aires to enjoy ourselves by helping others enjoy their lives more, with the pesos "liberated" from Freya Bolitho's sickly, insatiable avarice. Remember: you were the one most enthusiastic about our idealistic tour for the sake of others . . . and now you go and plant yourself in the ground. You vegetalize yourself. Because he who dies is planted, becomes a vegetable. He puts out branches and roots in the intimate landscape of the earth. And disperses the seeds of his blood very far below or very high up above men . . . Why leave this way, so suddenly? Why did you, such a skilled, resourceful survivor, break down and die, tearing yourself away from our nucleus? Life is conviviality. No one really lives just for the sake of living, not even the super-egotist. Life is worthless except in the company of friendship. A man like you, who now increases another's solitude*

by drawing yourself apart toward the sweet fields of henbane, per-
petrates the worst kind of felony. The lovely thing about our tour
was the imperceptible, unspoken coexistence, in which we passed
our hours. Oh, the symbiosis of seven disasters into which our conscious decrepitude was fused! I can't forgive your sudden flight. You
really should have stuck around. Why did you sever ties and flee?
Yes: you fled. You were the creative director of our dereliction. One
carries many deaths around on their person: the daily deaths that
shape the long agony of our path. That's life! What amnesia, what
clumsy distraction induced you to forget it and take the fatal step?
I don't want to know. Quiet! I'm not asking. Be quiet! The anguish
sunk deep in my heart asks, and the ID card found in your valise
answers. Shut up! I know. You were fed up with your dependen-
cy, chained to this world. Shhhh! You wanted to finish it once and
for all? And us? How could you renounce our expectations? We depended on each other. Your irresponsible choice cancels and ruins
our faith. The faith that—the same for us as for Saint Paul—is
the nature of the things we anticipate and the evidence of invisible things. No, Lon Chaney: I will not deify you. Your death will
make our existences even more precarious. One lives for their pos-
terity, not for themselves. You should have remembered that. And
you should not have left, there among your papers, that iniquitous stanza of Laurent-Atthalin. That tidy, solidly bourgeois stanza, obese with nostalgias and plumply self-satisfied with indifference, which you copied out so tediously. That indignant stanza,
stunning because it points out that your death was a suicide long
desired; a renunciation decreed in secret when we, overcoming an-
imality, wanted to experience the maximum tragedy of every single
stertorous death rattle. That despicable stanza, which pleased you
so well, which I refused to inscribe as your epitaph:

O Maître, j'ai compris; la douleur a parlé.
Elle m'a dit tout bas les approches de l'Heure;
J'ai rangé tout en moi, j'ai blanchi ma demeure.
Et, sur le sueil usé, j'ai deposé la clé.

DIJUNTO:

Ah, if only you could rebound from the tomb quick as a Basque jai-alai ball! You can't imagine my sadness, Lon Chaney. Our sadness. All together we were a nursery of hopes. Each plant giving sprouts and shoots for the future. Now spreading out, dispersing, who knows where, we will become dry branches. Withered leaves. Fertilizer. Ah, if only you could turn back the calendar like the odometer on any good old Ford. I can't believe that you've died. You, who knew how to sweet-talk both God and the Devil with a thousand wiles. You, who knew how to paint a donkey to look exactly like a tiger. You, who knew the secret hiding places of the many beings inside of you. I can't believe that you didn't avoid slipping and falling! That you didn't throw down a mannequin in your place! That you're going to let both your horse and your prick rot away in the pasture! Come on, Lon Chaney! How long until we see this is just a clever trick? Or did you really want to die? Or did you really want to die?

LONGINES:

Death is a vulgar short circuit. The fuse blows and good-bye! Who brags about a major disaster? If we only we never had to be wounded! ... If we were like those precise, infallible watches whose mechanisms never lose a second, because they function thanks to the oscillation of the atmospheric pressure, as well they should! ... But man is really a stupid, fragile clay cylinder. Instead of taking advantage of natural life forces, he uses them to kill. In truth, man doesn't die: he commits suicide. Yes: to you I say it. To you, who are fattening the mixture of sand, clays, calcium carbonates, iron, magnesium salts, phosphates, and humic matter among the earth. What? You think you've pulled off some amazing feat? Bah! You've got to wear death like a pair of tight trousers, like your very skin itself. Dying isn't that posthumous joy that delights you, but rather the decision of stripping bare the soul to the elements; of skinning off, every day, the tattoo of the adventure itself. Dying without dying. Rodenbach gave me the key: Pour vivre aprés ta mort sois donc mort dans la vie.

APARICIO:

I knew a blind man who stood and faced the rising sun every morning, swearing at it and insulting it. It irritated him so much, until one day a ray of light penetrated his retinas. But instead of illuminating the world for him, it only lit up the cellar of miseries he was living in. No less blind than before, he began to say such transcendental things that the whole town began to take him for a sorcerer. How could he know the human psyche so well if his eyes were still blank as a statue's! Cursed, whipped, mocked, scorned, he was driven from his town and exiled into the depths of the night. I saw him often, wandering around alone. It was pitiful to see how he loudly denounced the clairvoyance of introspection. Beware, Lon Chaney! Don't strut and amuse yourself with false hopes! There is no greater blindness than not knowing how to look at oneself!

FORTUNATO:

When the Montgolfier brothers ascended into the sky, a woman who witnessed their flight began crying and moaning: "What a disgrace! They've found the way of never having to die. And I have to stay down here!" Seeing you in the sky, I'm like the woman in that story. Happy are they who can loosen the body's ballast and soar upwards on the breath of the spirit! Happy, yes, happy! I'll always be a captive balloon. Moored to a gilded mast, my heart palpitates among terrible gasses that never explode. The worst tragedy! Craving the liberating catastrophe but tolerating the tidy normality of everyday life!

VIEJO AMOR:

Poor Lon Chaney! What good did it ever serve you to be decent? I remember our confidential late-night conversations, when you always insisted that: MARRIAGE IS THE TOMB OF LOVE. At your side, my bachelorhood as an old satyr was ennobled. Your conjugal pain justified my conduct. I love all things that can be loved with all the force of instinct. Shame, depravation, baseness exist not only

in morality. Your error was believing that your own morals have
something to do with morality itself. Your desperation discovered
the truth too late: when it was impossible to give up hope. At your
expense, others conjugated the verb "cocufier," to cuckold, which so
mortified you. I belong to "the others." And I've always cuckolded
others. In my life I've cuckolded as many husbands as I could. I will
cuckold as many as I still can, in juicy, meaty, succulent collabora-
tion with their wives ... Love's great technique consists of detest-
ing words and respect. In rooting around and stirring things up.
Groping in the dark. Being discreet and cheeky. Catching females
the way one catches turtles: flipping them over on their backs ...
Whipping them the way you do with camels: forcing them to kneel
down, so you can mount them ... "Cocufier," what a fine verb,
Lon Chaney! Oh, how I wish to God I could carry out my dream: an
adultery agency that makes house calls, delivering infidelity right to
one's front door! ... A business similar to those that flush out plumbing and water lines and sewers ... What an enterprise! There are
so many individuals, who, unlike you, enjoy and admit to plunging
their spoon into another man's pudding! Yes, old man: that's how
it is. Don't grumble any more. Don't be disgusted. You're in heav-
en, at the right hand of Our Lord. He will say to you in Latin, like
Katanga: AMA ET FAC QUODVIS. Yes! Love and commit all the
madness that you like. You'll see that when it comes to love there
really are no sins. Don't be thick. The great stock of love shattered
by your wife and family, was saved by the tenderness of Eglantine.
Enjoy it. There are eleven thousand virgins ... Don't be a fool! ...

THE DRIVER:
One hundred fat, shining pesos! I wish to God there were accidents
like this every day! With four crashes like this I could pay off my
little house and the moneylender would stop screwing me over. A
hundred silvery smackeroos! You never see them all together in your
hands at once like that! I liked that guy's confidence, paying me in
advance. GO URGENTLY AND FETCH A DOCTOR: I almost
killed myself but I brought him in time. A hundred pretty pesos!
It's enough to make you dance for joy. But you've got to watch your

step. *Why do these people think so much? Maybe the guy who bit the dust is some eccentric millionaire. They all look like . . . I don't know. They look like criminals but they act like playboys. A hundred sweet simoleons! If I can, I'll demand extra payment for driving the body and all the others. So . . . Knowing how free and easy they are, I'd be a blockhead for not taking a shot at it . . .*

THE SECRETARY:

Death is an accursed phenomenon on the gaming table of chance. Let us be a nation of tragic gamblers. Let each one place their bets! I've placed mine in front of the political cardsharps. If my ideals win, fine. I'll continue the game in successive wagers. I'll reap the glory that emerges from fortunate bets. All the same, if I lose I'll sink down and hide in the void with the resignation of an expert gambler caught up in fraudulent schemes. And in the great beyond I'll embrace the specter of myself, to console myself about my earthly end . . . Not even a grimace. No macabre histrionics. We have the opaque phlegm of the predestined, and the impassivity of the mystic sense of the world. Let us be aesthetes of the final end. Must we die? Fine, we die. Let's die smiling, taking a certain delight in the hygienic sensation . . . The same as the gambler who forgets the concept of money, let's lose the notion of existence. Life only has value as triumph! In other words, I do not assign it any value, or any merit. My plan is to compromise it, always for the sake of adventure: because risk draws great arcs of pleasure, because audacity poetizes enterprises, and valor is the only generosity! . . . If we can conquer hostile difficulty, let us enjoy the voluptuous sadism of triumph. And let us be cruel. If our urgent work fails to effect the downfall which we plot, let us not be afflicted. What for? Suffering is a morbid form of enjoyment. Let us rejoice like the masochist in the claws of some strange wickedness! . . . Let us make our soul a naked soul. Without the heavy clothing of hypocrisy. That it show itself as is, whole in its ascendency above riffraff and glebe. Let primary sentiments remain in their element, dauntless of culture and plundering feudalism. And let us stamp our mark of passion in any place, with an idiosyncrasy that disdains clever altru-

*ism and cunning piety, so that we might live, without compromise,
the heroic life which sublimates suffering ... Existence is an appalling enterprise if it's not adorned with the pleasures of audacity
and danger. Let us run its course with profound chivalry and lib-
erality of sentiments, as one speeds through a tunnel with a light
at each end. Let us never be detained by the wounding blackness
which lies in wait. A distant splendor illuminates our longing. Let
us defend everything, against everything. Against our peace, before
anything else. Because the only thing that excites the true courage
of honest men is death. Death: light hidden in the dark shadows
of the beginning and the end! Death: light that emerges upon the
intimate horizons with the anguish of the primordial soul! Death:
light that unites the confines of being, and fulfills it!*

CORRALITO:

They left the boarding house in Rumipal late in the afternoon.
The landlady dispensed a year's worth of smiles and a lustrum
of solace as she bid them farewell. By the end of their stay she'd
come to understand the caliber of her guests. But so much
gushing irritated Longines. And when she reluctantly asked
them to pay up before leaving, he felt like reminding her of her
initial reproaches.

The sun painted the trailing brushstrokes of its evening rays.
Heading for Corralito, the cars drove along soft, deeply rut-
ted dirt roads. Whirling clouds of golden dust went balloon-
ing along the ground behind them. Higher up, the thrushes,
with their dark wings, and in mid-sky, flocks of ducks in V formations.

The day was dying. The sunset breathing deeper and wider
into a velvety twilight of mimosa shadows and barking dogs. And
the night came on like a poncho thrown over a nest of rheas.

Sorrowful, downcast travelers. Tired shadows, dragged
through the gloom.

Motors and hearts, nothing more.

Now and then the startled bolting of some wild horses. The magical quietude of a lost, wandering cow. And the flashing hallucinatory apparitions of the nighthawks.

They were getting closer. The fairy lights of scattered houses. The black mouth of the night lighting up its cigarettes here and there.

They passed by the farmhouse of the Italian Viccario. Sudden, unexpected carbide lamps lit up the soup and polenta. The hullabaloo of wealthy settlers.

As they topped a rise, the first electric floodlights appeared. Lights more dangerous than the will-o'-the-wisp: the *luces malas* ... They'd arrived.

The strident diapason of hearts and motors ceased.

The station platform lay in darkness. Twelve minutes until the train from Rosario arrived. They leaned up against the white fence, right next to the station sign.

The breeze anointed their heads. Their senses sunk into the darkness of the train yard. And below the dome of each forehead, the sonorous pulse of the crickets and the soft brilliant light of the lightning bugs spun a web of tranquility and oblivion.

The warning bell to clear the tracks broke the spell. Katanga handed a fifty peso bill to the driver.

"Go buy six second-class tickets for Córdoba."

"Why buy them?" interrupted Dijunto."Let's play the counting crows game."

"Not tonight. We're not up for that."

The Secretary became curious. Anticipating his question, Katanga, laconically, explained:

"It's one of Dijunto's cons. With so many people traveling it's easy to avoid paying for some of the tickets. It all consists in moving from one side of the train to the other, in coming and going, in crossing paths in the coach, while the railway inspector checks the tickets. No doubt, you must understand the difficulty of counting a flock of crows in flight, right? Good. Well, we apply this principle to railway travel. It never fails. With all the confusion already inside the coaches we just add to the disorder. The inspectors always mix up their tally. They often get quite angry because they assume that someone is messing with them; but in the end, they stop counting and go away . . . It's a very comical ruse . . . Dijunto's own invention . . ."

A clever ruse for another time.

Coming into view from the south, the locomotive's cyclopean pupil sprayed its sparks along the tracks. Then the heavy vibration of its steel hulk. Their driver returned:

"Here you are. It cost twenty pesos, ten *centavos*."

"Wonderful. Keep the change. And thanks for your help."

"Thanks? Thanks to you all. I've never worked for such generous people!"

"Blah . . . blah . . . blah . . . So long."

As the driver said good-bye to the others, Katanga took the Secretary's hand. Bidding him farewell, he passed him a wad of bills.

"No, no! Where does this end? Enough!"

"Lower your voice. This amount settles everything. Take it." Their two faces were illuminated by the engine's igneous splendor.

"Just take it," Katanga insisted. "That way you'll be able to act, to do some good. And wipe out that herd of despicable scumbags who seek to oppress the farm workers in this area."

Contracting his facial muscles in acceptance and resolve, the Secretary pocketed the money. Quickly, to prevent the emotion welling up inside him from spilling out, he redirected it into six brusque but cordial embraces.

Once they were seated inside the second-class coach, the Secretary came up to the window.

"Don't worry. We will shed blood, sweat, and tears. The encouragement you've . . ."

The conductor's whistle sounded.

". . . given has moved me like never before. I always wanted to achieve my dream. From now on, I swear to you, I'll fight for the dreams of all those who suffer. In your company I've found . . ."

The locomotive blew its whistle for departure.

"... a great, passionate understanding. I was lacking faith
..."

The steam shot out with deafening blasts.

"... in human solidarity. I've got it now! You can trust in
me. I'll write to you. You'll hear from me!"

Katanga put his head out of the window to dissuade him:

"We'll never hear from each other. I need to tell you. Our
address is ..."

The train was rolling.

"... false. Please forgive us! Learn as we have the great wisdom of simply ignoring it all!"

"............!"

Astonished, the former; smiling, contented, the latter; each
stared back at the other until their separate gazes took flight in
the darkness.

MONTE RALO:

People on the move. Peasants rolling home drunk from the corn
harvest. Sloppy farmers eating and spitting without a sideways
glance. Married couples with mischievous little children. Humble families without the least notion of manners or hygiene.
And the inevitable mother with young daughters—all dolled
up and melancholic—superior to the second-class coach,
resignedly suffering the disorder, rudeness, and general filth.

However much they scanned the carriage up and down, they
could find no better spot than the one they had; near the entrance, choking on ash and clouds of dust; near the door, slam-
ming thunderously five times a minute; near the toilet ...

The toilet expelled heavy malodorous wafts right into their
noses. Katanga stood up to close the door. Impossible: the
latch was missing. His attempt to block it shut with a brusque
push failed; he accidentally lurched inside. Ooof! He thought
he was going to faint. Vomit, piss, garbage, excrement in the

toilet bowl, on the floor and walls. Ground zero for the most
nauseating fetidness. Pale, dizzy, eyes watering, he stumbled
back to his seat. He stuck his head out the window to catch the
fresh air afforded by the speeding train. And he stayed there a
long while, many miles, until he heard the voice of Viejo Amor
suddenly by his side:

"Katanga! Katanga! . . . Look . . . It's Lon Chaney! . . . Standing there on the platform . . . Yes . . . That red eye, barely blinking . . . That extended, waving arm . . . He came to say good-bye
to us . . . Poor fellow! . . . How he'll cry for our departure! . . ."

A rapid glance convinced him he was not dreaming. He
scrutinized the shadows far away to the south. Indeed. In the
distance he could still see the red lantern and stiff bar of the
railroad crossing. But the illusion was perfect in his mind. And
to not dash Viejo Amor's reverie, he agreed:

"You're right . . . It is Lon Chaney. . . I see him there, desperate, on the platform . . . Not on the platform we left from
. . . On another . . . Waving his soul in the shadows . . . Trying
to discern the reason for our absence . . . Yes, yes . . . It's Lon
Chaney! . . . Don't you feel his spirit caressing us? . . . Don't you
feel his goodness abounding with smiles and tears? . . . Oh, the
inner echoes of death, which resound in our anguish! . . ."

And still leaning on the windowsill, they passed a hand over
their eyes and forehead.

After a moment Longines interrupted with a complaint. His
ocular and olfactory inspection of the car had infuriated him.
Scraps of food, gobs of spit, empty cans and bottles, streams of
children's urine, fruit peels, and rotten fruit heaped up in a fetid garbage pile. Who could stand this pestilence, made worse
by the reek of stubbed-out Avanti cigars, stale armpit sweat,
dust from rags, dirty feet? . . . No decent person. And he stood
up. His eyes shone with a sickly light and the wings of his nostrils flared in disgust:

"This train is a real shit hole!"

"What, you, so tolerant of everything!"

"This is a train! A public conveyance! And you have to pay!

And there are sanitation rules!"

His plucked-eagle's head whipped about in bellicose agitation. He would have doubtless continued protesting if someone had answered him. Fortunately, everyone remained silent. And after chewing up his anger, he washed it down with grouchy curses.

Longines had changed. Since that morning, since the moment of Lon Chaney's accident, his psyche had been disturbed. His parsimonious words and actions turned to quick, biting sarcasm. His ingenuity and prudence devolved into stubborn, irascible outbursts. And he, who customarily displayed nothing random or imaginative, showed, at each step, the intemperance which results from misperceptions and their incorrect processing in the brain.

It is easy to be confused by certain emotions — commotion, shock, trauma — the inner disruption which overwhelms a person's soul when their attachment to a friend is broken. Easy and convenient. But it is not the burst of emotions that annuls or dulls one's ability to reason. It is the enormous work required to overcome the grief; the mental fatigue of trying to resolve, in the deepest ravines of consciousness, the isolation that results from the rupture of friendship. Because friendship, for men of Longines's character, is not a trivial, sentimental thing but the strong, subtle union of two intellects. Because being a friend means thoughtfully prioritizing a companion's entire world. Because Longines believed that if love is a tangent which penetrates the confines of inner life, friendship diametrically crosses all moral and abstract matter with the purest and most noble fervor.

A man appeared, with a pinched and bitter face, wearing a round bronze pin on his lapel. He demanded to see their tickets. It was Katanga's job to show them, but before putting his hands in his pockets, he examined the man from head to toe.

"Tickets, sir," the man rudely insisted.

"And who are you to ask for them?" Katanga answered in the same tone of voice.

"Don't you see my badge? Railway inspector."

"Sorry, I'm short-sighted: I don't see any badge ... I only show my ticket to someone wearing a uniform. That's according to railroad regulations, y'know, the letter of the law. . ."

"Oh, you don't say . . . is that right?"

He gave a thin smile of annoyance, before seeking legal recourse himself:

"Guard: make these passengers show their tickets."

There was no need. Katanga handed them over to him:

"Here you are. No problem. But please understand, sir, that you can't fool us or push us around . . ."

"Oh, is that right . . . I can't?"

And he furiously punched their tickets.

Taking a long step forward to continue his job, the railway inspector bumped into Longines. Face to face they seemed a mirror image of each other. The two of them were the same size. Hatchet-faced, sharply lined from the ears to the nose. Bony torso. And gnarled fingers. Continuing his comrade's phrase, Longines told him stiffly, quietly:

". . . and you can be sure, my good sir, that we are going to submit a formal complaint about the lack of hygiene in this car ... we will ..."

"You're the ones making it dirty."

And he lurched away, disrespectfully.

"Don't be a blockhead!" cried Longines. "I won't have it. Haven't you seen that we just came on board? Perhaps you didn't read our tickets? Go clean the bathrooms! Railway inspector? ... Bootlicker. Creep. Pimp."

Longines had hit the bull's-eye. The conductor, who was observing the scene from his place at the back of the car, could not ignore the inherent justice nor fail to take delight in their indignation. The inspector was, after all, one of those servile employees which the company quietly planted on the lines to sniff out and report those conductors who took a cut for themselves. This one had a reputation for being a real swine. Inflexible in his fawning meanness, he would never hesitate to ruin the careers of long-time employees, his own co-workers. Once, after getting off the train at Retiro Station, a conductor who had been fired because of him, gave him such a beating that he was hospitalized for two months. In Villa María, another conductor, after his racket was discovered, fired two shots at the inspector, but missed. Just a short time prior, with the train stopped on the tracks between two stations, he had caught a coworker by surprise, a twenty-two-year veteran of the company. The charges against him: five passengers without tickets! Nine pesos short of the total annual balance! Fifty-four *centavos* stolen from the British stockholders! . . . Now, demoted thanks to the inspector's malice, the former conductor worked picking up litter on the beach in a very miserable little seaside town.

Despite the pleasure the altercation gave him, the conductor was uneasy: he had been harboring a stowaway since Berrotarán. He was well-trained in the dodge, to be sure, but not astute enough to win out against the inspector's close scrutiny. The conductor was trembling, his pulse racing. He was on the verge of retirement and evidence of even this minor transgression could prove fatal: he could lose his benefits. Lose his job. Go hungry.

While the inspector avoided further confrontation with Longines, stepping up to the next seat, the conductor had a black presentiment. And he said to himself:

If only all passengers were like that: dignified! If only a stowaway wouldn't put me at risk. If only! . . .

He could not continue. The inspector was now in a bad mood, which was very worrisome to the conductor.

Aparicio, who occupied a separate seat with Fortunato, stood up and came over. Although the shaking and noise of the train had prevented him from hearing anything of the exchange, his sharp wits sensed something:

"What's the matter with that guy there?" he asked Longines. "I didn't like him from the moment we got on. His sallow color reveals his bad heart. Must be one of those guys with no guts and no soul."

"Go figure ... he's a railway inspector ... You remember that fat one in Junín: *Choose, it's one of two things: either you ride in second class or pay extra for riding in first.* And how Lon Chaney answered him: *One of three things: either you eat less, or you shit more, or you explode ...*"

"How could I forget!"

"Exactly ... Arrogant. Bad tempered. He's got a bug up his ass."

"Yes, a bug up his ass!" roared Longines. "I'm sick of bad tempers! Let every person fix his problems in his own way!"

He spat out his words with biting malice. Even his suppurating eye acquired an unusual vivacity. And thinking inscrutable thoughts, he slowly took his seat: facing the doorway, turned away from the toilet, its fetid stink making the menacing curl of his nostrils even fiercer.

The high-voltage of hatred leaps across angry nerve endings. But phlegm, stealthily, stores it up to be put to better use ...

Longines was a deep well of antipathy. Sunk in his thoughts, life around him vanished. Based on his outward appearance, no one would have suspected the relentless percolation of his thoughts. Nor the effort he made in searching his system for the proper mode of humiliation. Nor his interest in exhausting all scruples from his ego. No one suspected the revenge he was plotting.

Longines was a wellspring of cunning. A horrendous image reached the parapet of his eyes. He closed them modestly. And an ambiguous smile swelled up inside his being. Then, a sharp scream—of air sucked in through clenched teeth—a flash of momentary panic. Something serious, to be sure. Perhaps a projection of the steel wheels' grinding groan, the metal torn apart by the magnitude of its friction. Perhaps a bucket, filled to the brim with ferocious designs, which fell from his hands and, plummeting within his conscience, splattering the face of falsehood. Perhaps ... No one suspected a thing.

Longines was a well of silence.

Suddenly, the crying of an infant was heard from the far

end of the coach. A cry of illness. A tormented and torment-ing wail.

All the passengers turned their heads in sympathy.

The crying continued, monotonously sad. Crying and cry-ing. Penetrating, with its incessant drilling. Overcoming the hubbub of the train. Piercing the walls of vexation.

Many passengers, annoyed, turned around to look.

The crying increased. Its melody became lugubrious, with phlegmy, gurgling warbles. A lament. Lamentably lamentable.

Several passengers hissed and snorted audibly.

But the baby kept on crying. It cried and cried. Making false stops, distressed gagging. Crying ... Crying ...

Some passengers sketched theatrical gestures of resignation. Aparicio and Viejo Amor among them, thinking themselves magnanimous ...

The railway inspector reappeared, fierce and freshly deter-mined:

"Can't you make the child be quiet?"

"What do you want me to do, sir! He's sick."

"Sick? Do you have an authorization?"

"Authorization for what?"

"It's prohibited for sick people to travel aboard this train. You, conductor! How did you let this happen? Perhaps you don't know? Any contagious person can cause big problems for the company."

"It's just a hernia," clarified the father. "Nothing to worry about, it's not contagious. Don't get mad."

As if on purpose, the baby accentuated the fury of its tan-trum. Its crying was flooded with tears. Its pupils disappeared beneath the viscous liquid, displacing the refraction of the overhead electric lights. Its face, the color of fired clay, seemed to be breaking apart from his continuous hiccups. But no mat-ter how much the child exerted himself, the cry was diluted by its distressed, disconsolate, harrowing tone.

It was then that Katanga suddenly turned his head.

More than the child's crying, he'd been thinking about Hi-

laire Belloc's essay "On the Tears of Great Men" whose epi-
graph, from the Gospel of Saint John—"And Jesus wept"—
was for him like a generous glass of *Lacrimae Christi*. Belloc's
thesis also argued for the romantic reintroduction of the era of
tears. There was no reason that the custom of weeping—one
of the most gracious expressions of human nobility—should
suffer further proscription. Crying, provided it does not become a jeremiad, is thoroughly salubrious. It restores equilibrium after emotional upset. It compensates for the deficit of
negative balances. And the tears' powerful bactericide even dis-
infects the eyes and the nose. True. Katanga was familiar with
the work of the London physician J.A. Goodfellow on the benefits of crying rivers of tears, and the defensive and antiseptic effects of lachrymal therapy. Therefore, the lachrymal se-
cretion—which many cowards swallow "to make themselves
strong" and which hack actors fake with drips of margarine—
must not be suppressed by the dams of fashion simply because
it causes makeup to run, nor by the dams of affected virility
which conspire against integrity. No, sir! If crying is physical-
ly and morally useful, then why continue to support the current intolerance which imposes such severe control, denouncing crying as some sort of "weakness"? Why resist those natural
impulses which seek, through tears, to level broken, sorrowful emotions and acutely anxious thoughts? Katanga cried often, openly: to cleanse the cornea of floating dust and his eyes
of all they had seen along the way. And he cried astutely, with
frequency, to cleanse his spirit of turbid wantonness. For any
reason. He did not examine the factors. The important thing
was to cry. For him, tears were the best eye drops and the finest soothing agent. And he would keep on crying, wherever,
before whomever, either authentically, or for the camera, or
with the tears of a crocodile; Buddhic, sardonic, or Sarah Bern-
hardtesque; like Scipio, with relish, before the fall of Carthage;
like Thiers, out of pity, in the presence of Bismarck; like Von
Moltke, enraged, before the defeat of the Marne; whenever the
opportunity might present itself. Had he not cried, for exam-

ple, before the examining magistrate in Río Cuarto, and when confronting the inevitability of Lon Chaney's death?

Katanga suddenly turned his head and leapt up from his seat:

"No doubt about it: that crying child belongs to Don Rufo."

Dijunto and Fortunato automatically turned their eyes in that direction.

Indeed.

Don Rufo!

He was standing up, arguing with the railway inspector.

Katanga had the urge to go over immediately. But prudence gave him pause. He had already crossed words with the inspector. Any further incident could prove harmful for all of them.

"You go, Dijunto. Just go over casually and see what's up . . . Give our regards to Don Rufo. And tell him we're here on the train as well."

As soon as Dijunto got up, Katanga leaned over insinuatingly toward Longines.

"What do you think? Now that miserable inspector is harassing Don Rufo. What could such a manly man as Don Rufo have done to offend him?"

Longines had no response.

He was a well of silence. He continued plotting in his mind.

Serious, laconic by nature, Longines's life was ruled by the most rigorous canons of duty and chivalry. While the others argued or blew-up at one another, he gave his opinion, then said nothing more. With very rare exceptions, no idea or individual inflamed his temper. His passive attitude in that moment was the culmination of the strange events of the day. Never before had they seen him move with such temperamental zigzags. Nor so mysteriously sink down inside himself as he had there on the train.

Katanga observed him intensely.

Longines's expression was now touched with a certain pinch of cynicism. Katanga could not fathom his attitude. Why the change in character? What distortions had corrupted the pulchritude of his judgment? What overlapping intentions fed the confusion roiling in his psyche?

Katanga shrugged his shoulders in a sign of ignorance. But ever intrigued, his innermost thoughts verified the workings of a latent pathology, slumbering lethargically until now.

Dijunto returned. As he sat down to relate his findings, Longines focused his attention by cocking an ear. Katanga noticed the especially attentive interest in the angle of his head. And as the two of them listened, Dijunto went over the details:

"Well, you see: the argument wasn't with Don Rufo, but with the conductor. But it started with Don Rufo, who was traveling without a ticket. That inspector—he should have his ass beaten!—was so furious he wanted to kick him off the train. For nothing more than one ticket! Well, a ticket and a half. Kick them off! The trouble came from the little one's crying. As soon as Don Rufo told him that he was taking him to Córdoba for an operation, that fucker started in with all that business about infections and contagions and about what fatherhood really means, just a big fuss, all holier than thou. After accusing the conductor of letting sick passengers travel without authorization, he asked Don Rufo for his ticket. And when Don Rufo told him that he'd had no time to purchase one, the inspector gave both of them a dirty look. And he said: *Really . . . ? Well I'll make arrangements for the both of you . . .* This guy's a cunning bastard, no doubt. Instead of asking Don Rufo the station where he got on, he went back three seats and asked some poor woman: *Tell me, madam: since when has that child been crying?* Without knowing what dirty tricks he was up to, she answered innocently: *Since they got on, at Berrotarán.* Then he retraced his steps and asked Don Rufo where he boarded the train, and when he answered him: *Monte Ralo*, the Inspector turns white as choler, froths up like boiled milk. He shouts at Don Rufo that he's a liar, and calls the conductor a swindler. They almost came to blows. I arrived at that very moment. The conductor was roaring: *What do think, goddammit, that I'm going to get my hands dirty, for one ticket, for three lousy pesos, after twenty-nine years of service?*

Quiet! . . . Don't insult my intelligence. . . You've been ripping off the company for years. Now you're caught! You'll see . . . And it's not one ticket. Two tickets!

Two tickets?

Yes: two tickets. The little boy has been taking up the whole seat since Berrotarán, lying there in ponchos and blankets. I dare you to deny it. He's got to pay the corresponding fare. You'll see. You're gonna remember me the rest of your life . . ."

The train was coming into a station.

The engine was slowing down.

The railway inspector, who had started jotting down information for his report, stopped writing.

Crossing over to them, he kept on spluttering at the conductor:

"As soon as we pull out, I make my report. Doesn't matter if you don't sign it. There's more than enough proof. You're finished, you prick . . ."

Hearing this, Katanga turned around in disgust.

"Did you catch that?" he asked wrathfully. "Could there be a worse son-of-a-bitch than this anywhere?"

Longines barely shook his head. His suppurating eye stared back so sharp and cold that it made Katanga shiver.

At the far end of the car, in despair, Don Rufo sat suffering for the misfortune that his baby boy's distress had caused the conductor.

....

DESPEÑADEROS:

When the train had pulled out again and resumed its journey, the inspector and the conductor went up through the cars to first class. While the conductor had to stop and check the tickets of the recently boarded passengers, the inspector went straight on to file his accusations.

Using the telegraph at the station in Despeñaderos, he had verified his certainty about the conductor's "arrangement," communicating with the stationmasters in Berrotarán and Monte Ralo. The facts and evidence they gave were decisive. All that remained was to write up the report required to make it official.

Katanga, meanwhile, was alarmed to notice that Longines was missing. On the pretext of buying fruit, he had surreptitiously descended to the platform. Katanga looked out the window and saw him hiding in the darkness, creeping along slowly behind a privet hedge. And then he swung up into the shadows of the train which was now rolling again.

As if he'd been given an injection in his backside, Katanga's intuition did a somersault. He felt the certainty of the unavoidable. And with no time to lose, he launched into an invented story, talking loudly to cover Longines's momentary disappearance, slightly more emphatic than usual, so that no one at all would perceive the slipperiness of his maneuver. It simply added to the lively atmosphere inside the coach.

A short while later he was chatting with Don Rufo when he saw Longines come back and very casually return to his seat. He stifled a sigh. He held his handkerchief to his mouth. And he coughed to expel the pent-up air of his anxiety.

Aparicio was leafing through *La Prensa* which he held open to block the view . . .

Viejo Amor and Fortunato were shifting their bags around in the middle of the aisle, without any particular purpose, just to block the way.

Dijunto gave the order to take their seats like before.

With everything back to normal, Katanga turned the conversation toward another theme:

"I suppose, Don Rufo, that you must have heard about Lon Chaney."

"No. Has something happened to him?"

"Something, no: a great deal. He died this morning in an accident at the dam."

" . . . "

"It's overwhelming. The man who falls to his death gives us the saddest image of life's instability. One wrong step, one misfortune, is enough to demonstrate how fragile we are."

"That's right. My poor friend! Seems like he loved the peace an' quiet in the country so much. I remember his words when we were sayin' good-bye. He'd fallen in love with the place. Wanted to stay."

"Well, he got his wish. He's not far from your place: in the cemetery at Santa Rosa."

"Oh, my poor friend! Just like the world itself. You sing with pleasure today and tomorrow you're squashed like a toad."

"It says in the Bible, Don Rufo: *In another time you sang a song of life, now a lament for death.*"

"Bad luck, you said?"

"An accident. He slipped and . . ."

"Well, the thing is, there's a real villain on this train, and he's gonna bring me some bad luck, y'know?"

Katanga cut in:

"Excuse me a minute. I'll be right back."

"Of course! Go on. See you in a minute, then."

As he sat down next to Longines, he instantly recognized that the friend he knew so well had returned. He was no longer a man accosted from the inside. A man barely smothering his delirious rage. Without exchanging a word, he knew as he watched him that his capacious reason had triumphed again. And arrogance now extinguished — through violent repulsion and drastic actions — his whole inner-being was delightedly recovering its peace of mind.

"Longines!" he pronounced in admiration.

And he went sliding down the slippery slope of a fatal understanding:

The mind makes extraordinary concessions. The emotional awareness of normal people is, by nature, clear, uniform, and plastic. Plunging into it, the heavy hoof of nightmare rips open unfathomable chasms, which displace sentimental matter into rough escarpments. Melancholy is the void; hatred the protuberance. The work of the humble soul consists of patiently scaling the walls of their uneven passions. And to sweetly erase, with slow efficacy, the cliffs and canyons in the enormous, complex task of using the gravel of solace to fill in and level out the precipices of love. But there are proud beings, whose desire for kindness and common good is staunched, who refuse to accept the anxiety caused by gradual effort, who do not want to find a path through their own labyrinth; and overleaping the anfractuosities of the self, prefer to follow the short-cuts of personality, to flatten the unevenness with one single gigantic effort. They are titanic beings who, causing disaster equal to what they have suffered, level the sentimental terrain, smooth the sensations, and thus enjoy the glory of cenesthesia. Longines! Longines!

....

RAFAEL GARCÍA:

The conductor was extremely puzzled when he did not find the railway inspector writing his report. The man had gone off in a rage to do exactly that.

Don Rufo, who had the price of the ticket ready, as well as the money for the fine, to try to sort out the mess, sat expectantly with his pesos in hand.

One facing the other, they waited a long time for him to arrive. The conductor's hands and mustache trembled. Don Rufo lamented the conflict and its consequences.

"It's not right that you might lose your pension benefits on my account. It can't be! I'll pay whatever amount he demands."

Speaking, speaking without ceasing, about the possibility of finding a solution, interceding with requests, witnesses, and mediators, they didn't notice that the train was pulling into a station.

Crestfallen, resigned, the conductor busied himself with his duties on the platform, between the shrieking of brakes and the puffs of steam, which were compounded by his own sighs and huffing in the complex mechanism of his spirit.

The brief stop did nothing more than accentuate his anxiety.

Could he be, perhaps, in his compartment, writing the accusation?

The signal for departure given, he boarded the train, keenly desirous to make sure. The inspector's cabin was empty! He sped along the corridors, checking the toilets.

God, I'd love for him to need my help for something. If I found him sick somewhere, maybe . . .

Not in any of the toilets!! Then, extremely alarmed, it occurred to him to check the dining car. Not there!! The only place remaining was the boxcar. Pressured, feverish, he tried all the doors. And after asking the postmaster and the guard on duty, swaying in time to the rocking of the train, he exclaimed in a fluster:

"He's nowhere to be found!!"

They were pulling into Bower station.

BOWER:

Maybe he's gone and hidden in the locomotive. That swine, to screw me like this, he's capable of anything!

He ran through the train like a man possessed.

"The inspector . . . have you seen the railway inspector?" he anxiously asked the engineer.

"I don't give a shit about that asshole," the engineer replied without looking up from the connecting rods he was oiling.

"And you, Don Bernardo, you haven't seen him? . . . he got on in Despeñaderos . . ."

"Me? . . . It's none of my business. Let's hope to God he fell off! . . ."

"Hope to God he fell off!" the conductor repeated, opening his eyes, as wide as possible, as if just now, pronouncing the sentence, he'd perceived its meaning. "Let's hope so . . ."

He went striding off to speak to the head conductor:

"The inspector! . . . The inspector! . . . Send a telegraph to Despeñaderos and Rafael García . . . The inspector! . . . He's not on the train! . . ."

"Just get out of the way. What's your problem? Move. Get out of the way. Hurry up! I'll find out and communicate with the station at Colonel Olmedo."

The conductor blew his whistle twice. He waved the open-track flag the wrong way. He stepped up on the metal rungs of the ladder, almost slipping. Spluttering, he gestured, wildly, exasperated, trembling, confused, overjoyed, OVERJOYED, OVERJOYED.

....

COLONEL OLMEDO:

When they reached the next station, Longines seemed completely given over to the softness of sleep.

The second-class coach had stopped just before a sign with glowing white letters, phosphorescent against a blue background dark as the night.

The conductor ran across the platform.

"Colonel Olmedo, if I'm remembering correctly, commanded the Córdoba Battalion in the War of the Triple Alliance. Thanks to us, those of the eastern band, the war was won. If not, the Paraguayans would still . . ."

The conductor was signaling to the stationmaster.

"Please, Aparicio. No history lessons. South Americans have a propensity for exaggerated eulogies about any historical stupidity. Look at the hubbub the Argentines got into because Sergeant Cabral gave his horse to San Martín or because French and Berutti handed out little two-colored ribbons on the twenty-fifth anniversary of their independence. There's no sense in such commemorative nonsense. We give away handfuls of cash, and, as you see, it's nothing . . . *(The stationmaster and the conductor boarded the train.)* As for the rest, the current fashion around here of giving railway stations famous names really annoys me. Who are Gigena, Berrotarán, and Rafael García? Famous men who remain anonymous despite having places named for them. Rich men who donated the land for the stations to the English. Heroes whose greatest exploit was to be friends with the Minister in charge of doling out glory . . . *(The stationmaster took down information from Don Rufo and those around him.)* Yes, Aparicio, *je m'en fiche,* the notoriety that train conductors spread just by shouting out the name of each station to the sleeping passengers. For me, a name's legitimate renown lies in the owner's wisdom as he carves it into the block of the human heart. I detest that farcical fame which only rings a bell in the public ear. We must reclaim the meaning of things. I admire the temple of Pasteur, which turns his name into the verb which pasteurizes the world. I love Volta, Ampère, and Watt, who have become monads of the electrical enigma. Freud, pioneer of the subconscious, who founds an ecumenical enterprise to colonize it. Taylor himself, whose principles were spoiled by the iniquitous Taylorization of the effort. And even Victor Hugo, creator of empty and emphatic Hugolatries . . . *(Departing, the stationmaster paused on the coach's steps.)* This is what matters. Make a neologism from one's own personality! Graft from your own neologism an immortal tree! Renown that can never be abolished by decrees. Fame that escapes the reaction of little tipstaff ministers, little tin-soldiers, mini-presidents. Glory shed down from above."

"Finish already . . . Enough babble . . ."

(People crowded around, examining the steps on the side of the coach.)

Katanga stopped talking. He pursed his lips as if sealing them.

"Bah . . . you were getting heated . . ."

"Not at all. I was thinking about my disaster. Abd-ul Katam ben Hixem will not leave behind a lasting name but rather the burlesque epitaph of his nickname: Katanga! ... *(The conductor, now calm, was pointing out several signs.)* I could have been someone. To characterize my period of life with some brand name. My tricks, my feats, my traps, my stage machinery were special devices in the intrigue of illusion. With my name, I was able to conjure up a certain kind of human artifice. Like Cagliostro, like Thurston, like Pickman. To leave behind my word. Blondin: blondiste. Fregoli: fregolism ... *(The stationmaster called the police sergeant over to the car.)* But, oh! Doctor Inhell got mixed up in the inferno of philosophy. He wanted to know too much. To transcend grace and ingenuity by shuffling concepts. And his tricks, stunts, traps, and equipment all fell into the formidable contrivance of sophism. He got burned, of course, in the slow fire of meditation and in the hot coals of his own inquietude. And he became this, what you see here before you, a walking nickname: Katanga!"

"*Catanga bostera! ...*"

"Exactly: *catanga bostera* ... a dung beetle, an insect which rolls along his chosen ball of excrement—reflections, remembrances, etcetera—to nourish himself in the flooded winters of desolation."

(By the time the stationmaster and police sergeant stepped back down to the platform they seemed convinced.)

The whistles for departure were blowing.

Longines seemed to wake up. He opened his eyes: one a hawk's eye, the other a little boy's. And lowering his eyelids he mused rapturously into Katanga's ear:

"You're the craftiest, most inveterate rascal I know. An actor through and through. Your name should perpetuate the skill of artistic simulation."

"And what about the skeletons in your closet?"

The train now in motion, the conductor returned to the second-class car. He crouched down in the aisle in front of them. And after scanning the floor, he drew near to converse:

"You two didn't notice? You didn't see anything? The inspector has disappeared. There's no sign of him. Everybody thinks that he must have slipped off while the train was in motion. The police have recovered a banana peel caught in the metal rim along the edge of the step. Seems a clear sign that he slipped. Frankly, I wouldn't wish anyone to die, but . . ."

His conversation was no more than a monologue. He was so euphoric that he left no chink where one might introduce a sentence, an objection, a response. He went from seat to seat. Talkative. Full of atrocious deference. Repeating the remarkable occurrence and its details. Hardly varying the inflection of his voice: solemn, exalting "the divine justice" of the accident; pompous, proclaiming, "the irrefutable proof of his innocence" and compunctious, dissimulating his effusive happiness in front of his audience of passengers.

Longines roused himself and stretched, bored, disgusted, and disdainful.

In a few minutes the train picked up speed. It rolled along, through gullies, alongside a steep cliff. Turning to the left, a panorama of Córdoba suddenly opened up on the opposite side, and they found themselves rolling through the electric constellation of the San Vicente district.

"Finally, we're here!" exclaimed a strapping young boy in loose trousers, sitting up in his seat. I feel like I've been whipped on the bottom. We're gonna get off the train with our butts as sore as prisoners . . ."

"That's the purpose of the rear-end: a pound of flesh made to spend . . ."

The little old lady's voice provoked an uproar of laughter.

A cloudy tumble of alleys and barking dogs, the suburban quarter opened out toward the city center. To the left of the Pucará sports and boxing club, the bend of the Suquía River shone like a bright scimitar. And amid the joyous ringing of bells they reached the asphalt platforms of the train station, thick with imminent embraces and heavily loaded porters.

Their little band bid farewell to Don Rufo, setting a date to meet in the coming days. And then they were lost in the bustling crowd, each one carrying his bundle.

Amid the tumultuous throng bubbling over with insincere delight, Longines commented:

"Horrible trip, don't you agree?"

....

CÓRDOBA:

They had now been in Córdoba for four days.

Dressed for town, each man wearing a fresh set of new clothes, they strolled their skepticism through every part of the city. Restless. Tireless in the cause of leisure—a most difficult task to maintain by day—the provincial sluggishness imprisoned them in its treacle. Yawns. Empty hours. Useless nights. In its gestures and expressions, their indolent activism became weak and inhibited. They were fed up with pious, churchgoing women in their lace veils and sweet cakes with syrup. They felt the stagnant tides of tedium. And skilled at salvaging the spirit, feeling increasingly rancid and mucilaginous, they resolved to get mixed up in something.

"To start with, let's make a count of all the bronze plaques hanging in the vestibules."

Just like peasants visiting Buenos Aires who break their necks craning to count the floors of skyscrapers one by one, they indulged themselves with the earnestness of full-time university students. That task consumed two full days.

"What a racket! Whoever's not a lawyer around here must have a hard time scraping by."

"Currently, there are around one thousand two hundred of them in practice, spitting fire and lava, like active volcanos."

"What a stink!"

"Do you recall that fellow we followed along Calle 27 de Abril, from the Cathedral to Calle Santo Domingo?"

"Of course. That was hysterical, dodging lawyers and beggars on the sidewalk: *Hello, counselor; pardon me, brother. Hello, counselor; pardon me, brother. Hello, counselor; pardon me,*

brother . . . But even better was all the confusion with the porters, the night we arrived. Do you remember?"

They nodded unanimously, reconstructing the scene. A true
spectacle, symptomatic of the juridical spirit of this landlocked
city. Two porters, hauling two valises each, had just finished
stowing a tourist's luggage in the taxi. The owner of the bags, a
haughty woman from Rosario, asked them how much tip she
should give. With unflappable decorum, the oldest man said
to her:

"Please, you may pay us whatever you think is fair."

"Well, you see . . . I don't know the price . . ."

"The standard fee."

"Isn't one peso enough?"

"Personally, I won't file a complaint. As for my counterpart,
you'll have to pay him the same as me. He's my helper."

"Fine, here's another peso. But let's be clear: this is robbery."

"No, ma'am, it's justice."

They were dressing to go out to visit Don Rufo.

Viejo Amor and Dijunto were uncomfortable in their new
clothes. For them it felt like a disguise: something which suppressed their idiosyncrasies. Accustomed to loose garments
and wide, unconfined movements, their snug new jackets and
trousers cut into their armpits and squeezed their buttocks,
prompting an endless string of snorts and grimaces.

"*Hombre,* don't I look like Don Hangin' Ass himself in these
clothes?"

"No. They're a little tight on you, but you should stop worrying about it."

"Look who's talking! . . ."

"I've always worn good clothes and shoes," boasted Aparicio.
"Of course I've had to go hungry sometimes. We *Rioplatenses*
take pride in our appearance. We don't skimp on clothes."

"Yes. All dressed up, you make for some fine and dandy packages . . . so tightly wrapped that we foreigners have to
break your wax seals . . ."

From the next room, Katanga heard the conversation. He judged it both good and bad. The day before, without meaning to, he had witnessed a *Te Deum* in the Cathedral. And he remained firm in his opinion:

"Here, as in Buenos Aires, as in Montevideo, people spend ridiculous sums on clothes. But they don't really dress well: they puff themselves up! It's one thing to wear fine, impeccably cut suits, and another thing entirely to wear them well. There are very few men here who don't block out the waist, who don't pad the chest, who don't show themselves off as graceful and pretty ... Specifically, most people—the sheepish mass of fashion followers—do contradict the natural instinct of elegance. They don't understand that tailors are vile merchants of vanity. That grace and slenderness are attributes, neither given nor lent nor pawned ... despite the price difference for the leather—for gloves or shoes, let's say—I prefer kid skin to nutria, gazelle to guanaco. Around here they're all guanacos, clumsy bumpkins ..."

He paused before continuing:

"Yesterday I observed some prominent Cordovans. But these men clearly needed a lesson in dandyism. Better yet, a whole course. Still, they're a far cry from that contemptuous hierarchy where morality cedes to an excess of grace, scrutiny, and conformity. The men renewed in me a strident memory: how Roosevelt was received with fresh paint and new curtains. The fetid frocks stinking of mothballs at the official banquet. And the ridiculous photophilia of a whole city, mad to pose alongside a head of state ... *(Bending over, he smoothed out the crease in his trousers.)* It's true, Aparicio, here, very few men really know how to wear a suit. The majority are unaware that the first rule of elegance is forgetting about your apparel. But they strut about, pampered and conceited. And violate the unequivocal precept set out by George Bryan Brummell: 'Being well-dressed means not drawing attention to yourself.' *(He deliberately wrinkled his tie.)* Here in Córdoba, actions, and the mimicry of actions flow so thick that it sets one's teeth on edge.

They're lacking that monopoly of sagacious intelligence which stamps its 'label' of personality. Or which makes them different, in the end, from current foolish trends. Fashion makes everyone equally idiotic. And even vengeance, a beloved pleasure, is carried out with dull piety, when it should be an exquisite poem of satisfactions. Isn't that right, Longines? *(The man shrugged as if to say: What difference does it make to me?)* That's why all of us dandies are proud. We're enthusiastic about the luxuries we enjoy. And we don't offend refinement by making contact with what's crude ... *(He smudged the shine off his new shoes.)* Aulo Gelio, in a few words, summed up the classic hatred of elegance. This was already his family distinction. Anyone can awaken love, but hatred? Over the centuries no one has successfully eclipsed him. On the contrary, throughout the promiscuity of the ages, he has always maintained his reputation as arrogant, remembered for his enchanting affectations that can only be gifted by nature ... *(He soaked his handkerchief with opopanax.)* When it becomes common knowledge that "the world belongs to cool, calculating spirits," as the author of *The Prince* predicts, humanity will have reached a beautiful stage of social *souplesse*. The heat of passions and plots weighs heavy as chains and shackles. Because, as soon as the transitory fire of enthusiasm and impulse is spent, its dark ash falls into the depths of temperament ... *(He bent his hat a little bit out of shape and placed it on his head.)* It's necessary to cast off from the soul all dead weight that impedes the harmonious interplay of ideas and sensations. To be spiritually agile. To have an aesthetic awareness of attitudes. And to bask in the knowledge that superiority is enjoyed through the disdain of others ... *(His tidy negligence was silhouetted in the light from the doorway.)* From Alcibiades to Boni de la Castellane, life has sown beings of that variety. We must emulate them with the unaffected admiration demonstrated by Barbey d'Aurevilly in his ode to the handsome Beau Brummell. Thus, by example, will we learn what's most important: getting to know ourselves: in order to polish the sharp roughness of individuality. In short:

we must not be disgusted by our own self-conception!"

The cobblestone pavement, full of potholes, gave Calle Santa Fe the look of a dry riverbed. The weeds in the gaps and the
fresh tufts of grass that decorated the sidewalk accentuated the
rustic tone. As a finishing touch, they turned the corner to see
the cow and calf of a traveling milk wagon. The afternoon was
filled with clinking and lowing. A milkmaid and her little boy
with curly ringlets dismounted from the front seat and filled
two glasses with frothy milk.

In the shade they spotted the three students from their
boarding house, more stretched out than seated in folding
chairs, with books closed on their laps. The moment he spotted the milkmaid, the student from Rosario crossed the street
to flirt with her. Rescoldo was snoring. Patay was following the
flight of some pigeons . . .

The streetscape with its pastoral scenery paralyzed all six of
them:

"Are we here in Córdoba or are we witnessing one of The-
ocritus' Idylls?"

"Honestly, there's nothing missing: cowbell, colloquies,
snoring . . ."

". . . stones, clouds . . ."

". . . milk . . ."

Patay let out a cackle of laughter, applauding the accuracy of
their critique. And in a Santiago accent, replete with sibilant S's,
he recited, by association of ideas, various bucolic examples from
literature . . . That was all he knew: brief stanzas, short fragments.
Nevertheless, his pompous speech sounded like a real lecture.

So they terrified him with a vulgar, practical question:

"Could you tell us which tram takes us to the Children's
Hospital?"

"To the Children's Hospital . . . none. Take the line one bus.
It will drop you nearby. Get off in front of the Argentine Central Railway Station. Go two blocks south."

"Excellent. Thanks."

"Have a lovely time."

Since the first moment, they had become friendly with them all. With Rescoldo, from Rioja, for his austerity in silence and humility. With Patay, for his crafty imagination. And with the one from Rosario—whom they called Fenicio, "the Phoenician," after his native city's nickname—for the easy, lyrical freedom of his bohemian attitude.

Twenty minutes later they were approaching the hospital.

"That's Don Rufo's boarding house. Number 550. Right next to the lottery office."

"Plain as day: *GOLDEN DREAMS:* LOTTERY & OFFSITE BETTING."

"Football pools and double betting . . . Some golden dream that is . . ."

"Why so pessimistic? Can't you just see it . . . income securities, funding bonds, debentures, and spare change?"

"What a fortunate fortune, Fortunato!"

They went into the boarding house. Don Rufo was sitting up in bed reading the newspaper. They walked right in, taking him by surprise. Confused by their sudden intrusion, backlit as they were in their new clothes, he thought for a second that the police had come to arrest him.

"Hey! Watch out, tough guy!"

"Look, we've caught the *gaucho* with his guard down!"

"Of course . . . Suddenly like that . . . Anyone would be surprised . . . That mess with the railway inspector still has me jumping with fright . . ."

"Stop being silly. Your boy, how's the little boy! Did they operate on him?"

"Not yet. He's under observation. According to the sister, the doctor ordered a preliminary treatment. He's in good hands. It's nice to see the li'l pup. All cleaned up, so comfortable . . ."

He made an effort to contain his emotion.

"C'mon. Don't get upset. Everything'll be fine."

"You already know: you can count on us. It . . ."

"More than ever!"

Viejo Amor—thoroughly uninterested in children like any

good Don Juan—had picked up the newspaper from the bed.
Seated comfortably on a bench, he was reading peacefully.

Aparicio gave a start, as if drawn by a magnet. The enormous
heavy type on the back page! Without warning, he snatched
the paper away from Viejo Amor. He showed the article to the
rest of them. And he plunged into the sea of headlines:

CRIME OR ACCIDENT?
TRAGIC DISAPPEARANCE OF RAILWAY
INSPECTOR LEFÈVRE
SUICIDE THEORY DISCARDED!
ALL RESOLVED TO CLEAR UP ENIGMA:

SLIP OR SHOVE?
FATALITY OR VILLAINOUS INTENTION?

SCIENTIFIC EXAMINATION:
TRACES OF EVIDENCE FOUND IN TRAIN CAR AND
ON SOLES OF VICTIM'S SHOES

VISUAL INSPECTION OF CRIME SCENE

JUDGE TRAVELED BY HIGHWAY!
BLOOD STAINS ON BRIDGE AT TERCERO RIVER

SENSATIONAL STATEMENTS
FROM FARMWORKER
WHO FOUND BODY FLOATING IN WATER!

LOCARD AND LACASSAGNE
OFFER OPINIONS ON
SHOVES AND SLIPS IN CONNECTION WITH BANANA
PEELS

LACK OF EVIDENCE!
IN DUBIO PRO REO: INSUFFICIENT PROOF TO
DICTATE TEMPORARY CUSTODY

WILL THE MYSTERY BE REVEALED?

YESTERDAY'S LEGAL PROCEEDINGS
FROM THE EXAMINING MAGISTRATE

WARM PRAISE FOR THE POLICE

AN ADMINISTRATIVE DIVISION
WHICH BRINGS HONOR
TO THE GOVERNMENT AND THE PROVINCE!

Aparicio reached the end, diminished, dispirited. But something urged him on. He scanned the pages anxiously. He couldn't find any real article. It was a typical "investigative" account. Half a page of headlines, a miserable little column of unconnected text.

When he finally found the piece, he had the impression of climbing into a bathtub after having swum through a sea of ink.

"Read it out loud," demanded Don Rufo.

Aparicio complied:

Authorities yesterday continued their ongoing investigation to clear up the death of Railway Inspector Mario Lefèvre, whose disappearance occurred four days ago on the train from Rosario to this town, by way of La Cruz. The Examining Magistrate, along with technical personnel from the department of "Personal Security," verified two legal proceedings of capital importance: the examination of the second class railway coach, and the visual inspection of the bridge near Despeñaderos. The results of the expert investigation ordered beforehand do not point to any specific imputations. The mystery remains unfathomable.

The Conductor's situation has improved tremendously. His release, granted in his favor for lack of proof, makes clear that the charges against him and the various suspicions have been completely cleared up. Tomorrow we will publish the

opinion of several celebrated experts about the banana peel
that was discovered as circumstantial evidence of the crime.
Additionally, other valuable information which the tyranni-
cal restrictions of space now oblige us to hold in reserve.

Despite the fact that the mystery has not yet been solved,
the Judge has sent a note of congratulations to the Chief of
Police, for the zeal and efficiency shown by his junior officers
in cooperating with judicial investigations. If that has happened already, when nothing has yet been discovered, our
readers can predict the praise he will receive once the investigation is complete. That offers further proof that our Police
Force stands as a badge of legitimate pride for the current
government, which embodies and interprets the popular will
with wisdom; and a stinging slap in the face for the opposition who deny the achievements of the Police Force, as they
angrily wallow in their ostracism.

As Aparicio read, his olive-hued face, at first stunned and confused, was transfigured and illuminated with a smile that began
to grow inside him. Finally, reaching the last paragraphs, his
muscles convulsed in tremors of laughter:

"What a way to lick the boots of the police! This is a reputa-
ble newspaper, this?"

Still absorbing the news of the conductor's release, Don
Rufo nodded, barely uttering:

"Yes. It's the paper of record."

Longines wound his watch . . . During the reading, like a solitary man full of information, he entertained himself by tun-
ing into the others' psychic waves, without showing anything
other than his patient indifference. But, deep down inside, he
felt a warm radiant happiness. Happiness with himself and his
comrades, for the nobility of his action and the secret solidarity that it created among them. Light, resoundingly proud of
himself—his emotional battery charged up by the nightmare
of Lon Chaney's death now totally spent—he remained, he let
himself be, he was . . . And he kept on winding his watch . . .

Viejo Amor shook everyone out of the uncertainty of the moment:

"See? There was no need to get upset ... Should we go take a walk around?"

"Let's go."

As they headed out, Katanga, adjusting the knot of his tie, bumped into Longines on purpose. They waited a second. There was a slight hesitation. Then two tenderly malicious glances ...

They reached the Bar L'Aiglon by way of Avenida Olmos. One side of the street was quite old, the other, an ungainly clash of structures. At first, a rough extension of gouged and cracking walls. Then, nearing the downtown, a slenderness of uniform buildings. Finally, at the far end, a squalor of vacant lots choked by posters and handbills.

All of Córdoba was like this: a double face, a double expression, like Scopas's athlete who forever laughs and cries simultaneously. Stumbling blocks and progress. Devout sisters in habits crouching behind Spanish wrought iron grillwork, the flapper in a bathing suit that highlights her natural charms. Rancidness and *plein air*. Propaganda touting virgins and swimming pools ... From Sarmiento Park they had contemplated the city skyline. But they remained taciturn: rough inequality. Imbalance. Disharmony. Insolent churches surrounded by mud hovels. Hulking mills bordered by tin shacks. Modern palaces next to squat red-brick houses ... a horrible, displeasing, broken perspective: arrhythmia of vacant lots and towers. Of presences and shadows. Dissonance of opulence and misery. And they categorically repudiated the absurd subjectivity. Above all they loathed the decadence and luxury of religion—in the brilliant cupolas stacked like temple dancers' breasts, the altars carved and encrusted with adornments, and embroidered cloths worth millions of gnawing appetites—holding sway over the smooth cement tendons of factories, markets, and workshops ... They continued their stroll through the streets and plazas. A greasy city of obese friars. An infirm city of sick people without beds. A waspish city, stung, driven, and zipping with deceit, archbishopricked with dogmas. They were pained by the stubborn bronze likenesses of local grandees and the conspicuous absence of statues of the great national leaders, excepting, of course, José de San Martín. All of Córdoba was like this: contrasts, without links between the counterparts. Incongruences, with no unity in the opposition. Something irrefutably contradictory ... They saw it as a shoddy colonial rubbish pile, full of spurious art which perpetuates its outdated values while opposing new perspectives which prioritize the living. The stupefying theologies of the fifteenth century, which still manage to assert themselves as souls immune to error and faith. And the fossilized clay monuments of cloisters and museums, which only serve to document the prevailing fetishes, given that they lack the dignity of olden days or the old age of dignity ... Bitter, disappointing hours passed. It wasn't possible! Where were the promised tourist attractions? Where the beautiful scenes that the railway propaganda grinds into our eyes *velis nolis*? Nowhere! All of Córdoba was like that: ancient inheritance and *sans façon*. Charity and usury. Prayers and cocaine. A city clogged with convents and hovels. A city which aspires to elevate itself while breathing through the spigot of the university prick; unable to extend its spirit beyond the circle of hills and gullies. A city made wretched by bureaucratic marasmus, retching on the saintly odor of vice and the stench of congregations ... Tacitly, they were already disposed to leave. To abandon that urban crock, boiling over with suffocations of every kind. They, who were a *coincidentia oppositorum*, could not tolerate disparity when combined with inconsistency. But ... there was also something stupendous about Córdoba: the climate. And for three consecutive afternoons they walked up the hill to Sarmiento Park to watch the sunset and the evening close in around them. There, facing the panorama of the corrupted city spread out below, they experienced the joy of life which the Athenians enjoyed from the Acropolis and the Romans from atop the cliffs of Capri; the happiness that the English, eternal refugees of fog and mist, drink in from the heights of Funchal, Taormina, and Sintra. Then, emphatically, they resolved to stay. For the weather, if nothing else: to feel the warm caress of the sun as it slips behind the screen of the mountains; the silken hand of the tenuous shades of sunset; and the exultant melody of the breeze fanning through the plane trees . . .

They occupied two sidewalk tables on the terrace outside the Bar L'Aiglon. Tablecloths of Basque weave. Chairs of colored wicker.

When the waiter arrived, Katanga got up from his seat, trading places with Fortunato.

"Excuse me. It's just unbearable. Hunger produces in me the worst revulsion. I can't sit and watch people eating giant sandwiches."

The waiter and a few patrons turned their heads. All in unison. A slender young woman, with an angular face, dry skin, and strong teeth, was devouring a triple-decker sandwich.

"Imagine that!" murmured Aparicio. "A skinny little slip like her; she looks like a badly painted sigh! . . . If you didn't see her eating, you'd think that she fed on slices of air smeared with butter . . . And every mouthful a perfect bite of nothingness . . ."

"Ugh, we get all kinds!" commented the waiter, before asking: "Ready to order?"

"Chops. Seven chops."

"No. For me some Amontillado sherry," corrected Longines.

"And for me Byrr with soda. Five chops, nothing else."

"We don't have Byrr, sir."

"Kola, then."

As soon as the waiter went away, Dijunto turned to Katanga:

"It's curious. Such an elegant café serving *Cola de caballo*. If I'd known I would've ordered a *Carqueja* tea, good for the liver . . ."

"You're confused, old man. It's not some herbalist's remedy. By the way, where do you suppose the *Yuyero* is hiding out now? Such a pleasant *criollo!* The Kola is a really good drink for digestion. It's made with herbs from Central Africa."

"Near your country."

"What do you mean my country? I'm from . . ."

"From Katanga . . ."

"Very funny! Longines will do anything to get a laugh . . ."

"Isn't Katanga a region of the Belgian Congo situated in Equatorial Africa, near Rhodesia? Then, what's strange about there being Kola in Katanga?"

"As if a *catanga* had a *cola* . . . Beetles don't have tails."

"Such a rich, radiant pun . . . *catanga* is a black man, and a dung beetle, and *cola* is also tail, and ass, and glue and queue, and *cola de caballo* is a horsetail fern, the digestive herb, as well as the horse's tail, and the horse turned into glue! Whew."

"Your joke would be even better if you knew that Katanga has the richest radium mines in the world . . ."

"You're right . . . now I get it . . . You'll even cure cancer, just by talking!"

Katanga was lost in thought.

The laughter leapt, still rowdy, as the waiter served them.

The day was hot. The first sips were delectable, comforting, revitalizing.

Suddenly several stinkbugs came plowing boldly across the table. Flicked away, they plinked against the appetizer plates, leaving a foul stench between their fingers.

More gulps. The presence of more stinkbugs produced frowns.

No time to waste, they stopped jabbing the olives with tooth-picks and simply, delightedly, began to pop them into their mouths, as they also stopped jabbing Katanga with their jibes.

"Still more beetles. What a stinking plague of stinkbugs!"

"It's the weather. It's going to change for the worse."

They watched the sky. While they did so, a phalanx of bee-tles marched with impunity among the plates of brined cock-les, peanuts, and potato salad. Irascible blows from their hands. Imprecations.

"A damned plague!"

"Such bad luck: the things that bug you always come in a bug dance!"

It was strangely hot. The asphalt absorbed the burning heat of the day. The imminent storm loosened its net of shadows. A humid, penetrating heat. A heat of nocturnal hues, with all the blushing color of the warm, tropical gusts.

The stinkbugs invaded everything. The sudden infestation shattered their composure into violent gestures and contortions. Annoyance broke out everywhere. The owner of the bar intervened. He mobilized the dishwashers. Brooms and rolled-up newspapers and stomping feet. The siege was partially abated. But, soon, the stinkbugs' strategic instinct had them retracing their steps. And they retreated into the hidden places no one could see . . .

Only Katanga remained calm. Observing them. Serenely startling and flicking them away. He exhibited an extraordinary good humor. As if the others' annoyance prompted in him a secret complacency. Longines was about to reproach him, when he noticed Katanga dissuading him, demanding, with an open palm, silence. He coughed fictitiously. And noticing that the three handsome young ladies seated to their right were listening to him, he declared:

"Come on . . . don't curse . . . What do you gain by getting angry? Look! Like so many human insects, beetles also like a good game. They have a mountain climber's mania, which is disconcerting thanks to its pertinacity. In all animals, death and frequent danger generate a defensive instinct. Not so for beetles. The rapid and energetic flicking that knocks them off your lapel, as if it were the acroterion of a building's facade, has not yet hardened the obscure forces of their subconscious . . . Perhaps it's an exaggeration to talk about the subconscious . . . Perhaps an exaggeration. But thinking about images, what difference is there between a beetle with its hard shell and the hard-faced guy driving a 1930 hardtop model Ford? Absolutely none. The two of them, with consummate ease, expose themselves to death by the annoyance they create ... Because you've got to make fun of the emissions of these stinking, hard-shelled beetles!"

He checked the effect of his joke and, spirited on by their three smiles, continued:

"Fabre, the formidable poet of the insects—in whose post-humous homage the roosters of Rostand muffled their strident crow—could not explain the beetles' ambulatory and ascensional mania. All his entomological recollections, full of sweet pantheistic goodness, touch upon man's tenuous comprehension. That is why, here at this boulevard café, amid clouds of stinking exhaust from cars and the essence of stink beetles, I am going to undertake the research in question. Nevertheless, I have doubts about its success. I recall the case of those learned Germans who wrote five volumes in six-point type on the subject of: 'Why cats do not inhabit the workshops of marble masons.' And I fear, as well, an incontestable conclusion like the one they reached, upon affirming that 'cats flee from the workshops of marble masons because they believe that the fragments which fly off at each chisel blow, as the mason chips away at the marble, are thrown at them intentionally' ..."

Longines and Aparicio grasped his intention ... The ladies were laughing.

"Well, then. Beetles possess a full and urgent curiosity. They are not content, like so many usurers, to live exclusively within a tiny hole, barely large enough to contain them and their avarice. They emerge from recondite places, with the fixed idea of spying into the actions and lives of others around them, to judge whether it is, in fact, worthwhile to become a man in their next metempsychosis. Nevertheless, they depart from a false premise. They believe that humanity is the highest peak to be climbed. That's why, as soon as one sits down, they scale the ramp of the calf, take a light rest on the mesa of the thighs and ascend, audaciously, along the straight parapet of the back. At last they reach the summit of the shoulders. There, they pause to enjoy the view. They shake their patent-leather elytra, shiny as the hood of a limousine. And prepare for the greatest venture: to discover if men or women use better perfumes than they do."

The ladies whispered audibly, casting him sidelong glances.

"Beetles are cautious and they explore the lapel, neckline, and cleavage. Now, whatever attractions that the folds of lapels, necklines, and cleavage hold for the stinkbug is another matter requiring serious investigation. These are the very spots where ninety percent of the tragic flicks and fillips take place. But such caution is fruitless. However much one might grimace thanks to some vile whiskey or malign cocktail, those little tiny feet crossing the skin of the neck provoke a sudden sensation that causes one to twitch, ah! in nervous somersaults. And then one flails one's arms about as if choking to death on mustard gas . . ."

As he looked around, Viejo Amor began to glow with pleasure. A sharp elbow calmed him down.

"It's evident that we act in error. If each person possessed the exquisite goodness demonstrated by the *fioretti* of Saint Francis, our 'brother beetle' could amply satisfy his curiosity, sampling the cologne or lotion that perfumes us. But, no: our panic prevents them. And to humiliate our trifling, artificial scent, while our hand flails about, struggling to knock them away, they release into that same hand the decisive judgment of their foul-smelling emission . . ."

The three ladies sat up straight with easy grace and coquetry.

"The poor beetles meet the asphalt or tiles face to face. Our memory of their burning sting inspires us to step on them. At times . . . we remain with our deadly shoe suspended in the air . . . beetles comprehend the utility of cracks and gaps. And they dive into them, extracting from beneath their wings a kind of tiny white cape, like a challenge, as if to say: *See you next time* . . . Indeed. Moments later they will deposit, in our ice cream as it sits sweetly, innocently melting or in the puffed-up pastries, the fragrant calling card of their visit . . . After a while they move inside, underneath the pants or the skirt, to pinch their friend and imprint their stinking red signature . . . And, at last they return to their single-minded mountain climbing, once again showing their silhouette against the neck, to mock the hand's violent slap with their own transcendent fetidness."

Just as he had done many years before, after executing a brilliant illusion on the stage, Katanga lowered his eyelids, secure in his triumph. That distant applause was here transformed into the discreet whispering of the three lovely ladies. He had "performed" deliberately for them, innately discerning the nature of their spirits. He was not mistaken. Thanks to his homage, they spoke loud enough for him to hear their comments on "the well-ordered, careful grace of his speech, so full of kind, friendly remarks."

But the term "speech" made him twitch.

So with fine self-assurance he turned around, his head cocked to the right:

"Speech . . . God forbid! I cordially detest orators. A plague worse than stink beetles themselves. A Colombian friend of mine once rightly noted: "A book, a pamphlet, or a printed speech can be tossed out the window, can be sent as a gift to an enemy, can be hidden beneath the table. But you cannot treat an orator the same way, not without encountering serious difficulties."

Three splendid sets of teeth appeared along with their smiles.

"Well. *Pardonnez-moi la boutade.* If you wish to punish me, I will remove any impediments . . ."

But they had already paid the waiter. Now they stood up in a swirl of silks, gauze, and muslin, scattering the soft, subtle perfume favored by cultivated women, not unlike the pungent aroma of marinated meat; quivering flesh, ready to enjoy life's deepest pleasures.

While gathering up their gloves and pocketbooks, they added:

"In spite of the theme, how delicious your *causerie.*"

"You happen to be the only *pasable* Córdoban we've met."

"*Nous sommes d'Entre Ríos. La bas la chose est assez différente . . .*"

Katanga made a playful fuss:

"From Córdoba? Not I. *Cruz Diablo!*" and continued: "I discerned immediately that you ladies were not from around here. *Charme ... Gentilesse ...* Believe me: you have brought to my recollection ..."

"Good-bye."

"... the fleeting happiness of similar scenes, insubstantial but eternal ..."

"Good-bye."

"... which I experienced in the cafés of Montparnasse."

"Adieu."

"Merci. Au revoir."

They stepped into a luxurious Bordeaux-red automobile.

"After them! Follow them!" advised Viejo Amor excitedly.

"Silence! Don't be an imbecile!" Katanga growled.

And he followed them with his eyes until they were lost in the tangled uproar of the traffic.

He sat there, motionless, staring into space, his lips partially open.

As his gaze returned, his eyes were full of hallucinatory noises, spirals, and flashes.

And two lost tears.

That night Katanga couldn't sleep.

Enshrouded in his memory of the three ladies, he passed long hours watching the darkness. Watching his soul transcribed upon the blackness of the night. Gazing inside himself, but looking outward. Projecting himself. Because, with the sensation inverted, privacy became foreign, his forehead an enormous vaulted dome, and each thought, a luminous zephyr of intelligent *sephirot*. His ideas appeared etched across the sky in ectoplasmic calligraphy, as if some tiny, mysterious airplane were writing them. In this way, he neither thought nor spoke, he read these thoughts:

Is it possible to love three women simultaneously? Thousands; millions? The amor intellectualis *is not interested in possession, orgasm, horizontal happiness. But rather the amorous levitation of the body to the level of thought!*

The most intriguing aspect of flirtation is making things up as you go along, as if it had been destined. Secrecies. Crafts. Strategy. Instead of defensive measures, a plan of attack is devised. There is an accepted element of danger that has a beneficial effect. And one laughs because the phantom of love turns out to be a hilarious, disappointing joke in the vacant lot of the soul: a watermelon rind with three tiny shuttered windows, illuminated by the moon's reflection upon a tin can . . .

At my age, Chamfort's theory has, by now, become axiomatic: "J'hais assez les hommes et n'aime pasassez les femmes." But . . . Who can resist the ineffable delight of torching three heads like theirs on the pyre of the heart? Who wouldn't be tempted to trade anxiety for sighs in the holocaust of the ultimate illusion? Who shuns the aesthetic delight of burning perfumed incense in honor of the glorious, shining monument of love that is a woman at thirty?

By the way. I shaped the scene deliberately by speaking on behalf of so many battered beetles. Friction of words. Paradoxical massage. Excessive charity causes laughter. I know it. We all laugh. But, be careful creating too much friction . . . Rub two sticks together and the fire comes roaring out. Rub two membranes together and life bursts forth.

Oh, the cascading honey of her gothic tresses upon the marble bastion of her forehead! Oh, her Renaissance head with its pageboy cut, gilding across the gulf of her throat on the fiery reflections of her chestnut curls! Oh, her mane of ringlets like a Merovingian herald, thick with black waves crashing against the ivory curves of her neck!

How we looked at each other as we said good-bye! The woman's gaze seems to dress the man. From head to toe. The man's gaze undresses her. From her feet to her face. Hers begins at his hat, adjusts his tie, straightens his jacket, smoothes his pants, and shines his shoes. His gaze, sweetly lubricious, creeps up her calves, works its way underneath her skirts, caresses her buttocks, cuddles her pelvis, and runs up against the base of her breasts.

I did not find love floundering at the edge of desperation, about to be shoved by disappointment into the bottomless well of tedium. That's luck: to arrive before time runs out. I found love latent inside myself, and I saved it by washing away my putrid adolescence. Taking it out to do pushups in the face of mockery, sarcasm, and irony. Now I ask myself disconsolately, what for? I did nothing more than defile the contours of my soul and the composite parts of my conscience.

Poor Viejo Amor! I've got to make amends for my insult. He's a sharpshooter afflicted with a violent trembling ... in the drama of love, some people spend their entire lives rehearsing. But in the decisive moment, their nerve and tact fails them. Others, alas, make an impact on the first occasion that presents itself!

I admire the greatness of those who favor instinct over duty. I admire the ego of those who dauntlessly seek to satisfy those instincts, pushing every aspect of pleasure to the sexual wellspring where the soul lays stretched out. But I prefer to be what I am. A regressive man, who lives the abyssal drama of his solitude. And nevertheless, smiles ...

"Follow them ..." What a clumsy command! You follow and pursue women on foot. Seduction is a simple thing. "That man that hath a tongue, I say, is no man, if with his tongue he cannot win a woman ..." So says Valentine in Act Three of Two Gentlemen of Verona. Here and now, Act One of the Ford Era, is the simplest yet. Not even the tongue is needed to convince ... It's sufficient to court them in a Model A. In a private car from a well-known automaker, especially one with a hard top. The instantaneous magnetic attraction that draws the female is remarkable. The whole erotic substratum vibrates at the slightest wink from Don Juan at the wheel. "Self-destructing love affairs" are famous ... Several blocks or days of siege and that's it! They climb aboard the rolling boudoir. One gallant, fast-driving beau, and off to the lonely park they go, to the nocturnal alley, to the dead-end street. The automobile has certainly made for streamlined womanizing ...

Love is the image of the couple reflected in the pool. But, let an acorn fall, a flower ... and all is lost in concentric circles of pain, sorrow, nostalgia, and oblivion.

Don Rufo would say: There's no bull who doesn't become a steer ... Perhaps. I've practiced Fregoli's technique of transmutation by undressing and dressing myself in countless performances of love. Perhaps I was poisoned by le gourmandise. *Today—more than by the unctuous plea, more than by unctuous contact—I'm made content by a fleeting half-hour of cunning gallantry. Your clothes don't get wrinkled. And that voluptuous tingling lasts . . .*

Oh, that twisted verse that I once heard!:

Bachelor's flat
A crafty lad in
His hothouse
Spouting gallant lies
(Best if she who came
All the sooner flies.)

Here, the women stroll about still wrapped in men's protective respect. Born Aphrodite Pandemos, they live shy, cold-hearted, and loveless, like Artemis. Abolish such respect! Bring them to the communion of love. Return to them the sweetness and pleasure of self-determination. Abolish such respect! A vicious medieval habit with an unpleasant aftertaste, a modern chastity belt, it imprisons sex behind hooks and iron rods. Like the ones on display in the Musée de Cluny, its *cuirass withers youth and dries up the nourishing springs of the species. Abolish such respect! Because men's respect— cast in promises, embossed with artful lies, damasked with shrewd courtesies—is the artwork of their duplicity and concupiscence.*

His eyes were closing.

He could barely read his own thoughts now:

I feel the pain of never having been mistaken in matters of love; because therein lies the possibility of having been, however fleetingly, happy . . .

He sighed.

His eyes closed completely. There was a jungle of snores.

And in his dream, three dreamy orchids.

For several days they toured the most interesting spots in the mountains west of Córdoba. They had rented two comfortable autos and enjoyed the service of two volunteer guides: Patay and Fenicio.

The two young men worked tirelessly to show them the most popular routes, landscapes, and local curiosities. They knew the location of every general store and gas station in the district, as well as the prices of guest houses and hotels, and the names of the owners of chalets and mansions. Two very useful guides, but rather obtuse. They lacked a feel for the landscape. They held no bond with the agrarian soul, but connected instead with the frills and fripperies of summertime tourists who hauled the city along with them, transplanted in the form of *boîtes,* bridge parties, and *souperdansants.* For Patay and Fenicio the mountains were valuable only as a backdrop for bourgeois vanity. But their openhearted exaltation of futile things was charming. One day, in Los Cocos, Fenicio commented:

"That chalet over there cost four hundred thousand pesos. The owner is an importer from Rosario. His whole family has tuberculosis. The house is falling to pieces. Now this one on the right belongs to an old bachelor who's crazy about dahlias. He's invested more than a hundred thousand pesos in landscaping his gardens. See over there, up on that hilltop, there's a kind of fortress? It's Doctor Tumini's castle. It has a flagpole. When he's at home he flies his 'personal' flag. He's also from Rosario."

"No drawbridge?"

"No."

"That's a shame! What I wouldn't give to see him cross over it, brandishing his ridiculous coat of arms!"

"What! Don't you like it? The finest buildings are designed by Rosarians."

"Listen, my friend, how could I like such an affront to good taste? Don't you see that such things are simply the atavistic boasts of immigrants' sons?"

"True: the mountains would be more beautiful without any Rosarians!"

More given to reflection, Patay praised the spectrum of colors, the distinctiveness of each town, the picturesque qualities. Superficially.

"What do you all think of Old Tanti? The historic town with its little church, the creek ... Those thermal springs they call the Bishop's Bath! It's better than the New Tanti."

"Blah, blah, blah: tourism ... one place is as *Tanti*-lizing as another ..."

Going down the hill above the reservoir at San Roque dam, now well into the evening, Patay tried to vindicate himself. They stopped the cars. And from a hilltop he pointed out the metallic plate of the water, coppery in the sun; the shadow of the hills, silhouetting the chalets on the plateaus; the sleepy smoke from the chimneys floating above the vast stands of willows at the town of Villa Carlos Paz.

"It's poetic, eh?"

"Yes, it's poetic," replied Longines. "But neither you nor Fenicio comprehend nature. One from Santiago, coated with dust, the other from Santa Fe, stuck in the fog; you're a single, blind entity. The acacia thickets of the one place, and the corn fields of the other, have circumscribed your vision. You ignore the cosmic abstraction. The majesty of the mountain. The philosophy of the lakes. When you travel to Switzerland someday, then you'll understand ..."

Aparicio saved them.

"So, Switzerland immediately makes an appearance! All cantons, all cant. And not one little miserable revolution to help things ... Now, when I fought with the eastern band, under Commandant Borges ..."

The two students were shocked. Not that their good intentions were not fully recognized and appreciated. No. They were annoyed by their companions' systematic disdain and well-reasoned acrimony for the things they admired. For them, the beauty of the Cordovan Mountains was a matter of faith. Indoctrinated by the single-mindedness of propaganda and unacquainted with any other mountains they simply had no basis for comparison.

Speaking with Rescoldo about their new friends, they told him:

"They're all some educated old fellows, no doubt about it, but they're worse than stinging nettles. They complain about everything. I don't swallow that crap about how we Argentines go to the mountains to poison the landscape, overcome with a crisis of love, health or money . . ."

"Nevertheless . . ."

". . . or with the fanciful desire to show off bathing suits and play golf . . ."

"Ten points . . ."

"Now you sound like them, Rescoldo. You know what they liked on today's drive? Go figure: names! Tulumpa, Salsipuedes, Cavalango, Ischilín, Ongamira, Yuspe, Quimbaletes . . . That's how they are. They focus on stupid details."

"You think toponymy is stupid?"

"Who cares. Do you remember, on Sunday, in Cabana?"

" . . . "

"Yes. That discussion about the miner and the mushroom gatherer."

"It wasn't an argument, properly speaking. Barely a discrepancy. Something—how shall I say?—lyrical. It was nice, *che*, at the time."

Rescoldo—all sad eyes and sweet smile—took an interest:

"Let's see if you remember."

He was timid, shut away in himself, maturing the juices of his mental wineskin in silence and apathy. But of the three companions, his comprehension was the sharpest. He intuited something substantial and he pressed them anew:

"Let's see if you two remember."

"There's nothing special about it. Atop a mountain ridge, alongside a quarry, there appeared two men: one with a pick, the other with a basket. Each man got busy with his own task. One digging. The other gathering mushrooms. That's all. Aparicio and Katanga sympathized with the mushroom gatherer. Longines and Dijunto with the miner. And they got to arguing."

"But you've got to explain things properly! These guys maintain that the miner is profound while the mushroom collector is superficial. That the miner's impassioned faith is so strong that it eagerly bores down to profit from his dream. The first two renounced such virtue. They preferred indolence to effort. And they praised the wisdom of gathering mushrooms, by means of gentle twists of the waist, as opposed to the miner's colossal, often fruitless, fatigue. That was when Longines exalted stubbornness. Erect like an iron bar, the miner's willpower is a symbolic, virile member that penetrates the earth and reveals the fecundity of its interior. He is a mythic figure, like Osiris. By contrast, the mushroom collector is an impotent being, a parasite, who speculates with the parasitism of parasites just as vegetative as he ... And all hell broke loose! Their disagreement got louder when they touched on the superiority of nature's kingdoms. Between being a thing, a head of stone; or being alive, a head of cork. Katanga developed various theories about the mineral-man and the vegetable-man. About the slag heap and the wood pile. About the empty merit of being the offspring of metallic generations and the evident grace of shouldering the legacy of Dantesque forests ... They're cultivated fellows, no question; but more prickly pears than stinging nettles ... Being a student of medicine, they had me on my toes. Going from the gaseous and nebulous chaos of primitive condensation to attempting to justify the prevalence of inert substance. And, to justify the contrary, running through all the living world which extends from the division of unicellular amoeba to the vertebrate ... My head was spinning like a weathervane. They couldn't agree. The controversy only died down when Dijunto picked up a sparkling flake of mica, and Aparicio picked the moist umbrella of a mushroom. Concentrated on studying both fruits of the earth, they agreed there was a symmetry in the mushroom's fleeting life and the mica's eternal one. The subtle formation of multiple layers or membranes, of films of water and scales of light, was analogous in the artistry of each one. They established the fundamental similarity of two things so apparently different. Light: dry water. Water: liquid light. They proclaimed in one voice: *Everything is distinct, but it's the same!* And they concluded by cordially agreeing that their concepts may reside harmoniously in the pantheism that creates and sustains the mica and the mushroom, the spider and the cloud, the man and the tree . . ."

"Outstanding! Terrific!" Rescoldo burst out, laconically emphasizing his enthusiasm. "They're educated men, no doubt about it. As soon as I can, I'll drag them over to the university. I've got a harsh lesson for a whole lot of imbeciles with diplomas . . ."

In anticipation, he turned his eyes upward in ecstasy.

And felt a delicious, trembling tension.

SAN ROQUE:

Smug and mellifluous, Viejo Amor excused himself from that afternoon's excursion.

As a plausible justification, he claimed that he planned to look after Fortunato, whose rising fever concerned him. In truth, he had a different plan. This was evident from the euphoria that gamboled in his blood and the fallacious solicitude erected as a pretext.

Aparicio, who'd had a backstage view of Viejo Amor's burgeoning love affair with "Little Visi" the forty-something owner of their boarding house, gave him a wink as they said good-bye:

"Hope you enjoy your . . . salted hake."

"Salted hake? . . . Angel food cake!"

And twirling the tip of an imaginary mustache, Viejo Amor added, full of mockery:

"We'll see . . ."

The short trip by trolley car to the Central Station was too brief for Aparicio to work through his curiosity. It seemed impossible that a woman like that, so modest and excessively pious, would accept the advances of a man like Viejo Amor. Something else intrigued him immeasurably: their unbridled openness, their mutual enjoyment. There are some people whom love saddens: contrite young couples, predestined for misfortune; grievous spouses, arms hanging limply at their sides. Seeing those two, he didn't know what to think. They were radiant, illuminated with eroticism. More than envy, he felt confusion. Embarrassed, he clucked his tongue three times, as if saying to himself:

Well, it's their business . . . let them work it out . . .

But he couldn't shake the thought. He kept returning to the idea. As if lashed to a mental wheel he spun around, returning again and again to the particular interest which Doña Visitación had shown Viejo Amor: her attention to his clothes, how carefully she made his bed, their long chats on the patio, and her little gifts of cakes and sweets, served over *mate*, in pleasant *vis à vis . . .*

Climbing aboard the train, Viejo Amor's mockery still echoed in his ears. Aparicio clucked his tongue:

With his little senior-citizen cough! With his "We'll see" . . . so full of deception! . . .

Now seated, he addressed Katanga.

"Have you noticed Viejo Amor, how the old grouse is dragging his wings for Little Visi?"

"His *wings*? His balls, you mean. He thinks he's got a lot of masculine . . . pull. And he's an absolute fool who's going to end up getting us in big trouble."

"So then, you knew?"

"Obviously. I saw through him right away. She caught my attention the moment we settled in. Her modesty and studied squeamishness are, in my judgment, sure signs of perversion. The old saying is true: 'I never beheld greater license than love dressed in innocence.' You only have to observe her slack, puffy, bachelorette flesh awakened by desire, to deduce that she's a dangerous woman. And for good measure, her tiny little feet. When have you ever seen a female with little feet who's not wild-eyed for sex? *Parvus pes, barathrum!* Or better yet: tiny feet, gaping twat: the pit of hell!"

The National Railway locomotive took off rapidly. After crossing the Suquía River, the train traced a circular arc through the outskirts of General Paz and Alta Córdoba. The city lay in a sleepy haze, sizzling sunlight sparkling on the glazed tiles of the cupolas. Heading toward Las Heras Park, the train took a lashing turn to the right, then made a straight line for the villas and small estates along Los Bulevares and Rodríguez del Busto. And now in Argüello, it turned its eye resolutely toward the mountains. The landscape rose up into *pelouses*; shades of green; blue-gold air. At Km. 16 a waterfall and the rough contours of the Saldán ravine below the aqueduct sketched a fleeting romantic image. Then came a glimpse of Arcadia, a scene of willows and plane trees. Heading toward Caracól, the Suquía River Valley offered a clear, narrow, tree-lined route through a splendid gorge. The curves and straight stretches of the river sparkled like sickles and plowshares. Two quick twisting glances showed, to the right, the grizzled brown hulk of the cement factory, and to the left, the flowing tresses of a thousand nymphs combed fine by the Mal Paso dam. But the sights flew by too quickly to be admired. Their view dove down into the water with its gentle expanse of reflections then climbed up the zigzagging roads of the test mines and open pits of Dumesnil. Returning to the surface, skating upon the solar splendor, their gazes rested on the soothing green eyewash of the foliage around Calera. Jiggling and joggling through brusque switchbacks. In the red afternoon, the train's speed whisked away the stones, cows, trees. Fragments of images. Truncated flights. Enigmatic goats. The woodlands began to close in around them, the hills to confabulate. The Suquía, a luminous current, flowed away into shadowed channels. Misty darkness. The silent lakes of Casa Bamba, Perperina, and Berro. The tracks seemed headed for a dead end. Granitic hulks. Heavy shadows. One felt the suffocation of being trapped. And then it was night. A sudden and necessary respite from the emotionally charged landscape. Then, having passed through the tunnel, the sun immediately appeared. Clear. A cyclopean eye in the face of the sky. And cutting! Like the arch-angel's flaming, undulating sword, it fell in waves upon the flesh of the mountainside. And below, in the chasm, they heard the boiling blood of the torrent, while up above, threading through the perilous landscape, the locomotive steamed ahead, hurling into the abyss . . .

"San Roque Dam. Tickets."

They disembarked in the wink of an eye.

An aluminum vapor snaked over the edge of the reservoir until being lost behind road cuts and outcroppings.

They were directly in front of the dam.

With the scholarly innocence of schoolboys at the black-board, their gazes began to crisscross the wall from top to bot-tom, from the balustrade to the central flow; diagonally, from the spillways to the sloping staircase. In every direction. An un-interesting visual exercise for most of them.

"We'll break our necks yet . . ."

"Frankly, it's not even worth the visit . . ."

"I imagined . . ."

"What do you mean it's not worth it?" protested Longines. "By your reasoning, the Parthenon is a little marble farm house and the Leaning Tower of Pisa is just a lopsided silo. You've got to consider the passage of time. Measure works according to the technical and economic possibilities of each age."

"Yes, but . . ."

"Compared to the dam on the Tercero River . . ."

". . . this is a superior construction. It's functional. At Ter-cero they've invested years and millions, dozens of each, for what? So that the resident engineer can float by on his yacht and his British friends can fish for bream? There's still no ca-nal or water turbine to make use of the water. Here, at least . . . I could also tell you that the Tercero dam is nothing but a flea in comparison to the great Boulder Dam on the Colorado Riv-er, whose entire installations were built, from start to finish, in five years and two months, and cost millions of dollars more than the Panama Canal. Its massive wall is more than seven hundred feet high; the reservoir holds thirty-eight billion cubic meters. It's eighty times larger than the Tercero reservoir; any comparison is laughable! Not to mention the productive capacity of its generators, which produce nearly two million metric horsepower, an output which exceeds, by four hundred thousand horsepower, the combined energy of all power plants in Argentina! I'm not simply pleased with what's big for the sake of being big, but rather how much it benefits the public. That's why I soundly state my preference for the San Roque Dam. I'm not exalting the illusory. Nor do I digress."

No one replied.

Only a comment from Katanga, *sotto voce.*

"How nicely you've summarized that article from *National Geographic Magazine!*"

Crossing the bridge that crowned the wall, the puny bust of Cassafouth placed before the massive San Roque dam, angered Longines:

"It's an embarrassment! Look what the people's gratitude translates into ... twenty kilos of badly sculpted bronze ... How could they allow such ignominy, a dunce of a saint usurps the marvel of one man's ingenuity? At Boulder Dam, the reservoir is named Lake Mead, in homage to Doctor Elwood Mead, who was the project's chief engineer. Here, Cassafouth and Bialet Massé were thrown in jail ... How long will it be tolerated that San Roque claim an undeserved honor from heaven?"

"That's a question for the electricity monopolies ... You know that all the electricity in the country is cornered by two huge trusts: the S.O.F.I.N.A. and the A.N.S.E.C., Belgians and Yankees respectively. The local directors and lawyers are a bunch of traitors, fervent Catholics selling out their own country ... They might change the nomenclature on a whim! They exploit the customers in the name of God, or in the name of San Roque, which is the same thing ..."

Walking along slowly, lingering, they reached the restaurant on the left side of the dam.

Longines was still insisting:

"You've got to situate yourself in time! Fifty years ago! This was a fantastic creation. And it continues to prove useful; slender, bold, and high-spirited. There, on that little island, they should have built the monument to Cassafouth. Some gigantic thing, to match the dam, like the one for Count de Lesseps at the entrance to the Suez Canal. Or, if you prefer, worked into the living rock of that peak, an enormous effigy, similar to the three-hundred-foot heads that Gutzon Borglum sculpted from the granitic rocks of Dakota showing the faces of Washington, Jefferson, Lincoln and Roosevelt . . ."

Katanga again commented *con sordino*:

"You really squeeze a lot of juice from *National Geographic!*"

Aparicio, for his part, addressed him aloud:

"Tell me, Longines: was Cassafouth a Swiss?"

"*Hombre*, I don't know . . ."

"You don't know? Impossible! If he wasn't Swiss, he could pass for it . . ."

Settled into a garden gazebo bedecked with honeysuckle and bellflowers, they refreshed themselves, eagerly quaffing highballs of gin, soda, and lemon.

Cars and more cars pulled up on the terrace in front of them. Most wheeled around and drove back the way they came. Some parked. Their occupants got out. They stretched their legs, strolling along the top of the dam. They took the requisite snapshot and then, so long.

"From the looks of it, people don't spend much money here," Dijunto commented to the proprietor.

"Hardly any. Four or five owners have burnt out before me. If it weren't for the fact that I took a liking to the job, I'd be fried by now. What d'you expect from a whole lot of dainty prudes who drive cars? The money they spend on gas and spare tires would be better spent enjoying themselves, pleasing the body. They just snap their Kodaks. Fools, the lot of them. *Don't you have any panchromatic film? Supersensitive?* No. I have salami, *fernet,* Terrabussi snack cakes, kerosene. Ugh. It really pisses me off . . ."

"Well, it's no wonder."

"Places like this can only be appreciated by those who know how to admire beauty in a relaxed way," said Aparicio. "Tourists, so frivolous . . ."

"Tourists . . . And what about picnickers? God help me! I prefer the work crews and the country folk from this area . . . The only thing picnickers are interested in is proving that they've been up in the mountains. They come with cans of paint. Haven't you seen the bridge all fouled up with graffiti? There's not one post, railing, or rock that they haven't painted their names on. Then, photos; their goal is photos. They don't see anything, but they take home what the camera sees. True smugglers of the landscape."

"Landscape smugglers! What a splendid epithet!"

"It's not mine. It's from a very curious fellow who lives up around that bend in the road. We call him *El Chiflado,* the loony."

At that moment, two women alighted from a car.

They had taken a few steps when, going back, one of them shouted to the chauffeur:

"Can you bring us the paint and the Kodak."

"Not much light left for photos, ma'am."

"Bring it. We'll take a few shots."

The restaurant owner, with gestures of antipathy, pointed to the evidence:

"Didn't I tell you? Driven to throw away their money on photographs. Unbelievable! It really makes me crazy."

The owner was summoned inside. The moment he stepped away, Longines, his face pale, in a paralyzed stupor, caught the attention of the other three:

"Yes . . . It's her! I recognize the way she walks . . . Didn't you hear her voice? . . . It's her, Katanga . . . She . . ."

Their glances—flashing darts— bore into the woman's back.

"It's her! ... There's no doubt ... The other one is her daughter ... The one with tuberculosis ... I'm sure ... ."

"Sure, of what? C'mon. Speak."

"Say it already. You've got us with our hearts in our mouths."

"It's Freya ... Freya Bolitho ... The very same Freya Bolitho ..."

"No!"

"It can't be. All decked out like that ..."

"We stole everything she had ..."

It was Freya. But a very different Freya from that scrawny beggar with her haggard complexion, naked neck full of cracked wrinkles, and matted hair, ratty like the Gorgon's flowing head of vipers. Her disastrous loss had been instructive for her. Following a deep depression over having most of her savings stolen, she had reacted with impetuous energy. She deposited what remained in the bank. She condemned the sordid life of the wealthy beggar. But she did not totally renounce that ragged, ill-fated world. Instead, she began to wisely manage the business of pity and charity, hiring legions of young men, the destitute, blind, and crippled. She knew that compassion is the great tormenter of conscience ... She knew that everyone tends to be generous when mortified by diseases, blights, and defects that they themselves do not suffer, but whose presence momentarily looms over their conscience ... And now, well on her way to regaining the enormous sum she'd lost, she dreamed of revenging herself.

Ah, if I find Jarsolav and the Frenchman!

She'd sworn to kill them. They were the ones! The only person who had known her habit of hiding money inside stale loaves of bread was Jaroslav Kopecky, alias Fortunato. And although she did not witness the bitter scene of him absconding with her sixty-three thousand pesos, the only person capable of switching the loaves with such a feather light sleight of hand was the Frenchman, Lon Chaney. She was consumed with revenge. She didn't need to send the police after them. She believed that the delirious ostentation which infects those who get rich quick would be sure to give away their ill-gotten fortune. To find them, she explored every lead. Including self-improvement. Makeup and *haute couture*. Next, rejuvenated by hatred, she traveled from place to place, visiting the likely towns, one by one, surveying, sniffing, spying, her nerves steady in her design, and the Browning handgun waiting in her purse. Without success. Without any hope of success.

She'd been driving around the mountains for five days. It was not so much the telegram from her daughter Karen, as the need for rest which impelled her to travel. Passionate hatred withers the shrubbery of our nerves and dries up the fresh leaves of our blood. Forty-eight hours of languor were enough to calm her down. Karen's illness had been no more than a scare. The meagre, acrid woman who had arrived to Córdoba was now tempered through temporary distraction. Her daughter, in her illness, had once again become her little girl. And fortified by the effusive affection, her nerves and flesh began to sprout and blossom anew in the eternal spring of motherly fervor.

Now the two women were returning from the top of the dam.

The men's stubborn doubts melted away. It was Freya! The very same Freya Bolitho! Longines and Katanga rushed to intercept her.

They had all their responses prepared and agreed on, every possibility calculated.

She was so startled to see them, her only response was tears.

"Why are you crying, Mama?" asked a hoarse voice, made worse by several rattling, spasmodic coughs that sounded like a lugubrious cry for help.

"Happiness, Karen, happiness . . . ."

And she continued by explaining to her, in German, the joy of finding a friend like Herr Edmo Kumck. His kindnesses and support. His selfless help when, her spouse recently deceased, widowhood had caused her to see the world around her all black, black, black. His punctuality in assisting when, her spirit riddled with misery, she thought about throwing explosives into the void, but instead he shone a ray of light into it.

Longines protested that it was a very minor kindness. And

he reversed the gloomy theme which now began to upset the daughter.

Solicitously, Freya accompanied Karen to the car. She instructed her to bundle up and stay warm. Then she returned to Longines.

"My daughter doesn't know about any of this. For the last four years she's lived in Villa García, not far from here. The climate is good for her health but the absence of love and affection hinders her recovery. I've resolved to move up here in June, permanently. With the little bit that I saved from the disaster—about twenty-thousand pesos—and half of the income from my beggars—between a thousand and fifteen hundred pesos a month—I'll be able live independently without too much difficulty. My partner is an experienced professional. She knows the charity industry inside and out. And she's decent. Oh, if it hadn't been for those damned dogs, Jaroslav and Lon Chaney, I had nearly saved the hundred thousand pesos I needed to retire! But it doesn't matter. If I don't manage to avenge myself, the stolen money will avenge me; because money stolen from suffering people is a curse, like leprosy. I hope to God that their bodies and souls are already rotting away from gangrene! How I'd like to see them on their knees, defeated!"

"Freya, please: you shouldn't wish such bad fortune on anyone," ventured Katanga, dazed by the vision of Lon Chaney's fatal plunge and Fortunato's current condition.

"I do wish it. Yes. I'm being honest. I'd like to see them rotting away, covered with filth and open sores, dying without dying, in a squalid agony of spiders, misery, toads, moans, lamentations."

"Freya: let's change the subject," pleaded Longines.

"Why? Didn't I curse them just the same the very night of the robbery, when you were there to console me? Who else could it have been? Despicable men. Dogs."

Karen's persistent dry cough interrupted her. Freya hurried to leave.

"I have to go. Be sure to come visit me," she continued speaking from inside the car. "Remember: Hotel de Villa García, a little ways before Carlos Paz. I need to have a long talk with you. I know you'll come. It's absolutely necessary that you help me get my revenge on Jaroslav and the Frenchman."

It was a rapid and confused good-bye. Their farewells were mixed up and drowned out by the backfiring exhaust pipe. They held their arms up, their waves as violent as the woman's resentment. Longines and Katanga exchanged silent, inquisitive glances. They watched the car disappear across the craggy, scrubby landscape. And with their lips slightly parted, they lowered their arms at last.

Back in the gazebo, Aparicio and Dijunto were anxious to hear what had happened but the men were unable to say a word. Bitter curses mixed with tender affection and monetary sums; their encounter with Freya left them dizzy. They both shook their heads and clutched their jackets below their lapels. They both felt that something just below the surface of their consciousness was rapidly crumbling to pieces. They sensed a mysterious, transcendent virus, which existed both inside and outside of their bodies. Feeling the pressure to relay the news, they began their disjointed explanations:

"We're absolutely safe. But . . ."

"Indeed: nothing specific. But . . ."

Aparicio chided: "What does that mean? We're safe, *but* . . . , there's nothing specific, *but* . . . . Forget the *buts* and let's get to the heart of the matter."

It was hard to articulate. Freya hadn't the faintest suspicion that it was Longines who'd plotted the theft or that they had taken it upon themselves to redistribute the wealth obtained through the subterfuges and indignities implied in gathering sixty-three thousand pesos by begging. They would never be discovered. They could be sure of that. *But* . . . And their throats seized up.

"How many *buts* are there?"

Katanga made a great effort:

"You're perfectly right. The thing is that I believe in curses more than in threats: blasphemy is more effective than revenge. And the old woman Freya has shocked us with her curses."

"Not against us," corrected Longines. "You've got to explain things correctly. Freya vomits curses against Fortunato and Lon Chaney, whom she considers instigator and executor of the robbery. And the curses are now coming true: Lon Chaney . . . may he rest in peace. And Fortunato . . . fearfully sick in bed."

A premonition cast its shadow over them and they cut off the conversation. A gloomy pause. A bitter interlude. And suddenly they all signaled for the bill in unison. The owner came over. They paid in a flurry of useless gestures and expressions. They were urged on by a secret haste. For greater certainty they asked what time the last train would depart.

"There's no more trains."

"What! Doesn't it come after that last locomotive?"

No. The other way around. The last locomotive just left."

Silent, they gloomily resigned themselves to their bad luck.

The restaurant verandah was filling up with people from the public works crew. With the inevitable card games starting up, Aparicio and Dijunto felt drawn to the hubbub. On the pretext of seeking accommodations and preparing supper, they resolved to leave the gazebo. Standing up to confess their true aim, they hesitated a moment upon noting the low spirits of Katanga and Longines. Seeing them that way, like two sad phantoms sunk in the shadows of the sunset, they felt a pang of pity. But they realized the ridiculousness of the situation and each one chided:

"Don't be so glum, you're overreacting."

"It's annoying to see men like you, normally so rational, tormented by a witch's coarse remarks."

Dijunto and Aparicio cheerfully arranged the necessary accommodations. Rooms were available. They could spend a peaceful night in the mountains. And the next day, at eight o'clock, they'd be back in Córdoba. Nothing to worry about.

Dijunto ran back to the gazebo to relay the plans, certain of receiving their consent, and hoping to dispel the cloud of gloom hanging over them.

They were gone.

He didn't panic. He guessed they had gone to answer the call of nature and he joined Aparicio who was now itching to play a hand of *tute,* for starters.

The night was pure and the evening stroll was purifying for Katanga and Longines. Nothing clashed with the deep clarity of the sky or the grave dignity of the stars. The night was a temple and they were two supporting caryatids. They walked along in lively conversation. Cleansing themselves, their steady gait perfectly attuned to the sidereal harmony. They felt the enchantment of being two insignificant beings made gigantic by the static immensity of the night. The elusive, confluent line of the mountaintops matched the intellectual arabesque of their words. And the ideographic chasms echoed their interior silences. Soon they began to quiet down. To become classic statues. They were converted through the persuasive powers of stone. Its slender allegories. Its pantheistic flumes. Its philosophical arcana. Opaque, silent, they stood immobilized upon a plinth of rock. They stayed that way for long moments. More statues than ever. Enraptured by the hitherto unknown majesty of being nothing more than structures. And they achieved total oblivion, absorbed in the limpid task of contemplation.

Suddenly, a bulky human figure detached itself from the dark rocky scrub landscape. A living knot of stone or a stony knot of flesh? They couldn't see clearly. The darkness tightened the weave of its cloak. A rough raspy voice perforated the night like a shotgun blast:

"What are you doing there? This serenity is mine and I am its sole possessor. The landscape belongs to me. Away, tourists! Go away!"

"All right. Don't get mad. We're leaving now."

"But remember, even if the serenity is yours, the night belongs to everyone."

"Go away, I said! Quick. I don't want any romanticism corrupting my mountains."

"Tourists … Romanticism … Forget it!" Katanga reprimanded him, with short, clipped bursts of rage. "There are no tourists or romantics here. We're just as worthy as you. And we respect the solitude better than you do."

"Oh!" the voice stammered.

It was as if they had flashed their credentials. Drawing near, the gruff voice dropped its hostile tone:

"Beg pardon. Do as you like. I was mistaken."

Longines thought it prudent to explain.

"I'm Swiss and I know about mountains. I've spent many vacations on the shores of Lake Thun, in little remote villages surrounded by nothing but fir trees and avalanches. I know man's dimension in the immensity. I've measured it against the Jungfrau and St. Gotthard; and later beneath the Tronador and the Osorno. In gloomy hours of blizzard and hunger; in tranquil hours of comfort and calm. We are never more than a miserable atom. A hallucinated particle. Here, in the mountains of Córdoba, I've never felt insignificant. On the contrary. My presumptions prevailed. Tramping through the foothills for several weeks, I grew tired of their poor coloring, their scrawny vegetation, and the ridges' endless, repeated progression of semicircular arcs. I'll admit that I became annoyed by the predominant, sensual curve. Hills shaped like breasts and udders, like Percheron haunches and voluptuous buttocks . . . I confess that the sun, the mica, the bone-dry flanks and dusty roads of rocky Punilla or the rugged wilds of Calamuchita, mortified my retina instead of thrilling it . . . But I stand corrected. Today, a short while ago, I found myself surprised by their merit. I've just learned the grandiosity found within them. The night! Its nocturnal gala! The tremendous beauty of their nocturnal hours!"

The rough voice ran toward them, quavering among the cliffs and crags.

"Fantastic! Very good! I want to meet you. It already seemed to me that you weren't really smugglers of the landscape. Who are you? Me, I am the finger that probes the underbelly of the night!"

"*El Chi-fla-do!*" whispered Katanga, syllable by syllable. "The local loony!"

"Well . . . we're . . . beggars. Professional beggars, on vacation."

No longer filled with nourishing water, the lake was now a black diamond. The receptive ewer of the mountain. The perfect reflection of the solemn night in all its celestial ecstasy.

Turning back toward the restaurant they could just make out his silhouette. He was a handsome man, of Caesarean profile, perfectly clean-shaven. Broad shouldered, bent by height and years, his thick, coarse suit showed meticulous care.

"I sympathize with you because you've discovered what I've discovered. The night! Living by day is smothering. The daily invasion of tourists and the rabble of Sunday picnickers with knapsacks, destroying everything. Pests! Vermin! Locusts! They're possessed of destructive curiosity, no fondness for nature. They usurp, they do not contemplate ... You, however, are clearly gifted with reason. These mountains are female: spread out and rounded. That is why they are loved at night. The Alps and the Andes are male: abrupt and steep. That is why they are visited and admired by day. I've lived by night, in endless colloquium, for the last nine years. All of us who love these feminine mountains are their sad inhabitants. You'll see. The mountaineer of Córdoba does not sing, does not laugh, does not dance. The cueca, the sardana, and the tarantella; the chipper songs of Bavaria, Lombardy, and the Tyrol; the jolly traditional garb of Switzerland, the Balkans, and Provence reveal people of a fresh, agile spirit. They are spared the blight of love, which makes one miss out on all things. Free peoples! With an ability to collect the enchantment of the landscape, the glory of fresh morning milk, and honey-filled afternoons. Here ... Have you not suffered that feeling of abandonment, of things unfinished, the melancholy that overshadows the mountains by day? It's something quite overwhelming! Around here you'll find nothing firm, stout, or courageous. All anguish, enervation, discouragement. If it were not for the leaping goats and the plunging streams; if it were not for the galloping of the clouds and the colts, these mountains would be the very image of death. Ah, but the night! The sublime pomp of the night! I am the finger that probes the underbelly of the night!"

They reached the restaurant.

The owner was delighted to see them together, conversing naturally with *El Chiflado*. He held for the famed lunatic that protective sympathy which hypocrites who presume themselves sane often confer upon those cultivated men who are called crazy. A lacerating sympathy. His nickname proved the ignorance and stupidity of those who called him crazy.

Katanga and Longines noticed this immediately. And they vindicated it by offering him the confidence and intimacy of a long friendship. They spent a splendid hour at his side. From him they learned the cause of his isolation: a tragic love which required catharsis through solitude and silence. And through other locals—who exacerbated his modesty—they learned that he belonged to the Buenos Aires aristocracy; a once famous sculptor, his mountain home was a marvel of comforts built from rustic materials.

They effusively insisted that he dine with them.

"Impossible. My principles forbid it. I neither accept nor give. Even worse with you: it would mean sharing the alms you've received!"

"And so what? Does that bother you?"

"Of course it does!" he insisted, beginning to anger. "In all benevolence there lies a deadly irony!"

Something strange was at work in him. His face broke down into a grimace. His eyes swung from one guest to another. His egophilia, laconic and solitary, seemed to marshal its forces to repel the affront. Lowering his head, he seemed to gather his thoughts. A few brief seconds. And suddenly, convulsively, he attacked:

"Charity is the shameful way wealthy people have of granting justice to the poor. I am exempt from the viruses of misery and opulence. I hate them both equally. I don't need anyone's justice. Much less their charity, which most of the time is a repetition of exasperated remorse. *(His spittle splattered those nearest him.)* Charity always implies supremacy. The ones who give are either those who have already fulfilled all of their exorbitant desires or those who lack any desire at all and merely give in a crazed frenzy of mockery. If charity implied renunciation, alms would not wound human dignity. But those who give enjoy the cruel pride of superiority, or rather, a vile moral defect which induces in them a self-aggrandizement rooted in someone else's pain. *(He spat left and right.)* Charity will be abolished in some near future, because these dogmas cannot survive. Philanthropy itself will be offended by the similarity of all lives. Love for your neighbor will be trumped by the power of equality. Giving signifies nothing. Generosity is no longer bedecked with the golden coins of olden times. Being magnanimous is a vice. A vice of the rich, like ether, or morphine. And charity is a morbid curiosity only fulfilled with theatrical injections of vanity. *(He sputtered, choking with disgust.)* It's obvious that when this pseudo-virtue disappears, there will be no more beggars. And especially not beggars of your professional class, who speculate and exploit the dubious vulnerability of those who give. *(He coughed explosively.)* More than a social ill, begging is a collective swindle. It's a ruse, pulsing with feigned misery, designed to rip a penny's worth of pity out of people's hearts. Thus the beggar becomes wealthy and mocks his own misery. And this undermines the solidarity among men which should be found everywhere, shining like the light of authentic justice, given that we all come into this world wearing the same halo of rights. *(He heaved with nausea.)* There's no need to be clairvoyant. The suppression of charity will be a part of humanity's future. And you, vile pirates of emotion, are the black, moss-covered stones where the primary goodness of men slips and falls. *(He hawked up his phlegm with a rattling clatter and amid the rough noise he fled.)*

They were flabbergasted.

A few minutes later, the bad fumes of the diatribe dissipated, they commented:

"I don't understand why he should be so upset that we invited him to eat dinner."

"And even if it did upset him, what a sermon he blew out of his holy ass!"

The owner and a few other locals interceded good-naturedly.

"Pay him no mind; he treats everyone the same way."

"He flies off the handle about any damn fool thing."

"I told you he was a little nutty . . ."

Aparicio brought the scene to a close:

"A little nutty? The motherfucker is insane!"

....

CÓRDOBA:

At seven twenty-two they boarded the train.

After sleeping rather badly they had awoken to a foggy dawn. The shrouded gray mist of the morning settled down around the mountains, blocking their view and their moods.

They hardly remembered their unexpected encounter with Freya Bolitho. Nor her curses for Lon Chaney and Fortunato. *El Chiflado's* grinding nonsense still echoed below their skin, embossing their faces with its disapproval.

It's difficult to dismount from one's own high horse once it has reared up angrily.

Aparicio wished he could make them laugh at the absurdity to dispel their negativity and enliven the mood. But he didn't really know how. He bought a copy of *La Nación*. He opened it the way one opens a window onto the world. He stuck his head out. And counting on Dijunto, he chose a topic at random to help start up a conversation. No luck. Neither Katanga nor Longines withdrew from their self-absorption.

"Newspapers, magazines, Córdoba lottery," the vendor called out again.

Aparicio bought a ticket with a full set of numbers. He knew that Longines detested games of chance; it was a clear attempt to provoke him, to distract him with a fit of anger. But he didn't take the bait.

Trying a different tack, he asked Katanga:

"What do you think about number 21.147? Do you see the trick? Twenty-one, fourteen, seven."

"What am I supposed to think? At least, if you lose, you'll feel better. Magic charms and tricks are good for that . . ."

"I'm not looking for consolation," Aparicio proclaimed, fanning the flame of dialogue. "I'm so loyal to myself that I buy lottery tickets just so I have the right to curse my luck if I don't win anything; because a lot of people curse without ever playing!"

He smiled.

They all smiled.

The skeleton key had opened the lock.

"Now that's better. What do you gain by getting upset over some words from an old bird of ill omen and a mountain crank who's stark raving mad? We're way ahead of them. Even if they had started kicking, slapping, punching . . ."

"*Oui, Monsieur Truisme:* between words and blows, one must prefer words."

Then Longines joined in:

"Forget *Monsieur Truisme*: it's Mister Truncheon! Aparicio speaks from experience. Don't you remember the beating he got from the Amboy Police Captain and the Judge from La Cruz?"

"*Monsieur de la Police,* then . . ."

"Yes, fine, take it out on me. Just for fun, that's all. I ought to hire *El Chiflado* to teach them a lesson on how to respect people."

Katanga plunged in for a few seconds and declared:

"I'm not going to add my voice to the collective stupidity by stating that *I'm above every kind of scorn*, for the simple reason that I'm not above anyone or anything, but rather very distant from everything . . ."

"In appearance."

"But you've got to recognize that *El Chiflado* has class. That sermon he gave, he wasn't just blowing smoke out his ass, as I said, as a diversion. It was a rather well-aimed attack. And you told him we were professional beggars!"

"What could I say to a guy who proclaims himself the finger that probes the underbelly of the night?"

"The finger that probes the underbelly of the night?"

"Yes, Dijunto; a devastating digit that points to the stars but scratches for lice . . ."

The Uruguayan smiled radiantly, happy that he'd managed to stir things up. Nevertheless, the chatter was not sufficiently frank. If he'd been keener, he would have noticed. Katanga's reticence coincided with Longines's incidental remarks. Simple concessions to friendship.

Indeed. The vitriolic sharpness of *El Chiflado's* satire still burned in their private thoughts. The two of them, who'd heard Freya's anathemas against Fortunato, were then obliged to listen to the man's admonition against alms, which was Jaroslav's great bastion. All the fates seemed set against him. They thought of him back in Córdoba, sick, and they sank into a shadowy gloom; because predictions and curses are airborne viruses which undermine a man's defenses.

A sad and quarrelsome silence lingered over them.

The train pulled out of Dumesnil like a comet in search of the sun. Traveling through dense clouds, it found the woods at Km.16 veiled in gray mist and cement dust.

Aparicio succumbed to defeat, now infected with their collective sadness.

"Tickets: Córdoba"

The conductor's announcement shook them out of their funk. Each one felt the anxiety which afflicts passengers as they near their destination.

Katanga punctuated thirteen kilometers of silence with a few words of crafty knavery:

"Although unpleasant in many ways, this little trip has offered me something agreeable: I've learned that Longines's real name is Edmo Kumck."

"Edmo Kumck!"

"Edmo Kumck!"

"Yes: Edmo Kumck. What's the matter with that?"

"Nothing in particular. Except for the fact that Edmo Kumck was the *ever-loving friend* of Freya Bolitho ... That Edmo Kumck forged the plan to *amicably* rob her of the greater part of her fortune ... That the *amiable* kindness of Edmo Kumck acted so finely in the heist ... That the staged 'accident,' run-

ning over the boy who was helping her cross the street, awoke
in her the primary instinct of any mother: the urge to help a
child in distress . . . That only by provoking such a crisis was
there any possibility that Freya would let go of—even for a few
brief seconds—her bread-loaf piggy bank: the *amicable* objective of Edmo Kumck . . . That in his mathematical calculation
of the traffic accident-heist, the thing that was most admirable, for its diplomacy and subtlety, was the *amicable* conduct,
of which we had no idea, that Edmo Kumck displayed toward Freya Bolitho . . . I found out yesterday that his consolations were so profuse that the victim accepted the robbery and
muffled her wailing cry in the *friendship* of Edmo Kumck . . ."

From deep within the most recondite cell of his being,
Longines contemplated Katanga with proud satisfaction.

Excited, Aparicio patted him vigorously on the back:

"I didn't know those details. Like clockwork; a masterpiece!"

"When one is disloyal for the sake of the ideal, it's because
goodness requires supreme sacrifice. What a stupendous swine
you've been!"

Longines blushed with embarrassment: "None of that.
Edmo Kumck did nothing more than charge a fair price for his
kindness. He's not a stupendous swine. He's a tender swine!"

They were climbing out of the taxi when Rescoldo and Fenicio
appeared on the south corner, running at full speed.

They'd not even paid the driver before learning the terrible
news:

"We've been waiting for you. Or really, he's waiting for you.
The poor old man is slipping away! He might not even recognize you now. Yesterday, right after you left, he got much
worse, as if on purpose. Bronchopneumonia. Acute. He caught
it at the worst time. I realized it right away. I brought two of
the head doctors from the Teaching Hospital. They confirmed
my diagnosis. Fatal. High temperature. Rapid pulse. Labored
breathing. Cyanotic skin. There's nothing to be done!"

More than halted, they seemed paralyzed in shock.

"Come in. I just picked up some injections at the hospital pharmacy. Come in. I'll give them to him as soon as the priest finishes."

"The priest!" exclaimed Longines. "But he's a Protestant!"

"Details! This is no time for quibbling."

They strode resolutely across the patio. The half-closed door interrupted their momentum. Four sighs slid into the room.

The solemn scene of the priest anointing the sick, sweating, motionless man filled them with tears. And their hearts with sorrow. They would have liked to express their feelings. To surround the headboard. Make themselves heard by Fortunato. But the priest administering the last rites made them self-conscious. Their sobs were constricted and they were annoyed with the priest, praying ceremoniously, who stole moments which belonged to them. Their annoyance turned to hatred. They were on the verge of exploding.

They each took a deep breath.

The blessed olive oil—the *oleo laetitia*—infused with the Lord's compassion now moistened his eyelids, his lips, his forehead.

They crept closer, rapt in concentrated devotion.

To the beat of cavernous death rattles and sibilant inspiration, the last phrase of the sacrament fell sweetly:

"*Per istam sanctam unctionem indulgeat tibi Dominus quid quid delinquisti. Amen.*"

They were choked with emotion. They could stand no more. And before the priest could make the sign of the cross in the air, four voices broke out at once:

"JAROSLAV!!!"

The priest turned toward them in anger. Such scandal! They had shamelessly violated the beatitude of the act!

In their desperate effusion for their companion, the four of them moaned and moved about confusedly. Katanga wiped away the sacred unction with silk handkerchiefs soaked in water of laurel and cherry blossom. Dijunto rubbed him with gum benzoin. Aparicio wafted about the scent from a flask of

Balsam of Tolú. They felt a desperate desire to do something, anything, to stop the onset of death. It was then that Longines withdrew the crucifix that had been placed between the dying man's fingers. And amid the general shock, he gathered all the loose change from his pockets, and tremulously placed the coins in the dying man's right palm.

"Sacrilege! Sacrilege!" whispered the priest and the landlady.

But the coins worked their miracle! And the four voices again cried in unison:

"JAROSLAV!!!"

Anxious, agitated, Fortunato moved his head.

One by one, he observed his comrades there.

Now serene, his face showed the pride of an ineffable gratitude.

He tried to say good-bye. He made a faint effort. And the silvery money slipped through his fingers!

The music from the coins cast an air of enchantment around Fortunato's spent body. Longines threw himself to the floor. He frantically gathered up the coins. And making them jingle, he put them back into Fortunato's hand. The contact widened his final smile. He raised his eyes toward his friend.

They held the gaze for a moment.

And then the definitive drift towards death, eyes turned upward, sadder than any signal for the ace of spades that Aparicio's eyes had ever seen in any game of *truco*.

Viejo Amor summoned Patay, Fenicio, and Rescoldo:

"Do us a big favor. Take care of the necessary arrangements. We're just not up to it. Here's three hundred pesos to record the death at the Civil Registry, and to purchase a burial niche. Secure the use of the mortuary chapel and arrange the funeral for tomorrow. Spend what you need. We want a decent burial. A few cars. On your way, stop at the grocery store; buy food and liquor for the wake. If you run out of money, tell them to send us the bill."

He'd resolved not to consult the others. Deliberately. He knew that they would refuse any funeral arrangements, anything that would make a mockery of death. And pondering how this act of Christian devotion might enable him to win over Doña Visitación, he went against his comrades.

He had no scruples whatsoever about using Fortunato's corpse for selfish, sentimental reasons. Hadn't he agreed to the last rites only to earn her esteem? Why turn back now? He might as well carry out the customary wake and the prayers for the dead. Their affair, which had begun favorably and flourished with gifts of cakes, confections, and special dishes, would now be secured. In truth, ceremonies mattered very little to him. In accordance with etiquette he forced himself to suppress his passions and sought only to show his respects for the deep-rooted Catholic convictions of Doña Visitación, whom he now called Little Visi.

When the mortuary workers arrived with the coffin and the glass beads for the funeral chapel, Viejo Amor and Little Visi were sitting together in the entry hall. They watched the workers move about as if it were an everyday occurrence. They drank *mate*, chatting idly. And while Viejo Amor's audacious, roving hands provoked false complaints and affectionate flatteries, their mouths laughed, stuffed with cookies, syrup, and sweets.

Most people who repress their sexual desires have a real sweet tooth for candy, treats, and *patisserie*. Eligible young women, spinsters, nuns, choke themselves on bonbons, puddings, cakes, and other substitutes for pleasure. The gluttony of saintly laywomen, the voracious hunger of sacristans and candle-sucking Holy Joes, the bulimia of Carthusians and Mercedarians are all well-known. Their confectionary renown as producers of cakes, desserts, and liqueurs is, more than fame, the coefficient of the carnal appetite deferred by covetousness, onanism, and perversion. The deep connection between sweet fruit syrup and lack of sex is as cloying and sticky as it is certain.

He was biting into the half-eaten coconut macaroon she'd placed in his mouth, already bearing the marks of her teeth, when an urgent cry sounded from the patio:

"Viejo Amor!"

He recognized Longines's voice. He remained seated, savoring the delicacy of her hand and the flattery from her mouth:

"*Viejo Amor*—Old Love. How I love your nickname! God
willing our love will be an old love very soon! Because:

An 'old love' is not forgotten or forsaken.
An 'old love' if it leaves our soul
Never bids us farewell."

Another shout stubbornly repeated the call:

"Viejo Amor!"

Courteous, paying compliments to his lady—who continued humming the song she had begun—he stood up. And
earnestly begging her pardon, slipped away languidly, as if reluctant to leave the enchantment of her company.

They had gathered on the patio. Bluntly, angrily, they accosted him with a bewildering reproach.

"What kind of a farce is this? Who gave you permission to
make such a mockery?"

"You know the rule. So what's the meaning of this? . . ."

"It's not right for you to disrupt Fortunato's peaceful repose
by flouting his wishes."

"Did we bury Lon Chaney with such pomp?"

"You shouldn't waste the money on stupidities."

"Nor cause disagreements."

"Not to mention that Jaroslav wasn't Catholic. Why did you
allow that priest to torture him in his dying moments?"

"You should have followed our usual proto . . ."

"Enough! Listen. I never follow protocol. I never follow anything. Much less now."

"But, why priests . . . a wake . . . sacraments? . . ." asked
Longines, giving voice to everyone's thoughts.

Viejo Amor cocked his head. He cynically considered his response. But he didn't utter a word. Just a proud wrinkle in the
corner of his mouth . . .

Everyone understood.

The Swiss man grimaced in disavowal:

"This derails us. Say good-bye to our idealistic tour for the sake of others."

Swollen with scorn, Aparicio clucked his tongue. And added a finishing touch:

"You've got to be the biggest, most tasteless, idiotic boor! To think you — someone like you — could pretend to hang the flag of mourning from your old yardarm! Can't you just whip out the sarcophagus and amulets to get what you want from her? It's ridiculous! It's not right she mounts you but reins us in. It's not right that the flirtations of some old harpy . . ."

"Silence! I won't allow it!"

". . . interrupt our plans. You can't . . ."

"Be quiet, or I won't be responsible for my actions! Little Visi and I . . ."

The emotion choked him up in a modest pause.

"Doña Visitación and you, are what?"

". . . we're going to be married."

"   . . . . !!!"

They stood there with their mouths hanging open, their arms limp. Mentally crushed. With the shattered rubble of a thousand dreams lying at their feet. The air filled with the agonizing moans of discipline and solidarity — two faithful hounds — their necks both broken by disaster. They were caught in the full rapture of shock when the proprietress of the boarding house emerged from the drawing room.

Her silence weighed them down like a leaden sun, in their tormented disappointment of hot, flustered embarrassment and the stultifying mugginess of the afternoon, heavy with dark storm clouds.

As Doña Visitación walked past them, Viejo Amor gazed threateningly at Longines and Aparicio, more in anticipation of an outburst than in challenge. She felt the protective custody of his gaze. He was already hers! When a man looks out for you! . . . Her spirits swelled within her. And she continued to strut about in matronly fashion.

"Don't worry. We won't make a scene."

"I wouldn't allow it, anyway."

"This is finished. Tomorrow, the next day, or one day soon, we'll settle things."

"Whenever you like. Here, in the meantime, take this letter from Fortunato, for you."

Katanga's face had never fallen so deeply into shadow.

His bewilderment over his friend's death was complicated by the abrupt emotion of the quarrel. If agony makes the soul shrink before the incomprehensible dimension of the great beyond, discord shreds it with its rampant passion. He was unable to say or do anything. Inhibited. Tremulous.

The momentary calm was aggressively ruptured a second time.

"We won't be attending the wake."

"As you wish."

Their reciprocal hatred now violated the limits of correctness. Longines had spoken for the group and it pained Katanga to be party to such undignified conduct. And obliged by his affection for poor Jaroslav, he made a suggestion:

"You don't have to be so stubborn. The matter can be resolved. Today more than ever! Before the body of our comrade, all quarrels must be dissolved. Let us be united in peace. Let us sit down at the gaming table with death!"

There was a bitter consensus of suffocated rage.

Viejo Amor withdrew with a certain haughtiness. He joined Little Visi, who was coming out of the viewing room. And adoringly, innocently, they continued chatting.

"Yes. We must not sully Jaroslav's peaceful repose. I'll attend the wake. But after that . . ."

Aparicio led Longines and Dijunto to the viewing room:

"Don't worry. Let it go. It is impossible to renounce idiocy. He'll get what's coming to him. That woman will be our vengeance . . . Are you coming?"

"In a minute."

Katanga deliberately hung back.

His tolerant attitude had partially dissipated the lacerating cruelty of their stated intentions. Now he needed to erase the maliciousness from Viejo Amor's domineering attitude. To council. Pacify. Since a resolution was no longer possible!

With an almost paternal smile, he looked kindly on the "fiancées." Two adolescents: no more, no less. He admired the metamorphosis at work. Love rejuvenates, amplifying self-awareness and exalting the powers of the flesh. Why recriminate such a virtue! Never! The appropriate response is to denounce the notions which are born of prejudice. We must never vituperate the transformations incited by love.

Encouraged by a slight pout from Little Visi, Katanga walked toward them. Drawing near, he noticed something strange in himself. With each step his personality seemed to diminish. He was the same polished man, immutable and well-balanced, but as he neared them he was progressively reduced in size. Standing before them, the contrast perturbed him. Was it that the swells of love make lovers gigantic? Or were they actually plump and bulging with tenderness, brimful of sweet desires? He couldn't explain the smallness of his presence. And facing the fiancées, fat with caresses, obese with happiness, he delivered these words:

"I understand. Love also nestles in the fat-laden hearts of the obese ... Skinny people are mistaken when they think otherwise. In the forests of blubber, in the shadow of the well-nourished cells, the loquacious little goldfinch, which is born from glances, and flies on sighs, is wont to sing. *(The cold, disdainful face of Longines flashed in his mind.)* To see a fat man looking anxious alongside his beloved has always been a cause for ridicule. Such misguided ideas about life! Many believe it to be impossible. Many mock what they've branded as bacon-fat bliss. Such incorrect notions! They weigh the weight of ridicule where they had only to judge the ridiculousness of the weight ... *(The peevish face of Aparicio flashed in his mind.)* Thus we find the sad, silent nostalgia which fat people conceal within their jocund rotundity. Thus are they tormented by the fastidiousness of incomprehension. And let them be, in that vulgar metaphor that claims life is a sea, like simple buoys which mark the happy route for others. *(The timid face of Dijunto flashed before his eyes.)* I know that love also nestles in the fat-laden hearts of the obese . . . In their stout corpulence life's happiness has a plinth without equal. Never come down from it! But from its vantage point, Viejo Amor, contemplate your friends with affection. Don't curtail your kindness. Now, in the tender, luxurious softness of your beloved, you will find the peace which the poet sought. And, like him, you will be able to say to her: *Ton corps est la tombe de ma volonté morte.*

When the wreath of flowers arrived it was raining cats and dogs.

Rescoldo placed it ceremoniously upon the casket.

At first they didn't notice, because each one of the five men sat with his head hanging down or his hands covering his face. But, as soon as the penetrating perfume of hyacinths and spikenards spread through the room, their mutual gaze settled upon the unknown gift:

Who could be sending flowers to Fortunato?

They were sure it was a mistake:

Flowers? For Jaroslav?

One after another, the five of them stopped to look. As if under a spell. Covering their curiosity with diverse ruses: snuffing out the candles, adjusting the candelabra, speaking with the students.

Aparicio was the first to discover the card:

Pale, grief-stricken, he whistled furtively to his comrades. Amid a nimbus of roses, the card testified to something unexpected. Spontaneity. Sentiment. Courtesy.

It sent through them a shockwave of emotion with cordial repercussions. Copious tears began to flow. If the flower is a perfumed idea, the offering of the wreath symbolizes a ring of pure thoughts united by the faith of the heart.

They sighed in an attempt to disguise their anguish. Then Viejo Amor leaned forward to read the card. Touched as well by the thoughtfulness, he raised his remorseful face. He was about to step away. But his compunction found an unforeseen refuge. The trembling arms of Longines! And there was a communion of wailing grief from inside an impenetrable brotherly embrace.

The rain continued pouring down. It never failed to rain on the eve of Carnival, drowning parades and outdoor gatherings.

At midnight, three doctors showed up along with some friends, two male nurses. They wore a mask of sorrow. Not for the band of comrades in mourning, but rather for the Medical School's disastrous dance, which had been rained out. For them, the wake was a secondary concern. Patay and Fenicio had mentioned the large amount of high-quality booze they'd been sent to purchase. And with that in mind, they stopped by to express their condolences.

They came in soaking wet. Rescoldo, sensitive to the cold as always, shivered to see them. He urged them to take off their coats. He handed them a flask of Bols gin as a healing elixir for the body. Once the first one felt reinvigorated, he commented:

"*Che*, you're from La Rioja: you ought to be happy. If it rains like this on your vineyards!"

He smiled, wrinkling his nose, sadly thinking the contrary. Others responded for him:

"There's no worry. After God takes a piss on other places, he shakes it over La Rioja."

"Four drops. Is there any guy drier than this one?"

Fenicio introduced the interns, saying they'd been sent to express the condolences of the doctors who'd attended to Jaroslav. And the nurses, being pharmacy employees, had also helped with the urgent needs of the man's illness.

The austere formal obligations now fulfilled, the wake became a social engagement.

Busy talking with the man from Santiago, Katanga was the last to be introduced. The group did not especially interest him.

By appearance, all medical students look the same. He knew it. But he did not know that *in reality* they are even more alike. What made him bitter was the fact that the intimate knowledge that comes from the daily examination of pain does not add to wisdom, but diminishes it; the noble desire to heal is snuffed out in the face of so much chattering, brawling mediocrity.

One of the interns produced in Katanga an intense revulsion. As the introductions went around, he'd noticed the man's peculiar manner of shaking hands. Instead of stretching out his hand naturally, he was instead slow and methodical, simulating the gesture of giving an injection. Upon introducing him, Fenicio added:

"Varela works at the Institute for Syphilis Studies."

"Ah, yes, of course. Now I understand."

"Understand what, Katanga?"

"The way the man says hello ... when he shakes hands ... Pushing his thumb as if he were pressing down the plunger of a Pravaz syringe ..."

Varela was clearly an oddball. As he and Katanga exchanged words, the man's obsession with syphilis fought to penetrate the banal gaps in the conversation. Obsessive tendencies are always the same. The victim feels the need to communicate their obsession without the interlocutor realizing they have redirected topics, forced ideas, and steered the dialogue back toward their perversion. The purpose achieved, his sickly smile shone with euphoria:

"Yes, my mercurialized friend. Your comrade's death could have been avoided with a strong dose of Solu-Salvarsan. Syphilis is everywhere. Treat yourself. As a fourth-year medical student at the National College, I was sweet on a girl whose face was straight out of a painting by Murillo. To get what I was after, I bought her a pair of stockings at a clearance sale at Gath & Chaves, the kind which casts a light shadow over the calf. I had to spend three hundred fifty pesos ..."

"You call that a sale!"

"... for the corresponding anti-syphilis treatment! Trust no

one: syphilis is everywhere! There is no other remedy: intra-
muscular therapy! Get yourself treated!"

Varela's insistent allusion was reprehensible. Katanga had his
retort ready. But Fenicio winked at him and he chose instead
to keep quiet.

As he mingled through the crowd he heard, through Fenicio and the nurses, many anecdotes about the syphilitic doctor.
He was a cultured young man whose cheerful youth was often overshadowed by his darkness. His scientific delirium sent
him on exhilarating flights of fancy. A prisoner to his morbid
impulses, he ranted and raved about the world's leniency in
the face of the exponential advancement and concentric progression of syphilis. His intellectual insanity provided a counterpoint, then, to the disquietude of his diseased imagination,
and he invariably advised everyone to "seek treatment." A close
friend rebuked him: *Take up the practice yourself and be done
with it. You'll make bags of money. Nobody's more qualified than
you to open the "Get Treated Syphilitic Sanatorium"* ... When
Varela was given the task of making a press statement on behalf of the Institute Director, the newspapers printed black and
white proof of his aberration. In place of the typical opening:
"This release was communicated and the words transcribed, etcetera," he'd written: "This disease was communicated and the
treatment prescribed ..." Despite his fixation, he was authori-
tative and scrupulous. Prone to exaggerate already conservative
health precautions, he posted in his office, the now infamous
public notice composed by his own hand: DON'T BE NA-
IVE: USE FORMALDEHYDE IN PLACE OF HOLY WATER;
NEOSALVARSAN IS MORE EFFECTIVE THAN PRAYERS.
The archbishop intervened. And he had to muffle his outward
zeal, burying himself in the negative results of his Kahn and
Wasserman tests ...

Don Rufo had just arrived.

The news of Fortunato's death had surprised him just a short
while earlier, after a day spent at a friend's house on the outskirts of Córdoba. His condolences and excuses for arriving

late were delivered with such fervent perfection that Longines steered him out to the patio, so that the students' irreverent racket would not detract from his afflicted sincerity.

There, leaning against the wall, Longines offered Don Rufo a detailed account of Fortunato's final moments. And, in passing, demonstrating uncharacteristic confidence, he gave him a summary of Viejo Amor's love affairs. He was pleased to provide explicit details. Longines was proud to admit that he and Don Rufo were quite similar in character. And, in homage to the cordial effusion of the man's condolences, he took the opportunity to express his admiration.

Their mutual frankness filled them both with great satisfaction. The wisdom of the Swiss man's father bubbled in his memory: "*Give your friendship tacitly. To people who coincide with you in a definitive way. Remember well: the worst enemies are those who were once friends, who know your mistakes, defects, and weaknesses; because their swinish nature will irremissibly exploit them.*" And the *criollo's* sense of honor was immensely flattered by the Swiss man's trusting friendship.

Aparicio and Viejo Amor suddenly appeared:

"Here, Don Rufo, take your pick."

"Cognac or cherry kirsch?"

"Kirsch."

His choice pleased the Uruguayan who held on to the remaining drink. Before Don Rufo finished drinking, Aparicio had refilled his glass to the top.

"Whoa, friend, hold on. You're gonna get me plastered, easy."

"That's what life is for. See . . ."

"That's right. Lots of times I've wondered if I wasn't being foolish in avoiding alcohol. Every last drunkard looks happy! . . ."

". . . When they're sucking it down," interrupted Longines. "Sober, they're not worth a damn. Don't regret it, Don Rufo. Drunkenness is a slippery way to escape from oneself. The drunkard doesn't feel life. And the one who doesn't feel life, slips toward the void."

"That's what you say, because you've never gotten plastered," countered Viejo Amor. "But getting rip-roaring drunk once in a while is a healthy thing. It fans the fire in the blood. It stirs up the frozen air in the head. It makes hot coals and smoke. Love! Dreams!"

"Nonsense. You're mixed up. Pleasure isn't joy ... It's just quenched thirst. Delight fulfilled. Pleasure ... But pleasure is not happiness. For all the rest, completely useless. You can't keep hot coals in cellophane tubes! You can't keep smoke in a wicker basket!"

The harmony of the group, tentatively restored through sorrow, was again on the verge of being shredded to pieces. Viejo Amor, already slightly tipsy, detected an irritating allusion in Longines's reply. There was something there. He was going to answer him, reproachful. But several loud laughs were heard in the next room where the coffin lay. And in the light-hearted atmosphere the cloud of ill-will dissipated before they had finished savoring the liquor in their glasses.

They went in.

Many simultaneous conversations, memories from Carnival celebrations of past years. The old provincial parades, redolent with basil and perfume ... of rotten eggs and shantytown sweat!

The nurses were thinking back many years. Vivid tales of bacchanals and boozy parties. Confused chaos of customs that would never return. They painted their pictures with words and gestures. And young once more, they paraded behind— like in olden times—the costumed revelers they described.

Their voices became unctuous with nostalgia:

"You remember the kings, counts, slaves, street sweepers, the old black men and all the motley crew in bright colors, mirrors, and sequins? The devils on the loose and the bands of madmen: *Los Locos Unidos*? The fights between The Black Africans and The Star of the Orient? The rivalry between the troupes from Abrojal and those from Bomba? The chorus groups from

San Vicente and Barrio de la Hilacha?"

"How could I forget? Months at a time we went out at night, after school, near El Degolladito, to a vacant lot surrounded by houses and shanties, where the Sol Brillante de Cuba troupe had its rehearsals:

tum ta–rúm tum–tum–tum–tum tum tum–tum

tum ta–rúm tum–tum–tum–tum tum tum–tum . . ."

"It was a treat, especially on the eve of holidays, like today, to witness the dress rehearsal. The whole bunch of them giving their all to prepare their group's costumes. Silks, velvets, wigs, booties, bells. All the volunteer seamstresses to give the final touches. You had to see these poor ragamuffins who went around the whole year in straw slippers and t-shirts, so proud of their purple capes, ceremonious courtesans in their finery! And the candombe rhythm:

tum ta–rúm tum–tum–tum–tum tum tum–túm

tum ta–rúm tum–tum–tum–tum tum tum–túm . . ."

"The Sol Brillante de Cuba troupe boasted the best old black dancer in Córdoba. He was the trembler, the possessed old man of the tribe. It was really something to see when the director of the band gave him the cue: *Shake it, Earthworm, we're comin' up on the Press Booth.* And as if all of a sudden he was attacked by the shakes, tetanus, and Saint Vitus Dance all rolled into one, the guy started to trip, stagger, lurch, and stumble in a complete and never-ending vibration, in a frenzy that no modern dance can reproduce. He went on and on. Excited by the furious candombe drums and the hammering of the double bells:

tum ta–rúm tum–tum–tum–tum tum tum–túm

tum ta–rúm tum–tum–tum–tum tum tum–túm

tin ti–rín tin–tin–tin–tin tin tin–tín

tum ta–rúm tum–tum–tum–tum tum tum–túm

"And to incite more screaming clamor from the entranced crowd, Earthworm trembled, sweated, twitched, and twisted until, exhausted, the director held him up to present him to the reporters with the pride of the alienist exhibiting some strange creature from the insane asylum."

The drink flowed abundantly.

They were drinking everything, foolishly: gin, curaçao, beer, peppermint schnapps, cognac. Almost without pleasure. With the blind focus of poor students who won't get a second chance.

Varela, paralyzed from the large quantity he'd imbibed, sat with his head stuck to the back of the chair. Stiff as a mummy, he joined the conversation:

"I don't remember that. I was really little. For me the carnival began with the costume dance boom. That's when I first got gonorrhea. Since that year: 1915, I go only to amuse myself by seeing how much cotton blocks the urinals. And to calculate the stillbirths and babies to be born already infected with syphilis nine months later."

"You see it all black."

"Black? Three or four months ago I saw a *yellow* baby boy, splayed out. I was doing weekly rounds in the maternity hospital. A magnificent case."

"Wasn't it monstrous? . . ."

"Clinically. The obstetrician questioned the woman who'd just given birth: *Tell me, who's this child's father? We've got to inform him that the baby has died.* Panting with delight at the news, the young woman began laughing: *Don' know, doutor. It happen' during Carnival. A young guy dressed like a domino* . . . That's the Carnival I know! The Carnival of the pale-faced syphilis carriers disguised as dominoes!"

"Don't talk to me about dominoes."

"Dominoes, harlequins, and Pierrots have all spoiled a festival that was once so purely, perfectly *criollo* as carnival."

"They introduced a foreign taint."

"They grafted Nice and Viareggio onto the Afro-American jungle."

"Exactly," interjected Katanga. "Exactly. In the islands of the Caribbean and in Brazil one now perceives the decomposition of autochthonous values. I'm not aware of what the old Shrovetide days were like here; but once, in Pernambuco, I saw the impetuous strength and joyous frenzy of the blacks in the madness of their surging dances and wild revelry. Their vocation for monarchical pomp, mirrored escutcheons, and tinseled standards is something I didn't understand directly; but I did see the immense, absurd drama of their suffering, as they conquered the subconscious through the reality of the masquerade. Returning years later, the disintegration was visible. The exuberant enthusiasm and indiscipline were regulated and laid low. The Dionysian aspect—the innate furor bellowing in the forest of instinct—became an opaque parody. Constrained by urbanity, the energy of pleasure had been exchanged for the nostalgic circumspection of quadroons and mestizos. From what I hear, blackness does not even exist in these parts. It's been suppressed, de-authorized. It's regrettable in a way. Between the Mulatto troupe, which once a year reproduces the royal court of Martinique, and the aristocrats, who extend their own Carnival out all year long, the parody is preferable. It's far more innocuous, picturesque, and loquacious."

"You speak very well. You should have heard the hymns the bands played, the catchy voices of the regional choirs, and the verses, during the competitions. Delightful. Listen to this example:

Look at that poor slave
Dancing with thunderous sorrow
His father died in the jail cell
His mother in the bordello ..."

Various cackles assaulted the tale:
"Edifying."
"What an outstanding pedigree."
"Well, yes, a lovely lineage. It makes me think of the gypsy song:

My ma's a little match girl
My pa's a doggie barber:
My oh my! Such family honor!"

The nurses hiccupped with laughter. Drunk with nostalgia and the hodgepodge of sentiments, they missed Dijunto's quotation. They were smooching the bottle of anise liquor that Patay had handed them. And their misbehavior was even more distressing thanks to the hurly-burly of conga and candombe rhythms they were singing:

"Tum ta-rúm tum-tum-tum-tum tum tum-túm."

"All you pretty Córdoba girls, g'bye."

"Tum ta-rúm tum-tum-tum-tum tum tum-túm."

"So lovely up front an' from behind."

"Tin ti-rín tin-tin-tin-tin tin tin-tín."

"The troupe bids farewell."

"Till the next carnival."

"Tum ta-rúm tum-tum-tum-tum tum tum-túm."

Fenicio tried to intervene and get them to stop their irreverent racket. A difficult task. The drunks were so immersed in their roles, so identified with the objects of their memory. The only way to prevent more singing, contortions, and reeling about was to take drastic measures. They had to be convinced to go out and start paying for their drinks.

"All right. Enough. Finished. Let's go."

"Good . . . We're coming . . . *Hic* . . . Don' get mad . . ."

"You can count on us for your wake . . ."

At last, they left. Staggering, stumbling across the threshold. Slipping on the loose tiles in the patio.

The sky was pure, sparkling, washed clean.

The street seemed a trench, filthy with puddles and penumbra.

They disappeared.

Carrying the moon like a knapsack.

By dawn only Rescoldo, Longines, Don Rufo, and Dijunto were still awake.

Bitter hour, of biblical aridity, in which sleep and dream are frozen. An hour of enigmas borne through the night, which vanish into mist the moment the alarming sunlight comes flooding in. An hour which brushes the limits of anguish and abruptly delivers the ship of day to the shores of the flesh. A dry, sour, anguished hour.

Aparicio, Varela and Patay, the interns, Katanga, and Viejo Amor lay scattered about the room and the corridor in absurd positions, sound asleep or dozing in chairs, rockers, and couches.

They commented on the excesses of the previous night:

"Yes, that's how wakes are; whoever organizes one must be prepared to suffer an extravagant atrophy of moral sensibility! I prefer, a thousand times over, the dryness, laconism, and rapidity with which we buried Lon Chaney."

"Right: those kids were getting pretty out of hand . . ."

"Out of hand, out of their heads! Shameless. This wreckage couldn't be mended even by St. James the Apostle, may he rest in peace."

"I know that things didn't turn out well. I'm not going to defend them. However, I insist that it wasn't their fault, but Viejo Amor's. Sheer foolery putting Patay in charge of organizing the wake; his head is emptier than a mandolin! And Fenicio; noisier than a motorcycle!"

They continued complaining, their heads still pounding from the uproar. Rescoldo continued to defend his companions with his scalding sarcasm. A close friend of Patay, he heaped upon him the lion's share of blame—without implying disloyalty—the better to excuse the principal culprit, Fenicio:

"Not worth getting upset. Students. A word synonymous with mischievous spirits . . . Young fellows, from Santiago especially, are possessed of a great imaginative power. Ancient instigators of drought in order to help the crops that favor arid soil, they've been known for an eloquence whose salty wit surpasses the immense salt flats of their province. That Patay! I don't know . . . A prodigious leader when it comes to aberrant behavior. The shadow of the local mistol shrub, the perfumed nights of stars and peppermint, the longing for water . . . I don't know what explains his behavior. What's certain is that now and then he comes up with the strangest ideas, which deserve to be inscribed on twelve tablets of *quebracho* wood for the future temple of Eurindia."

Longines, sulking, replied squarely:

"All very well; but death, dear friend, deserves respect."

"I don't dispute that. I'm trying to get you to see that a man from Santiago with mannerisms like Patay is the closest thing to Dr. Pangloss that I know. Having a boozy party means that 'all is for the best in this best of all possible worlds.' Even disrespect and thoughtlessness. Don't you know he's a native of Santiago del Estero, where locust-bean meteorites fall with the same frequency as railway inspectors? Do you begrudge the locals the glory of having invented corn liquor, locust-bean mead, mistol balls? It shows a long line of debauchery."

Furious, sticking his nose up close to the man to smell his breath, Longines inquired:

"Tell me: are you drunk, too?"

"Those who know people from Santiago only through the stereotypes of Gramajo Gutiérrez or Gómez Cornet, are ignorant. And those that suppose them to have the same indolent or pagan rhythm as the dancers of Chazarreta, delirious. Look at Patay! In that province they wear different garments and they dance bandy-legged from whiskey and Carabanchel Anise, eluding both progress *and* the future."

Now it was not only the Swiss man. Dijunto and Don Rufo observed him with surprise as well. He made no sense at all. Such enormous absurdities . . . Maybe he really was drunk.

"You don't think so? You know what two of Patay's relatives proposed years ago? The engineer Palmeyra, and the Police Chief, Colonel de la Zerda? Something wonderfully Santiagan. Something which surpasses their porcine ancestry and climbs up higher than their patronymic heights. Nothing less than promoting aviation as a way to hunt cattle rustlers from the air!"

They deliberated in secret for a few, brief seconds. They agreed that he was crazy, not drunk. Now their grudging patience became a benevolent compassion. The young man had changed so dramatically and they finally understood why: Fortunato! Only a day ago the two had been happily chatting during the afternoon siesta. Now his submissive, flaccid cadaver lay in an oppressive zinc-lined box. Enough to drive anyone to insanity! They begged him to go and lie down. Patting him on the shoulder persuasively, they accompanied him to his room.

But Rescoldo crept back.

From the end of the hallway he delightedly confirmed the success of his strategy. He had ensnared the mourners in the net of his shameless rascality. He had deflected the well-deserved reproach meant for Fenicio ... He heard Longines commenting dispiritedly:

"Life is beautiful when happiness is balanced among health, honor, and good fortune. But the forces of the world always fight to break that equilibrium. There are inscrutable tragic counterweights. There's the proof. Poor Rescoldo. See the burden of fatality crushing him down into the abyss of delirium. Should one protest with tears? Vain undertaking. Watering sorrow makes it grow stronger, sadness extinguishes reflection so much the sooner. We must think. Think about this boy's goodness, his pureness, his eager efforts, the example of mourning which his conduct bequeaths us. And save him. Save him!"

The Riojan opened his mouth in stupefaction: "These guys ... have taken it all ... seriously."

He knew that comical themes could be gleaned from very grave matters. That the essence of hilarity is found buried in the flesh of a somber matter or in the cordial little frown of men with close, bushy eyebrows. But he didn't realize that the opposite was also true: that inane chatter could be taken so seriously. Chatter like his own, which employed exaggerated, banal topics ... to prevent his friend from being reprimanded.

He was going to confess his ruse. His sense of decorum was inflamed by any small slight. A beloved friend had once told him: *Your heart opens wider than a fool's mouth* ... But he was intercepted. The door burst open and someone stumbled hurriedly in.

In the long shadows of daybreak, it took them a moment to identify the intruder as he clapped the shutters and turned the key. It was Fenicio!

He was still breathing hard. He asked them to turn off the lights. He handed a folder to Longines. He collapsed into a chair. And panting, he explained to the four of them:

"Ian von Zuhlinder ... Ian von Zuhlinder's been robbed ... He's the assistant at the College of Natural Sciences ... A rabid Nazi ... What a whirlwind! ... They grabbed him around the neck, from behind, to rob him ... Four masked men ... When they saw me and the interns they fled ... No doubt I saved the poor Nazi from something worse!"

"And this folder?"

"I think it was premeditated ... The masks, to hide their faces ... They waited until he turned the corner ... In a vacant lot ... I don't know if you've heard about it ... On Calle Neuquén there's a Nazi committee operating ... Secret meetings ..."

"But, what about this folder?"

"The masked men vanished into thin air ... But they beat him good ... *Wham, bam, boom!* ... His face looked like a pomegranate ... They knocked him out ..."

Exasperated, Longines could hold back no longer:

"Details, Fenicio, specifics. Who gave you this folder?"

"Nobody. I found it and I hid it on me without anyone noticing ... It fell on the ground during all the fuss ... I suppose it belongs to von Zuhlinder ... To the Nazi boss ... He's the Nazi boss ..."

"The local Nazi leader?" Longines asked. And feverishly opened the folder.

It was full of typewritten papers. With drawings of butterflies and various classes of insects, finely painted in watercolor. With tables, graphs, and numerical scales in abundance.

He read the letterhead: INSTITUTE OF ENTOMOLOGY. Some diagrams. Various headings. He scanned it all, quickly but carefully.

"Nothing special," he summarized. "Scientific papers in German."

"That's why I gave them to you ... You and Katanga understand that language ..."

"I'd like to take a good look at them."

"They're yours ... But be careful! ... Don't let anyone know ... They could get me into trouble."

The room was filled with a dirty smell of stale alcohol, withered flowers, and burnt candles. Suddenly, with a loud groan, the disheveled Katanga stretched out his arms and legs. He slowly rose to his feet and slunk outside onto the patio, startling the group.

As the clear dawn shone on Doña Visitación's flowerpots, Katanga's slow, stealthy steps illuminated his friends' whispered conference.

And cast a Rembrandt light in Longines's mind.

The summary was very brief; the Swiss man informed Katanga in a few words:

"Be wary of believing that the truth is necessarily dense. It can be articulated through a thousand minor lies ... Like a viper slithering through a thousand rings. The truth is always venomous. My intuition tells me that here, in this folder, there's a great deal of hidden venom ..." His purulent eye winked with cunning suspicion.

Katanga nodded:

"Being as it's German, it doesn't surprise me: Protestantism, the categorical imperative, Hegelian philosophy, Romanticism, Imperial delirium, music. There must be a lot of music, too ..."

Laughter, bells, streamers!

From beneath garlands of light emerges the face of Momo, an ephemeral king's grotesque buffoon. Here he comes! Accompanied by a strange, extravagant cohort, crying aloud their joyous rites.

Evohé! Evohé!

Through air vibrating with confetti, the secular God shakes his symbolic rattle. As in ancient days, on the sacred hill, his body is garlanded with fresh vines and roses.

Laughter, bells, streamers!

A riotous mass of little children. A great strident noise of carriages. A polychromatic luxury of flowers and nectars. And a profane tickling runs through their souls.

Evohé! Evohé!

His followers circle round with profound frivolity. A philosopher shows his blighted pessimism. Seeing him, Momo whets an ironic grimace upon his face, painted as a crestfallen comic whose show's been cancelled.

Laughter, bells, streamers!

Peals of laughter fly like sonorous butterflies. Thrills unravel in the unwavering undulation of a sentimental streamer. And kisses are planted, compounded with perfume, on pale jasmine petals.

Evohé! Evohé!

Flee to the turbid swamp of the multitude, the eternally disguised. Who in the quotidian farce, donned the ragged chlamys of envy, interest, and evil. Momo is not the God of posthumous carnivals. That is why he hates them. And in the cackling of his rattle, the inexorable crows croak and caw.

Laughter, bells, and streamers!

Sorrow, anguish, tears!

Death arrives in procession beneath canopies of shade, immutable caryatid of life's temple. A throng of sad beings carry her and place her, fixed, immobile, in the frontispiece of a sepulcher.

Ananke! Ananke!

In a wasteland of black affliction, the Parca wraps her shroud round a clay dummy. Above the silent meadows are hovering, now and forever, browbeating parliaments of owls.

Sorrow, anguish, tears!

Sobbing men. Strident spirits moved to commotion. Screaming anguish of wails and laments. And a divine stinging pierces their souls.

Ananke! Ananke!

The burial procession circles round with austere gravity. Someone shows the branded welt of their fatalism. Seeing it, Death ridicules the learned ignorance that anticipates, doubly ill, the security of disgrace.

Sorrow, anguish, tears!

Sighs fly like parched, withered butterflies. Dashed hopes unravel from every wooden breast. And creeping through the dream, vile, expired, venomless occupation sheds its fledged feathers in the cave of the heart.

Ananke! Ananke!

Simple, guileless beings flee to the exile of their ego. Within life's heroic passion they refuse all simulacra. Death welcomes them to her antechamber of meditation. She loves them. And because in the barren wasteland they planted with love, peace germinates in them and flowers of serenity spring forth.

Sorrow, anguish, tears!

As the casket slid into its niche in the wall, none of them felt
satisfied with the ceremony. If they'd known beforehand, they
would have demanded the millenary custom of burying the deceased in the earth. Too late now. With the body stowed away
in a church vault in the Congregation of Our Lady Virgin of
the Rosary, the mason who cemented the stonework in place
told them:

"You can write in his personal information."

Katanga stepped forward. He accepted the pencil stub the
man handed him and, in the fresh whitewash, inscribed:

ƒ $ JAROLSAV KOPECKY $ ƒ

Below that he wrote the date. As a finishing touch, he engraved
a percent sign and encircled it with a heart. Then he murmured:

"Smetana, Smetana! Your *Moldava Suite* in this moment!"
And he closed his eyes in an attitude of devotion.

The interns and nurses in attendance looked at each other,
perplexed. They didn't understand a bit of it.

Now he spoke to himself:

*Death is an epiphonema. Not some contemptible plaque . . .
Epiphonema: the culmination and summary of a life. A life
worked out like a Parnassian sonnet, with the patience of artifice,
the gallantry of heroes or the subtlety of sages . . . This cement epitaph fills me with embarrassment. It buries the inner-emotion of
the once-living poem, without assigning it any merit. A common,
ordinary surface, which should be the screen of transfiguration, the
mirror of the soul!*

Suddenly, pencil at the ready, he turned to Dijunto, Aparicio, and Viejo Amor.

"What's your name?"

"Zenón Picalausa."

"You?"

"Fermín Hupoa."

"And you?"

"Olaf Olaffali. Why?"

"We're going to order two plaques made, right away. What we've got here is a disgrace. For many incompetents who commit suicide, for many fools who let themselves die, death is the *ultima ratio* with which they speculate to save their anonymity. For individuals like Lon Chaney and Fortunato, who've abdicated their own lives in order to save others, this is a mockery. It would be unfair to them if we simply did things the way they're always done. Betrayal, ever-alert, lies in wait for all those who get ahead; for all those who defeat the order of things with the shine of an authentic privilege. It mustn't be! I don't challenge what's unavoidable, but I do defy the crafty, infamous traps of oblivion."

Tense, concentrating, he closed his eyes again.

They all noticed the grimace of pain that crossed his face like the shadow of a cloud. And his inner tremor in the tremulous anxiety of silence.

The mourners began stirring to depart.

Someone snapped him out of it by inviting him for a stroll. He followed mechanically: his pupils glassy, his fists clenched.

Straying behind, Katanga let the other one go on. Now turning the corner onto the avenue of cypresses he stopped. He contemplated the sordid entrance to the cemetery. And smiling with grim incorruptible horror, he said *sotto voce:*

"Death is a portal upon the edge of a cliff. For myself, I want one that is sumptuous, majestic. Worked in the purest Manueline style: a mixture of sharp gothic ecstasies, arabesque minutiae of Byzantine sensuality, and strange Hindu imagery. A beatific facade of symbols and presentiments. Absorbed in its beauty, unaware, I will open the door and I will fall into the void . . ."

They stopped in front of the marble works.

The worker was fairly amazed to hear about the plaques they had in mind. Each of the two marble slabs — one for Fortunato, one for Lon Chaney — would simply show a seven-pointed star, with their seven different names — their real ones —

etched around it to form a sparkling radiance. In the center, the dead man's alias. And in opposing corners, a toad and a butterfly. Never, in forty years of funerary sculpture, had anyone placed such an order. In reality, the plaques were a hermetic homage to themselves. Stripped of their nicknames—their cloaks in times of chance and adventure—their naked identities showed them as beings with idiosyncrasies distinct from the associations forged by their monikers. But it was their real names now that allowed them to remain anonymous. Because reproducing something legitimate is always more noble than a legitimate reproduction.

They paid the marble worker half the amount in advance, with the promise of a speedy delivery. Don Rufo agreed to place Lon Chaney's plaque on his tomb. Refusing to keep the money the Police Captain from Amboy and the Justice of the Peace from La Cruz had paid back, he planned to use it to build a small mausoleum for him at the cemetery in Santa Rosa. Four hundred pesos would suffice for that. The remaining money—one thousand six hundred pesos of misappropriated funds, which the police had agreed to pay him in installments—would go towards his son's health and education.

As they got back into the car, Katanga and Longines became meditative. They had many impressions to share with one another but they were still processing the events of the past days and felt it better to remain silent.

Another funeral procession was approaching from the opposite direction.

The Swiss man burst out:

"The money that gets spent on these absurd trivialities! When I think how the funeral rites for Marie Antoinette, the Widow Capet, cost a mere thirty-one francs, I can only imagine Fortunato's astonished disgust if he could count the hundreds of pesos we've squandered on him."

"Not squandered."

"Yes: squandered. So much the more him being Protestant and opposed to stupid rituals. We should've buried him in the Dissidents' Cemetery, even if Viejo Amor and his 'fiancée' would've screamed bloody murder."

"Another fine idea! Now I see that there's disagreement regarding the nature of death itself! You can't be sure about anything. The proverb which says, 'Of those things most sure, the surest is doubt,' is right on the money."

The car was jolting along, hitting every pothole in the pavement. On the right-hand side, the incoming funeral cortege continued grinding along in an endless procession.

"Pretty long one, eh? Some big fat cat capitalist."

"Or many unemployed men coming along at his expense. If the mourners here paid for the hearse, the way they do in Spain, nobody would show up . . ."

Sarcasm seemed Longines's natural mode of expression.

His companion's face grimaced sourly. But the wheels of the procession, vibrating on the granite cobblestones, knotted his vision. Increasingly annoyed, shaking his head, he complained angrily:

"Wheels, wheels, wheels! Man's life is subjected to the tyranny of wheels! Turning and turning, from birth to death. Turning and turning in seven-year stages. Turning and turning, upon different wheels. Upon axles, be they joyous, frenetic, or squalling. Within hubs, lubricated by affection, passion, or misery. Playing, shrieking, or crying. Turning and turning! Now in the naive candor of baby buggies, tricycles, and roller skates; now in the youthful vertigo of bicycles, motorcycles, and automobiles; now in the adulthood of trains, horse-drawn carriages, and wheelchairs . . . Up to the age of sixty—turning and turn-ing!—here comes the hearse with its silver wheels pulling right up to the threshold of our house. For this! To drive life's broken-down chassis to a dusty hole in a tiny plot of ground . . . Wheels, wheels, wheels!"

Doña Visitación and Rescoldo offered some advice:

"The best thing you can all do right now is lie down and get some sleep."

"But sleeping like we do in La Rioja: several days on end. Bear in mind that the *Zonda* winds are blowing down from the mountains, cold and dry. Barricade your souls. Unplug your mental radio. And don't open your eyes until the storm inside you has passed."

They agreed without a second thought.

Emotionally exhausted, they dragged themselves off to their rooms.

Viejo Amor found his bed had been carefully made. A daydream coursed through him like a flash flood but the fragrant *lingerie* of Spanish lavender made him breathe so deeply that his sudden inspiration faded away in a sigh. As he passed in front of the closet, the seminal perfume from a great bouquet of spikenards accosted him with nostalgia. Scent of love! Feeling heavy and horny, he undressed as best he could, now obese with lust. Scent of love! And face down on the pillow, he stretched out his dream upon the hot, soft illusion of the flesh he craved.

They slept like logs.

Except Longines. Some preoccupation kept him alert. He and Katanga had undressed to the same rhythm, got into their beds, and turned off their respective bedside lamps. But Longines remained awake. While his companion filled the room with a symphony of snores, a wellspring of worries gushed through his breast.

Ian von Zuhlinder . . . Nazi chief . . . Ian von Zuhlinder . . . Nazi chief . . .

If he slept in some moment, the dream was only a prolongation of his vigil. The thought unraveled, spinning its thread. It did not stretch and slacken through the marasmus where logic and desire run aground. He advanced through intricate labyrinths of waves and murmurs. Active. With a pioneer's dauntless courage. His decision fixed on an objective still nebulous, but real in his intuition. Perhaps the secret forces which emerged from the depths of his subconscious had stepped forward to assist him. To carve out a path toward the enigma.

Something inexplicable happened. In the cloudy anxiety which disturbs those insomniacs who sleep without realizing it, he received a chance interference. A silent but potent voice, illuminating his brain, waking him up:

Ian von Zuhlinder, a spy?

Yes. Ian von Zuhlinder is a spy.

When he opened his eyes in order to hear more clearly— one hears better when staring into the darkness—his conviction vanished; he thought it must have been a deceptive auditory hallucination. But he listened very closely to the emptiness. There was a flexuose tonality circling in the air, similar to the vapor trail left by a scream. He fine-tuned his perception. Nothing now. He only heard the rapid beating of his heart.

His sudden fright made him leap up like a grasshopper.

In an instant, Longines was staring at the folder, with the spotlight of the bedside lamp focused right down on the papers, forming a luminous disc just the same as on a microscope's stage. He lowered his plucked eagle's head. And from the height of his intelligence, his one good eye shot forth a sagacious, perforating glance.

The papers revealed nothing. He meticulously read the pages as they were. Those dedicated to the horned beetle *(xylotrupes dichotomus)*, the giant American grasshopper *(tropidacris cristata)* and the common cricket *(pygnogaster graellsi)*. They refuted, *prima facie*, descriptions of the principal work of the British Entomological Society, and showed, in meticulous drawings, characteristics that had been omitted in the corresponding illustrations from the *Societé Entomologique* in Paris. Nothing of particular interest, except for the treatment which the learned English and French received in Ian von Zuhlinder's notes: *brutes . . . hypocrites . . . degenerates . . .*The unusual appearance of such terms in a scientific report captured his attention powerfully. He read again. And he fixed his eye on another allusion: "*. . . such swines as . . e.e . . eau, filthy gorilla of old yellow ivory, . . o . . eo . . e, an old maid's woolly fox terrier, who caused us* *so much harm."* The fugue of consonants — Clemenceau, Lloyd George — revealed the clue for him. There was indeed something hidden behind the apparent scientific purpose!

Eager to follow the path opened by these excoriations, Longines scanned the forty-two pages of German text. He was urged on by a deep desire to find more proper names, an incongruous presence within the naturalist's discipline. At first he discovered nothing. But along those lines, rather offhandedly, in a generalized allusion, Ian von Zuhlinder made reference to various South American presidents: *". . . they are all tsantsas, heads of state reduced to the size of a fist by Wall Street and the Foreign Office, tsantsas: dried shrunken heads of Indians and whites alike, a custom practiced by some tribes in the Upper Amazon."*

Such discoveries, hinting at a deception hidden in the text, filled him with the same certainty as his prophetic dream. And before becoming engrossed in the marrowy task of elucidating the encrypted details of the entire file, he plunged into his memory, searching his earlier years for the fountain that rejuvenates the strength of one's ideal.

He was a humble employee of the LONGINES WATCH FACTORY when he'd had his first contact with cryptography. For months on end his department was in charge of assembling certain apparatuses that greatly intrigued him: the celebrated Wheatstone cypher-watch! Its two dials, intricately inscribed with letters, and a disc that moved around a central axis, fascinated him. The small hand, driven round by springs finer than the typical coil, did not measure time. What, then? When he found out, he was disappointed. Accustomed to regular mechanisms for the exact measurement of fractions of seconds, this watch, designed to reveal man's hidden thoughts: a code breaker. It seemed to him, at first, a satanic contrivance. But it came to agree with him. And how! In the victory secured by the Watch Workers Union during the first strike against the Swiss Watch Factories, Longines's personal role demonstrated the efficacy of his services as an amateur cryptographer. He had discovered, precisely, the key word—DJEMNAH, he remembered it well—which linked communications and thwarted the resistance of bosses and directors! ... From then on, by mere intellectual dilettantism, he increasingly specialized in the thousand stratagems of the written cypher, of mysterious correspondence, and secret codes. His sharp skills were further honed by Fleissner's *Handbuch der Kryptographie*, and by Beaufort's recently published book: *A System of Secret Writing*. Edmo Kumck, young apprentice of Chauxde-Fonds then left the canton of Neufchatel, his family, and the workshops where his hands displayed exceptional skill at coordinating tiny wheels, cogs, pins, and jewels pulsing together in perfect discipline—a tiny beating heart—inside an engraved metal casing. A deep longing drew him to Geneva: to study and study. He wanted to sink down methodically into the profundities of the hieratic, the unintelligible, and the esoteric. The city's soothing calm, stretched out above Lake Léman, quieted his anxiety. And his tempered passion took pleasure in the lengthy investigations which uncovered the way some letters disguise themselves as others, figures as words, drawings, diagrams, and conventional signs. In this way he learned—advised by Porta, in *De furtivis literarum*, and Conradi, in his *Cryptographia denudata*—that bad systems and excessive artifices fill the mind with suspicions. And that the only indecipherable code consists of a dictionary of agreed upon vocables, of arbitrary and variable value, in agreement with surreptitious laws, set by the interested parties ... By now a skilled code breaker, his admission to the Swiss Chancellery as expert cryptographer was the corollary to various exceptional jobs. And his voluntary retirement, a stupendous performance:

The "Swiss Union of Watchmaking"—which sends forth the products of Patek Phillipe, Zenith, Vacheron, Baume & Mercier, Longines, Movado, Cyma, Duward, Omega, and other brands of lesser status—had received veiled references about a plan conceived by various rival establishments in France and the United States to usurp its primacy in the world market.

How? The Allied industries were shrouded in the most impenetrable mystery. However much the Watchmaking Union sent out detectives, buyers, and fictitious operatives, the result was always the most anguishing ambiguity. Certain of the attack, the Swiss factories found no other recourse than to cautiously restrict production. It was under these circumstances that someone mentioned to the Board of Directors the now famous personality of Edmo Kumck. The detectives had intercepted some copies of encrypted correspondence. Perhaps the former apprentice from the Longines Factories ... Placed in charge of the matter, his concentrated efforts were no match for the hidden contents, especially the term "Pascal," to which seven of the intercepted messages alluded. Therein lay the whole substratum of the mystery! His feverish search for the meaning threatened to blunt his sharp wits. He drew on his experience as the official expert cryptographer for the Swiss Chancellery, carefully trying out every possible means of cracking the code, from the skytale—a simple cylinder wound with an encoded strip of parchment—to the fixed and moveable columns employed by Hogg's code, to even the most abstruse procedures of military cryptography. An arduous case! He began to despair. The fatigue made his eyes and brain spin. It was then, in a rapture of skepticism, that he experienced a propitious inspiration. Seeking rest in distraction, but a distraction related to the cause, he took up Pascal's *Les Pensées*. He read without any specific aim, skimming here, skimming there. What balsam, *le différence entre l'esprit de géométrie et l'esprit de finesse*! Passing on to another topic, he was dazzled. There, in the tenth paragraph of the second section! Eureka! Eureka! There, where Blaise Pascal contrasts metaphysical time with real time. There, where he concludes: *"je juge par ma montre."* There was the whole crux of the matter! Eureka! Eureka! Because as Father Guerrier explains, Pascal always carried his watch tightly strapped to his left wrist. Thus, in the intercepted messages, "Pascal" effectively signified: *montre-bracelet*. So, after all, the plan of the rival consortiums against the Swiss Watchmaking Union consisted of flooding the world market with the frivolous yet useful fashion of the wristwatch ... What an apotheosis! With the nature and details of the industrial plot established, the Swiss factories followed his instructions and advice to the letter. It was an enormous mobilization, synchronized in silence, and supported by the most brilliant technicians. Production was organized in multiple shifts working around the clock to make up for lost time. The finest goldsmiths, silversmiths, draftsmen, planners, and engravers designed the wristwatches. With the very finest, most convenient special features. There was, by now, a notorious boredom with the outdated pocket watch. It did not respect the modern premises of elegance and common sense. The tyranny of the chain—onerous and bourgeois—made the product more expensive. The pocket, at approximately thirty-three degrees centigrade, conspires against precision; because the brusque changes in temperature as one checks the time cause irregular operation. Diverse professionals spoke up. Doctors especially, surgeons as well as clinicians. Taking the pulse, for example, watch in hand, implied, upon putting it away, pocketing viruses that may transmit illness to oneself and others. What a revolution! The wristwatch was the messiah of a new time! Its arrival had to be properly heralded! Edmo Kumck set the standard and marked the pace. Astuteness and foresight. The offensive attack hinged on advertising. Based on what he'd learned from the encrypted letters, a major marketing push would cause a huge impact two months before Christmas and New Year. The strategy took advantage of the holiday hubbub, launching the depth charge at the key moment, reaching distributors and retailers, with fair prices, quality, and style, in a dignified manner. Everything worked out according to plan. And the great battle of Christmas and New Year—classic dates for gifts, holiday bonuses, souvenirs—was gloriously won by the Swiss Watchmaking Union.

Suddenly, Katanga turned over in bed. He was talking in his sleep:

"What do you think? I'm not some nouveau riche of science!

Einstein disagrees with some of my postulates; but James Jeans
... in the 'International Union of Prophets,' I ..."

He continued snoring.

Longines folded in on himself, afraid. He gathered up his
nostalgic recollections. And he shut out the light.

He felt an instinctive panic, invincible but unfounded. It
seemed to him that his silent soliloquy had leaked and spread.
That all the diverse information that he held in his private
thoughts could be lost. He peered into the shadowy darkness.
He waited a moment. And shaking, blindly, he moved to the
bed.

"If only I could sleep!" he muttered. "Ian von Zuhlinder is
already in my grasp. If only I could sleep!"

But sleep would not come. As he calmed down, his brief
flurry of anxiety was drowned in a flood of memories. He
could not hold back the current of deserved pride as he over-
flowed with past experiences that fed the river of his inner
life! He lay in one of those states of exaltation in which repressed self-love erupts to reject the possibility of a future ster-
ilized by disaster. The tremendous applause at the coronation
banquet still resonated in his breast. He felt his ears deafened
by praises and congratulations. A thousand people packed the
best restaurant in Geneva! He saw, one after another, the President of the Swiss Watchmaking Union and the foreman of the
Longines Factories, rising to their feet to offer a toast in his
honor. And he saw Edmo Kumck, the Edmo Kumck buried in
the past, his other self of happier times, rise up in the full delirium of the standing ovation to answer and thank them: *I am
a loyal follower of a discipline honored by Plutarch, Bacon, and
Poe*... What a felicitous beginning! And how many interesting
topics in his speech! His retrospective enthusiasm settled on
some passages. How they had enjoyed the tale about the primitive trick employed by Roman soldiers and generals which
consisted of writing a secret report upon the shaven crania of
slaves. As their hair grew back, it hid the message entirely; all
that was needed to crack the code was a razor, the slave's head

was simply shaved clean again! ... And such avid silence as he
conceived of another revolution in watchmaking and proposed
manufacturing more logical watches: ones that follow the direction of earthly rotation; that is, that they move backward:
from left to right, from east to west, their hands marking time's
course as it was projected onto the world! ... His list of honors
was matched only by the long list of gifts conferred. Named
Exclusive Representative and Distributor for the Swiss Watchmaking Union in South America, with headquarters in Buenos Aires, the good star of fortune pursued him relentlessly.
His business negotiations were such perfect works of calculation and intuition that they deserved the praise of envy herself.
Triumph became a custom. Making money something banal.
A gift that degenerated into vice. And he was rich, bourgeois, a
magnate, almost by accident, as all around him buzzed the rage
of sterile effort and the hatred of useless sacrifice ... He came to
know the painful difficulty of eluding the watchful eyes of admiration: a kind of psychic gonorrhea, which comes from contact with another's ambition. His efforts to treat the affliction
were in vain; he was forced to tolerate it for a prolonged period, until the crisis of 1914 sent it feverishly packing ... When
fortune decreases, admiration—like a rat from a burning
building—is first to flee. He began to enjoy the isolation; but
a serious illness transformed pleasure into misery. He understood then that life requires compromise and so he placed the
entire weight of his stoicism on the scale, to bring it to balance.
But stoic beings, with their own moral receptivity, are the ones
most cruelly harmed ... Various subordinates combined forces in deceit, and he was ruined by an enormous fraud. And as
sickness kicked his legs out from under him, charges of embezzlement poured their burning pitch down from above ... He
was sacked, then fell into depression, from depression to ruin,
from ruin to vagrancy, all that was left was the path of the her-
mit which he traversed impassively, as go those conquered con-
querors, proud of their reversed honor, the *via triumphalis* converted into *via crucis*. There he was in Villa Desocupación ...

Rustling bedclothes cut off his breathing. He stayed alert. Bah. Katanga was speaking, again, in his sleep:

"Yes, sir. I belong to the Brain Trust ... Impossible to buy any toy in a ninety-five cent bazaar with ninety-five pesos of melancholy ... Of course! Give me one hundred million dollars and you'll see ... Just like Baur, the champion of genetics, he devoted himself to creating a breed of legless cattle. I will channel the Vale of Tears, I will exploit the Vineyards of the Lord ... And there will be wine and joy in the world! ..."

His head rocked back and forth on the pillow. Then he continued snoring.

Longines was exasperated. Unable to work through his harsh recollections or reconcile the dialectic between his dream and his wakefulness.

He got up out of bed.

Transparent dawn gently filtered through the gloom.

He opened the shutters.

He gathered up the scattered pages.

And he exclaimed:

"Shadows. What are shadows, shady von Zuhlinder? This. This! Sick light. Amputated splendor. Poisoned clarity. But I know the remedy. I know the remedy!"

And methodically, he placed page one of the file under his shrewd gaze.

Eight o'clock exploded with Longines's first shouts of joy.

Nine o'clock exploded with Katanga's first yawns.

Ten o'clock exploded with Viejo Amor's first reprimands.

The latter two had agreed to leave the house at nine o'clock, to pay off some of the burial expenses in the city center. Viejo Amor was annoyed by Katanga's slow start:

"When you say nine o'clock ..."

"That means eleven. That's always been my law. Waste time, procrastinate, delay: what a beautiful compendium of philosophy!"

"Informal philosophy!" he added irritably.

"Since when such punctuality? You know perfectly well that sleeping is my only indulgence. And that I'm faithful to it. Perhaps love has got *il signore* Olaf Olaffali in a hurry?"

"Don't be cute. Are you coming or not? I have an appointment at eleven. An obligation."

"Obligation? Our watchword is to have no obligations. No commitments. Never compromise."

"Cut it out! Are you coming or not?

"I'm not going! What kind of heavy-handedness is this? You've changed, Viejo Amor!"

Longines, absent from the scene, burst in, his arms raised high in absolute elation.

"That's it! I've got it! It's all completely clear!"

But his joy ran aground upon their sullen silence. Viejo Amor and Katanga stared back at one another with aggressive, unprecedented dislike; the former, fed up with mockery; the latter, shocked by the sudden reprimand. A minute passed with them glaring in this way. And suddenly, spinning on his heels, Viejo Amor abandoned the room!.

"THAT'S IT! I'VE GOT IT! IT'S ALL COMPLETELY CLEAR!"

Katanga remained immobile. He clenched his jaws. He fixed his gaze on the floor, ashamed of his conduct, and for having allowed himself to become frustrated by someone like Viejo Amor.

It's idiotic to diminish oneself, to yield. If you let them, any degenerate will climb the ladder of your kindness to become a peer. They become your peer and then execute their attack. They force themselves to reciprocate, wrapped in hatred, the smile which your pity first extended. There's no worse pity than the kind which intelligence extends to vulgarity. Ah, but it doesn't matter! I'll learn from the moral. I'll no longer dilute my pure mental qualities by alloying them with what is crude and coarse. I know how to handle myself. And I'll redirect his anger back onto him with my indifferent supremacy which he so reviles!

"Katanga: That's it! I've got it all figured out!"

His vexation had blocked his hearing. He scratched his facial muscles from the inside. He snortingly released his breath corrupted by rage. He lashed his nerves in continuous tension. And he scolded himself for having such difficulty in expressing his anger and for having shouted to defend himself.

A friendly shaking pulled him out of his abstraction:

"Katanga: I've figured it all out!"

"Ah! . . ."

"Yes. Everything! Ian von Zuhlinder, exposed to the light, revealed from head to toe . . ."

Longines noted that Katanga still wasn't listening. He explained himself. It's necessary to have some obscure place in the soul, an illiterate reserve, a cistern of ignorance, a basement storm shelter, a place to take the burning pessimism caused by the reverberant spiritual world, and plunge it into the dark water. If Katanga had possessed this, his anger now fallen silent, his cool composure would have again operated at the level of things and of men. But he continued to be lost in himself. Without listening.

Perplexed, faced with his companion's listlessness, Longines pondered how best to overcome it. Then, laughing at himself, he accosted Katanga, pulling on his arm:

"Do you realize? Olaf Olaffali is a monstrous *summum*. If only we'd known his name before! Olaf, inverted, is *falo*, phallus. *Fali*, read forward, is plural: phalluses. Four phalluses, at the least—two going backwards, two going forwards—hanging from one single man! It's something really unusual, mythic, similar to the Syrian Venus with her double row of breasts! . . ."

At first Katanga didn't catch the joke. But the seed had fallen on a fertile spirit. Hearing Longines laugh and laugh, Katanga examined the phrase. Soon an analytic laugh began mumbling within his mouth. And now, without repressing it, his full, chiseled lips let the expected cackle escape.

"Fantastic! Olaf Olaf-fali. *Falo* + *falo* + *fali* . . . four phalluses . . . True: if we'd only known his name before! There are names that crucify and lash, because they predict and forewarn. Key-names, mysterious, capable of clarifying everything."

Longines took advantage of Katanga's understanding and his words:

"That's right: now everything is clarified. Something amazing! Ian von Zuhlinder is a dangerous spy who threatens the security of South America. Something huge, Katanga! Come and see."

He moved to show him the conclusions of his sleepless night. But he still hadn't quite captured his attention. Katanga seemed blocked, caught up in the memory of something:

"Olaf . . . Olaf . . . Yes, now I remember. As Doctor Inhell I happened to be named a knight of the order of St. Olaf! During a *tournée* through the Nordic countries, the royal family of Norway 'permitted itself the honor of insinuating my presence' at a benefit to raise money for the poor neighborhoods of Christiania. That's how kings ask: they insinuate . . . I agreed. In those days, kings "asked" me for favors. *Sic transit* . . . Doctor Inhell . . ."

"Three in one: Thurston-Houdini-Fregoli . . ."

". . . the benefit show was an extraordinary success. I contributed two thousand crowns of my own money to the cause. The check was presented to Her Majesty, the Queen, Honorary President of the Red Cross. Two days later a chamberlain came to pay homage to me. And on the eve of my departure, I received the Cross of Saint Olaf, that fierce, untamed, fanatical Viking canonized for his Christian zeal and his maritime feats. Olaf II, "the Saint," carried the faith of the martyrs to the Orkney Islands, nearly five centuries before Columbus set foot in the New World . . . and ten centuries before I would, under bitter circumstances, take the decoration to a pawn shop in Valparaiso. Do you know the Orkneyinga saga? Do you know its legend told through the 'song of the skalds'?"

"Right now I don't know. Nor am I interested in hearing any more about it. Put multi-phallus Olaf aside for a while. The important thing is right here! The thing I've just confirmed! Ian

Zuhlinder is an ex-treme-ly dan-ger-ous spy!"

Seeing the pages covered with annotations, drawings, signs, diagrams, brought Katanga back to the complete possession of his senses. The anger and delirium which had momentarily driven him to distraction were followed by a cold, stubborn longing to verify the information. They sat down next to each other. Page by page, they checked the texts in German and the details of the drawings. Urged on by Katanga's interest, Longines indicated where his cryptographic investigations had begun: the denunciations against Clemenceau, Lloyd George, and some South American magistrates. He continued, showing the curious ironies interpolated in the description of fleas *(Pulex irritans)*. A brief phthiriological sketch mentioned Count Luxburg's famous insult to a certain chancellor: "You are a louse trapped in tar" ... And rounding out his preliminary analysis, the allusion to the venality of the press in the Southern Hemisphere, written beneath a perfect illustration of the common cricket *(Acheta campestres)*.

"Up to this point, as you see, the references are discernible but, shall we say, 'candy-coated' to appear rigorously scientific. The coating, nevertheless, is highly toxic. Substituting England where it says 'Entomological Society,' then France for 'Fabre,' Germany for 'Zoologisch Institut,' Italy for 'Rivista Coleotterologica,' the United States for 'American Museum of Natural History,' Brazil for *papilio*, and League of Nations for *Thysania agrippina*, I was immediately able to detect the existence of a secret glossary. This kind is the most difficult to crack. But intuition pierces everything! *Thysania agrippina* gave me pause; it's the moth with the largest wingspan in the world, followed by the *Papilio homerus*, a swallowtail butterfly in Jamaica, with a seven-inch wingspan. The League of Nations was hidden below its ten-and-a-half inch wings! Making the respective substitutions, the meaning of the text changed immediately. I was spellbound. Now the truth became clear: a plan of invasion and conquest! ... by the Reich! ... *manu militar!* ... Nothing less than all of southern Brazil! ... a portion of Uruguay! ... and the

Misiones province of Argentina! ... As if it were the African territories all over again!! I couldn't believe the revelation! ..."

"And you shouldn't. That's crazy."

"Crazy? There's nothing crazy in the empty-heads of the heads of state, except for the nationalism of the Junker, the racist, or the Nazi. This idiot von Zuhlinder proves it. His patriotic faith ... But let's go back. I want to convince you. Look closely."

Still speaking clearly and precisely, Longines decoded the pages in extensive detail. Slow, prolix, meticulous, he left nothing unexplained. He showed fifteen pages of his own handwritten notes, containing his personal conclusions. Fourteen instances of high espionage appeared most clearly elucidated, specifying the meaning of signs, cyphers, and words, and the corresponding military snares concealed within the outlines, diagrams, and artistically rendered entomological drawings.

Katanga's discomposure prevented him from thinking clearly. Suspicious, he demanded visual evidence. And Longines had it. Plenty of it. And when Katanga finally understood the ruses and simulacra hidden within the innocuous text, he turned pale and went to sit on his bed.

Soaked in sweat and certainty, the Swiss man urged him:

"Pull yourself together. Come here. Now let's examine the butterfly illustrations."

He gathered his wits and went over.

It was a heavy bombardment of unnerving shocks. The first struck as Longines revealed the faint sketch of the fortress at Porto Alegre, inscribed within the body of the *Anaea suprema*. The second, marked out in the wings of *Cyrestis thyodamas*— the famous common map butterfly—the tacit cartography of Rio Grande do Sul and Santa Catarina which bordered the Misiones Province of Argentina. The third, a strategic map of São Paulo, threaded through the beautiful patterns of the gran amazona: *Argynnis childreni*. The fourth, within a splendid example of *Callithea sapphira*, the location and strength of federal troops echeloned from Uruguay to San Borja, on the Brazilian side; and from Monte Caseros to Concepción de la

Sierra, on the Argentine side. The fifth, as revealed in the eight
white spots of each lower sector of the *Catagramma cynosura,*
the planned location for the site of Las Posadas. The sixth, the
bridges and streets of the city of Blumenau, in Santa Catarina state, which he made out within the drawing of the *Zeonia
sylphina* butterfly. The seventh was hidden within the absolutely diaphanous wings of the wondrous *cristalina de menandro,*
its subtle nervures tracing out the hydrography of Rio Grande
do Sul with its fordable streams. The eighth, lines of small forts
and military outposts along the Uruguayan border, carefully disguised in the drawing of the *Catagramma cajetani.* The
ninth, he showed him encrusted in the beautiful polychrome
of the *Agrias amydon boliviensi,* the principal schools, factories,
and broadcasting stations infiltrated by Nazis as centers for espionage. The tenth, on the same page, two butterflies typical of
Argentina: the *Colias lesbia* and the *Danaus gilippus,* their modest designs concealing names of chief officials, instructors, and
school teachers scattered throughout the region. The eleventh,
the best roads and trails through the state of Paraná, blended
into in the white striations slicing through the dusky brown
of *Papilio philolaus.* The twelfth, transcribed in the dead nervures of the common *Danaus erippus,* the convergent routes in
the outlying areas of São Paulo. The thirteenth, the cadmium
spots that embellish the *Dismorphia fortunata* sketched out, according to Longines, the probable airfields of the expeditionary
forces. The fourteenth, by his appraisal, the number and importance of pro-Hitler legions among the settlers, disguised in
the grizzly-brown stripes which cross the *Papilio epidaus feno-
chionis.*

Katanga sat back stupefied.

Bowled over.

Poleaxed.

Slack.

That night, after two o'clock, Longines slipped out surreptitiously with Fenicio and Rescoldo.

Presumably to verify some information. To ascertain certain details. To clear away any doubts about the conclusions he had reached. Katanga did not ask but it was all implied in the Swiss man's light, joyful step. Katanga knew from experience the metamorphic powers of optimism. The transfusion of euphoria which enlivens even the laxest laxity and the most incorrigible indolence.

But to keep from slowing him down he said nothing.

For his part, he needed sleep, and so he lay down to take his rest.

In vain.

His peace was a silence choked off by the confused bustle of his thoughts. His repose fatigued by dour, threatening frowns. His imagination a complex frieze of multicolored butterflies, gray-brown spies, and monocled Germans.

Tying up loose ends in the darkness—like telephone company workers setting up new connections in their underground cubicles—Katanga remembered an article in *The Times* about German propaganda in Brazil's southern states. The concomitance of purposes reinforced Longines's confident conclusion. The methods of espionage and counterespionage implanted by supposed "settlers." Teutonic education and upbringing imposed on their descendants; sworn loyalty to the Reich over the country they called home; their disdain for the local language and predominant Catholic religion, were all clearly demonstrated. No doubt remained, then, that Nazi emissaries were working as direct agents of the National Socialist Party, controlling the activities of the "German settlements," whose obedience to the Reichführer quashed any doubts about them possessing the discipline necessary when the time came for takeover and consequent annexation.

Hitler's primary idea, taken from Gobineau: extreme, out-and-out racism, which heralds the supremacy of the Germanic people, was palpable in that propaganda. The prohibition of settlers marrying native people; the embarkation order for all mothers close to giving birth, in order to shelter their offspring under the flag of the fatherland; fomenting the birth rate through subsidies from Berlin; the orientation of children within the German tradition, were all flagrant testimonies that the German settlers in no way accepted Brazilian sovereignty. The humiliation and poverty resulting from the disastrous chaos of the Treaty of Versailles would be vindicated here, where the trusting hosts were unaware of the imminent, slashing blow.

Katanga was personally offended by the ignominy of such ingratitude. The decoding of Ian von Zuhlinder's portfolio provided clear evidence of a meticulously planned attack and the assured predominance of the evil plot designed to usurp Brazil's unarmed innocence.

When a nation exhausts its scientific inventiveness in a search for synthetic products with which to cover its lack of resources, the natural abundance of raw materials in underdeveloped countries becomes a difficult temptation to resist. The *wollustra*, bauxite, synthetic buna rubber, desperate German substitutes, were evidence of their zeal to take over new territories. Textile fibers, metals, rubber are not easily replaced. Costly combustibles invented in laboratories such as "lactic wool" made from casein, and "artificial thread" manufactured from cotton and jute residue, did not solve the problem but, on the contrary, filled the spirit with a sense of privation. Chemistry had failed the Germans in their attempt to supplant nature. And with these attitudes of dominance now unmasked, he could clearly see the aggressive will of a people who know how to methodically prepare its plans of conquest.

An invasion and usurpation were perfectly feasible, so much the more given that England and France, firmly resolved not to return the former German colonies of Togo, Congo, and Cameroon, would turn a blind eye to the invasion . . . Given their scant investments in that part of South America . . . This would allow them to satisfy, without any risk to themselves, Germany's imperious zeal to secure the virgin territories needed to supply raw materials, indispensable to its population and industry . . .

Turning over nervously in bed, his mind lit up by the scintillating truth, he spoke aloud in a persuasive voice, as if to Longines:

"Enough! *Probatio probatissima!* What we need now is to get to work immediately. Without fear or delay. We must rally the unity of the continent. Shake up the chancelleries. Put the people and the state on guard. *Probatio probatissima!* Thoroughly expose the Nazi plan, making their blood run cold with our boldness! The deciphered documents will ruin the final act, so close to being carried out! German expansion at the expense of America's naive democracies will be thwarted! We hold the proof of proofs. Only one thing is needed: tact, caution, astuteness. Such a stunningly audacious plan requires that we act swiftly, verify it beyond the shadow of a doubt so that it does not evaporate in the face of popular disbelief. Such enormous evidence will not be accepted without justification. Watch out, Longines! Let's ensure that the proof of its existence is not ridiculed and reduced to absurdity. Be careful! The Pan American Union and the League of Nations must mobilize together as one. The United Press and Associated Press will not be on our side. After Brazil, the United States is the most threatened power; because Argentina and Uruguay . . ."

Longines suddenly turned on the light.

He'd heard it all.

"Are you the one calling for tact, caution, and astuteness? The whole neighborhood just heard you . . ."

Sad, discouraged, his face glowing in the semidarkness, he appeared exhausted and dejected. For a moment. But the Swiss man's natural ability to confront difficulties won out. He understood the many childish senilities that run amok in an aging fool. And Katanga's anxiety was pacified.

He undressed rapidly. A feeling of tumultuous vehemence filled him with satisfaction. This hostile enigma lay under his control and he felt ready to take various proactive gestures. He turned off the light. And through conduits of shadow he debriefed Katanga on his latest assertions:

"Now, nothing remains to be clarified. The proof becomes even more disgusting when you consider how much there is. Beneath the guise of a pigeon-breeder, Ian von Zuhlinder owns a dovecote that is in continuous activity. I won't bother to specify the quantity and quality of messages he transmits and receives. Under the pretext of radio-telegraphic experiments, one of his subordinates runs a short-wave long-distance broadcasting station. Unnecessarily powerful when you think about it. At the Munich Bar, Rescoldo gathered some stupendous gossip from the mouth of a waiter who'd been fired from the German Club. Turns out that his scientific excursions to the Misiones Province are actually scouting missions. There are real chains of spies throughout Brazil and Argentina. Corpus, Puerto Mineral, Eldorado, Apóstoles, Irigoyen, are all linked to Blumenau and São Paulo. According to Fenicio, there's no end to the strange, crazy tasks they assign Zuhlinder at the Institute of Entomology. He's a remarkably adept deceiver. He uses those resources as a guise of normalcy, to hide his Nazi-loving ways. Masks! But now we've pulled off his masks!

"*You've* pulled off his . . . don't be humble."

"Entomology: a mask. Drawings and diagrams: a mask. Did you see, according to my key, how the silhouette of the last butterfly reproduces the entire coastline from Santos to Punta del Este? It's interesting. And their design indicates the most likely ports for unloading, the best coves for dropping supplies, and the strategy for attacking Paranaguá, Florianópolis, Laguna, and Río Grande."

"Yes, Longines. All of Ian von Zuhlinder's butterflies are marvelous. Better yet: they would be marvelous if they weren't infected with pro-Hitler hysteria . . . Among the Greeks the word *psyche* signified, simultaneously, both butterfly and soul. Nazis today are sick butterflies: souls that do not fulfill the progressive evolution of karmic law. Their beastliness takes them backward. They are low, cringing larvae squirming through life. Dead chrysalises that will not open. Butterflies that will never take flight toward immortality."

"   "
 . . .

It was five o'clock in the morning.

Ash Wednesday.

The five of them were in a taxi, heading for Sarmiento Park.

They crossed the city in the thick, sleepy heat of the after-noon. Empty streets. Here or there a gardener at work. Throats and cornets hoarse from overuse. Ashes of streamers and con-fetti on the ground. Ashes of insomnia in the passing faces. Ashes of merriment in the air. The fleeting celebration had de-canted the people's exhilaration and sudden raptures, leaving behind a gray tedium of sediment.

Ash Wednesday.

The five of them were in a taxi, heading for Sarmiento Park.

Ascending Avenida Argentina, the breeze struck their faces with increasingly pleasant gusts.

"Velocity, the only freshness available right now," pro-nounced a languid Aparicio.

Nobody said anything.

The automobile turned left, went speeding past the Fine Arts Museum. Now well above the city, they all breathed in deep-ly, filling their lungs, feeling the cooling breeze filter through the endless foliage. Katanga thought about the murmuring for-est of Wagner's *Siegfried*. The others were thinking of nothing at all. They let themselves be carried along, looking at the trees, the clouds, the birds.

Suddenly, *whizz! boom! crash! smash!,* the commotion of an ac-cident. The sudden snap of insults and swearing. The car in front of them had just been violently broadsided by another driver.

From the nearby bar, the traffic warden came running out:

"Barbarians! Nowadays you can't even go in to have a drink of water!"

"I was driving on the right side."

"So was I. Is it my fault if the trees block the view?"

"Doesn't matter: who drives that fast through here? You must be an idiot!"

"You're the bigger idiot. This driver here can tell us how fast you were going."

"I didn't see anything."

"How could you not see, the crash happened right in front of you?"

"I didn't see a thing. Maybe the pedestrian . . ."

"You, sir, could you tell me . . . ?"

"Look, officer: I was just walking by, cooling my head. I'm going crazy thinking about a bill that I've got to pay by tomorrow. I'm walking along thinking about how to deal with that . . . What do you expect me to see?"

Longines urged them to keep driving. He did not want to get mixed up in other people's problems. When the taxi pulled away, the victims of the accident, now enraged, were calculating the cost of their respective damages. The taxi driver—lean and nervous, in leather cuffs and cap—poured out in a Catalan accent all the pus of his vocabulary against the traffic warden.

"It's the fault of that stew-brain, *dat pe'l cul,* with his head up his ass. For not being on his post. For not directing the traffic properly. He should pay the damages."

"It's your drivers' fault," refuted Dijunto. "You're the ones who run people over, you kill them, you respect nothing. The poor pedestrian walks along, always ready to jump out of the way thanks to your insolence."

"True," added Viejo Amor. "Rudely blowing the horn, near misses, splashing huge puddles on purpose. Drivers are perfect savages. Yesterday I almost got creamed by two cars as I was crossing Calle San Martín."

"What bothers me is the vigilance itself," pointed out Aparicio. "There shouldn't be traffic wardens. That way fear would keep drivers cautious. Do you see pedestrians waiting for someone to direct us? That's how they'd learn. I'm sure that'd put an end to accidents."

"The remedy for resolving the traffic problem is quite simple," intervened Longines. "Canceling the license of any driver who hasn't paid off his car yet would do the trick. Cars are pure ostentation! Car culture is the biggest 'circulating debt' in the country. That way you'd have less than ten percent of the cars in circulation that are currently infecting the streets . . ."

"What burns me up," indicated Katanga, "is just what a hurry so many lazy drivers are in when they're behind the wheel. Hurry for what? For nothing. One guy's in a hurry to win the race, for his own ego, or so others admire him; they'd never rush to do something so imbecile as trying to connect with themselves . . ."

The driver abruptly stopped the taxi:

"You'll excuse me. But you'll have to continue on foot. The spark plugs are starting to fail, *voto a Deu*."

"What's starting to fail is your decency and . . ."

". . . intentions. We were going to get out right here, anyway."

"Good. It's three pesos forty."

They handed him four pesos.

Walking along the asphalt road bordered by Carolina poplars, they reached the statue of Dante.

"Good thing it isn't written in German. Durante Aldiger . . ."

"*Alighieri, tedesco? Va vía.*"

". . . with stupid plaques and inscriptions. I always remember that monument covered with titles in Costanera: 'To Achával Rodríguez: Jurisconsult, Orator, Diplomat . . .' as if they were virtues on the same level with being cultured, honest, and good!"

The words were barely uttered before a terrifying roar forced them to jump up onto the base of the pedestal. Without stopping, screaming right along with his engine, the taxi driver hurled a fistful of coins and curses at them:

"Eat shit, you assholes! I don't want tips from idiots with their heads up their asses, *dat pe'l cul*."

Spinning round in a perfect half-donut turn he left them choking in a burning curtain of exhaust fumes. Trembling.

Paralyzed with fear. Shouting, without a word to say. Shouting with gestures and thoughts.

It cost them much effort to soothe their irritation. Heading into the gardens they felt their senses overwhelmed by the raging tumult. They walked across parterres bursting with white lilies. The flowers' perfume failed to soothe their inner tension. Following a quiet path, their familiar aplomb began to return. They sat down on two benches—one facing the other—beneath a rose-studded trellis. At last, the beauty of the spot soothed their eyes. And they settled back into themselves, turning upon the hinge of custom, in the calm afternoon.

But each one's spirit was ground down by the scene just endured and by the various issues to be discussed at the present meeting. They all felt the silent rebelliousness of individuality that had taken root and grown up between them; envy's implacable antipathy for the excess of ideals; and the miserly fury of stinginess against the excesses of altruism. They each carried established prejudices, irreducible antagonisms, and hidden renunciations, ready to bleed the moment the debate ripped open the scab of shame which kept them silent.

Katanga and Longines wanted to dispel the impending discord. They could feel the hostile tensions created by the impulsive need for immediate satisfaction. They sensed suspicions emerging like waves and trespassing into consciousness while remaining resistant to reason. They grasped the disenchantment bubbling around them, and filled with misery, heavy with disappointment, they looked at one another and understood.

"Well, friends: let's speak as such, given that we still are. For the next hour, perhaps . . ."

"What kind of words are those?"

"I won't allow it."

"I understand myself. The predominance of individual desires becomes clearer and clearer. Not just the weaknesses of the flesh. Its power expands and amplifies the more it evolves and develops, despite the barriers of egoism and trenches of cunning which lie in its way. Let's get straight to the point.

Let's face up to the personal failure we are all guilty of, the collective failure of our tour. Our bond is broken! We're a scattered pack. The virtues of former times, which led to magnificent achievements through heroic solidarity, have been traded to satisfy abject ambitions, and filthy, vulgar vices. We can accomplish nothing this way! Let's confess it openly. The best thing we can do is scurry away like rats, each one through his crack in the wall. It's painful but it's true. Because the ideal lies above, in the head—not at the level of the crotch or the earth—and it can only be reached by the cable-car of a strong will. With you now . . ."

Viejo Amor and Dijunto protested emphatically:

"The fact that I'm engaged to be married is neither a betrayal nor a weakness."

"The fact that I aspire to settle down in the countryside implies neither rebellion nor ingratitude."

Aparicio had the urge to defend himself as well. But he suddenly felt inhibited and uncomfortable. In truth, he also wanted "to be finished once and for all." To get his share of the money. Dissolve their headlong impetus. And go his own way freely, without criticisms or censures, to move forward with his political campaign.

The difficult silence which settled upon them brought a certain air of mistrust and reproach. Katanga, revolted, thought to challenge them, to trick them into healing their discord. But he bit his lip instead. Better. What could Viejo Amor possibly prefer over his cloying love for Doña Visitación? What dream could overcome Dijunto's happy vision of resting his bones in the rich soil and fresh pasture? What authority could ever outsmart Aparicio's roguish caprices? He let them sway in their foolish stubbornness. And crossing his legs, his disdain offered up the elegant homage which courtesy customarily pays to obduracy: he smiled.

Longines kept watch, from within his trench of silence. He kept watch, lying in wait with Fortunato's letter and von Zuhlinder's papers, two grenades ready to be hurled. He suffered stoically. A crisis of nerves, so discreet as to be almost puritan, made his whole body vibrate. He thought he would suffocate from holding back his explosion of rage. And he continued choking on his constricted anguish, trembling to keep from shouting.

The mistrust and reproaches broke through:

"Fine. Let's stop talking uselessly to ourselves. Let's take account of things."

"Yes. Accounts; tallies not fairy tales."

Longines hunched down over his pockets. Feline, his hands twisted into talons, to extract his treasurer's notes. He was responsible for dispersing the funds "liberated" from Freya Bolitho. Faced with their upwelling scorn, he pulled out the money:

"Here's everything: the cash and the ledger. Take it. Examine, check it over. Whoever wants to leave, let him go! Let's see: draw up your complaints . . ."

"These one thousand pesos . . ."

"You've forgotten already? They were meant to be paid as the sum demanded by the bosses from Río Tercero to free those settlers about to be deported."

"Isn't that this figure?"

"No. It's all written here. That was given to Don Rufo as payment for his hospitality."

"Yes; but Don Rufo agreed to collect that money from the Judge from La Cruz and the Captain from Amboy. Did he collect or not?"

"Some of it. But the amount he collected was meant for his son's operation."

"Yes, fine, all right. I forgot."

"Viejo Amor, I demand that you sharpen your recollection. Getting into situations like these, every man should know his own business exactly, down to the last detail."

When two men fear one another is when they are closest to coming to blows. As in the tale by Shestov, reciprocal fear provokes threats, and sharpens passions. And a false sense of courage precipitates the clash and the drama. The only fearful one now was Viejo Amor. He knew that in matters of punctuality and exactitude, Longines was a marvel, a chronometer. But Viejo Amor took solace in a particular memory: one day Longines had stepped inside a fancy clock shop to check the exact time. His eyes scanned all the clocks ticking away, on the walls and columns and in the display cases. Nothing more impossible! Seeing the disparity between so many precision instruments, he walked out disappointed: without learning the time, of course!

The memory strengthened his resolve. Why not challenge Longines? So he ventured his observations, with the false boldness which fear provides: first of all, to avoid being made a fool in the very meeting he'd insisted on calling; second, to be consistent in his habit of "taking chances" ... He was a specialist! On innumerable occasions, feints of love, he'd utilized his audacity—in reality: a harried sexual hunger—and the joy of surrender was his prize. With identical intention, he now organized his doubts about another kind of audacity—in reality: a harried moral fear—in hopes of achieving a monetary surrender.

This opportunity, nevertheless, crashed into something hard: the fortress of honesty that was Longines. A man who was skilled, like few others, in the ancient art of honor! And figure by figure, item by item, Longines overwhelmed him with the crystalline clarity of his computations:

"Summing things up precisely, then: of the original sixty-three thousand pesos, there remain thirty-eight thousand five hundred. Here they are. Your share is five thousand five hundred."

"Five thousand five hundred? What do you mean? Seven thousand seven hundred! Why do you two get to divide up the shares from Lon Chaney and Fortunato?"

His accusation instantly inflamed them. Katanga unleashed a furious, wounding, whiplash glance across the offender's face.

Longines curled back his nose and stretched out his lower lip, spluttering a rebarbative curse. They could not rush to the attack; any real aggression would have implied weakness. But they didn't give an inch. And they continued furiously, one with the cutting look, the other with a vomitous voice, harshly criticizing, spraying spittle on Viejo Amor's face, now flushed red with shame.

At this point, Aparicio intervened. He considered the disparity and sidestepping their anger, he smoothly opined, for everyone's sake, that the best thing was to give each man his seven thousand seven hundred pesos and be done with it.

Katanga's whiplash glance softened. And covering his ill-will with smiles, like wrapping a cobblestone in serpentine streamers, he faced Aparicio:

"*Che*, haven't you been listening? . . . The amount we each get is five thousand five hundred . . . Lon Chaney's and Fortunato's shares don't belong to us . . . Lon Chaney's we have to resolve by majority vote, and Fortunato left behind a will . . ."

"A will! What d'you mean!"

"Yes: the letter he gave Viejo Amor is a last will and testament . . . Let's read it . . . Don't interrupt . . . That's why we're here . . . So much grasping greed is repulsive . . ."

The Swiss man read aloud:

Dear friends:

Any one of these nights you'll find my dead body. I feel death approaching, prowling around me. It won't be long in coming because I've opened the door to it. I would like to die during the day so that my vital flame is not visible as it is snuffed out. Forgo any kind of funeral. You cannot light the candles from both ends! No flowers on my coffin. They only bring to mind the sweaty odor of fornication! Let my burial be as simple as possible. I can't stand hearse drivers in their frock coats! I know what I'm talking about. I was once a bank manager in Prague. I once was, and through my own fault I am no longer. One is guiltier of triumph than of defeat. As a manager, I embezzled three hundred thousand crowns. Being an expert in fraudulent rackets and financial schemes, an un-

*lucky junior-level employee was made to take the blame: Vik-
tor Zilahy. What a comfort it is to tell the truth, here, within
this vessel of putrid flesh which commands both human and
divine lies! May Viktor Zilahy forgive me just as I forgive his
vulture of a son!*

*After the father's suicide and his family's disgrace, Markus
Zilahy arrived in Buenos Aires. He came to murder me but
chose instead to torture me. Yes: to torture me. Listen carefully: the victim always conquers the delinquent! To agonize, beneath the perennial threat of being denounced, is the worst
pain that can be suffered. It means enduring the vampire's
soul-sucking jaws, without being able to frighten him away.
It means living in continuous psychological anemia. None of
you will ever know what I've suffered for the last nine years.
It's indescribable! Dragging your skin and bones along in anguish and dismay! You inner shambles crawling with affliction and desire! And unable to die, because someone enjoys
the luxury of killing without killing!*

*Oh! I always said it: heroes are those individuals who play
all their chips, who bet it all on the gaming table of destiny, and win! I needed to pile up coins and coins, in order
to buy the big chip of my liberation. I never made it. Begging and begging, nine years of wandering about beneath his
vigilant hatred, I've handed over to Markus Zilahy twenty-
eight thousand pesos. I still owe him seven thousand pesos, to
emancipate myself from his cruel inexorable rage and from
my own remorse. Pay him, please! From the hovel of my soul,
with a pleading, hangdog face, I beg of you.*

*How bitter! The one who dies loses his position in the bu-
reaucracy of humanity. But there are post-mortem decorations
for those who insist on making the sacrifices necessary for retirement in eternal peace. Perhaps I do not deserve it. But be
generous. Do not allow my soul to be unraveled by damna-
tion! This is not some foolish whim of a dying man. It is the
cry of my dignity! It is the dignity of my bowed honor on its*

bended knee! I know what I'm talking about. I was once a
bank manager in Prague.

Thank you, my friends. And may my silence in the tomb,
paid for in advance by my silence in life, grow ever greater!

JAROSLAV KOPECKY.
P.S.: Markus Zilahy lives at 3714 Cochabamba,
Buenos Aires

Their disappointment was tremendous. Adverse circumstances hit home with true ironic marksmanship, destroying their
unconscious hopes and well-reasoned demands. They could
see the choking burden which had squeezed Fortunato's soul.
Viejo Amor never expected that ending. Had he guessed it, he
would've never delivered the letter! He'd supposed the contrary: that Jaroslav was going to do them a favor, using his own
portion to augment each man's share of the money. Dijunto
gulped. The house he'd planned to buy cost eight thousand
pesos. Aparicio saw himself compelled to conform. The three
of them were, if not destroyed, resentful of the bleak Mephis-
tophelean power of chance.

Master of the situation, Longines straightened out his voice
and his pride:

"All right. Let's sum things up again. The bottom line is:
each of us has, as his share, five thousand five hundred Argentine pesos. I propose that we take from Lon Chaney's share
the fifteen hundred needed to fulfill Fortunato's last wish. That
would leave four thousand pesos to divide among five."

"I refuse. I'm not obliged to repay anybody's embezzlement."

Viejo Amor's words dropped like molten lead. To mention
embezzlement in that moment of crisis smacked of treason.
Perhaps the money should be divided up ... But they were
too ashamed to demand it openly. Katanga was on the verge of
coming down hard but he controlled himself again. It wasn't
worth getting angry. There he was, face to face with a fiery, lu-

bricious satyr, newly tamed by "love." One of those "automatic-zipper" types who fly open, and "expand with a flourish," the moment a woman winks her eye. It pained him. Katanga glimpsed Viejo Amor's destiny which, with any luck, would render him the worst punishment. The punishment which defeats all those depraved, clumsy oafs: marriage ... And breaking the pensive impasse, he expressed himself:

"Stop worrying about it. I'll make up the necessary sum. You're exempt from this pious obligation. I have the honor of "being dead" along with Fortunato. The dead oblige the dead ... not the living, my dear Viejo Amor."

Aparicio's sense of gallantry was touched by this noble pronouncement. From the dock where his longings lay anchored, he advanced, diligent and honest. He silently approached his friend. And discharged these words into his ear:

"Honestly. This prick's behavior embarrasses me. I've never seen so much falseness and duplicity. He is, and always has been, a hypocrite. He's shown his true colors. Allow me to contribute to fulfill the bequest of the deceased."

Katanga pulled him close to his chest, squeezing his right arm:

"Thank you. Thank you."

He said no more. He had noted Aparicio's shy, embarrassed attitude at the beginning of the meeting. It would not do to trust him too much.

Why did he not declare his support, sing it out loud? Perhaps his secret anger was the feigned anger of the dishonest gambler whose *modus operandi* ... and *vivendi* are discovered. But his next words vindicated him from any suspicion:

"I just offered him my contribution."

"We all should."

"I'd do the same; but ..." insinuated Dijunto with broken inflection.

"I repeat: there's nothing more to say. For me, it's no sacrifice. My money is ..."

It took Longines only a few moments to calculate the aliquot quotas. To the base sum agreed upon for each, he added eleven-hundred pesos more from Lon Chaney's ownerless portion. And he doled them out.

From the amount corresponding to him, Katanga subtracted one thousand five hundred pesos to be added to the sum owed by Fortunato. He handed them over to Longines:

"Please. Take this. Tomorrow, pay off that hangman. Send him the money."

Reduced by his own jealous desire to emulate, Aparicio solemnly insisted:

"I've said that I was going to contribute and I will contribute."

"There's no point. Keep your money. Tonight Longines will propose to you the most stupendous investment that can be presented to a patriot like you. It's a business deal of outright glory and fast fortune."

The liquidation had reached its conclusion. Now there was nothing left to be done. They began to head off indifferently. Perhaps they could have offered up a few words as an epitaph for the solidarity of their quest. But nobody demonstrated any interest in saying them. Perhaps the futile benevolence of a few sighs would not have been unwelcome. But none of them even sighed. It was a vulgar scene—like all things definitive and unredeemable—the last scene of their company's sinuous, factional journey of joy and tears.

Scattered, shabby, shambling, they were heading for the gate, when they noticed Dijunto's absence. They retraced their steps. Like a clod of dirt upon the bank, like a thorny acacia among the roses, they found him with his money in his hand, pale and grief-stricken, weeping, sad, moaning:

"Active misery, always miserable! Idle wealth, always miserable! Active misery, always miserable! Idle wealth, always miserable!"

Nobody understood the meaning of his words, except Katanga.

"C'mon. Don't make yourself sad. You'll have the house you

dreamed of for your old age. You don't have enough, do you?"

Dijunto shook his head.

"How much more do you need?"

"Nine hundred pesos."

"There, there. Don't you worry. I've got the eleven-hundred from Lon Chaney right here. C'mon, then. You're going to get it . . . deed and everything."

He looked at him.

They looked at each other, one with the humble stare of an ox; the other, with the tearful eyes of a man.

It was ten-thirty at night and Aparicio still hadn't arrived.

They'd agreed to meet in Don Rufo's room to avoid the least suspicion. Ian von Zuhlinder's report lay spread across the table, methodically dissected. Like a cadaver, the Nazi plot showed its scientifically tattooed skin and fetid entrails of out-sized ambitions. The most recondite enigmas lay exposed and clarified. Each intestine stuffed with "artfully woven tissues" of lies, how many "communicating vessels," how many nerves trained in the betrayals of espionage! Longines's patient, meditative labor desired nothing more than for the impending scandal to be recognized, to be authenticated by public consensus as a paragon of wisdom.

It was a quarter to eleven and Aparicio was nowhere to be seen.

For his part, Katanga had prepared a massive publicity campaign. The plan filled seven pages of lined paper. Publicity was necessary to polarize international attention with the incredible thunderous revelation and the credible details of the plot. Imagination, unity, calculation! He had rigorously considered the diplomatic and journalistic aspects on their own terms, with the central idea of stimulating America's adverse sentiments and inspiring confidence in the democratic destiny of its southern brothers-in-arms. From his own experience, Katanga understood the value of propaganda. He knew that the publicity agent is a psychologist who studies the flow coeffi-

cients of the way human suggestibility is powered by words, artistic fads, and self-interest. He weighed the situation and the
opportunity. It was the perfect moment to fulfill his top priori-
ty: to put the oscillations of political conscience to the test. The
Americas must speak against Nazism with unified, unequivocal animosity! And he was well aware of the cumulative valor
of repetition and the decisive charm of vivacity. He drew up an
orderly list of the ways he intended to broadcast the plot and
to provoke its repudiation.

Eleven o'clock sharp and Aparicio was not there.

Longines held out a few minutes more. But then he could
stand it no longer:

"This is insulting. I can endure injustice but never a lack of
punctuality. We agreed to meet at ten o'clock. At ten! . . . There
are always false coins and false men in circulation."

Aparicio walked through the door.

"Speak of the devil," said Katanga. "We were just talking
about you . . . I yield the floor. Longines is in charge of the first
part of the explanation . . . Meanwhile Don Rufo and I will go
and have a coffee."

The Swiss man immediately began to pour his heart out.

"All right, Aparicio. Let's not waste time. Hold on tight, it's
going to get rough. In twenty-four hours you'll be the most
famous man on the continent. All the newspapers in South
America will blazon your name on the front page. The revelations that you'll make, in a thousand interviews with special
foreign correspondents, in secret meetings with government
officials, diplomats and technicians from Uruguay, Argentina,
and especially, from Brazil and the United States, will add up
to more fame than you've ever dreamed of in your life. All this
enormous documentation, in code, that has reached my hands
by a mere coincidence, irrefutably proves the existence of the
rashest, most audacious plan of conquest ever known. Brazil,
Argentina, and your own country, Uruguay, will be the target-
ed nations."

"My country!" he babbled, choking with emotion. And,

suddenly, reacting with energetic impetus: "What do you mean my country? Why my country?"

Longines spent forty minutes providing him with a circumstantial explanation of the vast proportions of the Nazi plan. He left out no detail, however small, elucidating clearly and concisely. Each drawing, diagram, and schematic aroused in Aparicio two correlative sensations: admiration for the spy's ingenuity, and triumph for the cryptographer's shrewdness. The Swiss man placidly accepted his vote of confidence. He continued speaking with the mental sovereignty conferred by certainty, and the authority of an impeccable conscience. He spoke of his cryptological studies and his portentous knowledge of espionage. He connected his personal experiences at the Chancellery of Berne to the exploits of the Intelligence Service in London. And laughing delightedly about the sport of "spy hunting" during the war, he pointed out his own unstained satisfaction of being a "hunter of enemies" during peacetime.

"Well, Aparicio. This prey—much sought after by Sir Brazil Thomson and General Baden-Powell to add to their collection—has been collected for you. And you will pluck its feathers; or better yet, its multiple wings, to show the world the falsity of its colorful lines and patterns. To reveal its thirst for conquest and the plan it conceives . . ."

"Why must I be the one? This task is beyond me."

"Because of all our group, you're the only South American. Because your temperament agrees with the fervor this job demands. And because, when the nation is in danger, strength rises from weakness with the vehemence of youth. This is your chance, Aparicio!"

He was convinced. Silent. Calculating the responsibility which it occasioned and—why not say it?—the impending excitement, the approaching fame, and the sure apotheosis of his name."

"I accept; but I want to make sure I understand everything."

"Have no fear. In three days' time, I'll have you so well-informed, so saturated with information, you'll be able to hold forth, and with absolute sufficiency, on any question they put to you. Besides . . ."

When Katanga returned there remained almost nothing for him to cover. Amid the general enthusiasm, Longines had carefully explained all the details of the publicity campaign to the Uruguayan. The first task: to procure the support of worldwide media corporations. Next, telephone conferences with the Foreign Ministries and Defense Departments of Brazil, the United States, and Uruguay, secured through their embassies in Argentina. And finally, the direct, formal dealings with the local government.

The transcendent continental sweep of the affair and the prospect of becoming a great person upon his country's stage, exceeded Aparicio's imagination. His pock-marked, olive-hued face seemed to become smooth with the responsibility. His habitual reluctance gave way to a haughty nobility. Full of distinction, he now felt himself the recipient of a higher destiny. And he was going to bring it to a climax by employing the same faith as the great producers of the collective soul.

"Katanga will now explain the rest to you."

"Enough, Longines. I think I've got it all figured out. Now we've got to get to work."

"We're getting to that. He'll explain what we've estimated as . . ."

"Yes. You've got to contribute five thousand pesos, at least."

" . . . !"

"Ah! You're one of those fellows who think that glory comes dropping down from the sky, eh? Well, you're naive. Glory doesn't come from above. It rises from below. And only after enormous sacrifices does it take shape in the heaven of the ideal. Every ascent costs something. Don't be alarmed. That sum alone won't be enough. Longines will also kick in five thousand. And I'll give three out of the four thousand I've got left."

"All for my sake!"

"Yes: for your sake and to preserve the integrity and liberty of America. I've got my share right here."

"And here's mine," ratified Longines.

Tense, overwhelmed, with the bills in his right hand, Aparicio rocked his body to and fro in unexpected indecision. Quickly, furtively, he considered the triumphant guarantee implied by their offer. And putting the money away, his hand sought out those of his friends to tender them his joyous thanks for their glorious alms.

They informed Doña Visitación that they'd be away, traveling around for three or four days. And they departed ... to the center of the city.

In the finest tailor shop each man bought several suits. Straight-cut and double-breasted. Some in dark tones, others, discreetly elegant, for afternoon and evening meetings. More, in loose flannel, saxony, or tweed, for everyday wear. They spared no expense. White shirts made of soft, genuine silk with stiff collars. Gloves, colognes, creams. In short, everything necessary for an impeccable and sober *tenue*. After much self-inflicted neglect of their personal grooming, they returned to the cult of appearance, which is the cult of the faithful without fervor.

Stylish and elegant, their composure immediately acquired the distinguished, measured restraint of polished "men of style." They saw fit to make their arrival at the Bristol Hotel in a luxurious automobile, and to take up rooms in the hotel's finest suite. The courtesy shown by the employees and servants was the gentle reverse of their own tempered, circumspect gravity.

The moment they turned the key to lock the door, they began to cast their net. A net of cables and telegrams. A net of influences and resources.

The three telegraphic conferences they carried out yielded the desired result. The very next Panagra flight brought the combined military attachés of the United States and Brazil. The sub-secretary and the top cryptographer from the National Ministry of Defense flew in together on a military plane.

The conclave took place in the hotel and in various locations in the mountains. Long meetings, with voices hushed and brains on fire. Within the protective circle of protocol, all the specious detail of the Nazi plan was exposed. Hours of documented evidence. Hours of restrained emphasis. Aparicio would have enjoyed some more effusive praise and applause. He seemed suffocated by the climate of reserved approbation. By contrast, Longines and Katanga breathed easily. They knew that coexistence of diplomatic vehemence and passions controlled by coldness occurs only in a hushed atmosphere.

The next day, at first light, the top directors of the United Press and the Associated Press arrived by train. Everything was ready! The stupendous mechanism which blends the word into news and then divulges it was standing by, awaiting their orders. It was a day of buzzing telegraphs and purring telephones. The respective ambassadors followed the meeting's progress, step by step, consulting with their official spheres about effects and alternative outcomes. Conferences with Washington and Rio. A direct line to the Itamaraty Palace and the Casa Rosada. Consultations with delegations. Dispatches to consulates.

News technicians arrived in the afternoon. Checklists and messages. Photographs and communiques. The final meeting that night, carried out in the Sierras Hotel in the town of Alta Gracia, was conclusive, definitive. Aparicio played his role with a fluency of manners and firm mastery of the matter at hand. Experts and diplomats were persuaded of his knowledge and patriotism. He attacked Ian von Zuhlinder's document with a sharp phalanx of reasonings and deductions. His explanations abounded with countless connections between various topics. And the truth advanced in a squadron along the grand avenues of thought. Hidden in side streets and alleyways, doubt and skepticism took their aim. He happily responded, seizing the opportunity to annihilate them with his dialectic, crushing even the most recondite bunkers of subterfuge. That evening's triumph was sanctioned shortly thereafter. Then the wavelengths again hummed feverishly. Two intense hours of sharp telegraphic tachycardia and radiotelephonic otitis. And then everything was settled.

They returned from Alta Gracia at three-forty in the morning.

They surrendered to fatigue.

Washing their hands in the bathroom, they had the final conversation of the day:

"Well, Aparicio: you can't deny that you are now a *vir clarissimus et ilustre.* Your prestige now circulates in the highest centers of power in the Americas. And tomorrow ... what a day awaits you! When the Foreign Ministries of Brazil and the United States reveal the *affaire*, your name will resound with echoes of admiration in the concert of humanity."

"Tomorrow ... I would have preferred it today. I don't understand this delay."

"It's logical," added Longines. "The Ministries must advise the republics of the Pan American Union. To combine efforts, perhaps, a joint action ..."

"I would've preferred today. The press could initiate my ..."

"Never. Hierarchy and protocol. The press will do its job later. Soon the ears of the world's free consciences will thunder with the letters of your name. What an apotheosis your name will enjoy, Aparicio!"

A sad grimace trimmed the edges of Katanga's lyrical tone.

"If only I had a name ... instead of a nickname ..."

Seated on the edge of their beds, taking off their shoes, they seemed to stop moving for a while. Indeed. There they sat, lost in thought, "where action is not yet the sister of dream." Taciturn. Abstracted.

The Uruguayan tried to restart the dialogue:

"I would've liked it today. To carry our good news and rewards back home to the boarding house ..."

"No doubt ... Of course ... But first things first. Let's go to sleep now ... It's not dignified to tackle such issues of international protocol in shirtsleeves."

At eleven the next morning they were up and about.

"You stay here, just in case," suggested Katanga. "We're going to the post office. We'll telegraph Doña Visi about our arrival."

"Why don't you send a messenger with the news?"

They went out without answering.

Their main purpose was somewhat different.

In the Panagra office, without answering the employee who greeted them deferentially, they took out their wallets.

"I've got five hundred pesos. You, Longines?"

"Nine hundred sixty-three pesos and seventy centavos."

"All right, sir. How far can we travel with one thousand four hundred pesos on tomorrow's plane?"

"Twenty pesos more would get you to Callao ... Carrying standard baggage, the ticket costs seven hundred ten pesos."

"Fine. Then, two tickets to the stop before that, wherever it is."

"To Mollendo?"

"Yes, sir; to Mollendo."

Delighted, they commented festively:

"*Macanudo* ... Very exciting ..."

"And we've got a few pesos left over for the initial expenses ..."

They reached the boarding house on Calle Santa Fe in the hazy hour of sunset, unexpected by Viejo Amor and Little Visi. Walking in like they owned the place, they suddenly noted a fuss in the front room:

"Do the gentlemen require anything?"

Their attire gave weight to their bearing, their stylishness lent distinction to their appearances. Doña Visitación, confused, grew anxious as she turned on the light in the room. For a moment she was speechless:

"Ah! It's you! No one would've recognized you!"

Viejo Amor's eyes inspected them inquisitively. Especially Aparicio. After three days of absence his manner was changed.

They had been three intense days, during which their old withered dreams were fattened by pleasure. Aparicio had become the living embodiment of satisfaction. His chest swelled. He asserted himself . . . Neither Viejo Amor nor Doña Visi comprehended his transformation. Logically: they were unaware of the events that had unfolded. The three men were fully aware. The Uruguayan's self-infatuation resulted from his successful role in the proceedings. He now fully identified with the messianic character he'd been portraying; his ego caressed by the official recognition of the magnitude and transcendence of his information. He not only permitted himself a few touches of bitter irony against various delegates but, becoming foolishly high and mighty, against the very authors of his sudden apogee. One night after dinner at the Bristol, Longines had remarked to Katanga:

"This poor devil really gets under my skin! Just yesterday he was chewing over his misfortune in exile. Now, look at him . . . Leaving his caviar canapés half-eaten; his glass of '*vieil armagnac cuvée Van* 1884' unfinished; his splendid Hoyo de Monterrey barely smoked! . . . These resuscitated lice really irritate me! I can't help it."

"In my opinion . . . it's best not to say anything," Katanga whispered in his ear. "This is what's repugnant about the men of the River Plate. They act like arrogant know-it-alls when they're really brutes . . . Talking like brash playboys when they're simply destitute . . . No other people manage to be quite so vain as they are. No people trick others nor fool themselves so naturally. Pretty little good-for-nothing scoundrels! They turn what's soft and smooth into something rough and weathered, they take what's humble and complicate it . . . All that, despite the good, prudent pleasure found in what's pure, simple, and easy!"

Doña Visitación joined them for dinner that night. The lady's presence kept the conversation dignified. Their typical anecdotes were put on hold. No talk of fleecing teachers, colleagues, and nurses . . . Viejo Amor delivered a small tribute to Dijunto. New owner of his much-desired country house, he would be departing in a few days. In truth, Viejo Amor couldn't care less about Dijunto's status as a homeowner; the toast was an excuse to pompously announce the date of his wedding. It was an awkward moment, but quickly saved by the students who launched three stentorian hurrahs, and Katanga, with his customary delicacy:

"In the name of my comrades, allow me to offer my most sincere congratulations. Man — the wave of an enormous tide — has the responsibility of not wasting away on the beach of the world; he must propagate the species, through books, inventions, and children; in the trinity forged by the soul, the spirit, and the blood. Well done, Viejo Amor! May happiness and good fortune shine always upon your new home!"

But the exact opposite appeared to be true: the new groom really only desired a "pleasurable femsocket" to appease his libido. His deformed morality would, in short order, smother any possibility of happiness. And seeing Viejo Amor so subdued after "his conquest," Katanga's keen perception saw beyond the festive congratulations to his companion's interior bubbling malice . . .

Longines read and reread the letter from Markus Zilahy, not present for the occasion, acknowledging receipt of the seven thousand pesos. He was joyously radiant. When the couple was ready to take their leave and new hurrahs broke out, his happiness found an unimagined spigot from which to gush forth. He stood up and said:

"If only I were less moved by strong emotions in this moment, so that I might add a tiny sprig of orange blossoms to Hymen's crown. *(General surprise.)* I've just seen the funeral plaques we commissioned for Lon Chaney and Jaroslav. *(Sudden fright from the bride.)* I've just confirmed the liberation of Fortunato's soul, as well as Dijunto's voluntary enslavement of his bones by Mother Earth. *(Stupor.)* I've just glimpsed Viejo Amor behind the mask of romance, moaning between whispers, as we did in the good old days:

Mon ca ur soupire
La nuit et le jour.
Qui peut me dire
Si c'est l'amour?

"*(Sarcasm.)* Such happiness makes me tender. Because it is born of death. Because the flames which are extinguished, in turn, spark work and affection. *(Contempt from Viejo Amor.)* Meanwhile, those of us who resign from life in the full flush of triumph—Katanga and I—snuff out the candle of conscience and offer glory as a gift. *(Deaf reproach from Aparicio.)*"

Aparicio was deeply disturbed. So many subtle slights could not be processed all at once but rather in fractional shards. The fiancées left the dining room. She, sighing sweetly. He, proud, gliding on her sighs with a skillful air of superiority over the diatribe.

The students remained, lording over the after-dinner conversation.

By midnight, Katanga was the only who still remained in their company.

Up in his room, Longines was restless, roiling with anger, excessively meticulous in organizing his bags. Better to say, in preparing his abandonment. He didn't want to leave all his things in promiscuous disorder like so many castoff goods, so many submissive souls. He opened his suitcases. He checked their double-linings and hidden springs. He cleaned the latches. He carefully packed his clothes. After painstakingly polishing his penknife-fork-spoon-punch-can opener-corkscrew-awl-screwdriver-glass-cutter-scissors, he sat at the table, and wrote:

Aparicio:

When you come calling for us, we'll be who-knows-where. We'll have bored through the walls of aether to elude the glorious responsibility we leave behind for you. Those of us who thrive on continual evasion have no tolerance for the mockery of praise and fame. May the burden of your apotheosis be light! May this disloyalty—

*our only regret—fall not into the past dressed in memories but
in the naked future of this pair of fugitives. LONGINES and
. . . .*
    *I leave all my things to Rescoldo, except the "Ten Command-
ments," which I'm taking with me.*

When Katanga came into the room, he read the note without
any show of emotion. He added his signature and these lines:

I beg you, Aparicio, to be generous with Patay, Rescoldo, and
Fenicio. Their exams are coming up and they may need some
financial assistance. They've also been a factor in your exaltation. May your nobility shine splendor on them, too. And
when you visit Dijunto and Viejo Amor: be tactful! Let it not
be derision that knocks upon the door of another man's weeping disaster . . .

And so as the Uruguayan slept peacefully in the best suite at
the Bristol, the implacable solitude of Longines, and the doc-
ile solitude of Katanga melted together into the solitary beatitude of sleep.

*It was natural that they might slip down the smooth declivities of
dreams toward nightmare. The secret of their true plans carved a
slippery slope between the scheme and the subconscious. From atop
two peaks of pleasure they rolled downhill. From the Star Palace of
Yildiz, drunk with the blood of the last Ottoman Turkish tyrant,
Katanga bore the head of the Red Sultan to his father. Longines
from the consecration of Geneva, holding aloft the chalice of vengeance, toasting the railway inspector's death, Freya Bolitho's curses, and von Zuhlinder's hatred. And they plunged into an atrocious
dungeon, a bloodcurdling cavern. There, boiling away in a cess-
pool of viruses, fermented scabs, a crowd of constitutional pariahs,
conventional idlers, and international scoundrels: hungry-faced
drifters; blind, lynx-eyed sharpers; one-legged va-nu-pieds crawling with lice and wanderlust; sad, withered sidewalk-smoothing*

almoners; bald, crapulous hobos; obscene, filthy globetrotting vagabonds; threshold-polishing panhandlers fattened on diatribes;
lümmels *in rags;* one-eyed pickpockets; atrium-assed alms-beggars;
sickly accattoni; *hunchbacked vagrants with lumbago; vinous
limping clochards; paraplegics on skates; pokey little deaf-mutes;
beachcombers with rancid mollusk skin; wall-pissing tramps with
zippers agape;* steel-shod lausbuben; *trolls lurking under bridges;
bandy-legged, knock-kneed men on creaking crutches . . .*

When they got to their feet, amid vomitous vapors, tannery
stink, and plague-infested tunics, a harsh voice rang out loud and
clear, making them shrink back in astonishment:

"I've got my hands on you at last! Don't you remember me?
You're the drifters I was looking for!"

"We're not drifters."

"By the worst estimate we're simply idle unemployed, vagabonds . . ."

"It's all the same."

"It's not the same. The vagabond is a cultivated man, a loiter-
er, who takes delight in his leisure; the drifter is a poor devil, on
the move, who can't stand tedium. The vagabond asks, he utiliz-
es pity and forgiveness; the drifter steals, he frightens with hatred
and cruelty. The vagabond is a satiated tourist, skeptical, cruising
through life; the drifter is a hungry traveler, a deluded dreamer,
marching toward death. It's not the same!"

"Nonsense . . . Let's see your hands! You can't fool me. There are
no cretinous Police Chiefs or posh Judges here . . . In this dungeon,
I'm in charge!"

Stupefied, they now recognized him. It was the angry detective
from that night, under the bridge, in Río Cuarto. *The professional
doubter! The explorer of the lie! The only one they were never able
to persuade or convince!*

"I've got the criminal charges right here. Conspiracy. Robbery.
Terrorism. Bloody Murder. Let's see your hands!"

How could they surrender, allow themselves to be clapped into
iron chains? They writhed around in choking convulsions. The
twisted bedclothes flew up into the air.

Their terror exploded in gusts of fire.
They docked in the roadstead of wakefulness. Free once more!
Submissive, amid the spermy shadows, the pack of hounds from
the nightmarish lesson licked at their feet.

As they passed through the front door where Doña Visi stood
speaking to the deliveryman, she asked them:
"Will you be here for lunch?"
"Probably never . . ."
"Maybe someday . . ."
Their response—a flock of gray words—floated for a moment in her spirit.
They caught a taxi at the corner: "To the Bar L'Aiglon."
They rode in silence, but radiant. Coffee. Cognac. Newspapers.
The front pages, plastered with enormous headlines, announced sensational news: top-secret information offered up
for public consumption:

UNITED STATES LEASES
TWELVE DESTROYERS TO BRAZIL!
YANKEE WARSHIPS TO PATROL
SOUTH ATLANTIC COAST

NORTH AMERICAN OFFICERS
AND BRAZILIAN TROOPS
DEFENSIVE COOPERATION?

They read no more. Why bother? The international pabulum
had begun. Soon the powder kegs of the press would blow up.
"Quel brouhaha! Quel tohu-bohu! . . ."
"Péle-méle et tóle-tóle ensemble! . . ."
They smiled Machiavellian smiles.
Three-quarters of an hour later, they were at the airfield,
scrutinizing the upcoming midday flight schedules.

The plane ready for departure, a feverish individual hurriedly climbed on board. The trimotor was ready to take off but a telephone warning delayed the *décollage*.

Two detectives removed the anxious passenger from the plane.

"What's going on?" asked the copilot.

"Spy."

The sullen, laconic response winked an eye at their intuition.

"Ian von Zuhlinder?"

"Yes. Ian von Zuhlinder."

Boulders, glosses of distance, went rolling past as they flew up and away, borne aloft by a spiritual wonder:

Wings of knowledge ... Feathers of luminous kindness ... now cleaved the smooth lines of silence and blue sky.

Serenely.

And they were lost in the heavens like the shadow of two birds in memory.

JUAN FILLOY was an excellent swimmer, dedicated boxing referee, and talented caricaturist; he spoke seven languages and he practiced as a judge in the small town of Río Cuarto. A world-champion palindromist, he utilized obscure words, coined new ones, and gave all of his novels seven-letter titles. He received various distinctions during his lifetime and was reportedly nominated for the Nobel Prize. He died in 2000 at the age of 106.

BRENDAN RILEY is a teacher, translator, writer, and editor. Among other works, Among other works, he is the translator of Álvaro Enrigue's *Hypothermia*, and Carlos Fuentes' *The Great Latin American Novel*.